MIDNIGHT FIRE

"If you make a wrong move, or even so much as think about screaming, I'll wring your neck." His voice was abrupt. "Do I make myself clear?"

Nicki Sue gave no further thought to her vulnerability or to the fact that she wore only a wispy nightgown. "Yes," she spat. "I understand you perfectly. Now, what do you want?"

"My, my, but we're a feisty one," he said softly. Suddenly his eyes darkened and he jerked roughly on her wrist. Nicki's body came in contact with one lean, hard thigh. "You've got exactly two minutes to get up off that bed and get dressed—or face the consequences."

Her head flew up and she glared at him. "Let go of me," she gritted from between clenched teeth.

"Don't push me, lady."

Jesse studied her closely. She really wasn't Evanson's usual style. This one had too much fire. He slipped lean, strong fingers beneath her neck.

"Maybe there is something I want after all," he said huskily. "Let's see if you're worth what he pays you."

OUTLAW'S CARESS

MARY MARTIN

ZEBRA BOOKS
KENSINGTON PUBLISHING CORP.

ZEBRA BOOKS

are published by

Kensington Publishing Corp.
475 Park Avenue South
New York, NY 10016

First printing: May, 1988

Printed in the United States of America

This one is for my brother-in-law and sister-in-law,
Bob and Elaine Martin,

and

two very dear *friends, Darrell and Jean Hamer.*

Prologue

The Sacramento Valley, 1870

The frieze of darkly clad riders watched the Simmons's ranch from a hill overlooking the lush valley. They were armed and ready, their clothes and weapons in sharp contrast to the peaceful surroundings. Hidden within a copse of pine trees, they went undetected, yet were able to observe everything that moved in the valley below. The sun sank steadily in the western sky, vivid streaks of gold and purple beyond the distant treetops.

Hat pulled down low over his eyes against the slanting rays of the sun, the leader swung his gaze to the gay party scene in the front yard of the Simmons's home. He was well aware that Peter and Delores Simmons were giving this party in honor of their daughter's engagement. He wasn't surprised that none of them had received an invite. After all, they had absolutely nothing whatsoever in common.

It was growing steadily darker. The stars came out and the moon rose in silver brilliance.

The party was in full swing now, no one aware of the hostile eyes following their every move.

Peter Simmons appeared almost euphoric as he meandered about the yard greeting old friends and accepting their congratulations. He'd been one of the earliest arrivals in the Valley; he'd sought his fortune in the gold fields, sold off his nuggets and dust, and had settled on a choice section of land, where he planted orchards of fruit trees. His orchards had turned into a prosperous business venture, and today there were no money worries. He and his family lived well and were respected throughout the Valley. On this particular day he was thinking how all of the hardships they'd endured had been worthwhile. He had everything that he'd ever dreamed about. Life was good. Yet he could not stop his gaze from wandering toward the surrounding hills; nor could he stop the frown that briefly furrowed his brow. He stood unmoving for several more seconds, then, with a slight shudder, turned away.

The leader of the group hidden in the hills was a short bear of a man with a pockmarked face and small, dark eyes. His eyes narrowed with deadly purpose as they followed Peter Simmons across the yard. As the shadows deepened around them, he reached for the nickle-plated .44 on his hip. Removing it from the holster, he spun the cylinders, checking each chamber carefully by the light of the moon. Seeing that one was empty, he filled it, and with a flick of his wrist, snapped it closed. From the corner of his eye he detected a fleeting movement beside the lake in the distance. A revealing shaft of moonlight streaked down from the sky and caught in its light a smiling young couple who had slipped quietly away from the party.

Hand in hand they walked beside the water, oblivious to anything but each other.

The man was tall and dark-haired, the girl petite and fair. The girl's pale blond hair, adorned with buttercups, shimmered like spun gold in the gleaming moonlight. The couple paused to stare out over the lake. Across the wide expanse of water a coyote barked balefully at the moon, an owl hunting flew whisper-soft overhead, and in the tall reeds beside the water, pack rats scurried about.

Throughout the Valley, a host of distant insects in cadenced harmony blended peacefully in nature's song. The girl held up her left hand to catch the moon's rays. She smiled serenely.

"It's such a beautiful ring, darling. I can't tell you how happy you've made me."

The man gathered the young woman in his arms. "I'm glad that you like it. Your happiness means everything to me, Allison."

Her heartbeat quickened as she stared up into his handsome face. "You make me feel so cherished." Moisture welled up in her eyes and clung to the tips of her golden lashes. Her young man appeared immediately concerned.

"What is it, darling?" he inquired anxiously.

"Our love is so perfect . . . ," she explained almost shyly, ". . . that sometimes . . . I'm afraid I'm going to awaken from this beautiful dream."

Deep blue eyes, as dark and seductive as the night, met Allison's luminous gaze. "What we have is no dream, sweetheart. It's very real." He pulled her close in his arms, his head dipping forward to claim her soft mouth. He kissed her until she knew for certain that he did indeed exist, as did his devotion. When the kiss ended, Allison was breathless, yet absolutely certain of his love. She shivered with emotion, and he smiled gently.

"Do you need any further convincing?"

Her features brightened with happiness. "With that kind of heavenly persuasion, I could just be tempted to say yes." She laid her cheek on his broad chest,

adding softly, "All I want is to spend the rest of m
life with you."

"And you shall, so quite worrying your pretty littl
head."

"I believe you. It's just . . . that sometimes I wis
we'd run off and married quietly like we wanted in th
beginning." She hesitated shyly, then continued. "W
could already be living together . . . as man an
wife."

He smiled gently. "You know I want that more tha
anything, sweetheart. God knows leaving you eac
night isn't easy. But we've only a couple more week
until the wedding. And I know our families are gla
that we decided to wait until they could share the da
with us." His lips brushed her temple. "And this way
I'll have the ranch all shaped up before I take yo
there as my bride."

The girl sighed resolutely. "You're right, of cours
I'm just being selfish. Sometimes I think that I car
for you too much." She drew back to gaze enrapture
into his eyes. "Correction—I know I care for you to
much."

"I feel the same way." He closed his eyes and in
haled the delicate scent of her hair. She was every
thing he'd always wanted in a woman. Gentle
soft-spoken, with a fragile beauty that took his breat
away every time that he looked at her. Petite an
feminine, Allison instilled in him a fierce need t
protect her from any hurts or dangers.

Laughter drifted across warm breezes to disrupt th
intimate moment. Allison reluctantly moved out o
the circle of her intended's arms.

"As much as I want to stay here with you, I suppos
we really should return to our guests?"

He nodded, then gave her one last quick kiss. "
love you more than life itself. Always remember tha

Allison."

"Yes, my darling," she said softly. "I'll remember."
Then she gently took his hand and turned in the direction of the brightly lit yard, where her family and their closest friends were gathered.

It was a rare evening to see the people of this valley so free of worry or care. All about them tonight the land seemed at peace. Allison could not help but recall the past several months, and the dissension that had run rampant through the Valley with the arrival of that awful person. The past weeks had been like a nightmare. Her parents had told her that it wasn't as bad as she imagined, that it had been far worse once before, when the Sacramento Valley had been the heart of Gold Rush country. Her parents had decided to settle here after their strike. They'd been lucky and had realized their dreams early on. It had been her mother who had talked her father into homesteading. It was a good life back then, they'd said, but not without certain perils.

With the Rush came scores of immigrants who converged upon the Valley eager to join in the feverish search for gold. A tidal wave of humanity spilled over the sleepy town of Sacramento, with murders and robberies becoming a daily occurrence. Homesteaders, like her father, were driven to carrying guns at all times and guarding their property with their lives. Even their pickers were given weapons to carry, and to use if they found it necessary. They had been forced to do so many times. At last the Rush dwindled, and the blood that had been spilled and the gold that had precipitated it became just a memory. Yet it would forever remain a very bitter one for the families who stayed on to live simply in the fertile valley, plant orchards, and produce succulent fruits. All had remained quiet, until several months ago. Another in-

11

terloper had come seeking a means to get rich. And
he was persistent, and had proven a deadly adversary.

As in earlier years, Allison's father, joined now by
her two older brothers, had defended their holdings
and Allison calmed now, remembering that they had
been successful. There had not been any real trouble
in weeks. And there wouldn't be, ever again. Turning
her thoughts away from grim memories, the girl concluded once again how lucky she was to have found
such a wonderful man to love. It was not the time to
reflect on the past, but a night to rejoice in the future
and to definitely cast aside dark thoughts.

Shortly thereafter the couple rejoined their guests
and the celebrating continued far into the evening.
Eating, drinking, and dancing became the order of
the night; and it was heartily agreed by all that the
Simmons family sure knew how to throw a heck of a
celebration.

At last the pace slowed, and there came grateful
sighs. The rousing rhythms of the guitar and fiddle
drifted into a mellow waltz. Young couples came together and swayed in each other's arms on the raised
wood dance platform. The older members took this
as their cue, the men meandering to a grove of cottonwoods to swap stories and pass around a jug, the
women following Delores Simmons into the house to
find a quiet place to sit and talk.

Delores glanced back over her shoulder one last
time at her daughter and her fiancé before she disappeared through the wide oak door. She smiled almost
wistfully at the sight of Allison with her cheek pressed
close to her young man's. He was a good man, and
she had every confidence that her daughter would
have a fine life. From the first, she'd known he was
perfect for her shy, reticent daughter. Delores was
content in the knowledge that she would not be losing

12

her daughter, but gaining another wonderful son.

It was sometime later, almost midnight, when the far-off wail of a train whistle echoed faintly through the surrounding hills. Peter Simmons's head shot up and a curse lingered on his lips. He stifled harsh expletives, reminding himself not to overreact, that nothing was going to go wrong. He mustn't allow himself to believe for even a moment that his daughter's engagement party would not end on the same happy note that it had begun.

"Everything's going to be okay . . . ," he muttered, feeling moisture suddenly form on his brow. With an almost desperate motion he removed a handkerchief from his pocket and dabbed at his forehead. There wasn't any reason to suspect trouble. After all, things had been quiet in the valley of late. There was some comfort in that thought at least, Peter reassured himself. He glanced across the yard at his two sons, who were dancing with their sweethearts. He remembered Mark, his eldest, having cautioned him about relaxing his guard too much, even for this one night. But Peter had shrugged off the warning, and listened to Delores. His wife had been adamant about leaving their guns in the house. He recalled her exact words that had swayed his thinking.

"No, Peter. I will not have our daughter's engagement party marred by having rifles about everywhere. I just can't stand the thought. Put them all in the gun cabinet . . . and leave them there for this one night." She'd turned pleading eyes upon him. "Please . . . for Allison."

Mark had looked to him also. But in his son's eyes there was an underlying fear he would not speak aloud before his mother. He knew his mother's request should not even be considered, and why. Delores had been sheltered from the latest trouble by her husband and sons. She had no idea how serious things were. And Peter knew that Mark was stunned when his father had agreed with his mother. And later, when he'd found time to speak to his father alone, he'd relayed his feelings and misgivings. They'd be helpless, like ducks in a open pond, he'd said. But Peter had brushed aside his words. And now, finding his gaze meeting Mark's, he knew a terrible sense of frustrating anger. Why hadn't he listened to his own inner voice? Mark sent him a questioning look. The music stopped. Folks began gathering their loved ones for the long ride home. Peter observed Mark exchange a few words with his younger brother, then both boys began walking in his direction. He saw that their steps were a bit unsteady from too much drink, and of a sudden, Peter had this terrible sense of foreboding. The air had taken on a damp chill, and glancing up, he saw the moon lying partially obscured by tattered clouds. It was an eerie, discomforting sight.

Another long, low wail seemed to drift across those clouds, and Peter Simmons shivered. The damned train whistle, he thought; it did it to him every time. And the whiskey that he had drunk wasn't helping matters. He rubbed the back of his hand across his eyes as if to wipe away an image before them. Suddenly he froze in motion for what seemed an eternity. Something was amiss; the familiar rhythm of the night had been disturbed. He glanced furtively off in the distant hills. A silence blanketed the valley, a disarming kind of hush when it seemed even the smallest insects were frozen in motion.

Allison Simmons's intended noticed the stillness too. He was standing beside her saying goodnight to a family who lived on the next ranch. He cocked his dark head and listened.

"What is it?" Allison's voice held a breathless note

14

as her eyes searched his face.

"I'm . . . not sure, exactly," he replied with a slight frown.

"It's so still—"

"Allison," he cut in sharply. "Get in the house." When she didn't move, but stood there staring at him as if finding it difficult to believe that he had spoken to her in such a manner, he grasped her arm. "Move—now!"

Her large, expressive eyes, which had been so luminous only moments before, grew wide with unknown terror. "I don't want to leave you. Come with me . . . please!"

He stared at her with imploring eyes, but she would not budge, and in that instant he found himself desperate to put to memory the way she looked at that exact moment, and keep it safe forever within his mind's eye. She had never appeared lovelier to him, or more precious. Silk-soft curls cascaded about her bare shoulders, and wispy tendrils framed her heart-shaped face. Her off-shoulder gown had been ordered from San Francisco especially for this night: a pale peach satin, with yards and yards of cream lace adorning each flounce, enhancing the creamy smoothness of her skin. Long, feathery lashes could not conceal the growing alarm in her blue eyes. The air around them seemed to quiver with expectancy. It was then he heard the faint jangling of metal bridle bits and the thud of iron-shod hooves on hard-packed ground. Riders . . . a lot of them, were headed their way.

They had waited in the cover of mist-shrouded hills, twenty or more men, their faces concealed by masks, their guns primed for action. And when they felt the time was right, and the odds in their favor, they moved out toward their targeted destination.

"Remember, ride in fast, do the job, and then move out," the head rider yelled out. He turned in his saddle to glare pointedly at the masked group. "Stay on your horse. If you fall—you're on your own."

One rider reined his mount in beside him. He was a big, rawboned brute with narrow, cold eyes. The leader watched him closely. He knew him for a trigger-happy sort: a man you did not like to have at your back.

"Yeah, what is it, Tim?"

"I just want you to know that I have the explosives we were talking about the other day. Just give a holler when you want me to toss 'em out." His voice was devoid of emotion.

"You sure are itching to start some fireworks, aren't you?"

Tim's eyes narrowed to evil-looking slits. "That Simmons fella made fools out of all of us the last time. I'm gonna make certain that this time . . . I have the last laugh."

"Just be absolutely sure that none of our own men are in the way," Waco spoke again.

"I was an explosives man in the war. I can handle myself just fine."

Waco nodded briefly, his eyes burning from beneath dark, bushy brows. "Yeah, so you've told me time and again. Well, you're going to get the chance to prove all them big stories of yours true."

"I can, and I will," Tim replied confidently.

"Then I expect there won't be nothing left breathing or standing when we ride out."

Tim chuckled. "I'll blow that place so high and wide there won't be even a splinter left."

The riders moved onward through the dark night

16

Without incident they rode onto Simmons's land and reached the outer perimeter of the yard, where the last of the guests were departing.

Peter Simmons was the first to see the lead rider gallop forth from the trees, a rifle in one hand and a pistol in the other. Helpless, weaponless, Simmons spun about with an angry cry of frustration and made a dash toward the house, and his rifle. He didn't take three steps before Waco's rifle cracked and a bullet tore into his spine. Simmons froze in motion even though his brain screamed inwardly for him to run. He knew he had to reach his gun . . . he had to.

"Damn you . . . damn him," he groaned as he struggled to stay on his feet.

Peter Simmons never saw the face of his killer. The last thing that he heard before a bullet slashed through him was the sound of cold laughter.

The vulnerable party-goers were easy targets for the shooters. They dashed madly about like frightened game whose pursuers knew no mercy. Death rode rampant through their midst.

Allison Simmons was in shock, her eyes glazed with the horror she was witnessing. She watched as her father was cut down before her. From the house she heard her mother's screams, the terror-filled cries of the other women. Her brother Mark was holding the lifeless form of his sweetheart in his arms. He was weeping brokenly. The back of a rifle butt slammed into his head. Allison began screaming and could not stop.

"Murderers! Filthy animals! Leave us alone . . . leave us alone!"

Tears flowed from her eyes, and her heart was overwhelmed with pain.

"Run, Allison! Run, darling!" she heard her beloved yell from a distance, but found her feet would not move.

Her fiancé finally reached her and grabbed her by the arm. She pulled free of him and began running toward her father's crumpled body. His killer watched her from behind slitted eyes.

"Allison, come back here!" her intended yelled over the din of noise and confusion. He dashed forward to reach her before it was too late. But knew even as he did that it was. He saw the man watching her, the killing look in the horseman's eyes. And then watched helplessly as the man took aim with a big Navy Colt, and fired.

His own body jerked when he heard the sharp retort of the pistol and saw Allison's slight form hurled backward by the force of the blast. Even so, she refused to fall and fought vainly to remain standing. The deadly pistol flashed several more times. Her body was jerked about in a deadly dance like a puppet whose strings had suddenly been pulled up short. It was a horrible scene to witness. Her fiancé cried out in anguished rage. With a choked sob she tumbled to the ground. That sound tore through his heart.

She was already dying when he reached her.

"Oh God, Allison, don't die . . . ," he begged, falling to his knees and taking her into his arms. Bullets slashed into the ground around him. He barely felt the pain sear across his right arm, then another in his shoulder. A burning sensation tore into his back. With no thought for his own safety, he gathered Allison close to shield her from the barrage of bullets. One hand caressed her pale face, imploring her to live. His eyes searched her own, and with horror, he realized he could not save her. He cupped the back of her head, his long fingers entwining in silken hair and flower petals wet and sticky with her life's blood.

Allison's body gave a slight shudder, and was still.

18

The light had gone out of her beautiful eyes.

A red mist of fury veiled his pain. Gently he laid her down, then, swearing violently, he leaped to his feet. Allison's killer had wheeled his mount around to sight down on another helpless victim.

Waco was so caught up in killing blood lust that he never saw the lithe figure hurtle from coiling shadows to knock him from his horse.

The two men rolled over and over on the ground, their grunts and snarls muffled by the screams of the dying. The air was so thick with gun smoke that it was hard for Waco to discern his attacker's face. They were both panting from the exertion. Waco knew by the strength in the other man's hands that he was battling for his own survival. The hoarse voice near his ear gave him chills.

"I'll kill you for what you did to her."

Waco could feel his grip on the pistol loosening. His fingers made a desperate grasp for the trigger. He felt himself hurtled onto his back, and the gun tumble from his grasp. Relentless hands closed around his throat. His eyes bugged from their sockets as talonlike fingers squeezed with unbelievable power. Waco knew he was going to die. Fear curled in his belly and spread to all of his nerve endings.

Out of the night, a gunshot resounded. His attacker fell sideways off of Waco onto the ground. Blessed air poured into Waco's lungs. He focused his eyes on one of his men, who loomed above him, a smoking pistol in his hand.

"Thought you was a goner, didn't you?" the man chuckled, as though finding it all very amusing.

Waco rubbed his aching throat. "I was beginning to wonder." He got stiffly to his feet and glanced down at the still figure lying on the ground. He was amazed to see that the man's back was riddled with countless

19

bullet holes. His gaze swung to the other man. "And how come I'm thinking that under that mask you're grinning from ear to ear, Shawnee?" He nudged the inert form sprawled in the dirt with the toe of his boot. The man didn't move. "This one ain't going nowhere."

Shawnee leaned over in the saddle and extended a hand. "Come on, we're wasting time. Let's hightail it away from here while we still can."

Waco laughed. It was a relieved sound. "People have to pay for their mistakes, don't they?" He swung up behind a grinning Shawnee.

"Ain't it the truth," Shawnee snorted.

The sound of gunfire and the screaming voices were quiet now.

Suddenly a blast seemed to shake the earth, and orange tongues of fire lit up the night sky. The gunmen watched as the two-story house quickly became a mass of smoking rubble.

"Wooo-eee!" Shawnee yelled.

"Tim's as good as his word," Waco laughed shortly. "There isn't even a splinter of wood left."

Shawnee spat a stream of dark tobacco juice on the ground. "Time to gather 'em up, Waco."

Waco gave a sharp whistle. The men quickly banded together. They surveyed the grizzly scene one last time, satisfied that they had accomplished what they'd set out to do.

"Good work," Waco told them. "The boss will be happy."

Tim relaxed in the saddle with a satisfied smirk on his face. "You think these fools would get smart, wouldn't ya?"

"They never will," Shawnee snorted. "And that's okay, too. Because, in a manner of speaking, these fools pay our salary."

20

He didn't know how long he'd been lying there listening to the unearthly stillness. The shooters were gone, fading into the night as swiftly as they had come. Strangely, he felt no pain, and thought that perhaps it was like that when you were about to die. He didn't care. Nothing mattered anymore. His eyes found her: his beloved Allison lying within an arm's distance. He wanted to touch her so badly, but he could not move. His gaze lingered on her face. She was still beautiful, even in death. A burning vengeance was born within him. He'd loved her so . . . and they'd taken her from him.

Overwhelming hatred consumed him. He recalled the cold gray eyes of Allison's killer. He knew than that he would come back from hell to find him, and make him pay.

Chapter One

The young woman's lips twisted into a wry smile as she read the social item in the *San Francisco Call*.

San Francisco, Calif., June 10—saw the wedding of Miss Nicole Suzanne Norris to Mr. Patrick W. Ryan. The ceremony took place at Saint Patrick's Cathedral. The bride wore a gown fashioned in lace and white satin trimmed with quills of silver ribbon and embroidered with tiny seed pearls. She was attended by four maids in ice-blue gowns. Mr. William Chapman, esteemed banker and family friend, escorted the bride down the aisle. Immediately following the ceremony, the bride's aunt, Miss Lorna Hamilton, was hostess to a lavish reception in honor of the newlyweds at her home in Rincon Point. There were many noted citizens in attendance. The happy couple boarded the noon train for their sprawling ranch near Bodie, California.

Nicki Sue removed her gold-rimmed spectacles and tossed the newspaper aside. She had not expected to see the announcement in the newspaper this soon; after all, her wedding had only taken place that morning. Yet, knowing Aunt Lorna as well as she did, she knew she shouldn't have been surprised. Lorna Hamilton was a pillar of society, and had tried many times to mold Nicki in her image. At this, she failed miserably. The young woman obeyed her aunt's edict (on most matters) because she felt it only right, considering how Lorna had taken her in when she was left all alone in the world following her father's untimely death. But even though Nicki was modest and kind, she did possess a streak of stubborn pride that even her Aunt Lorna's unendless castigation could not bend.

Her mother, who died when Nicki Sue was eight, had found her daughter's indomitable spirit delightful. The girl had many fond memories of the laughter-filled hours they had shared. But life with her mother's sister proved quite different. Nicki Sue soon learned that in Aunt Lorna's home there was little laughter. Life became nothing but a series of disagreements. Every day Lorna found reason to criticize Nicki. And worse of all were Lorna's cutting remarks when she happened upon Nicki wearing her spectacles.

Not that the girl looked unattractive wearing them. On the contrary, the slender gold wires were fashioned becomingly and did much to emphasize her beautiful tawny-gold eyes. It wasn't as if Nicki wore them all of the time. She did not. She only needed them when she was reading, stitching, or attending the theater.

In the beginning she didn't understand her aunt's disapproval, but as she grew older it became quite clear. Aunt Lorna was worried that Nicki would fail to attract a man's attention. Her verbal tirades increased, until finally she simply forbade Nicki to wear her spectacles in public.

"It's time you considered the consequences of your actions. Why, you shall never receive a proposal from ome nice young man at the rate you're going," Lorna Hamilton would carry on. "It's absolutely absurd, Nicole Suzanne, the way you defy me at times. I'm beginning to believe that you deliberately go out of your way to provoke me."

"That's not true, Aunt, and you know it," came the cool reply. "And I resent your implying such a thing."

"You just don't like hearing the truth, that's all," Lorna would respond waspishly. "But it's true enough, all right."

Nicki looked up from her embroidery to meet her aunt's heated gaze. "I try hard to please you in most everything. However, if I am to enjoy needlework, and a night at the theater, then I simply must be allowed to wear spectacles. Is it such an unforgivable thing to be seen in glasses?"

Lorna leaned over her niece and abruptly snatched the delicate wires off her nose. "Yes," she replied, frowning with disapproval, "it is!" Laying the spectacles on a side table, she swept from the room.

Her aunt's implication that Nicki deliberately went out of her way to shun potential suitors' advances was far from the real truth. Nicki desperately wanted to find someone who would love her and take her as far away from her aunt Lorna's scolding tongue as possible. But she was beginning to think that she would never find such a man. And then when she least expected it, Patrick Ryan came into her life, and despite her aunt's doomful prediction that the romance wouldn't last if Nicki didn't stop wearing her spectacles, Patrick had asked Nicki Sue to marry him. Nicki was flattered, but she wasn't absolutely certain that he really loved Patrick; and being the honest person that she was, she had discussed her doubts with him.

"I do care about you, Patrick," she had said softly, "but . . . ?"

"No—don't say it, sweet," Patrick had hurriedly injected. "I'm aware that you . . . don't feel the . . love that I feel for you—but I have love enough for both of us." His shining eyes had mirrored nothing but kindness and devotion. "Please, give me a chance to make you truly happy. Let me take you away from here. I want you to come with me to my ranch. You'll be free there, and I promise I'll never place any restrictions on you."

Nicki's eyes had misted. "I don't wish to hurt you in any way, for you are a dear man. But . . . I don't think it would be right of me to marry you when I don't love you. A man like you needs a wife who will make him happy." She'd sighed deeply. "And I honestly don't know if I can ever give you that."

"In time, I believe you will," he'd murmured tenderly, enfolding her hand within his. "I want you, Nicki Sue. Please—don't turn me down. Do me the honor of becoming my wife?"

And Nicki Sue, who had endured her aunt's criticism far too long, and wanted to believe she might yet find happiness, had agreed to marry him and live with him on his ranch in Bodie. It was enough that he promised to give her a good life, and loved her very much. She didn't want it to matter to her that he was considerably older than she, or that when he kissed her, fireworks didn't go off in her head. And she absolutely refused to think about the nights ahead when as her husband, he would want to touch her . . intimately . . . and love her . . . completely. It was too distressing to think about, so she simply closed her mind to any worries and concentrated on the preparations for the wedding. She was ready for a new life, and more than willing to live on Patrick's isolated ranch and help him turn it into something special.

Thoughts returning to the present, she gazed down

at the wedding band on her finger, and a frown furrowed her silky brow. Patrick had surprised her with his mother's ring at the church. To her dismay, when he'd slipped it on her finger during the ceremony, it had been too big. He promised to have it taken care of as soon as they were settled. Suddenly fearful of losing the cherished keepsake, Nicki regretfully slipped it off her finger and wrapped it up in her lace handkerchief. She then put it away in her carpetbag, where she knew it would be safe.

"Nicole Suzanne," she murmured thoughtfully, snapping the bag closed. "I doubt whether you will ever hear anyone call you that again . . . or suffer further abuse under the lash of Aunt Lorna's scolding tongue. Your life will be wonderful. . . . I'm certain of it."

And then her thoughts turned to the forthcoming night, and stark reality set in. She remembered what her two girlfriends, Margo and Gaylene, had told her about her wedding night. Margo had been married for three years, Gaylene for two. They were direct, and left no intimate detail unexplained. Nicki had sat red-faced, but enthralled

"It's terribly painful the first time, but it's over before you know it . . . and it can be endured," the bold Margo had drawled over her chicken-walnut salad. Fork poised in midair, she viewed Nicki's stricken face. "And if you're real lucky, he'll let you keep your nightie on."

"Margo!" Nicki had choked, then grabbed for her wineglass to take a fortifying sip. "You make it sound . . so . . . awkward."

"It is, my dear," her friend Gaylene had chimed in, chewing methodically on a bite of lobster. She had cast Margo a sideways glance. "You are the lucky one, dahling. My Freddy expects me to welcome his

27

kisses and caresses." Her eyes shifted to Nicki Sue's astounded face. "*And* he likes the lamp turned up a bit . . . so he can watch."

"How dreadful!" Margo had gasped.

"Yes," Gaylene had agreed.

"Oh my," Nicki Sue had groaned, then stared balefully at her friends.

"I hope Patrick feels it's perfectly acceptable for one to keep the covers up to your chin and your nightgown on the entire time."

"You do what your husband wants," Gaylene had stated firmly.

"Absolutely," Margo had said.

Nicki had felt nauseous.

"Patrick will want to do what makes *me* happy; I know he will," she had managed to stammer.

Her two friends had exchanged smiles and considered they'd done what they could to prepare their naive friend. She would just have to endure her husband's manly urges as best she could.

Nicki's cheeks grew rosier by the minute now as she reviewed their conversation, which had transpired two days before her wedding. She glanced nervously at the clock on the nightstand. Patrick would be joining her before long. Very soon she would know what it was like to be a woman in every sense of the word. She could not help becoming nervous as visions of Patrick holding her, kissing her . . . and . . . She swallowed painfully. This is it, Nicki girl, she thought. Your wedding night. Glancing about the lavishly appointed sleeping car, she strove to quiet her racing nerves.

"Now, just calm down," she murmured. "Margo said it could be endured. She wouldn't lie." She placed a trembling hand to her throat. She was glad that Patrick had been ever thoughtful of her feelings and having sensed her apprehensiveness after they'd fin ished dinner, announced that he was going to walk to the smoking car and have a cigar, and perhaps talk for a while with Lars Evanson, the Pacific Gold Coast's owner.

Nicki Sue reconfirmed how lucky she was to have found a man who considered her feelings before his own. And even though she was not looking forward to his lovemaking, she knew that she could expect him to be a considerate lover, and she *was* eagerly anticipating the special bond that they would share after this night. Having known so little love in her life, Nicki was eager for affection. And longed to return the same to her adoring husband. Soon, she thought, you'll begin to feel love for him. It will just take time, and you have that. This is just the first day of your life together. There will be many, many more. She kept reminding herself of this as she took off her traveling suit and began her toilette.

Opening her valise, she withdrew the pale ivory satin gown that she'd chosen especially for this night. She caressed the delicate lace that adorned the low neckline and was aware of the sheerness of the flowing gown. It was beautiful, and she hoped that Patrick would find her beautiful in it. She slipped into the ensemble, then brushed her long hair until it drifted around her slender shoulders in a cloud of dusky brown. She walked over to study herself in the dressing room mirror. She thought the clinging gown a bit too provocative, but Margo had been insistent that she buy it when they'd been shopping for her trousseau. But now that she was actually going to wear it in Patrick's presence, she found the material much sheerer than she'd first imagined. She recalled the plumper, rounder proportions of her girlfriends, and felt even more dismayed. Suddenly her hips seemed too narrow, her legs, too long and gangly.

Actually, the only part of her figure that she was satisfied with was her bosom. She did have nice breasts, she surmised, turning this way and that before the mirror. They were lush and full, with an enticing valley in between. Most of her friends had been considerable less endowed, and simply green with envy. And Nicki had to admit that she didn't mind their envy a bit.

Her eyes staring back at her through the looking glass were wide, slightly tilted at the corner, and a brilliant tawny gold. Her skin was creamy and smooth, and her mouth . . . ? It was here that Nicki Sue faltered just a bit. Her Aunt Lorna had always said that her mouth was definitely too generous in proportion, and in opinion. Now, feeling suddenly, defiantly, unrestrained, the young woman smiled undaunted at the image in the mirror.

She pinched her cheeks until they were becomingly rosy. Yes, that was better. Patrick was certain to think she looked beautiful.

"From this day forward you have only yourself to please, Nicki Sue. For your husband loves you madly just the way you are."

After dabbing a touch of the French perfume that Patrick had given her for a wedding present behind her ears, she removed her delicate wire spectacles and put them on the bureau. Then she slid into bed to await her husband's return.

Patrick Ryan was staring at his cards, unseeing. Every few minutes he'd pull out his timepiece and check the hour. Then he'd catch Lars watching him, and he'd smile a bit sheepishly and resume concentrating on the cards he held in his hand. He'd discovered Lars in the smoking car playing poker with

30

several other men, and while he hadn't wanted to become involved in a long, drawn-out card game on this of all nights, he was well aware that it was Lars's generous offer of his private car that would allow Patrick to spend his honeymoon night with his bride in style. After a short deliberation, he agreed to play just a few quick hands with Lars and his friends.

Patrick accepted one more glass of smooth Irish whiskey from the porter. The wind was whistling through the cracks in the windows and howling about the door. It felt good to be inside, where it was warm and a good drink was at hand. Some of his tension eased, and he began to relax.

"And there's plenty more where that came from," Lars replied, picking up a deck of cards and reshuffling them carefully.

Grinning, Patrick shook his head. "Not for me, I'm afraid. I don't think my new bride would appreciate my overindulging in the spirits tonight."

"You need to quit worrying so much about what the little woman thinks, Patrick ole boy," Lars said as he dealt out the cards with quick moves. "Put her in her place early, and keep her there."

Patrick picked up his cards. "That wouldn't work with this lady; she's someone real special, and I'm lucky to have found her."

Lars smiled and gathered up his own hand. "No insult intended, I assure you. I guess you have a gal with spirit to willingly give up a nice life in San Francisco and begin her married life in an isolated mining town like Bodie."

"Bodie?" another man at the table echoed. "Why, you are brave, taking a new bride to live there. Everyone knows that the smoke of battle barely clears off the streets before more appears. Heard tell it's a real shooter's town."

31

"It's not all that bad," Ryan chuckled. "And my wife will be just fine. Nicki hasn't lived all of her life in a big city. She's been around mining towns before. I know she's got what it takes."

"Well, take some advice from an old married man," one of the players, called Mort, interjected. "Leave the lady wondering where you've gone now and again, and she'll be thrilled to death when you finally come walking through the door. It works every time on my Hazel." He winked at Patrick and puffed on his cigar.

"Mort's right, you know," Lars said, studying Patrick's ruddy face in the muted light of the overhead gas lamp. "You're going to have the rest of your life together—but you've only got one chance at this sizeable pot here in the center of the table."

Everyone laughed, and Patrick just shook his head. He really was sorry now that he'd even allowed Lars to talk him into playing cards. His mind wasn't on a game of poker. It was on Nicki Sue. And right now that's where he truly wanted to be. But he continued to pretend interest in the game for another couple of hands, until finally he decided he'd had enough.

"This is my last hand," he stated as he studied the fresh deal. "There will be other nights for poker, but a fella's only got one wedding night, and a gal like my Nicki Sue. It doesn't set well with me to leave her alone any longer."

There were disgruntled looks from everyone, but Patrick remained firm in his decision.

"That's the way it has to be, gentlemen. My mind's made up."

"Whatever you say, Patrick," Lars forced himself to reply congenially.

"You can't blame us for trying to keep you from getting away with all of our money in your pockets." His gaze flicked over the neat stacks of gold coins in front of the Irishman before lingering with interest on Ryan's countenance.

Ryan was a big man, with wide shoulders and massive arms. His fiery red hair clearly bespoke his heritage, and his weathered face indicated the time he'd spent outdoors in the hot California sun. Lars knew of the Irishman's love of ranching, knew of it very well, as a matter of fact. Countless times he'd offered to buy Ryan's sprawling ranch, which was located in a desolate area outside of Bodie, California, and had his offers rejected. Lars didn't like rejection any more than he liked Patrick Ryan. Both got in the way of his plans. And he had plans for that land. Big plans. Ryan didn't appear to be doing anything with it. Of course, there wasn't much the average man could do with sand and rock. Worthless acreage that wasn't fit for man nor beast. But Ryan held fast to it for some reason. Purely sentimental, he'd told Lars. Hogwash, Lars was quick to surmise. Plain and simple. The Irishman was an emotional fool, but one thing he wasn't, and that was stupid. And to hold on to that barren property the way he did, when Lars had made him countless generous offers, just didn't make good business sense. Lars had persisted, making Ryan yet another proposition just a few minutes ago. And gritted his teeth again when Ryan had refused to sell.

"The answer's still no, Lars," the Irishman replied. "And I really don't wish to discuss business on my wedding night. I'm sure you can understand that."

"All right, all right, Patrick," Lars was able to respond lightheartedly. "No harm in a fellow asking."

Inwardly he was seething. He hadn't allowed the newlyweds his private, lavish accommodations simply because he felt like being generous. No, he'd been plotting ever since he'd learned from the conductor that Ryan was on board with his bride. He'd gone

33

personally to the passenger car and extended the invitation to the couple simply because he knew that it never hurt to sweeten the lure with a little honey. He'd been delighted when they'd unhesitatingly accepted. And Ryan's bride had been so sweet when she'd smiled at Lars, blushing prettily as she'd thanked him for his generosity. Lars had ordered his personal porter to see to their every need, even went out of his way to send the newlyweds a bottle of imported champagne from his private stock. And as he'd hoped, after Ryan had seen to his wife's comfort, he'd come to the smoking car to personally thank Lars for his generosity.

Lars was thinking at the moment how marriage seemed to have instilled in Patrick an even greater desire to keep the land. No doubt the old fool was thinking about raising a bunch of kids who would one day inherit the worthless place. Lars almost cursed out loud thinking of yet another obstacle that he might encounter. The Irishman's offspring! Who would undoubtedly share their father's love and devotion to the land. No! he wouldn't allow that— couldn't let this unsettled business with Patrick Ryan go on any longer. Within Lars there was building a coiling tightness that was making it difficult for him to breathe.

It was then Patrick threw down his cards with a flourish and a lopsided grin. "Guess this is my lucky day all the way around. Three kings and two ladies. Read 'em and weep, gentlemen."

Clamping his teeth down on his cigar, Lars tossed down his hand in disgust and watched Patrick rake in the pot. It wasn't his poor run of luck with the cards that prompted him to glower stormily at the Irishman. But Patrick didn't know this. He just chuckled gleefully, misinterpreting the reason for Lars's sullen expression.

"Sorry about fleecing you tonight, Lars," Patrick said. "It sure doesn't seem right in view of your kindness to my bride and me."

Lars grumbled under his breath and held up his empty glass to the hovering porter. It was promptly refilled. Sipping slowly, Lars found himself wondering once again what this man found so enthralling about the hellish property in the middle of nowhere. There wasn't a damn thing the average man could do with it but listen to the wind blow. Was it possible the Irishman knew something about that property no one else did? Lars snorted disgustedly to himself and tossed down another shot of bourbon. He knew he had had enough and should stop before he was roaring drunk, but having to accept defeat from anyone was not something Lars Evanson was accustomed to, or tolerated well. He did not accept the word *no* in his vocabulary.

Glancing downward as he reshuffled the cards once more, Lars considered the few remaining obstacles. He called to the porter to refill the Irishman's glass. A frown marred his brow when Patrick adamantly refused.

"No more for me, Lars," he stated quickly as he drained his glass and prepared to rise. "I meant it when I said I had to leave."

"Don't go rushing off so quick," the man called Mort interceded with a friendly smile. "It's still early. And you've got to give me a chance to win some of my money back. Fair's fair, you know."

Patrick waved a brawny hand through the air. "Some other time, perhaps." He suddenly appeared jovial. "After all, this is my honeymoon night. It wouldn't be good to dally with the fellas and chance missing it altogether."

Lars saw no way to object further. And the other men remained quiet. Lars raised his glass and studied the Irishman's rugged features over the rim. "No, I suppose it wouldn't at that. I guess we'll just have to continue this at another time. Goodnight, Patrick."

"Perhaps," Patrick returned with a nod. "If our paths should ever cross again." He picked up his hat and nodded. "Goodnight, gentlemen."

"Oh, I think we'll be seeing each other again," Lars called after his retreating form. "After all, we've hardly gotten to know one another, and I have immensely enjoyed our acquaintance so far."

"Until later, then," Patrick responded, barely considering his reply. He was suddenly anxious to leave. He was envisioning his sweet Nicki Sue waiting in that feather-soft bed for him. His blood heated in his veins. No longer attuned to Lars or the other men, he strode down the narrow aisle and opened the door. The clacking sound of the wheels immediately filled the car. He went through the door, calling back over his shoulder. "Thanks again for the use of your private car, Lars. I owe you one."

Lars leaned back in his chair and tried hard not to allow his thoughts to prod him to move too quickly. His companions, their enthusiasm dampened by their heavy losses to Patrick, immediately gathered up their remaining coins and called it a night. Lars was left alone with the sound of the train creaking and rumbling over the countryside, and the dark, blanketing night outside the window. Although he barely noticed. He was busy thinking, seeking a foolproof solution to his dilemma. Weaving drunkenly, Lars got to his feet and ambled past the porter, the only other occupant in the smoking car. "I think I'll call it a night, Leon. See to cleaning up, and then you can catch a few winks."

"Sure thing, Mr. Evanson," the man replied with a grateful smile, then added solicitously, "You be careful out there on that platform with the wind ablowing the way that it is. Don't take much for a body to get caught in the draft and get blowed overboard."

"Yes, I will," Lars replied, and shut the door behind him.

He ambled unsteadily through the next two cars. It was then he spotted Patrick just ahead, saw him pause on the platform leading to the private sleeping car. Lars hastened to the door, and it was then he observed Patrick leaning over the rail, appearing as if something had caught his eye.

Glancing around him, Lars made certain that no one was paying attention to him before he opened the door.

The train lurched around a sharp bend and Lars made his move.

Chapter Two

A revealing shaft of moonlight pierced the cloud-covered sky and slanted off of sheer granite walls to brighten the bleak landscape. The wind cut through the rock strata like a sharp-edged knife, its howl reminding the man who waited in the concealing darkness of a hungry wolf.

Jesse Kardel turned up the collar of his sheepskin coat and pulled the brim lower on his Stetson to ward off the biting wind. He'd known many nights liké this one. He'd felt a part of the night for a long time, and of the wolf who prowled the shadows in search of the kill. There was nothing he hadn't been through to have at last arrived at this point. A long, lonesome wail echoed through the valley. Jesse tensed in the saddle, listening. One corner of his mouth briefly twisted upward before tightening to a thin line.

"Fortune's coming around the bend," he told the man behind him. Get ready to ride."

Robert Bodine Kardel, Jesse's brother and lieutenant of the Kardel gang, struck a match against his thumbnail and cupped it in his palm. Pulling his timepiece from his pocket, he checked the hour.

"The Pacific Gold Coast is right on schedule. I guess we'll go join the rest of the boys."

"I knew we could set our watch by Evanson's train,"

Jesse said. "He's become real predictable over the years."

Robert Bodine glanced over at his brother, his expression tense. "Been waiting for this a long time, haven't you, Jess?"

"A lifetime, Bo." Jesse's words were tinged with bitterness.

"I can't wait to see the look on Evanson's face when he finds out his train's making an unscheduled stop," Bo stated humorlessly.

Jesse cocked his head, his smile grim. The train was less than a quarter of a mile away. He nudged his sorrel stallion with his knees. "Or better yet . . . when he hears it's being robbed."

Jesse was well aware that Lars Evanson boasted no outlaw had ever molested the Gold Coast's cars, and Jesse's own men (when they'd ridden the train to scout things out) had reported seeing sacks of minted double eagles enroute to the banks in Nevada County lying unguarded in the baggage cars like so much petty cash. But then, train robberies were still something rare.

There was a rumor that the James boys had recently robbed the Chicago and Rock Island Railroad in Iowa, but no one had ever held up a train without having it come to a full stop. Jesse wanted the element of surprise on his side. There wouldn't be any time for the train crew to sound a warning. The steam locomotive would be overtaken so swiftly and efficiently that it was certain the express messenger wouldn't have time to lock the connecting doors of his car. The train would not be halted until Jesse had managed to swing over to Lars Evanson's private car. The outlaw wanted to inform him personally that his boast of having the

39

safest mode of travel was about to be shattered.

The rest of his gang, six men who were some of the best riders and fast guns in the West, would await their leader's signal before spreading out through the cars and bringing the train to a halt.

Jesse and Robert Bodine sent their spirited horses flying down the mountainside, the thrill of the moment pumping adrenaline through their veins. They heard the cast-steel drivers of the steam engine protesting the curve, and caught their first glimpse of the locomotive as it sped out of the trees and into view.

Dakotah Smith snapped the lid of his watch closed after having glanced quickly at the hour. A tall man and a half-breed Mojave, his vigil inside the PGC passenger car had been a tense one. His long legs felt cramped and stiff in the confining space between the narrow wooden seats. He shifted in his seat, careful not to bump elbows with the snippy matron sitting to his left.

Moisture formed on his brow. It was warm in the car despite the cold night. Or perhaps it was just him, he reasoned. He didn't like being closed in for any length of time. It made him edgy, reminding him too much of the jail on the reservation he had frequented more often than he liked to remember. A trickle of sweat ran into his eyes. Removing his hat, he ran strong brown fingers through his flowing hair. His grandfather chided him about it, calling it "half-long," a Mojave expression. But his wife liked it. And that was good enough for Dakotah. His astute, dark-eyed gaze studied carefully each unexpected movement of the passengers. Out of the corner of his eye he observed the woman beside him cradle her cranky

40

baby protectively closer and move over yet another inch on the seat. She'd been glancing nervously at Dakotah like a mother hen protecting her chick ever since they'd left the station back at Eagle Rock.

He favored her with a bland smile. The woman's pinched nostrils distended. Dakotah's eyes turned glacial.

"Don't you be fretting so, ma'am," he drawled. "I only eat little babies when the moon is full. And tonight—it's only three quarters." He was rewarded with a disdainful snort before he swung his gaze to stare out of the window at the dark countryside.

"Smart-aleck Injun," he heard her grumble under her breath to the man sitting across the aisle from them. "If any of them would just take a little pride in their appearance instead of deliberately trying to look so savagely heathen, they might find decent folk would treat them better."

The perfectly groomed man nodded in agreement. He looked over the top of his spectacles at Dakotah's hawklike profile caught in the moon's light. "I couldn't agree with you more, madam," he said with obvious disdain. "They insist upon interacting with us, yet they don't know the first thing about good manners. Someone should have taught this young man a thing or two before they allowed him to wander off the reservation."

Dakotah, who was known to stare down even a killer grizzly when he chose, turned his head to pierce the man with an icy glare.

"Anytime you'd like to give it a try, mister, you just say the word."

The heavyset conductor bustled down the aisle, his face flushed from the exertion, and stood with arms akimbo before Dakotah. "Listen here, Injun. There's to be no trouble out of you, or I guarantee you this train will be making an unscheduled stop." He pointed a fat finger at him. "Do I make myself clear?"

Dakotah leaned back in his seat with a crisp nod and switched his gaze once more out of the window. This train's going to make an unscheduled stop all right, he thought smugly. But it won't be because of your order, Mr. Conductor. He failed to suppress a derisive smile, certain that when it came time for him to convince the passengers to stay in their seats, the conductor and the big mouth across the aisle would be singing a different tune.

Jesse observed the big headlight of the eastbound express slicing through the night. As the steam locomotive came full around the bend, he urged his horse into a laid-out gallop. Faster, faster, through the thick covering of towering pine and spruce, into the shallow stream before the big grade, and then out onto the flat stretch beside the tracks. Ahead of him the Kardel gang were swinging aboard the train, each man intent on his designated car and position.

The switch from horseback to the side of the caboose went smoothly for Jesse. He swung agilely onto the ladder and climbed up over the top. He ran along the roof of the swaying, rumbling car and leaped effortlessly onto the roof of the next car. Three times he repeated the same action, his long legs easily clearing the open space between the cars until he reached the stylish private car of Lars Evanson.

Without making a sound, he dropped to the platform.

* * *

Nicki Sue was feeling miffed. She'd been lying in bed waiting for Patrick to return for over an hour. He'd been gone so long that if she didn't know better, she'd think that he'd forgotten about her. Well, wedding night or no, she was getting sleepy. Yawning, she was just reaching to turn down the lamp when a hand on her shoulder made her jump. Her annoyance evaporated immediately.

"I was beginning to wonder if you intended to come back tonight," she said softly. She felt the mattress give beside her as he sat down. She turned her head to offer him a welcoming smile, and froze in motion. Sitting beside her was a complete stranger! She blinked and blinked again as she tried desperately to focus her vision clearly on the dangerous-looking man before her.

He was big, with obviously wide shoulders covered by a thick sheepskin coat. And the dark profile of his face revealed a predatory expression that sent every nerve in her body a warning message. Nicki had never felt so afraid in her life. With a shiver she drew back from him, only to freeze in motion when he smiled as though her fear somehow amused him.

"What a pleasant surprise," he said almost casually.

"Who . . . are you? . . . What are you doing in here?" she managed to gasp.

"Guess I might ask you the same question," he drawled.

"I have no idea what you're doing here—but I am supposed to be here!" she replied, astounded by the audacity of the stranger. She could feel her cheeks begin to burn beneath his probing stare.

He was studying her with the coldest deep blue eyes she had ever seen. "A very pretty blush, one I'm certain you've worked hard to perfect."

The obvious note of disgust in his voice stung her pride and she would have liked to slap his face soundly; however, she was no fool. Nicki Sue knew by the look of him—his clothes, his manner, and the guns tied down on his hips—that he was a man who didn't take chances, or abuse from anyone. He was here for a specific reason, and she could only hope that whatever it was did not involve her. Bravely, she drew a deep breath.

"Look—you'd better leave here this instant, or I am going to call the porter."

"You're not going to call anyone."

"We'll just see about that!" she shot back, her anger overriding her fear.

She opened her mouth as if to call out, and immediately his hand rested threateningly on the handle of his gun.

"Believe me, lady, you don't want to do that."

Nicki Sue stared dumbly at him, unable to tear her gaze away from his face. Time appeared to stand still as he drew her to him with his eyes. She felt pinned beneath that hard stare and mesmerized by his deep, commanding voice. A shadow of a beard covered his jawline, and she found herself thinking ridiculously that his jaw would no doubt be lean and square without it. But then, why should she be considering anything about him? He sure didn't give a damn what she thought of him, or that she resented the insulting way he let his gaze wander over her, almost as if he were envisioning her without any clothes. Perhaps she would do well to wonder more why he was here. Sobering, she considered the possibility of his being a killer . . . or a violator of women? Though more likely, simply a thief who skulked about in the night. She regarded him warily as that big hand moved to tilt his dusty Stetson back on his head. Coal-black hair tumbled across thick, dark brows.

"That's better now," he said when she quieted, his eyes narrowing on her face. "I take it your man's due back soon?"

Furious and fearful both, Nicki couldn't find the words to answer. The menacing scowl returned.

"Answer me, lady; I don't have all night."

The way in which he spat the word "lady" left no doubt in her mind of his contempt.

"No . . . no, he's not." Nicki Sue hurled the words at him, her heart racing.

"What time you expect him?" he demanded in an impatient voice.

"I . . . I'm not certain," she stammered, trying to regain her composure. The last thing she wanted to do was tell this man anything about her husband. Something about the look in his eyes — and yes, that cruel twist of a smile — clearly bespoke his intentions. She vowed resolutely that he could beat her black and blue and she would tell him nothing!

"How come I don't believe you?" he said in that cynically mocking voice.

"I . . . I don't really care if you do or not!" she half screamed at him.

"You should," he stated deadly soft. "If I were you, lady, I'd care a whole lot." He picked up a silky strand of her hair and toyed with the end. "Because it could make the difference between me staying here with you until he arrives — or leaving you alone."

Her eyes flew to the insolent grin now lurking around his mouth. There was a savage carnality about his lips that kept her gaze there. She could not help noticing how startlingly white his teeth were against the copper brown of his skin. Nicki deliberately

45

avoided looking into those chilling eyes, fearing what she'd discern in their depths. She was certain now that he was after Patrick, and trying to frighten her into revealing her husband's whereabouts. But she wouldn't tell! Even though she wanted desperately to tell him anything just to be rid of him. She couldn't let this man intimidate her! Her jaw set mutinously. He watched her eyes. They were beautiful and revealing, their cat-gold depths spewing fire at him.

"What's your name?" he asked, breaking the pregnant moment of silence.

Pulling the covers tighter about her, Nicki hissed. "Look — I'm not telling you anything, so you may as well be on your way."

Something close to a glitter of fury sparkled in his eyes. Nicki was scared to death but refused to cower further, instinctively realizing that it was the worst thing to do. He kept toying idly with the strand of her hair, wrapping the dusky brown tresses around and around his long fingers. She could feel her knees beginning to shake. He was close to shattering her weak shield of bravado. Her nostrils quivered slightly at the man smell that assailed them: horses and leather intermixed with fresh air and the wildness of the night. It was not an offending scent, nor unfamiliar, but of a sudden, seemed very threatening. Every instinct she possessed screamed at her to get away from him fast. Yet before she had a chance to move, he released her hair only to grab hold of her wrist.

"If you make a wrong move, or even so much as think about screaming, I'll wring your neck." His voice was abrupt. "Do I make myself clear?"

Nicki Sue gave no further thought to her vulnerability or the fact that she wore only a wispy nightgown. If he meant to rape her, or . . . even kill her,

46

she could not just lie here and let him do it. She glared up at him, sparks shooting from her eyes. "Yes," she spat. "I understand you perfectly. But whatever it is you plan on doing, mister, I won't make it easy for you." She could feel the heat and strength of him through his clothes, he was so near, and the thought of what he might do to her prompted her nails to curl into claws.

He noticed, and amusement crept into his voice. "My, my, but we're a feisty one," he cajoled softly, deceptively. "And that surprises me a bit. I would have thought he'd like them weak and submissive." Suddenly his eyes darkened and he jerked roughly on her wrist. Nicki's body came in contact with one lean, hard thigh. "You've got exactly two minutes to get up off that bed and get dressed — or face the consequences."

Her head flew up and she glared at him. Amber-gold eyes met the deep dark blue of his probing gaze. "You're hurting me," she gritted from between clenched teeth.

"Don't make me do anything more," he responded tautly.

She shuddered at the implication. There was absolutely no mercy in his eyes or his manner. "I don't know why you're doing this. If it's money you're after, take it. There isn't much —"

His short bark of laughter sent needles of anger piercing through her.

"What makes you think I want anything from you? Could be I just dropped in to pay my respects to your man."

"I don't know what to believe!" Nicki snapped, goaded. "The least you might do is offer some believable explanation."

"Don't push me too hard, lady."

She saw the truth behind those thick, dark lashes and fell silent, brooding now over her fate.

Jesse studied her closely. She wasn't exactly Evanson's usual style. He generally preferred voluptuous blondes with sugary voices and no sass. This one had plenty of fire; too much for the railroad man. But then, from everything that he'd heard about the man, he figured she was just a diversion for the night, bought and paid for. He shrugged mentally. What did he care anyway? He'd use her too. And this unexpected little surprise would only make the thrill of conquest even sweeter. Imagine Evanson's fury when he finally cornered him and just happened to mention what a fine time he'd just had with his little bedmate. A hot rush sizzled through his veins. He was living life on the sharp edge tonight, and he felt exhilarated by it, and her. He slipped lean, strong fingers beneath her neck.

"Maybe there is something I want after all," he said huskily. "Let's see if you're worth what he pays you."

Nicki went rigid. She couldn't believe what he'd just said. There was a determined set to his jaw and a glimmer of desire in his eyes. "You're the lowest form of—"

"I'd say it's the other way around," he cut in dryly. "Anyone who'd bed down with the likes of our friend appears to fit those words real good."

"I beg your pardon!" Nicki Sue gasped in outrage. She was seething with anger. No one had ever dared talk to her in such an insulting manner in her life.

"You heard me right," he said brutally, holding her head still by exerting a hint of pressure around her neck.

Her cheeks burning, Nicki lashed back. "I realize

your kind only knows a particular sort of woman . . .
but I am not that kind."

One dark, slanted eyebrow quirked upward. "I take
it by the look on your face that you expect me to
believe you?"

Nicki Sue's chin lifted in a stubborn gesture of
pride.

"It's . . . true. . . . You must have me confused
with someone else."

Jesse allowed his gaze to roam over her bare creamy
shoulders, fix upon the twin mounds that rose and
fell in rapid succession beneath the thin cover, then
slowly work their way over her slender form outlined
so temptingly beneath the tangled sheet. His breathing quickened and a coiling heat knotted in his belly.
She wasn't the most beautiful woman he'd ever seen,
but she had a way about her; and beneath that sheet
he had little doubt she was all female and very enticing. He drew the sheet slowly off her shoulders, his
fingers straying to the ribbon of lace that adorned the
neckline of her gown. He hadn't been with a woman
in weeks. And this one intrigued him. It was certainly
the wrong time to be thinking about it; but he was.

His voice held a husky timbre when he spoke. "I
haven't got anything about you confused. I know why
you're here, and who it is that you're waiting for. Now,
let's quit playing games. . . . We're wasting a lot of
good time."

Nicki's mouth quivered. "I won't allow you to touch
me, mister. I'd rather die first."

He made no move to release her. "And I think
you're lying."

She started to protest, then realized it was pointless.
He sensed her fear, her instinct to survive, and knew
damn well that she didn't want to die. He was staring

49

at her with a triumphant gleam in those chilling orbs. Nicki swallowed painfully, and to her mortification, tears stung behind her eyelids. She was innocent in many ways, but not so much that she didn't understand what was about to happen. "Leave me alone . . . just go away and I'll not tell anyone that you were here."

One long finger drifted downward across her breast, traced teasingly its round perfection. He could feel her heart beating in rapid tempo. She was a brave little thing and she had spirit. It was too bad for her that she'd taken up with Evanson.

"I'll go away . . . ," he replied whisper soft, "but when I'm good and ready." His hand left her neck to lace strong fingers through her long hair. He gripped the silky tresses tightly this time, then very slowly he drew her face close to his. He breathed inward slowly. "You smell real nice . . . like apple blossoms."

They were so close, their breaths intermingled and caressed each other's lips. She felt his hand slip inside her gown. It was burning hot against her cold flesh. Pride forced her to stifle a cry of terror. When his thumb flicked across the velvet texture of her nipple until it grew pebble-hard, she choked back a strangled moan. This man was taking liberties that only her husband was entitled to. He was intending on . . . on . . . Rational thinking escaped her — she could feel evidence of his desire for her préssing hard against her hip. He forced her head closer, and before she could do more than gasp, his lips were capturing her half-open mouth in a demanding kiss. He was aggressive and bold, his tongue stroking over her lips, her clenched teeth, demanding she allow him to awaken slumbering passion. Nicki did her best to refuse, trying hard not to whimper as his stubbled jaw grated against her chin. His kiss was so like him, she thought: consuming, demanding, overwhelming. One arm like steel banded around her. She knew it was useless to struggle, but she couldn't help herself. She arched upward and twisted in his arms.

His mouth withdrew a fraction from hers. "You sure are trying hard to convince me that you're new at this, aren't you?"

"I could never want you," Nicki managed to gasp, her eyes wide and vulnerable.

He held her pinned by his passion-darkened eyes. "But I want you." His hands came up to cup either side of her face, burning where they touched.

Tears of frustration and rage blurred her vision. He was threatening to blot out everything she had ever believed in. This man barely held in check a savage rage that lurked just beneath the surface of that cold, hard veneer. His very nearness, the absolute masculinity that emerged from him, was far too disturbing and overpowering. She let forth a cry of protest.

"Stop it! Just leave me alone."

With a sudden movement, he yanked the sheet away. In the struggle her gown had shifted up around her thighs. The cool air against her skin made her shiver. She struggled to get away. He held her tighter, his body moving to cover hers, his hand returning to her heaving breast. She shouldn't just let this happen! But what could she hope to do against his formidable strength? Nicki's reaction was prompted by stark fear. She bit down on his bottom lip. The acrid taste of blood met the tip of her tongue. She freed one hand to pummel him on the back. With a snarl of undisguised rage, he flung her roughly back on the bed and gripped her chin relentlessly between thumb and forefinger.

"You little hellcat," he growled. "Do you know how easy it would be for me to have you?"

"You'll have to knock me out or kill me first," Nicki Sue replied hoarsely, knowing full well that she meant it.

"Or maybe just stake you out — Indian fashion," he said, eyes glittering ominously in the dim light. "You know what that means?"

Nicki could feel her face fuse crimson at the lewd suggestion. She'd heard tell of things Indians had done to their captives. "Bastard," she growled low in her throat, "no-good—"

"The real you is starting to emerge, isn't it, lady?" His fingers had twisted in her hair, drawing her head back. "Your innocent act was almost convincing, you know that?" he said in sneering contempt. "But we both know that's all it is, just an act." He was glaring at her as if he hated her more than anyone or anything.

Nicki was past rational thinking, she was so frightened. She only knew that this man was beyond any depth of human emotion. He was absolutely ruthless, and now she knew, he'd really come here tonight to kill. But why would he want to hurt Patrick? Bile rose in her throat. The bunched muscles of his arms held her prisoner and, she knew, gave only a hint of his true strength. She lay completely still now, barely breathing, and watched him closely. He'd loosened his grip slowly. "Now — I think we understand each other perfectly. You just be a good girl and tell me exactly what I want to know, and you can make it easy for yourself."

Her hands came back on either side of the pillow, then burrowed beneath it. "Why are you doing this?" she asked, her eyes huge in her pale face. And then,

"You wouldn't even hesitate to kill me if you had to . . . would you?" She saw him watching her, but he didn't seem aware of her right hand inching under her pillow, groping for the derringer she always kept there, no matter where she was. It was a protective measure she'd learned from her father after they'd taken to living in one mining town after another. She'd been alone most of the time and had quickly learned to shoot a gun.

"Kill you," he laughed softly. "The last thing I would want to do to someone who looks as good as you would be to kill you."

"But I know now that you wouldn't hesitate . . . if you had to."

He took his time in answering, as if he were considering his reply.

At last he said, "No — I wouldn't hesitate."

Moving fast, Nicki withdrew the derringer and pointed it at him.

"I feel exactly the same," she stated calmly.

If he was at all surprised, he did not show it. His gaze narrowed. "Then you'd better pull that trigger, for if you don't, I guarantee you that you're going to regret it."

It was then Jesse heard the distinct sound of gunfire outside. The signal. There was no more time to waste on the woman; he had to make his move fast.

Nicki flinched, thinking momentarily that she'd somehow pulled the trigger and shot him. Before she realized the gun had not discharged, he'd grabbed her hand and yanked her off of the bed. She fell to her knees in front of him, her hair cascading in a wild maelstrom around her.

He seemed so tall and formidable towering over her, and his voice when he spoke was without one shred of emotion.

"Remember this for future reference. As soon as you draw down on someone — shoot them. Don't take the time to think about it, or it damn well might be the last thing that you'll ever do."

Chapter Three

Nicki felt numb with shock. Outside the plush car in another part of the train, shrieks of panic echoed through the night. Bewildered, feeling as if she'd become a part of some terrible nightmare, Nicki stared wild-eyed at the man looming over her. There was something about the merciless gleam in his eyes that sent a warning message to her brain. Careful, Nicki, her inner self warned, for he can read your eyes and know exactly what you are thinking. Her stomach fluttered in fear as he reached forward to entwine his fingers in her hair, then slowly drew her to her feet. Nicki was tall for a woman; her eyes, almost directly meeting his, gave no hint of the tumultuous emotions inside her. There was something about him that held her spellbound, and it took the crack of a rifle shot, followed by a hoarse cry, to send him hurtling away from her.

Jesse immediately forgot the woman. His razor-sharp instincts were always attuned to any danger. There was no doubt in his mind that something had gone wrong.

"Damn it!" he growled, and spun away from Nicki and out the door.

Nicki was too frozen in fear to move. One minute he'd been standing there before her, and the next, it was as if he'd never really been there at all. She glanced furtively around her. She had remembered his muttered curse, had stared in numb disbelief as he'd whirled away from her and tore from the car. He truly was gone! And she was alive! Her heart was pounding hard against her rib cage as she scrambled quickly to her feet, every muscle quivering in reaction. She tried to think calmly what she should do. The sounds of gunfire had diminished, but the screams continued. The train was slowing, the wheels shrieking in protest. Nicki's pulse beat wildly as a vivid picture formed in her mind. She had heard tales of a new breed of outlaw that had emerged to keep pace with the times.

"Train robbers . . . . ," she breathed shakily. With chilling clarity the full import of her words hit her. "The train is being robbed!"

And Patrick? Where was he? Terror consumed her, prompted her to hurriedly fling off her gown and pull on a dress, then scramble about for stockings and shoes. Glancing about, she did not see her derringer, but there was no time to waste looking for it. Flinging open the door, she hurried forward to the next car, her only thought to find her husband. The smoking car was empty except for the porter, who was huddled in a corner, an expression of stark fear on his face.

"I'm looking for my husband," she told the man. "He was supposed to have been here earlier. . . . He has red hair. . . ." He was staring blankly at her. "Please! Patrick Ryan? Do you recall the name?"

The porter shook his head. "I never seen nuthin' . . . ," he babbled, "just heard all the ruckus . . . and then . . . Mr. Evanson, he came tearing back through here like a madman—"

"Was Mr. Evanson with anyone?" she interjected.

The porter shook his head furiously. "No . . . no, he was alone."

56

"Did he tell you where he was going?" Nicki persisted.

"Never said nuthin'—but I expect he was after them robbers."

Nicki heard her worst fears confirmed. Overwhelmed with urgency, she tore from the car and made her way to the passenger coach, praying that she would find Patrick there. As she opened the door, Nicki's vision riveted immediately on the man standing in the aisle brandishing a gun. Nicki dared not move. Their eyes met. His were black as night and glittered with reckless lights. He motioned her forward with the gun.

"Get in here and don't make a fuss," he demanded brusquely. When she remained frozen in numb horror, he snarled. "Move, lady! Don't take time to think about it!"

Nicki Sue saw at once that he was not the same man who'd accosted her earlier. This one had long, dark hair and ebony eyes. He was of medium build and everything about him looked Indian. The frightened passengers were huddled in their seats, their faces frozen in masks of absolute terror. Nicki stepped quickly by him and took the first available seat. A woman was pressed in the far corner of the wooden bench sobbing uncontrollably, a screaming baby grasped to her bosom.

The train was coming to a grinding stop, the cars shuttling their couplings, the unexpected braking nearly flinging the passengers from their seats. The screams of terror from within the public coaches became more frantic.

"All of you folks just try and stay as calm as possible!" the outlaw yelled above the din of noise. "I'm not going to harm you none if you just do as you're told!"

"You gonna rob us, mister?" one young boy around twelve asked bravely, his round face as white as the shirt that he wore.

Dakotah glanced over at him. "No," he said simply.

The lad appeared disappointed. "You're not?"

"That's what I said, didn't I?" Dakotah replied, somewhat amused.

"You like the Jameses—don't steal from plain folks?" the precocious youngster persisted.

"If you don't pipe down, boy, I might make an exception," Dakotah told him with a meaningful glare.

The conductor, who when he heard the word robbery had attempted to run from the passenger car and sound a warning, was lying slumped over the city slicker who'd scorned Dakotah earlier. Jesse had made it clear to all of his men that no one was to be hurt if it could be avoided. Well, Dakotah had tapped the conductor with the butt of his gun as lightly as possible. And it had been necessary. Everyone was stunned as they realized that they were witnessing an honest-to-God train robbery. So far, no one else had tried to act brave.

Dakotah was glad that the woman who'd entered the car had unexpectedly settled down. When he'd first glimpsed the look of desperation in her golden eyes, he'd been prepared for anything. It was vital that everything went just as they'd planned. He was the only member of the Kardel gang who chose not to wear a mask, stating with an amused chuckle that most folks claimed one Indian looked about the same as the next, so he figured he had little or nothing to worry about by exposing his face.

"Young man! how long are you going to hold us up

58

like this?" an elderly lady sitting beside Dakotah's intimidating form inquired boldly. She wore a hat adorned with purple flowers and impatiently waved a pearl-handled cane. Her sharp eyes scrutinized him.

"Not much longer, ma'am," Dakotah replied politely. "Now, would you please stop thrashing that walking stick about? You're beginning to make me real nervous."

The old woman's lips pursed sourly. "Well, I hope that we won't be detained much longer. Because my son is supposed to pick me up at Whiskey Flats. And he does not like to be kept waiting."

"I'll be out of here directly," Dakotah sought to reassure her. "So just quit your fretting." The plan was for him and a few of the men to guard the passengers in the coaches while Robert Bodine and Smiley hit the express car. Jesse was to take care of his own business, and afterward he would join them. The sound of the door opening once again drew his immediate attention. His gaze riveted on the intruder. His expression was somewhat bewildered when he saw Robert Bodine enter through the door when he'd been expecting to see Jess.

"Is everything all right?" Dakotah asked.

"There's been some trouble," a masked Robert Bodine said upon reaching Dakotah's side. He kept his voice low. "One of the passengers is dead."

"Damn," Dakotah muttered. "How'd it happen?"

"No one's really certain. It appears the guy took a tumble off the train. I saw him going over the platform outside the smoking car as we were riding up. It was chaos at first, but we've got everyone calmed down a bit now," Robert Bodine explained. "There were several passengers who must have been looking out the windows about the time it happened. They went crazy. We just got them quieted down." He shrugged. "Guess he just lost his balance."

"Does anyone know who the guy is?"

"Not yet. I just caught a glimpse of his red hair. One passenger mumbled a name . . . Brian . . . ?" He shrugged. "Something like that."

"Shouldn't we go back for him? Maybe the poor bastard's still alive."

Robert Bodine shook his head negatively. "He's a goner for sure. No one could have survived that fall."

Biting her lip to hold back hysteria, Nicki Sue listened to what they were saying. Her stomach had knotted when she'd heard the one bandit mention the unfortunate man's red hair, and the name, Brian. Brian? she wondered, or perhaps — Ryan?

Dakotah took a deep breath. "I expect our man is riled plenty."

Robert Bodine glanced around him and saw several of the passengers straining their ears to hear their conversation. "Yeah, he is at that. Guess we'd better keep it down. Everything in here seems under control. These folks don't appear to have seen anything, and we sure don't need to excite them unnecessarily. They'll have to go back for the body later."

"I reckon that's all we can do," Dakotah agreed.

Suddenly Robert Bodine's mood brightened and his eyes gleamed. "Jumpin' Jehoshaphat! But wait till you get a look at the minted gold pieces we took out of the express car. It was overflowing with double eagles, just like you said it'd be. We'll be holding the train so that Smiley can bring the horses. You just keep these nice folks company awhile longer and then it's 'Adios, amigos,' and outa here."

"Just give a holler when we're ready to ride," Dakotah said, his face suddenly breaking into a smile. "I sure would like to have seen the look on Evanson's face when he heard his train was being held up. Bet he's madder than all get out. Too bad—that money's going to help a lot of folks where I come from."

"Evanson was fuming all right. He turned into a madman. Strange thing, he wasn't where Jesse expected him to be. He almost got the drop on us in the express car, but we took care of him before he realized what was happening."

"Bet you had a real good time doing it."

"Yeah, I did," Robert Bodine grinned. "I managed to sneak up behind him just as he was coming at Billy. I grabbed him in a bear hug and just shook that big forty-four right out of his hand. We even made him help us gather up the money. You should have seen it! All the time I was explaining to him how he could count on getting together with all of us again real soon. Whoo-eee! if looks could kill, I'd be dead right now!" Robert Bodine pounded Dakotah on the back good-naturedly before turning about and striding down the aisle and out of the car.

Nicki Sue felt sick to her stomach. She clenched her hands in her lap, a pitiful sob bubbling in her throat. Where was Patrick? A man with red hair had fallen off the train—Patrick was nowhere to be seen. And something within her was screaming that it was because he was lying dead back there on the side of the tracks. The image in her mind was so painful that she could not bear it. He was such a big, vital man, and so able to take care of himself. How could he have simply fallen off the train? Hysteria overruling common sense, she jumped up from her seat and darted past a surprised Dakotah toward the door. She was certain now that Patrick must have confronted the robbers unexpectedly, and they'd pushed him off the train.

"Lady! Where in the hell do you think you're going?" Nicki heard the bandit snarl, and when she ignored him, "For God's sake, lady, don't make me shoot you!"

Nicki reached for the door handle.

The stunned passengers watched the scene unfold with horror on their faces. An expectant hush settled in the car. The deadly click of the outlaw's gun hammer sent a ripple of nerve-tearing sobs through the passengers.

"Damn it! Don't shoot her!" came the familiar deep voice, and Dakotah swung his gaze over the woman's head to see Jesse stride through the car door. He stepped in front of the woman's path.

"I don't think it would be a good idea for you to leave here, ma'am," he told her, moving to take her arm. Nicki Sue eluded him and he frowned. "Let's not make this difficult. . . . Just return to your seat."

Nicki shook her head wildly. "No! you don't understand . . . I must find him! Let me pass." She glanced upward at the tall, imposing figure blocking her path. Her eyes fixed upon the hard glare above the mask covering his lower face—and she knew him then. "You—!" she spat.

He reached out for her and she shrank back from him—then suddenly came at him like a wildcat. One hand swung outward. Quickly, Jesse dodged the swipe of her nails. He was cursing heatedly under his breath, wishing that he'd taken the time to tie her up before he'd left Evanson's car. Now he didn't know what he was going to do with her. But one thing was for certain. If he didn't manage to get the little wildcat quieted immediately, she just might stampede the entire bunch of them. And then they'd have one heck of a mess.

"You'd better settle down," he murmured harshly, "or I'm going to have to settle you down myself."

Nicki Sue kept fighting, forcing him to get rougher than he liked.

Dakotah stood by staring nervously, careful to keep one eye on the passengers as he tried to explain to Jesse what had gone wrong. "I don't know what happened to her," he called out to him over Nicki Sue's unladylike shrieks. "I sure am sorry. She caught me by surprise going loco on me like that. I didn't have a chance to catch her before she was past me."

"Save the explanations for later," Jesse ground out. "Just keep these people in their seats until I get her out of here. Then you follow us — we're about ready to ride."

"Sounds real good to me," Dakotah said, keeping one eye on the stunned passengers and the other on Jesse and the crazy woman. She had effectively twisted away from him. White teeth bared and those cat eyes spewing hatred, she was giving Jesse one heck of a time. Dakotah breathed a sigh of relief that he no longer had to deal with her.

Jesse caught Nicki deftly to him. He tried to hold her, but she fought him with proud defiance.

"Let me go . . . you don't understand . . . ," she half sobbed, thrashing in his arms in a desperate effort to break his steel-like grip.

"Shut up," Jesse snarled at last, having noticed the passengers squirming edgy-like in their seats. They were just about to bolt too. He saw the glimmer of panic in her eyes, and fear on her face, but knew she wouldn't quit fighting. It was just her nature to give as good as she got.

"I won't let you keep me here — I must go to him!"

she hissed.

"You're not going anywhere!"

She looked up at that, and appeared as if she'd like to scratch his eyes out. Jesse wasted no further time, but snaked an arm around her waist, and before she could protest, he'd scooped her under his arm and strode briskly out the door and onto the platform. Dakotah warned the passengers to stay seated and hurried to follow behind Jesse. To Nicki, who was imprisoned rigidly beneath one of Jesse's arms, it seemed suddenly as if the whole world had gone mad. Up ahead, the steam engine huffed in protest as the engineer closed the throttle, then turned to glare at the man holding a gun to his head.

Lars Evanson, who was slumped beside the empty safe in the express car still unable to believe that his train had just been robbed, gingerly put a hand to his bruised ribs. They hurt like the devil. He cursed his inability to have gotten the drop on that smart-ass outlaw before he'd jumped him and shaken him senseless. And the other one—the leader with the cold eyes, who had come in at the last and had taken such pleasure in goading him about stealing his money. He had told Lars that they'd be meeting again soon, to remember that. He'd remember him, Lars thought, and those eyes of his: cold, hard, midnight-blue. They had glimmered with killing intent at Lars, and he'd thought it best not to push his luck too far, so he'd kept real still until they'd gone. And just as the menacing leader had turned to leave, throwing a sack of money over his shoulder, he'd told Lars with sneering contempt that the next time he saw him, things would go smoother, and he'd make certain Lars paid even

64

more for a debt the railroad man owed.

Lars grunted to himself now. Debt? What was the outlaw talking about? He didn't owe anybody anything. Although now—he owed that son of a bitch a heap of trouble for stealing his gold. That outlaw was a walking dead man. Nobody robbed the PGC without asking for trouble. Shakily he rose to his feet, intent on retrieving the Winchester that was kept next to the safe. The express messenger was lying unconscious next to the rifle, and Lars stepped over him without concern. Snatching up the weapon, he lunged toward the doorway. He peered cautiously about outside at the group of outlaws who were preparing to mount up. They were laughing and having a real good time while they were hauling off his money.

"You aren't going to get away with this," Lars growled.

The moon was cloud-covered and the light was bad, but Lars was still able to sight down on the tall cold one who was the leader. He was real careful not to expose himself and take the chance of getting his head shot off. He saw Nicki Sue trying to pull away from the outlaw, and sighted down on the struggling pair. He didn't care if she was in the way. Perhaps it might even work out to his advantage if he got her. Nothing mattered to him as much as trying to stop the bastards who had stolen his money. The last thing he needed now was his railroad developing the reputation of an easy road to rob. He had enough problems, what with finding it increasingly difficult to raise enough money to lay more track. He was certain his little road had great prospects; he'd been successful in luring investors when he'd first begun years ago on the outskirts of San Francisco. And even though he had to bleed the line many times over for need of short-term profits, he had still been able to continue to attract investors and sell bonds.

But lately the picture was looking less rosy. The Pacific Gold Coast was slow to build because of Lars's own personal greed and, over the past year, Patrick Ryan's failure to allow the road passage over his land. Without Ryan's approval, the road would have to divert around the Ryan property; and that meant laying track through granite instead of the softer earth and straighter section across Ryan's spread. For if Lars would opt to build around him, it would take months, and vast sums of money, to blast through the granite hillside north of the Ryan property. It was turning into an unpleasant situation, and even the ever-faithful Krystal King, who awaited Lars in Bodie, was becoming less enthused about investing any more of her money in his road. Lars couldn't have that. He needed to put all obstacles in his road's path aside. By God! He had worked too hard to have everything go awry now! He would see his dream of connecting his rails with the transcontinental railroad through the Nevada Summit. And no one was going to upset his plans.

Jesse had hurried down the steps and greeted his men, who were beginning to congregate from their assigned posts. When they caught sight of the disheveled Nicki Sue wedged firmly under their leader's arm, they took to hooting and hollering like a pack of coyotes.

"Taking along a souvenir, big brother?" Robert Bodine couldn't resist saying.

"Help yourself to the pick of the litter?" came another voice.

Laughter rippled through the group.

"Yeah, and all the time he had us convinced he was staging this job for money," the man they called Smiley chortled.

"When you're all through carrying on, I'd like to get out of here," Jesse said, his eyes unreadable above the black mask. He'd released Nicki and had taken his horse's reins from Smiley. He glanced briefly over at Nicki as he swung up in the saddle. She was quieter now, appearing somewhat in shock. At least she wouldn't be causing any more trouble for them. It was then he felt it—that same sense, or maybe even smell, of danger that he'd learned to recognize and act upon. Without hesitating, he leaned over the side of his horse and reached out for the woman just as a shot split the air beside her. She didn't even flinch.

Robert Bodine stood in his stirrups for a hard look at the train cars. He turned to his scowling brother, who had grabbed the startled woman by the hand. "It looks like Evanson. We've got to go—now! Leave her!"

Jesse would have liked nothing better, but something wasn't right; one of those shots had been aimed for the woman. Why had they been deliberately fired at her?

The horses threatened to bolt, and the men had their hands full trying to keep them under control. Several shots were exchanged. Smiley reined quickly in beside Jesse.

"Jess, this job's going to go haywire if we don't get out of here real fast!"

The Winchester opened up again, a bullet whining past and into the trunk of a nearby tree. Jesse was glad that Evanson was a poor shot. He knew he had to act quickly or see everything fall apart. His men

67

were scattering, and soon someone was going to end up wounded, or dead. Evanson never did give a damn about anyone but himself, and of course, his railroad. Jesse's eyes fell on the woman he perceived as Evanson's high-priced lady. He saw her eyes widen in surprise when, with a sweep of his arm, he swung her up behind him on the horse.

"Hang on tight, lady; you're going for a little ride," he called over his shoulder.

Nicki Sue was terrified, but when she felt the horse surge forward, she flung her arms around Jesse's waist and held on for dear life.

Jesse waved his men onward. They took off for the hills. Their first train robbery was over. And it had been an adventure to fire the blood and provide incentive for their next ride. And there would be another. Jesse had no doubt about that.

Lars saw them retreating and eased the hammer back to full cock. He sighted down on the Ryan woman's back.

"Such a convenient way to eliminate unwanted obstacles," he murmured under his breath, then cursed when he heard movement behind him.

"One of the passengers has been killed, Mr. Evanson!" the conductor blurted as he rushed into the car. "There's talk all over that one of the outlaws tossed the man over." He was waving his arms frantically. "You've got to go back and get the body, sir. Or we just might have a riot on our hands."

"Son of a bitch!" Lars snarled at the untimely intervention.

The conductor's head bobbed excitedly. "Ain't it the truth, though! I sure never dreamed we'd have to worry about this train being robbed." He fell silent beneath Lars's chilling glare.

Outside, Nicki Sue held tight to Jesse as he sent his big sorrel into a full gallop to a covering of pines. She bit back a scream of panic. Somewhere back on the lonely, dark tracks, Patrick lay dead. And she would be lucky if the same fate didn't befall her. Holding back a sob, she closed her eyes against the biting wind that stung her eyes and sent needles of cold into her skin, knowing she had to concentrate her thoughts on how to stay alive.

Jesse caught up to the other gang members after a half mile. When they were certain that no one was following them, they slowed their mounts to an easier pace. Nicki Sue was barely aware of the exchange of words around her. She was numb with fear and cold, but her mind was already racing with thoughts of escape.

"Why in the blue blazes did you bring her along?"

Jesse fixed a hard stare on Dakotah Smith. "We need her. She's Evanson's woman. And having robbed his train, you can bet he's going to have a posse hot on our trail within hours."

"How's she going to help us?" Dakotah asked, his dark eyes uneasy.

"Well, think about it. If we get cornered, we'll have some bargaining power."

Dakotah stared at the merciless eyes of his friend. "You can't really be planning on keeping her with us. She'll slow us down."

"She's our ace in the hole. And we do—what I say." Jesse gave a quick jerk of his head. "Now, let's quit talking and do some riding."

Without further argument, the group headed due west.

It was sometime later, when they were certain they were far enough away from the scene of the holdup, that they banded together beside a river running parallel to a range of cliffs. The men dismounted and led their horses to water. They removed their masks, comfortable with the knowledge that it was too dark for the woman to clearly discern their features; and Jesse had taken her down to the river, where she could not see them. The men congregated on a rock ledge hanging over the river to roll cigarettes and ease jangled nerves. They'd had one heck of a good time; but it *had* been nerve-wracking with dodging bullets and a screaming virago to disrupt their smooth plans.

Jesse slid out of the saddle and pulled the woman into his arms. She was light as a feather and, surprisingly, didn't protest his assistance. Involuntarily, she clutched at his shoulders as he tumbled her into his arms. He didn't fail to notice that she smelled nice; sort of like apple blossoms in spring. His eyes found hers, which were wide and staring with condemnation at him. She sure looked a sight, with her hair long and windblown around her shoulders and her face smudged by tearstains.

Against his will, an emotion he'd thought long buried stirred. With a smothered curse, he strode toward the river. He didn't know at the moment what he really intended to do with her, or how he'd eventually use her, but he had considered on the long ride that she might have some information about Evanson he could use. It was then Nicki stirred against him, her body feeling all soft and warm against his. Trying not to think about what he would do with her when she was no longer of any use to him, Jesse hunkered down beside the river. His gaze traveled over her face. The moon shed enough light for him to clearly distinguish

70

her arresting features.

He remembered the feel of her hair in his fingers, soft and luxuriously thick, like the mane of a thoroughbred. And those incredibly long-lashed cat-gold eyes where magnificent, even when they spewed hatred at him. Somewhat wryly, he caught himself thinking that she might be passably pretty if she were cleaned up some. He brushed the back of his hand across her cheek just to see her reaction, and saw her nose twitch as if his very nearness offended her. He was not in the least surprised to find that even after that hard ride, her spirit remained intact. For the first time, he wondered if he'd borrowed himself more trouble than he might care to handle.

Nicki Sue stared up at him, and found her worst suspicions confirmed. It was, indeed, the same man who had burst into the private car and accosted her. She had not gotten a very good look at him before, what with all of the confusion and her concerns for Patrick foremost on her mind. But now she studied him closely, and knew beyond any doubt that it was him. She watched warily as Jesse slipped the scarf from around his neck and· dipped it in the river, then squeezed out the excess moisture. When he went to wipe off her face, Nicki tore out of his arms to sit back on her heels and glare at him.

"Don't you touch me — you! If you do . . . I'll . . . I'll scream."

He paid her no mind but reached forward and brushed back the hair from her cheek. "Go ahead," he stated blandly just before he swiped across her startled face with the cold cloth. "No one here cares, so scream yourself hoarse if it will help settle you down any." His expression was as impassive as his Indian friend. He was in total control.

71

Pent-up fury surged through Nicki, and she knocked his hand aside.

She was begging for a fight, and Jesse knew it. Christ, but he'd never known a woman who was such a scrapper. He could feel the enmity radiating from her. Well, enough was enough. He grasped her behind the neck and held her still. She grabbed hold of his wrist. His eyes pierced her.

"We're not going to have us another tussle here, lady. I've had my fill of wrestling with you for tonight."

"The feeling is mutual, I assure you," she responded acidly.

Jesse loosened his grip, and Nicki failed to suppress a sigh of relief. He grinned sardonically at her before shrugging out of his jacket and draping it about her trembling shoulders. "Sorry we had to leave before you could pack, but your friend didn't leave us much choice." When she would have brushed off the coat, he threw her a meaningful scowl. "Keep it on. The last thing I need is for you to come down sick."

"Who are you referring to when you speak of my friend?" she inquired with a puzzled frown, not daring to toss aside his coat.

"You know good and well who I'm talking about," Jesse scoffed.

Her eyes widened with awareness. "Perhaps . . . you mean Mr. Evanson," she stated in complete innocence.

"Yeah, Mr. Evanson," Jesse snorted. Nicki looked genuinely puzzled. He considered her coldly, assuming that she was being coy, trying to make him think that she meant nothing to Evanson in order to save her own skin. "Call him anything you want, lady. But I was the one in the private car, remember? And you were the one waiting there all tucked in real cozy-like beneath Evanson's sheets."

Nicki's face fused scarlet. "Just what is it that you've been implying from the first?" she asked, her tone acid.

"That your 'friend,' Evanson, is more than a casual acquaintance," Jesse stated bluntly. "And he pays cold, hard cash for your company."

Her eyes widened in shock. "That is absurd!" she cried, jumping to her feet.

"I don't think so," Jesse said, his voice hard and unyielding. He was before her in an instant, grasping hold of her arm. "You keep him company on those long, lonely trips he takes, don't you, sweetheart?"

His crude accusations shattered her nerves, but Nicki quickly vowed not to offer him too much information for fear of jeopardizing her well-being. But he was treating her abominably; she vowed when she finally did get away from him that she would go to any lengths to make certain that he was caught and punished for everything that he'd done. But right now she had to think about how she would eventually escape him. For she was certain he would never let her go; she was the only person on the train who could identify him. A passenger had been killed. If he let her go, she could put a noose around his neck; they both knew she would—and picnic beneath the gibbet. Determined to remain strong, she forced some semblance of composure and offered him an explanation she hoped sounded plausible.

"Not that it's really any of your business; however, I feel the record should be set straight. I *was not* in Evanson's private car for the reasons you claim. Why, I hardly even know the man. We're acquainted through mutual friends, and when he found out that I was traveling on board, he was kind enough to offer me his private sleeping car." She shrugged. "That's really all there was to it."

Jesse smiled disagreeably, thinking what a consummate little liar she was. Why, she didn't so much as blink an eyelash when she spouted that one. "I remember a lot of things about our first meeting—and you were damn well expecting someone. Evanson sure wasn't very happy seeing you with me." His gaze narrowed. "He would have shot you if not for me—or have you managed to put that out of your mind?"

Nicki vaguely recalled seeing someone (who could have been Evanson) standing in the express car door just moments before the gunfire had exploded. It didn't make any sense. Why should he want to kill her? But in thinking back, he certainly hadn't seemed to care whether she was in the line of fire or not. Nicki's eyes met the outlaw's. A chill swept down her spine. Then—she knew what this man was trying to do. He wanted her to think that Evanson had been trying to kill her so she'd have doubts about going back. And it was clear that he obviously remained convinced she was Evanson's paramour. He was going to use her: barter her to the law should they catch up to him. The full knowledge of her precarious situation made her tremble.

She could not let this outlaw know she was Patrick's wife. If he learned her name, and the dead man did turn out to be Patrick, he'd make certain she didn't tell what she knew. She had to keep him guessing if she was to protect her own life; and then she'd see this bandit in hell with a smile. She allowed a brief flicker of pain to cross her face.

"How can you be so cruel? Things aren't as they appear."

He smiled lazily at the pitiful look in her cat-gold eyes. "You're really very good, but not quite good enough."

There followed an intimidating silence. Nicki studied the sinister half smile that played about his lips. Her mouth felt as dry as cotton, and she was on the edge of hysteria. She was beginning to realize that she wasn't really any different from this man. When it came to survival, you would do just about anything to stay alive, even contemplate taking a human life.

Finally he said, "Look — just don't go trying to put anything over on me and we'll get along a whole lot better. I'll be watching you real close — and you won't stand a chance if you try and escape."

Nicki did not flinch, but stood her ground with seeming compliance. "I'll do exactly as you ask, mister," she said with forced calm, praying he'd believe her.

He was watching her with frigid eyes, judging her carefully. God, Nicki, don't let him goad you now, she thought. She was filled with vengeful wrath, but wisely refused to allow him to taunt her into revealing her true emotions. He was cunning, but then, so was she. It would be interesting to see who got the better of whom in the end.

"For your sake, I hope so," he finally murmured.

Suffering beneath his humiliating treatment, Nicki was forced to bite down on her bottom lip to keep from shouting at him. She never wanted him to know how very much he set every nerve in her body on edge.

For the next twenty-four hours Nicki Sue brooded over her fate, and could not help but wonder if he meant to kill her when she was finished serving a purpose. The train robber (as she silently referred to him) said very little to her. They had separated from the others, and where they were headed, she did not know. They were forever riding, just the two of them, their final destination unknown. But the long, silent hours gave her time to think, and plot, and wait for just the right moment to make her move. For now she knew she had to escape. It was her only chance of getting out of this alive.

She had observed that every few hours he would stop the horse and take out his field glasses to scan the distant horizon. She'd think then of sliding off the horse and dashing away. But there was never a place with decent cover to hide, and she knew he'd find her if she didn't seek just the right place.

As she visualized what he might do to her should he catch her, her stomach knotted and a quiver raced through her. She settled back to wait awhile longer.

By the time that dusk was settling, Nicki Sue thought she'd best make her move. She waited until they had stopped to stretch their legs and share a bite of supper. He didn't appear to be paying her any mind, but stood with his back to her and adjusted the saddle pack on his horse. She quietly began walking toward a scraggly group of thorny bush on the edge of towering fir trees. He had afforded her little privacy, except when absolutely necessary. She hoped this was one of those times he'd assume she was answering nature's call. And then she felt his eyes bore into her back, like twin shards of ice between her shoulder blades. Purposely, she spun slowly and faced him down with all of the dignity she could muster. She should have remembered that he was no gentleman, and that he cared less if he appeared crude in her eyes.

"Is something the matter?" she asked with a

haughty toss of her head.

He didn't answer, just turned casually away and resumed his task. Somehow his indifferent attitude did little to bolster her bravado. She knew how fast he could move, and could well imagine how deadly accurate was his aim. But he had to be tired; he had not rested all day, while she'd been able to nap while they were riding. Even though she had not been tired, she'd forced herself to catnap. She had prepared herself for just this moment—and now she was going to escape. That single thought gave her the added boost of nerve to keep walking. When she was behind the bushes, she looked through the branches to see if he was still beside his horse. He was checking the sorrel's hooves, that tall, lean body seeming almost casually relaxed.

Her pulse raced and her heart pounded as she began to edge her way backward toward the sheltering trees. He still hadn't turned around. Several times her shoes crunched lightly on gravel beneath her feet, and she paused, cringing, listening for his footsteps. They never came. As she darted quickly into the shadowy cluster of fir trees, she remarked to herself how easy it was, and remembered with chilling clarity how silently he'd invaded the private coach.

"Going someplace?" he called out suddenly in a taunting voice.

His voice was closer than she had expected, and she flew onward over the uneven ground like the devil was in pursuit. She raced blindly through the unfamiliar terrain, forging through the thick shelter of trees, oblivious to the scratches the low-lying branches inflicted on her arms and face. She had misjudged him, and his wrath would be fearsome if he caught her.

It took him longer than he'd first imagined to catch her, and then, remembering those long, coltish legs that had enticed him so when he'd first come upon her in Evanson's car, he understood her fleet-footedness. He caught her, though, bringing her tumbling to the ground with a bone-crushing hug that tore her breath away. Their legs and arms became a tangle of limbs as she fought him with everything she had to give. Her knee caught him in the stomach, and she felt brief satisfaction when she heard his soft grunt of pain.

Jesse knew she was trying to put him out of action with the deliberate way she aimed lightning jabs with her feet. Her face was flushed and moist from their struggles, and when she arched up against him and he felt the heel of her slipper glance off his hip, he knew exactly what was on her mind and quickly rolled to one side for fear of losing more than his pride. He was surprised by the show of strength in her slender body. Finally he pinned her beneath him. She lay spread-eagle in the dirt, her breasts heaving with exertion, and her eyes no longer cleverly concealing her hatred.

"You bastard! One of these days you'll pay for this!"

"Enough!" he snarled at last, grabbing hold of one flailing leg and sinking unrelenting fingers into the soft flesh of her thigh.

She went suddenly still, all of her strength gone. He stared down at her; a single tear had left a dusty trail across her cheek. But it left him unmoved. His face was set like granite.

"You've been wasting a good deal of my time, lady. And I'm not going to warn you again about trying to get away. Next time—I won't have to take a step to bring you down." He saw by the look on her face that she understood his implication perfectly. Abruptly flinging her away, he sprinted to his feet.

Nicki struggled to sit up, and gave a sharp gasp of pain. Her leg burned like it was on fire. Looking down, she gave a slight gasp, noticing that her gown was torn and tattered, and along her thigh there was a bloody gouge. The first shock waves of pain coursed through her, and her face went pale.

"I can't get up . . . My leg . . . it's been hurt," she gasped, her voice breathless with pain.

He stared at her for a moment with a flat look that chilled her soul, and then he said, "I don't know how you're going to ride now."

Nicki felt an even greater fear than before. Around them, night was closing in fast, and she knew that soon the four-legged animals would be about hunting. She would be easy prey for yet another species of killer. She swallowed her pride and said slowly, "Don't . . . leave me here all alone. . . ."

He turned his back and began striding purposely away.

"Please . . . I'm begging you. . . . I swear not to cause you any more trouble," she blurted.

He just kept walking. Then he stopped. Nicki held her breath as he turned around to assess her face from afar.

"You'll do exactly what I say from now on?"

Nicki Sue nodded miserably over the lump in her throat. "Yes, I promise." He had her exactly where he wanted her now. But at the moment there was little else she could do.

He strode over to where she sat huddled in watchful silence. After a moment's pause, he went down on one knee, then gathered her in his arms. The tense white lines around his mouth made it clear to her that she had finally managed to pierce his steely control.

Yet the knowledge did not make her feel triumphant.

"Just remember this—whether you live or not from now on depends entirely on you. I'm through making deals with you, lady." His tone was brutal, and Nicki had little doubt that he meant exactly what he said.

It was very late. They had stopped to camp for the night inside a cave that he'd seemed to instinctively know was there. He did that a lot, she'd noticed—as if he either knew the area very well, or harbored a sixth sense out here in the wilds, which she had to admit was amazing.

Within no time he had a fire going, his gear unpacked, and they were sitting on opposite sides watching the flames bouncing cheerily off the gloomy interior walls. A coffeepot on a hot rock near the fire vented forth an ambrosial vapor of steam, and turning on a spit above the flames was the crisp, brown carcass of a rabbit. Her mouth watered, but she refused to ask him for anything. He hadn't spoken to her since their earlier confrontation. The new arrangement suited Nicki Sue just fine. She completely grasped her situation now, and while she hated to admit it even to herself, there was no way to escape him. Her only hope was if someone rescued her. But no one knew where she was, she thought pitifully.

Jesse reached for a tin cup. "You getting hungry?" he asked, breaking the silence between them at last.

She met his gaze. He was sitting Indian fashion in front of the fire, and now he was watching her closely.

Her stomach growled loudly. No sense in trying to lie about it, she thought, and nodded slowly.

"Food's almost done. There's plenty here for two." His manner was more relaxed than it had been, but she knew very well how quicksilver his moods were.

"Would you like some coffee? It's good and hot."

"Yes, please," she replied quietly, then added, "Where are we?"

He filled a tin cup and handed it to her. She wrapped her hands around it and savored its warmth.

"In the mountains. We should reach our destination after sundown tomorrow."

Nicki sipped at the strong, hot brew. She had a sudden longing to shrug off his sheepskin coat, feeling suddenly that it symbolized an intimacy between herself and this man that unnerved her. But knowing that it would likely anger him, and knowing how fearsome he could be when provoked, she did nothing.

Jesse's gaze lingered on her, taking in her riotous long hair lying tangled, yet enticingly, about her shoulders, her golden tiger eyes that seemed to always pierce him chillingly, and he was more certain than ever that with this woman there would never be any peace. Just because she was quiet now did not mean that their stormy days were behind them. As soon as she recovered, she'd be at him again.

Nicki watched him over the rim of her cup and found herself thinking that she had never seen a man's eyes that reflected so little of his soul. She hoped by now that the authorities knew that she had been taken hostage by the train robbers. She could only pray that someone was, even at this moment, searching for her. Her shaky indrawn breath prompted him to inquire, "Would you like a shot of whiskey? It'll help dull the pain."

"No, I'm all right."

He shrugged indifferently. "Suit yourself."

She was suddenly so weary and could not help snapping. "What would suit me is to have *never* laid

81

eyes on you."

Jesse laughed harshly before rising to his feet and walking to the entrance of the cave to stare out into the darkness. "You don't know how many times in the last few hours I've found myself wishing that exact same thing." He reached in his shirt pocket and withdrew a rolled cigarette.

Nicki smiled icily. "Well, just remember — you're the only one here to blame for this awful situation."

He nodded slowly. "Guess that's one thing we can agree on." He placed the cigarette between his lips and struck a match against his thumbnail. When he looked at her again, his eyes were veiled. "It was definitely my mistake when I saved you from being gunned down — no doubt I'd have been a long way from here by now if I'd just minded my own business like *you* keep telling me to do."

Nicki's nostrils flared and her cheeks pinkened. But before she could recover her composure to fling back a nasty retort, he sauntered through the cave's entrance and was swallowed up by the night.

Chapter Four

The cave suddenly felt as confining as a tomb. A log popped and crackled in the fire, sending a shower of sparks spiraling upward. Lazy wisps of smoke curled into the shadows, and Nicki found herself thinking how quiet it seemed without his presence. She stirred uneasily, knowing if she continued to notice every creak and sigh around her, she'd be shaking with fear in no time.

Placing her empty cup aside, she struggled to sit up. Her head swam with dizziness and for a moment she was fearful that she might be sick. She was just very weak, she thought, and knew if she didn't force herself to eat something that she would become ill. Despite her discomfort, gnawing hunger urged her to help herself to a piece of the rabbit. Although the meat was stringy, it was tasty and filling. As she ate, Nicki considered what there was about the train robber that intrigued her. She could honestly say she despised everything he represented, yet from the beginning he'd set her blood racing through her veins with his unpredictable moods and rugged good looks. She told herself that looks did not make the man, and what was within a person was all that really mattered. He left a lot to be desired in that area. But yet, she could not deny that when he was near, her pulse raced. In her wildest dreams she would never have considered such a thing possible with a man like that. She was a woman of virtue and, if she was being completely honest with herself, rather prim standards. She had always accepted responsibility for her actions, even looked upon life's twists and turns — no matter how dire at times — as a challenge. But this was one time fate had dealt her a mortal blow. How could she remain optimistic facing such contradictions? Her head began to throb, upsetting her stomach even more. Glancing down at her greasy fingers, she swallowed back rising nausea and quickly wiped them on the folds of her skirt.

She sat back and started to wonder if perhaps she was partly responsible for her present situation in some way? Of course, he had abducted her and she'd been helpless against his strength, but why . . . oh God, why did she find her heart racing when he came near? What was wrong with her to be affected by him so? She'd heard some people could appear perfectly normal, yet harbor within them a dark, perverse side that they kept cleverly hidden behind their moralistic views — until somehow, it was awakened. At the thought, her mind rebelled. No! That is impossible, she quickly assured herself as she sank down on the bed of pine boughs and leaves and pulled the blanket around her. She was confused over the way he made her feel, but after all, she had to remember she was dependent upon him right now. He was all that she had to protect her from the dangers that loomed large and ominous in this untamed wilderness.

Without her being aware, her eyelids drooped sleepily, but then came the chilling howl of a coyote and her eyes flew wide open. To add to her misery, knifelike pain lanced through her thigh, setting her nerves on ragged edge. She wondered now if it had been wise to decline his offer to doctor the wound. But just the thought of him tending her, touching her intimately, had been too much to bear. When he had casually offered just before he'd left earlier to find food, she'd nearly choked, and had reiterated peevishly, "Absolutely not! I'll manage fine without your help."

His expression had closed off and he'd looked down at her. "I wouldn't let modesty stand in my way if I were you," he'd warned her. "You won't like what will happen to that leg if an infection sets in."

She remembered having mumbled rather stiffly, "It . . . will be just fine. . . . I'll take care of it myself."

"Have it your way," he'd said, and had picked up his rifle and announced he'd return shortly with fresh game.

Thinking he'd only be away a short while, Nicki had quickly tended her injury, and after cleansing the wound and binding her leg with strips of cloth she'd torn from the hem of her gown, she'd settled back to await his return. But he hadn't come back, and she began to get anxious. The pain in her leg intensified, and she thought then how foolish she'd been not to have at least asked him for some whiskey to disinfect the wound. She pressed the back of her hand against her mouth, then wiped at the beads of moisture dotting her upper lip. Was she developing a fever? She quickly felt her forehead and, to her relief, found that it was still cool. A movement outside the cave drew her gaze to the entrance.

"Where are you?" she found herself whispering, then praying for his return soon. She realized he was becoming more important to her as the minutes dragged by. Although she found herself injured and removed from all that was safe because of him, her contempt had given way to new feelings — truths that she did not like admitting, but nonetheless were there. She was miserably aware of her absolute dependence on him, and was both disgusted and terrified all at once. How she loathed him for having put her in this awful situation! She rubbed one hand across her tired eyes. Yesterday she'd been confident she would escape, and it had been her single foremost thought. The wind howled in the passages behind her. Waiting was becoming unbearable, and just when she thought she might surely go mad if she had to spend another minute wondering if he might be thinking of circling back after she'd fallen asleep and riding out alone, she caught a fleeting movement outside the cave entrance. Her nerves stretched taut, she called out in a hushed voice.

"Is . . . is that you?"

"Go to sleep," his familiar voice called back to her, and Nicki could not help the half smile that curved her mouth. With a sigh of relief she pulled the blanket up beneath her chin and immediately fell asleep. And no dreams came.

It was very late when she was drowsily awakened by the feel of a hard, muscular arm draped across her waist. She did not protest when he pulled her close, fitting her against the curve of his body. Nicki simply sighed gently, her sleep-drugged mind accepting the imprisonment of long arms and legs, and only stirring when his warm breath caressed the back of her neck. She knew she should not allow this, but then he whispered something near her ear and her fears evaporated.

Tomorrow, she thought, will be soon enough to face her conscience. For tonight, he was all that she had to keep fear and despair away. With a sigh of acceptance, she instinctively moved closer. His body seemed to fit around her slender form as if she had been made exclusively for him; and Nicki Sue, who had never slept with a man before in her life, felt her body automatically respond, and lure him.

Involuntarily, his hips moved against hers in a sensual, coaxing motion that made her pulse beat wildly out of control.

"I think you need to lie still," she heard his husky voice murmur near her ear.

"Mmmmm . . . you do the same," she replied drowsily.

"I was just accepting your generous offer, ma'am," he said, tauntingly.

She felt that caustic smile in the dark, and her eyes flew open. She could not deny that she was very much aware of the feel of his body against her, and the unwelcome stirring of heat in the pit of her stomach that he alone evoked and controlled. Having never known such raging desire like this before, Nicki Sue refused to acknowledge that with this outlaw—this callous, abrasive man—she felt very much alive, and all female.

"You're shaking," he murmured, gathering her closer. "Let me give you some of my warmth."

"I don't need your warmth," she replied stiffly.

"Yeah, you do, but you're too much of a hardhead to admit it," he stated dryly, forcing her still against him.

"You're enjoying this immensely, aren't you?"

"What do you think?"

"That I find it hard to believe you would enjoy anything without violence associated with it," she could not help but fling back over her shoulder.

She heard him laugh softly.

"Even train robbers have their weak moments."

Suddenly she wished he'd resume that contemptible tone of his; anything was preferable to that husky drawl which sent gooseflesh scurrying along her arms.

They kept up the soft banter of words for several more minutes. She heard his voice, gentle for the first time, become low and coaxing, and despite the pain of her injury and the fact that she didn't even know this man's name or intentions, his warmth and comforting nearness had eased her misery.

"Relax, I'm not going to do anything to you," he murmured. He had to admit he liked the feel of her in his arms. She was warm and soft, and smelled damn good. He gently kneaded the back of her neck until he felt her body respond to his gentle persuasion. He held her, with neither of them saying anything more until they both quieted and at last he heard her deep, even breathing. She was asleep, and now he could do the same. But to his surprise, it was hours before he closed his eyes and put from his mind the already too familiar scent of her, and the many ways he envisioned making love to her.

Roughly persistent hands shook her awake. It is barely dawn, she thought upon opening her eyes and seeing the faint sunshine filtering through the cave entrance.

"Sorry to interrupt your beauty sleep, but it's time to get up and be on our way." His tone of voice was once again impersonal, his eyes without hint of compassion.

Nicki Sue blinked up at him. For some reason, this morning she longed to see a flicker of warmth in his eyes. But she wasn't surprised to find it was not there. She was given to wonder if perhaps she wasn't falling more beneath this man's spell with each passing day. He was lulling her into a sense of false security. She had to remember the stories she'd heard about women who'd been taken hostage by the Indians and how some had bonded to their captors so closely that they literally died from despair when they had been forced to return to their families. She recalled one such case she'd read that had intrigued her.

Cynthia Ann Parker, a young girl from Texas whose family had been brutally murdered before her eyes by a band of renegade Comanche, had been taken captive by a Comanche war chief and had eventually fallen deeply in love with him. She married him, bore his children, and became an Indian in every way. They lived as man and wife for many years, until one day a scout discovered her in the encampment during a raid and spirited her back to her white relatives, who forced her to live with them in the white man's world. She had literally grieved herself to death. Cynthia Ann Parker and her Indian husband had loved as few ever do. It was their son, Quanah Parker, who went on to become one of the greatest war chiefs of all time.

For the briefest instant her eyes met her captor's, and she felt her cheeks burn beneath that hard, piercing glare and the memory of how they'd slept so close last night.

"Give me your hand," he said, and reached forward.

Nicki Sue instinctively drew back. She had to fight this fatalistic attraction to him. It was just due to silly images that her mind chose to conjure up instead of allowing her to perceive him as he really was. It was merely a form of self-protection, and a way for her to cope.

"You can't bear having to depend on me, can you?"

"I'm not accustomed to having someone tell me what to do every time I move," she snapped, looking away.

He sighed. "We're wasting a lot of time arguing. I just thought you might find it easier if I helped you to the horse."

"I think I am capable of managing on my own," she immediately replied, wanting no part of his arms around her, confusing her.

There was a moment of tense silence and then he stated firmly, "Well, I don't." Before she could move away, he grasped her fingers.

Nicki glared at him. He stared unsmiling down at her, daring her with his eyes to defy him as he instinctively adjusted the sheepskin jacket snugly about her shoulders. "It's windy today. You'd better keep bundled up."

With one arm wrapped securely around her waist, he led her slowly toward the sorrel. His long legs brushed against her skirts, seared like fire through the thin material, prompting her to snap testily.

"Will you just stay away from me!"

Jesse stiffened and drew back abruptly. "Go on then," he said harshly. "I won't be offering to help you again — next time you can ask me first."

Nicki fought to maintain her balance after his arms abruptly released her. She avoided those rugged features set like granite as they coolly observed her, but slowly, determinedly, hobbled to the horse with as much dignity as possible, almost stumbling once, then finally reaching the horse's side. She was out of breath and fighting back waves of nausea, but she'd done it on her own. She knew he was watching her, felt those penetrating eyes.

"I don't know how you think you're going to swing up in the saddle," he told her. It did not surprise him when she cast him a knife-edged glare.

"From now on just keep your opinions to yourself." She stood there for several long seconds trying to figure just how she was going to put her foot in the stirrup. Pain seared through her thigh each time she moved, the muscles quivering in reaction. Dizziness swept over her, forcing her to bow her head and lay her forehead against the cool leather of the saddle. Was there nothing she could do on her own anymore? Under her breath she called him several very ugly-sounding names, and felt decidedly better after having done so.

"Change your mind yet?" he inquired quite calmly after several minutes.

Nicki was so angry she was shaking, but she had to admit defeat for now. "Very well," she gritted from between clenched teeth. "If it will shut you up, then I'll accept your assistance."

He came toward her. "I think you need to let me take a look at that wound first. You won't last the day on the trail if it isn't properly taken care of."

"No!" she snapped hoarsely. "I won't stand for it!"

He saw her face darken with fury, but reached out to take hold of her arm anyway.

"There isn't going to be a discussion about this, lady," he said flatly. "Now, come sit down and make this easy on both of us."

She had no wish to comply, but had to agree with him. Judging by the way she felt, she wouldn't even last an hour on horseback. "All right," she sighed at last. "I'll let you look at it."

When she was seated on a boulder and he was

hunkered down in front of her, he began talking quietly.

"I know this is upsetting for you"—he kept talking to her as he drew her skirt upward to her knees, then draped it across her thighs—"but it's something that's necessary, so try not to think about what I'm doing." He glanced up to observe her watching him, aghast. "For God's sake, look in a different direction. Count the cracks in the wall—anything—to take your mind off what I'm doing."

"That's far enough," she hissed as his cool fingers inspected the top of her bare thigh.

He sighed with disgust before snapping. "Do as I told you—now."

Nicki scowled, but averted her gaze to stare out toward the cave's entrance, even though it was impossible to completely dismiss the fact of what he was doing. She felt him unbind the crude wrapping, felt the cool air against her injured flesh, and suppressed a groan.

"I'll try not to hurt you," he said in a reassuring voice.

Out of the corner of her eye she saw him regard her injury impassively for several long seconds before he stood up.

"It's not serious," he told her, and she swung her eyes to meet his. "I want to put something on it that will protect against infection."

"You're not really asking my permission, are you?"

"No, I'm not," he replied without hesitation, "just letting you know my intentions."

She knew there was no sense in protesting. He would do what he damn well pleased no matter how much she fumed. She simply nodded tersely.

He explained he'd only be leaving her alone for a

short while to gather what he needed. She watched him leave, and did not like the sensations of panic that she felt as soon as he was gone. To her surprise, he was back within minutes, and Nicki could not help but wrinkle up her nose at the sight of the offensive-looking substance he held in his hand.

His mouth twitched suspiciously. "It may look sinister, but it will help you a lot."

"An old Indian remedy . . . no doubt?" she said in a disdainful voice.

"Yeah, it is," he returned quickly before going down on one knee in front of her. When his long fingers closed around her knee, she could not help but shiver. Swiftly he laid the cool, moist vegetation directly over the red, puckered gash.

Even though he was quick and gentle, Nicki had to close her eyes as needles of pain shot through her leg. A low groan escaped her.

Jesse heard her soft gasp and was surprised to feel his stomach muscles tighten when he noticed a spasm of pain cross her face. Yet she refused to cry out. He admired that kind of courage in a woman.

"I know it hurts, but just try to relax and concentrate on something other than the pain," he surprised her by sympathizing.

Nicki raised her head to glare at him. "That's easy for you to say; you're not the one who has been injured."

He regarded her keenly. "I know what kind of pain you're going through. But it'll pass. Just keep talking—or call me a few nasty names if you think it will help." He almost smiled. "I'm sure you've thought of a few."

Several, she almost shouted at him, but thought better of it. Suddenly she laughed harshly. "You

93

know, I can't help but think how ridiculous it is that I've been through so much the past few days because of you, and yet, I don't even know your name."

He slanted her a quick look. "Why is it suddenly so important for you to know it?"

"It isn't important," she hurriedly injected. "I was just curious, that's all."

Their eyes met.

"Curious? Or calculating?" he inquired with a trace of sarcasm tinging his words.

"Fine! Don't tell me your name. I really couldn't care less who you are anyway."

"My name is Jesse," he told her after a moment's pause. "I guess there's no harm in telling you that much."

She was openly surprised at his admission and, for some unbelievably strange reason, wanted to hear him call her by her name instead of snarling "lady" at her in that contemptible way of his. She sat quietly watching him efficiently tend her for several long minutes, then offered hesitantly, "Mine's Nicki . . . Nicki Sue."

He didn't comment. Suddenly he was very angry at himself, and her. Somehow, the careful boundary lines they'd drawn for each other were being set aside by their simple exchange. She wasn't beautiful—or even good-natured; and by God, if he hadn't risked life and limb for her too many times already. Yet he couldn't deny that he had enjoyed the way she'd fit so perfectly against him last night. He hadn't had this feeling about a woman in a long while. Protective; that was it. Christ! He didn't want to even consider it, not even to himself. Physical desire was one thing; a man always enjoyed the feel of a woman in his arms, the warmth of her kisses, yet afterward was relieved to find she easily slipped from his thoughts once morning came around. Well, it was morning, and even though they'd only shared a bedroll for a few hours the night before, he was finding it difficult to forget how she felt, smelled, and—damn it!—stirred his desire. You've just been too close to old memories the past few days, he reasoned with himself. And knew that that much was true.

He worked as quickly as possible, and after rebinding her leg with strips of one of his clean shirts that he'd taken from his pack, he helped her into the saddle.

To Nicki, who had turned her head to look at him, it was suddenly as if his face had been carved from stone. He grabbed hold of the pommel and paused to stare up at her.

"This is the last day we'll be traveling together," he said. "We'll be parting company real soon. Try not to get yourself into any further trouble—for both our sakes."

She glared at him, those amber-gold eyes filled with contempt, bringing to mind an angry she-cat he'd cornered once when he'd been riding one night through the mountains. Tiger eyes—that's what they reminded him of.

"Where are you taking me?" she demanded.

Ignoring her, he removed the canteen from around the saddle horn and placed it to his mouth. Tipping it upward, he let the cool water flow down his throat.

"I think you owe me an answer," Nicki Sue persisted.

His thirst slaked, Jesse recapped the canteen and looped it back around the horn. He took his time in answering, deciding finally that it wouldn't hurt her to know his plans, and perhaps it might even quiet her down some. "There's a place that's about a day's ride from here." He readjusted the stirrup and prepared to mount up. "The people there will be happy to put you up for a while."

"These people . . . ," Nicki said hesitantly, "are they friends of yours?"

"Yes."

"Won't they object to your leaving me with them?"

Jesse caught her staring apprehensively at him, and slowly shook his head. "No, they won't mind at all. In fact, they'll welcome the female company."

Nicki blushed, wondering just *who* would enjoy her company. No doubt a bunch of misfits who were on the run like him. She did not like to think about his leaving her with them, but she could not give him the satisfaction of knowing it. As casually as possible, she asked, "Will . . . you be leaving again as soon as you drop me off?"

"No, not for a few days. I need the time to lay low until I'm certain there are no lawmen in the area looking for us."

"Oh," she breathed, clearly with mixed emotions.

"You sound kinda pleased that I'll be around for a while longer."

"I am not!" she shot back defensively, really in no mood to fence words with him, yet unable to stop herself. There was a brief pause before she added, "Are these so-called friends . . . trustworthy?"

He watched her closely, one dark eyebrow quirking upward. "I really wouldn't worry any if I were you," he drawled slowly, his eyes raking over her. "I can tell you right now — you're definitely not their type." He swung up behind her with an amused snort. "Move your rump a bit, will you?"

She seethed with indignation. He was back to ordering her around as if he had every right to do so.

She ignored his request, choosing to sit with her back held proud and straight. He could just walk beside the horse if he didn't like the present seating arrangement, she thought angrily.

She'd been edgy all morning, and Jesse knew she was begging for a fight. She turned slightly to meet his gaze. He assessed her eyes, and saw no fear. But there was anger and undaunted bravado, and begrudgingly he had to admit he respected that. But enough was enough. He grasped her on either side of her waist and shifted her weight forward.

"I'm through arguing—just do as you're told."

Gathering the reins loosely in one hand, his arms encircled her.

"At the moment it appears that I have no choice. But, only for the moment."

His sharp laugh rang in her ears. "I've never met a female who could goad a man past his limits with their harping the way that you can."

Stung by his sarcasm, Nicki cast him a fulminating look. "I've never behaved this way in my life! It's *you*—you with your crass manners and your bullyish ways." Her eyes were shooting sparks at him, but Jesse only grinned. Nicki swung her gaze immediately forward.

"If I didn't know better, I'd say you were trying real hard to hurt my feelings," he cajoled in that now familiar mocking voice, leaning over her shoulder. "You know . . . I like you a whole lot better the way you were last night." He paused as though lingering over the memory. "You remember, Nicki Sue . . . don't you?"

She did. Her eyes squeezed shut and her face felt

hot. She remembered all too well the feel of him, the scent of him, the warmth that his body had emanated as he'd pressed so intimately against her. And how she'd ceased shivering and had at last accepted his embrace. And of course he loved reminding her! His disparaging tone had struck a vulnerable chord within Nicki. Tears of impotent rage threatened to blind her. Why did he have to be so cruel, seem to enjoy it so? She fought to hold back the tears. By God, she wouldn't give him the satisfaction of seeing her bawl. And she would never again weaken and relax her guard until he was gone from her life. She felt him knee the sorrel forward, and then they were on their way. And even though she could not see his face, she knew he was gloating.

The hours passed swiftly and it was growing warmer, the sun sometimes relentless as it beat down upon them. He seemed to know his way, even over the winding mountain trails and through thick forests of trees. It was late one evening when they came to the crest of a towering bluff and halted. Nicki licked her dry lips and stared down into the vast space below. In the distance, a lake cupped into the hills glinted like silver in the moonlight. It was quiet here, the earth seeming at peace, and the end of her ordeal near. She was relieved, yet apprehensive, and could not help wondering where he was bound to afterward. And where was she bound, she wondered? There was still Patrick's death she'd have to face. She hated thinking of Patrick again, and how awfully he'd died. She said a fervent prayer for him, and then a quick one for herself. She didn't know where her life would lead after this nightmare was over, but one thing she did know for certain, she would never again allow anyone to dictate her life. Even Patrick, as kind and loving as he'd been, had wanted her for his own so badly that he'd offered her marriage even knowing she didn't love him. He had been willing to settle for her any way he could get her. It had not been a good way to start a marriage. She could see clearly now that she'd simply been trading one set of problems for another. Nicki was still very frightened by her uncertain future but knew whatever lay ahead, she would deal with it, and finally make her own happiness.

Jesse's arms tightened around her at that moment, his breath whisper-soft behind her ear, and her heart raced despite her best efforts to remain indifferent to him.

"Are you okay?" he asked.

"Yes, fine," she replied, even though she felt far from it.

Emotions too turbulent to acknowledge warred within her, and Nicki was both angry and disturbed that this outlaw, with his quicksilver moods and commanding air, had the ability to make her feel more alive than anyone ever had before. He had hurtled recklessly into her life and had taken complete control of everything she did, and the course of her future. But he had also forced her to realize the shallowness of her previous lifestyle, and stimulated her to make a firm vow to change it.

"I have to know something, Jesse," she suddenly had to ask, then sensed an immediate wariness about him. "I . . . have to know if there was a man killed during the robbery."

"I'd be careful where I pried — you just may not like the answer," he was saying grimly, wondering if she had a personal interest in the guy who'd fallen off the train; then, remembering her panic when he'd interrupted her flight from the passenger coach, he be-

99

came even more suspicious. "What was that fellow to you?"

"I . . . was just curious . . . that's all," she managed to stammer and avoided answering his question. She was struggling with her emotions, suddenly needing to know if Jesse could have been involved in so brutal a crime. "Were you . . . did you . . . ?"

"I didn't kill him," he stated evenly, and Nicki was stunned to realize she wanted very much to believe him.

"Who . . . was the person killed?" she asked, her voice trembling.

"I'd say Evanson is the one you need to ask that question."

"Evanson?" Nicki breathed, her heart beginning to pound.

"You sound surprised," Jesse said, his voice hard-edged. "He knows more about it than I do; I'd be willing to bet you on that."

Nicki's mind whirled. "That's . . . preposterous! Mr. Evanson couldn't know . . ." Her words trailed off, for she was suddenly drained of all emotion, even grief. There didn't seem to be anyone she could believe in anymore.

"You'd rather go on thinking I'm the one, wouldn't you?" His hard voice interrupted her brooding thoughts.

"Of course not!" she quickly replied, but knew she had not convinced him.

"I haven't forgotten where we first met, who's coach you were in."

Nicki had forgotten how unscrupulous he could be, and even knowing she didn't owe him any explanations didn't stop her from snapping. "Mr. Evanson simply offered his private car for my comfort. . . . I

100

tried to tell you before—"

"You were waiting up for him," he interjected bluntly.

"No—not for him." She took a shaky breath, and knew that she just could not bear to tell him how she'd been anticipating her wedding night when he'd come along and had torn her life, and her future, asunder. No, she could not discuss it with him. It was too painful. But Jesse pressed to know more.

"For who then, Nicki?"

"Just what right do you think you have to ask that question?" she lashed back heatedly, turning away.

"Your being here with me now gives me that right," he stated gruffly. "I'd like to know who you are . . . who you really are, I mean."

Nicki took a tremulous breath. "I think you'd like me to say I was waiting up for Evanson, for then you could go on believing I'm a—" She caught herself and sighed deeply.

"Does that bother you, what I might be thinking?"

He had posed the question in a sneering voice, and Nicki felt her face pinken. She was glad he wasn't looking at her. "No! I . . . I . . . just don't like anyone believing I'm that sort of woman."

Nicki knew, until she could be absolutely certain of the facts, that she must be careful not to imply she was Patrick's wife. She could not forget for a moment that this man was on the run and, if forced, would undoubtedly kill her if he thought that she posed a threat to his freedom, or his life. There was something else she felt absolutely certain about: If Jesse was lying to her about being innocent of Patrick's murder, then she would tell the authorities everything she knew about him and his men—and see they paid for their terrible crime!

They rode quietly for a time after that, each lost in their own thoughts. Jesse knew Nicki was trying hard not to give in to her fear. She'd been through a lot, and was very near the end of her endurance. They both needed some good food and a comfortable place to sleep. She'd be fine in a few days, and he could be on his way just as soon as he made certain no one dogged their trail. Soon it would be over, and he would be free of this troublesome female. There was no doubt he'd taken a hell of a risk bringing the woman along, and could only hope that by separating from the men, he'd at least been successful in throwing the posse off their trail. He figured he'd left an obvious enough trail for them to follow him, but now it was time to cover his tracks and have those cocksure government men scattering in different directions like leaves in the wind.

He reined his horse sharply to the left and deeper into the nearby mountains, forging steadily through a cold stream and then across hard granite stretches, making it impossible for even the best tracker to follow.

His mood lightened when he considered he was almost at the end of his journey. He was going to leave her where she would be properly looked after until things quieted down. Soon he'd be finished with her. In a few days he'd be on his way, free of any ties once again, and could rejoin his men at Hawk Point (their safe lair far off the mainline track high in the Sierra Nevada mountains). He crested the steep incline several hundred feet upward, and came upon a mountain ledge. He looked past the sheer declivity before them, his sharp eyes quickly locating the obscure winding trail that very few knew about, and only those who did rode the outlaw trails.

"We'll be there soon," he said, and Nicki did not fail to notice the relief in his voice.

"Good, for I'm just as weary of your company as you are of mine," she sighed, running her fingers through her tangled hair.

"It's three more miles to Sandy Creek," he said. "There's a river just before we get there where we can clean up a bit. Sorry there aren't any clean clothes for you, but I expect where we're going they'll have something for you."

"Is it . . . a town?" Nicki was suddenly given to ask.

"Of sorts," Jesse replied, "although there's not much left of it anymore. Gold fever ran through it like wildfire a while back. Squatters came. They settled wherever they could find a level enough section to put up a shack. The fever made them all change." His voice lowered. "Didn't take much then to kill a man, or run his family off their land. Of course, it never does when a good deal of money is involved. Nuggets ran as much as ninety-eight percent pure, and I'm told a small sack of gold yielded around a hundred twenty-six dollars.

Nicki glanced over her shoulder, her face registering her amazement.

"It's true. But there isn't anything left. The only folks who live there now are those who remember the regrets of yesterday and want no part of anything like it again."

With a steady hand he guided the horse down the mountain pathway until they were safely on flat ground. Still they rode on, and it was sometime later when Nicki Sue looked up to see lights flickering through the trees. It was so peacefully quiet. Around them giant sculptured monoliths guarded their passage. For the last leg of their journey along the base of the mountains neither Nicki nor Jesse said a word. It gave one a sense of tranquility, Nicki thought, to ride along in the muted gray shadows of the towering giants who loomed large all about them, and seemed to protect them from the prying eyes of the outside world. The wind whispered through her hair, and the crisp air tingled in her nostrils. Her mind was alert to every sound. She was struck by the raw, savage beauty of the place, seeming to draw in the vitality around her through her pores until the adrenaline sang through her veins. She had never been more aware of the beauty of nature!

Jesse saw her observe her surroundings closely as they rode on the outskirts of the small town, careful to stay well out of sight, then onward a few miles until they passed a barn and a corral with several horses. He drew rein before a solid, well-built cabin.

"This is it," he told her.

"Are you sure . . . we'll be welcome?" Nicki inquired hesitantly. She was somewhat puzzled by the neat, almost homey, appearance of the place. Her gaze wandered over the cabin, observed the cheerful curtains at the windows and the flower garden in front of the house.

Jesse slid off the horse and helped her dismount. "Yes, I'm sure. They're real nice folks. They mind their own business and won't ask too many questions. I strongly suggest that you try to show them the same courtesy." He took a firm hold on her elbow, hesitating, waiting, it seemed, for her to reply.

"I understand what you're implying," Nicki said. "I won't cause any trouble for you." She peered up at him. "But on one condition."

"What's that?" he asked dryly.

"That you keep at a distance." Her eyes suddenly gleamed with battle lights once again. "I think we both could use some breathing room."

"Lady — you've got yourself a deal," Jesse agreed as they walked across the yard and stepped up onto the plank porch. "Just do what you're told and don't make a nuisance of yourself, and I won't be forced to ride roughshod over you." He knocked on the door.

Nicki mumbled angrily under her breath. A nuisance! Why, he treated her no better than some quarrelsome child he felt it was his duty to reprimand for surly behavior. Her unease intensified when after several minutes a sleepy female voice called from behind the portal. "Yes . . . who is it?" She should have known, Nicki thought with an inward smirk!

Jesse grinned laconically at Nicki's smug expression before replying. "It's me, Meg. I need a place to stay for the night."

The door was slowly drawn inward and a small figure stood back in shadow. "Jess? come in — my, it's good to hear your voice."

Jesse stepped over the threshold with Nicki before him. "Brought you some company."

"Any friend of yours is welcome here," Meg enthused.

Nicki glanced at the woman. She was thin, almost frail-looking, and appeared in her late twenties, although with the room in shadow, it was difficult to really tell. Her hair was dark and her eyes were gentle and kind. Nicki was decidedly taken aback by the other woman. She was definitely not what she had first envisioned. She thought she must have been very pretty once, before the harshness of the elements and the everyday struggle to live in this remote area took her beauty prematurely. She caught a brief glimmer of surprise in Meg's eyes when they beheld her, then a flicker of something else, before Jesse stood quickly between them, his hand tensed now at the small of Nicki's back as if in warning.

"It's good to see you again, Meg," Jesse said gently. "I'm sorry for waking you, but I'd be real obliged if you could put us up for a while."

The woman's eyes swung from Nicki to Jesse, and changed completely. Everything she felt for this man was revealed in her luminous gaze. Nicki wondered if Jesse had been right to have brought her here. Surely he knew how Meg felt about him, and what she must be thinking at the moment. But then, what did Jesse really care what anyone else thought of him?

"You should know that without asking," Meg told him softly.

"Thanks," Jesse said huskily. "I didn't want to intrude, but you're the only person I can rely on." He inclined his head at Nicki. "This is Nicki Sue, Meg. She needs to rest up for a few days, and then I'd like for you to take her into town and see that she has safe passage back to wherever she'd like to go." His voice was even. "Will you do that for me?"

Nicki could not help but notice how differently he looked at Meg. There were no burning lights in those blue eyes, but there was warmth and, for the first time, compassion. The harsh lines of his face eased beneath a rare smile.

If Meg thought his request strange, she was careful not to reveal it. "Of course," she agreed, her tired features softening. "It's so nice to make your acquaintance, ma'am." Her eyes did not linger on Nicki, but turned quickly back to Jesse. "You haven't been in these parts in a long time. Thought maybe you'd forgotten about us."

106

"You know better than that," Jesse said quickly.

"Yes, I guess I do," Meg responded, yet her voice held a measure of doubt. She caught herself and brightened. "Well—you're here now, and that's all that matters."

There was little doubt in Nicki's mind that Meg wished for more than friendship with Jesse. But how did he feel? She searched Jesse's face. If she didn't know better, she would swear he appeared uncomfortable beneath Meg's warm gaze. Nicki averted her own eyes and allowed them to wander over the dimly lit room.

It was a small room and held very little furniture. There was a half-open door leading to another room, and a ladder in the center of the floor that obviously led to a loft. Nicki was given to wonder just how many people occupied the cabin. Meg's voice interrupted her thoughts.

"You can bunk out here by the fire," she told Jesse. "And the lady can sleep in the spare bedroom in back." Her gaze fixed on Nicki. "It's not much on luxury, but it's clean and warm. I think you'll find it comfortable." She took note of Nicki's soiled gown and ragged appearance. "Looks like you two have been traveling hard. How about something hot to eat before you turn in?"

"There's no need for you to fuss over us," Jesse said. "You go on back to bed. I can rustle us up some food and show Nicki to her room."

"Nonsense," Meg replied. "It isn't often I get company. Let me just get a nightgown for Nicki and then I'll dish you up some leftover stew from supper—it won't take me a minute."

"I'd like to freshen up a bit first," Nicki stated softly.

Meg nodded. "There's water in a pitcher and some clean towels hanging on a rack in the spare bedroom. Jesse will show you where to find them."

"Thanks," Nicki said gratefully.

"Be right back," Jesse told Meg. He led Nicki into the back room.

The room was dark. The moon shining through the curtains on the wide windows lit a pathway to a lamp on a bedside table. Nicki watched closely as Jesse crossed over the floor and turned up the wick on the lamp. Immediately the room glowed softly with amber light. Nicki looked around silently. With casual curiosity she walked over to the windows and separated the curtains to peer out. Trees and boulders surrounded this side of the house, but it would have been possible to escape if one didn't have an injured leg. Grimly, she acknowledged her physical limitations. As much as she would have liked to flee from this place just as soon as he left her alone, she knew that for now, escape was impossible.

She turned around to examine her surroundings. It was a comfortable room, although there was a dry, musty odor as though it hadn't been occupied in awhile. She wondered where Meg slept, and why she didn't use this spacious bedroom. There were some lovely pieces of furniture. An iron bed with an ornately designed headboard took up half the length of one wall; there was also a rosewood dresser, a washstand, and two comfortable-looking chairs. A stitched sampler adorned the wall between the chairs. It was cozy and intimate.

Jesse stood several feet away, his presence suddenly overwhelming to Nicki.

"She shared the room with her husband." He answered the unspoken question in her eyes.

Nicki raised a speculative brow. "And where is he?"

"He's dead," Jesse said.

Nicki emitted a sigh. "Oh . . . how awful for her." And then her own set of circumstances, so closely parallel to Meg's, crushed down upon her and could no longer be held at bay. Tears welled in her eyes and she fought to blink them back. She was just tired, she told herself. Her shoulders sagged and she sat down on the bed with a tiny sigh.

Jesse saw the telltale glitter of moisture in her eyes, his voice coming husky in the shadows. "You'll be all right here." He drew a deep breath. "I know it's been rough on you the past few days. . . ." His words trailed off, and when he spoke again, his tone was again controlled. "Well, if you won't be needing anything else, I'll just leave you to your privacy." He walked toward the closed door. Meg's voice came from behind the portal.

"Here's a gown for Nicki, and the stew's about ready."

Nicki found herself wondering how long she'd been standing there.

Jesse opened the door wider and took the garment. "Thanks. I'll be right out." He shut the door tightly this time and turned back to Nicki. "Just in case I don't get a chance to mention it before we turn in. I'm a real light sleeper. And even though we both know you're in no shape to try leaving here unexpectedly, I thought it best to let you know that nothing gets by me unless I want it to."

"You don't have to issue threats," Nicki stated with a glare, reaching out to take the proffered gown from his hand. "I wouldn't know where to run even if I could."

"That would be the last thing I'd believe about you,

Nicki Sue." He suddenly grinned sardonically. "I've seen how observant you are. You don't miss a thing. You'd know where to head all right — if I'd give you the chance." His eyes darkened. "But you're not going to get that chance until I'm a long way from here."

She seethed silently as he left the room and closed the door firmly behind him. Nicki Sue sat numbly for a minute before removing his coat and tossing it aside. She felt very small and absolutely vulnerable. Her thick mass of dusky hair fell about her as she buried her face in her hands and sobbed quietly. After a while, she got up and walked over to the washbowl. She poured water into the bowl, and picking up a cloth and a bar of lemon-scented soap, she scrubbed her face and arms until she felt reasonably clean again. She longed for a hot bath, the tub filled with scented bubbles, but knew that would have to come later. Much later.

Nicki didn't know, in thinking about it later, how she'd endured sitting at the table with Jesse directly across from her, feeling those magnetic blue eyes flicker indifferently over her from time to time, making her think and feel things she didn't want to feel.

The food Meg served them had been simple, but tasty and filling; the homemade wine that had accompanied the meal was now making Nicki's thoughts swirl. How many glasses had she drunk? Nicki wondered now — and recalled Meg's promptly refilling her glass each time she emptied it. Obviously, she'd only been trying to make her feel welcome and at ease. Nicki wondered if she shouldn't have refused that last glass of wine. She sat there, saying very little, although neither of them appeared to notice, they were so caught up in their own conversation. Jesse and Meg had kept up a constant conversation during the meal, and Nicki did not fail to notice that he never once glared at Meg in the way that he did her. Meg could ask him anything, and he answered her without hesitation or a gruff tone. Abruptly, and feeling their watchful gazes, she excused herself and went immediately to her room.

"Sleep well, Nicki," Meg called cheerfully. "I'll have a hot breakfast for you in the morning."

"Thanks," Nicki responded.

Closing the door softly behind her, she undressed, and picking up Meg's nightgown, she drew it over her head. Securing the ribbons at her neck, she couldn't resist walking over to the door and listening. There was silence except for the crackling of the fire in the hearth. She wondered if they'd called it a night. And then, if perhaps he'd gone to the loft with Meg. She felt her cheeks grow warm.

Then she heard them resume their conversation, their low voices and whispered words drifting through the thin walls. Meg was doing most of the talking, her words spoken softly, yet still discernible.

"I thought after you were here last . . . and the way that I had behaved . . ." She hesitated, then forced the words. "Well . . . I wouldn't have blamed you if you'd never come back."

"Let's not talk about yesterdays," Jesse said hurriedly, sounding to Nicki as if he'd be happier if they talked of something else.

"I know how uncomfortable it makes you, Jess," Meg said, "and how you always shy away from dredging up memories."

"We both have things in our past it's best to leave buried," Jesse was quick to respond.

111

"Yes, we do," Meg sighed.

"I have only one thing on my mind right now," Jesse said.

"I know that too . . . and I wish sometimes you had room in your heart for something besides vengeance."

Nicki didn't want to listen, but couldn't stop herself. She leaned her head against the rough wood. Meg's voice bore regret, and was tinged with sadness.

"I know it's been difficult for you, and what you went through was horrible. But I've been through a lot too, and I know being alone all of the time makes it difficult not to dwell on the past . . . and those things we should forget. We could help each other." She hesitated momentarily when he didn't respond. "You don't know how happy I was when I heard your voice. . . . I was hoping that you'd come to tell me that you'd reconsidered what I offered you last time. . . . But you didn't, did you? You came . . . because . . . of her?"

"Meg, let's not spoil it," Nicki heard him interject gently. "I've never tried to hide anything from you. You are a wonderful woman, and you are special to me. But you know how it is with me."

"Yes," Meg replied with a definitive sigh. "I know very well how a man like you thinks and feels. And the main reason you come here at all . . . is your loyalty to Reed's memory."

Nicki heard Jesse snarl under his breath, his measured tread as he crossed over the room, and then a furtive rustle of movement as if Meg was being drawn into his embrace somewhat against her will.

"Stop it; I don't like it when you talk like that," he growled.

Meg sniffed. "It . . . is the truth, Jess. You just don't like hearing it. I wish I could make you feel

112

differently . . . but I know now . . . I can't."

"Poor, sweet Meg," he was suddenly murmuring huskily. "You didn't deserve either one of us, did you?" There was a brief exchange of whispered words and then Nicki was certain from the sound of their breathing that he was kissing her tears away. Breathless murmurs followed.

Nicki was surprised to realize she felt anger close to the surface; and not directed at Jesse—but at Meg! She hurried to the bed and sat down, expecting a shiver of revulsion to easily dismiss the visions in her head of Jesse kissing Meg, caressing her, and was stunned to realize she had to concentrate all of her efforts on trying very hard not to become breathless imagining Meg being held close in those powerful arms and kissed by that knowing mouth. Her stomach fluttered at her own recollection.

"No . . . stop . . . ," she whispered in anguish, never more aware that since Jesse had come into her life, her emotions were in a constant tug of war. Every sense now felt heightened, every nerve tingling with awareness. It was the wine, she told herself . . . only that. With a shaky sigh she lay down on the bed and forced herself to close her eyes.

If she had thought she was going to sleep without dreams, she was in for a shock. The dreams came. And in them she fought against the truth that, awake, she refused to fully accept. Now that she felt certain Patrick was dead, she had to face being alone again very soon. Loneliness was an awful thing, and when it invaded dreams, it was even more devastating. Nicki's hands twitched on the mattress. A man suddenly appeared in her dream—but he was not Patrick. This man was tall and darkly handsome, and his eyes made her feel warm wherever they lingered. His arms en-

113

folded her and his hands caressed her, and she felt as if she truly belonged to him in every sense of the word. This feeling of belonging was so real and intense that Nicki moaned softly in her sleep. With a pitiful sob she woke up and lay there trying to banish his image from her mind. When she realized it was impossible, she got up and went to the door. Opening it slightly, she observed Jesse standing with his back to her in front of the hearth. He was alone, and Nicki felt irresistibly drawn to him, just as she'd been to the man in her dream. She was drowning in a sea of emotions, swept past rational thinking by awakening senses that refused to be denied. Jesse had never tempted her more than he did right now.

Appearing darkly brooding, he stared moodily into the orange flames, his dark hair tousled, lying shaggy about his neck, his back bared to her wide-eyed gaze. Without his shirt, he seemed even more powerfully built . . . more fearsome . . . and absolutely spellbinding. His shoulders were wide and sleek with long, corded muscles, and his arms were thick and rippled with taut, sinewy flesh. He held a glass of amber liquid in one hand and he appeared restless, and for the first time, appeared troubled over something.

Glancing around the room, Nicki was glad she did not see Meg. Were Meg's words of earlier disturbing him? Something undefinable stirred deep in Nicki's soul, and she simply could not fight it any longer. She still did not know how she could hate someone so intensely, yet still find him attractive, and even wonder what it would be like to . . . But what did it matter at this moment? It was the dream making her feel this way, she told herself, all warm, yet strangely longing. Her eyes roamed over him and the warmth inside her intensified.

Heat shimmered around his tall form. Bronze muscles rippled and gleamed in the firelight as he rotated his shoulders slowly as if to try and dispell a coiling tightness. His movements were deceptively lazy; Nicki Sue knew this very well. He had been right in his warning. She wouldn't stand a chance of slipping past him before he'd spin about and be upon her. That lithe stride would be almost silent, those long fingers decidedly cruel as they grasped her and yanked her hard against him. Nicki quivered in acknowledgment, and wondered . . . how would a man like Jesse make love to a woman? Would he be fierce and demanding in passion as he was in everything? Or surprisingly gentle, a side that she had yet to see?

He took a deep breath and raised the glass to his lips to drain the contents. The molten gold shadows played across his bare skin, teased him like a lover's caress. Nicki's eyes wandered over the length and breadth of him, drinking in the sight of him — and she was suddenly stunned upon noticing the tiny puckered scars marring that perfection. They were round and lethal in appearance, a slight gray tinging the area. She had seen scars like that only once before when her father, who had been drinking heavily at the time, had accidentally shot himself in the hand while cleaning his pistol. They had been unmistakably caused by gunshot wounds: one in his shoulder . . . two in his back near his spine . . . and another above his waistband where his pants rode low on his hips.

Someone had cold-bloodedly shot him in the back.

Chapter Five

She was certain she had not moved nor made a sound, and could only stare stunned as he slowly turned and stood facing her, deep blue eyes glittering with reckless lights. Her heart began to beat frantically and she felt strangely numb and unable to move. Run, her mind commanded, yet she did not.

He came toward her without expression, his footsteps as silent as his emotions. And even as she told herself how much she despised him, that he was dangerous, rough-edged, and at times even cruel, she could not deny that she felt mesmerized by him, and experienced a shiver of excitement race through her. She was staring at him, she knew, but there was no turning away. He was all-powerful, all-daring, and more man than anyone she had ever met.

Her eyes drank their fill of him, almost as though she were seeking to quench some raging thirst within her even as she realized that she'd never quite be able to do so. She took in everything about him, from his dark, curly hair to his long, straight legs. She could not help but notice the taut muscles ripple across his chest as he came toward her, or the grooves on either side of his mouth deepen as he smiled lazily, purpose in his eyes.

"Couldn't sleep?" he asked her.

"No . . . I was thirsty . . . I was going to the well for a drink." Her thoughts were befuddled by the wine she had drunk earlier and her words were slightly slurred. She tried to read his shadowed face. He was studying her closely and her heart skipped a beat.

"You're dressed for it too, I see."

Her hands immediately crossed over her breasts. "I didn't . . . think anyone was still awake."

"You were listening to Meg and me," he stated without hint of anger. Their eyes met and Nicki's mouth went dry as cotton. She was captivated by that insouciant gaze.

"No . . . ," she automatically protested, but dropped her eyes guiltily. "Well . . . it is difficult not to hear with the walls being so thin."

"Did you hear what Meg was saying?" he asked softly.

"She cares very deeply for you," she heard herself blurt suddenly, and felt her cheeks grow hot. She felt so ridiculous she bowed her head and stared at the floor.

"Look at me, Nicki," he commanded huskily.

She was almost afraid to, but then she did, drawing a shaky breath. His midnight-blue eyes raked her from head to toe as she stood there before him not knowing what to expect. Strangely, she felt no fear, but something else . . . and it was a feeling she'd begun to know well, setting the pulse fluttering wildly in her throat. His eyes fixed upon the telltale throbbing, and awareness glittered in their depths. She sensed something different about him at this moment that lured her, even as she wanted to resist.

The firelight surrounded him, backlit his tall form

in golden hues, and even as Nicki told herself to be wary, her eyes savored the male beauty of him. His features were ruggedly handsome, his jawline chiseled and commanding, yet it was his compelling eyes that drew her to him almost as if she were under a spell. They were the deepest, darkest blue of the night, and held just as much mystery. Thick black lashes framed them and, even now, prevented her from assessing his mood, or his innermost feelings. He was a big man, although not bulky, but lean and strong, and breathtaking to behold. Wide shoulders taped gradually to a slim waist. Crisp black hair covered his wide chest, narrowing downward over his flat belly, and disappeared into the waistband of his snug-fitting trousers. To her horror, she found she could not help remembering how enticing those powerful limbs felt entangled about her own. She saw that he was watching her just as closely.

"Meg is a special lady — but she is *not* my lady . . . if you know what I mean."

She did, and was not ready for the peculiar pounding of her heart at the acknowledgment.

"I think I'd better go back to bed," she said quickly.

"Not just yet."

"Jesse . . . it wouldn't look good right now if Meg should walk in."

His hands moved to gently grip her shoulders to prevent her from leaving. "She's asleep upstairs, and this has nothing to do with Meg. This is between you and me."

Nicki clutched the door frame with one hand. The wine she'd consumed seemed to have befuddled her thoughts, and she felt as if her limbs grew heavy beneath his touch. Too many visual images taunted her now. Jesse, that night in the railroad car. Jesse, kissing her, wanting her . . . and her having tasted passion, unable to forget. She swallowed and managed a faint reply.

"You know there is nothing between us. . . . Please let me go."

His hands moved to the back of her neck, fingers lacing through her mane of thick hair. "You couldn't sleep because you were thinking about the same thing I was."

"I don't know what you're talking about." She could not seem to think clearly with those glittering eyes raking her from head to toe. His fingers gently kneeded the taut muscles at the back of her neck.

"You know very well what I mean, so quit playing the innocent," he said gently and without hint of sarcasm.

She had been unable to keep her eyelids from drifting closed with those long fingers lightly caressing her.

"It isn't how you think. I woke up and was thirsty. I didn't hear your voices any longer . . . and I assumed that you were asleep." She was struggling for some measure of control, trying not to think about the fact that they were both half-dressed and his skin felt so warm against her own.

"You assumed wrong," he stated huskily, and her eyes flew open to meet his. She saw what he wanted in his eyes, and her heart thudded even faster. Before she could utter a protest, he pulled her close, held her arms pinned to her sides. His body against hers was mesmerizing. She told herself quite rationally that it was to her advantage to fake some semblance of compliance, for she knew too well what a formidable foe he made. But it was a feeble excuse, and Nicki Sue whimpered in soft frustration.

119

Jesse felt her body surrender to the touch of his, the hot flush of desire radiating the smooth bare flesh of her back. She immediately went stiff. Gently, he kneaded the tenseness from her spine and objection from her thoughts. His fingers were so gentle . . . so soothing.

No — he should not be doing this. . . . I should stop him even if it does anger him. Nicki was certain he was just seeking to prove his dominance over her. It was so like him. She made an attempt to struggle, but he was having none of it.

"Who are you trying to convince again, Nicki? Me or yourself?"

Anger and indignation blazed from her eyes. "I don't need to convince myself of anything about you!" she choked. "I know what you are and the only thing you want."

"That makes us even," he breathed huskily, "and I'm suddenly real tired of talking." His hand grew bolder, slid over the curve of her spine, long fingers tantalizing the swell of her buttocks. They were sure and enticing, teasing slowly where they touched. She had expected them to be rough and uncaring as they moved over her. Her heart lurched madly as he caressed her with a lover's sure touch.

Nicki closed her eyes and swallowed hard. The room was spinning, whirling, everything seeming out of kilter. And then somewhere deep in her mind, she thought shockingly, perhaps it was *she* who was the one out of control. How could she experience pleasure from his touch? With an effort she struggled briefly, only to hear him whisper.

"Stop it, Nicki. . . . We both know this isn't new to you. You've been playing the tease long enough."

She could feel his breath, warm and scented with

brandy, against her cheek, and felt the pulse in her throat throb erratically. "You don't . . . understand," she protested softly.

"I understand more than you know," he soothed, murmuring other unintelligible words as his lips brushed across her cheek, her closed eyelids.

"Wh-what are you doing . . . ? . . . Please." She twisted frantically, desperately, and was surprised when he abruptly released her. Quickly, she took several steps backward.

Jesse watched her through narrowed eyes, found himself thinking what a consummate little actress she was, yet in seeing her panic-stricken eyes, knew a flickering of doubt.

Nicki wanted to turn and run, her emotions were so shaken.

He was so near and so overwhelming in size and sheer masculinity that Nicki felt seared by his gaze and unable to move a muscle. She didn't know how much he'd been drinking. It was hard to tell when he was always so much in control of everything he said and did. He came toward her. She noticed that his steps were measured and sure, his eyes as clear and piercing as ever. She wished she hadn't been so foolish to have drunk so much wine. With a shiver she crossed her arms immediately over her breasts in an effort to shield them from his eyes. A gasp escaped her when lean, strong fingers encircled her wrists and gently drew her arms down to her sides.

"Don't," he said softly. "Let me look at you."

He took his time, allowing his gaze to feast upon her femininity outlined so temptingly beneath the thin gown.

Nicki watched him with a guarded expression.

"You're a very desirable woman. It isn't easy being

121

close to you . . . and not touching you."

She told herself it was for certain the liquor talking, and that he was indeed drunker than she first imagined. No one had ever said anything like that to her before in her life. "I think . . . I'd best go back to bed." She tried to maneuver away from him, but it was useless. Nicki knew she should struggle harder, but her limbs felt weighted, and within the darkest passages of her soul the flames of desire burned stronger than her will. She knew then what was going to happen, what she wanted to happen. With a strange perceptive certainty, Nicki felt Patrick's death, knew beyond any doubt now that any life they may have had together was nothing more than a lingering memory. This man holding her was warm and vital and, at the moment, surprisingly gentle. She felt him cup her chin in one big hand.

"Quit fighting, Nicki; you know it's useless." Slowly he slipped her gown off her shoulders and lowered his head until his lips grazed the slender column of her neck and lingered on her bare shoulder. "You always smell so damned good."

His words sent uncontrollable heat curling through her and searing along all of her nerve endings. What was wrong with her that she should enjoy this man's lovemaking, and even wonder what it would be like to experience more? She was terribly frightened and confused, but at the moment, she had never felt more alive.

"Jesse . . . you mustn't; I don't . . . belong to you," she said shakily.

His lips continued their heated path along the hollows and curves they discovered. "I think you're wondering what it might be like, though, aren't you?"

"No, that's not true." Nicki Sue shook her head

furiously from side to side, refusing to openly acknowledge her need.

His lips were inches from her own, and even though she knew she should not want his kiss, she did, and her lips parted of their own accord. His mouth closed over hers, and time seemed to stand still. She felt lost in that kiss, possessed of no free will, and hungering for the taste of him against her tongue. Her head fell back and a soft whimper bubbled in her throat. Her knees trembled so badly that she would have fallen if he had not been supporting her with strong arms, crushing her against his naked chest until her senses were consumed with the now familiar masculine scents that were so much a part of him. She had never experienced anything like this in her life, and was stunned by the physical longing he stirred so easily inside of her. Nicki sagged against him when his tongue swept hotly across her full lips, then sought her own with hungry possessiveness. In passion, as in everything about him, he could not be restrained. His hands touched her everywhere, at last deftly untying the ribbons at the neckline of her gown and drawing it looser than before, exposing the creamy tops of her breasts.

Her breasts ached, they longed so to feel his touch, and her nipples grew flush against his chest, luring him to touch them, cup their quivering fullness.

Inflamed by his own need, Jesse snarled softly and touched the satiny round globes, filled his hands with their perfection.

Nicki's hands slid up his back, and her fingertips lingered momentarily over the two scars near his spine, and a tingling shock quivered through her. She wondered even as her fingers moved to touch him elsewhere, what had happened to him in his life to have made him what he was now? Somehow, she knew that the scars on his body were minimal in comparison to those seared into his soul.

Nicki could not explain then what happened next, or when she would recall it later, ever be able to. When at last his fingers slid downward over her lower abdomen and touched dusky curls, she abandoned the last of her will and met him halfway, arching her hips upward as one finger caressed deeply. It felt so good. She was on fire, liquid heat turning her bones to jelly. Her body moved involuntarily to the teasing rhythm of his touch. Breath coming in jerky gasps, Nicki blindly sought some unknown peak of pleasure.

"I want all of you, Nicki," he said thickly, and felt her quiver in his arms.

Their eyes met for only a moment, but it was enough. He read the acceptance in their tawny-gold depths, and his lips claimed hers. He kissed her so completely that all thoughts, save one, flew from her head. No longer were they simply the lady and the outlaw, but were being drawn inexplicably toward something more. She clung to him, feeling at that moment as if their very emotions mingled as one. Her lips moved beneath his, and slowly, very slowly, he eased her into the bedroom, and then there was only the soft clicking of the door being closed.

She was leaning against the wall and he was touching her again where he seemed to know the fires burned hottest.

Teasing and tasting the sweetness of her lips, the velvet hollows within, Jesse sought to make her completely his in every way. He slid the gown down her arms, very careful of the thick white bandage around her thigh. Her gown fell in a whisper about her ankles. His hands were gentle as they explored her lush breasts, cupped their fullness, and he bent his head to take one pebble-hard tip between his lips. Nicki purred her pleasure, her head immediately falling back, sending her sweet-smelling hair cascading about her slim thighs. It was the wine singing in her veins, she told herself, not heady passion that made her suddenly want him to do more . . . to teach her what it was like to truly be a woman.

As though he knew her thoughts, he swept her up into his arms and carried her to the bed. After that, her thoughts were a whir of jumbled images and vivid colors exploding behind closed eyelids. She felt his naked body pressed close to hers, his hand guide her fingers to touch him, and somehow knew the motion to use that would give him the greatest pleasure. His breathing grew ragged, and his kisses more consuming. He wanted more, would take more. She opened her legs to accept his touch, arching against those knowing, seeking fingers and experiencing pleasure so sweet she thought she might die from it.

He kissed her hair, her eyelids, the pulse that throbbed in the hollow of her throat. And he stroked her where she burned for him until she was moist and writhing for him to take her. Her thighs parted . . . her gently undulating hips urging him to a primitive dance of passion. A small gasp escaped her when he grasped her buttocks, the hardness of him pressing against her moist warmth. He was so hot and hard, yet unbearably exciting.

Jesse had the strangest feeling that somehow it had been Nicki who had seduced him. Her nails raked along his back and she nipped his shoulder with her teeth. His mind surfaced briefly from its fog of passion when he felt the delicate obstruction that met his

125

first thrust. He moved his hips and saw her bite down on her lip. Surely, he thought, it can't be. He had thought she was a kept woman, could have sworn that Evanson must have bedded her many times. But now he knew for certain she was not.

Nicki's body arched in shock as her tender flesh sought to accommodate all of him. Her head fell back and she stifled a soft cry. Hurry, she thought, hurry and make me yours. At the moment all she could think about was the two of them becoming one in the most beautiful way possible. She tried hard not to cry out. Her eyes flew open. He was watching her, those midnight-blue eyes piercing. She caught a fleeting glimpse of both surprise and confusion in his gaze. She caught her bottom lip between her teeth.

"Damn it, Nicki, why didn't you tell me?" he growled in a whisper, although he could not stop the demands of his body urging him onward to fulfillment. He thrust forward, stifling her whimper of pain with his mouth. And then she was returning his kisses, surrendering all to him.

Nicki had never imagined that it would feel this way. It was nothing like her friends had said. It hurt, of course, but strangely felt very good too, like molten fire slowly oozing through her and at last blotting out the pain. Lost within the throes of passion, she forgot everything else except how good he made her feel. Burying her face in the curve of his shoulder, Nicki felt herself spiraling with him into that vortex of pleasure. Faster, harder, hotter, both of them lost in fiery desire, and then ecstacy, and that shadowy void where only lovers meet.

When it was over, and they lay, bodies slick with sweat, passion sated, the full import of what had happened hit him hard. Jesse pulled away from her to

126

glare at her with sudden bitter contempt. She curled into his body with a sleepy yawn and a soft hiccup. Christ! But the little minx was half-soused on wine. He hadn't noticed it before, or maybe he hadn't wanted to, because it was easier thinking she was free with her favors, and absolving him of any guilt in the end. In two days she would be nothing but a memory. Jesse unbound her arms from around his neck and rose from the bed.

Unable to stop himself, he suddenly leaned over the bed and traced one long finger along the curve of her silken hip, the outline of her creamy white breast. She only sighed in her sleep. She had the most beautiful body he'd ever seen. He stepped back from the bed and, calling up supreme willpower, turned away.

"Jesse?"

He heard her sleepy voice and froze, kept his back to her. "Go back to sleep, Nicki."

"Can I ask you something first?" she whispered, her voice slurred by the wine and sleep.

He turned around and observed her propped on one elbow, her body all peaches and cream in the moonlight slanting through the windows. He took a deep breath. "What, Nicki?"

"The . . . scars . . . on your back . . ."

Tension quivered through him.

"You're wondering how I got them, aren't you?"

Flustered, Nicki stammered. "It . . . did cross my mind. I know that they're gunshot wounds."

He nodded crisply, then spun around and walked to the door, paused with his hand on the latch. "It was a long time ago, Nicki, when things were different."

"And the drinking . . . the outlawing . . . ?" she had to ask.

"What about it?"

"Does that help you to forget?"

"I can never forget — I won't let myself." His words were hard.

"I'm . . . sorry," she said, and knew immediately that she shouldn't have said it.

He ran his fingers through his hair, then glared at her again.

"For chrissake — go back to sleep. The last thing that I need is your sympathy." He was staring at her in that old hateful way, as if he would snap her head off if she came too near.

Suddenly feeling humiliated by his harshness, and the betrayal of her own flesh, Nicki Sue stifled a sob and buried her face in the pillow.

She heard the door close and rolled over to lay for hours staring up at the lacy shadows flickering on the ceiling.

Nicki Sue awoke to the sun streaming brightly through the window. She couldn't remember falling asleep, or at the moment, where she was, and why. And then with startling clarity it all came rushing back to her. With a gasp she sat up and swung her legs over the side of the bed. Her body ached and her head was throbbing. She wished that she could forget what had happened last night. But all that she could think about was how his lips had felt against her skin, ravishing her mouth, and the need he had awakened inside of her.

Meg's cheerful voice sliced through her recollections, and she gave silent thanks.

"Hello in there! There's some food on the table for you if you're hungry! Come on in when you're ready!"

Nicki couldn't help thinking with cool disdain how

Meg's tone sounded like she was radiating sunshine herself. She got up and walked to the washstand and splashed water on her face. She felt oddly flushed this morning, and picked up a damp rag and wiped it over her arms. She dried herself off, and hurriedly ran a comb through her tangled hair. When she was satisfied that it was free of snarls, she secured it on top of her head as best she could with some pins she found lying beside the soap dish. She assessed her image in the round mirror above the washstand. Well, at least she looked better than she felt. She studied her smooth complexion. The brisk scrubbing made her face tingle and gave it a healthy pink glow. With her thick riot of hair secured tightly back off of her face, her fine high cheekbones and cat-gold eyes were brought preeminently into focus. With a collective sigh, she dressed, then crossed the room and opened the door.

"Heard you moving around. I hope you slept well," Meg said, smiling at Nicki as she entered the main room.

Nicki Sue was surprised to see a young girl and boy sitting at the crudely fashioned wood table. The boy was about eleven, and the girl, barely six. They met her curious gaze, then resumed eating their hot corn mush. For some reason, she had not imagined Meg having children.

She tried not to appear surprised. "Yes . . . fine, thank you."

"How's the leg this morning?" Meg asked, her face concerned.

"Fine," Nicki returned. "Whatever Jesse put on it must have been some sort of a miracle potion."

"The Indians have many cures that seem like it," Meg commented, busying herself with refilling the children's cups.

"Wherever did he learn such a remedy? He's such a mystery to me, Meg," Nicki said tentatively. "I shouldn't wish to know anything about him . . . but I do." Then, seeing the strange look in the other woman's eyes, Nicki knew she shouldn't have spoken so freely. Whatever must Meg think?

Meg brushed a tendril of hair from her cheek. "I know what you are feeling, dear. Jesse is a confusing man, but he has a way about him that affects all of us." She indicated that Nicki should take a chair. "Now, you'd better sit down before the youngsters gobble down everything." She smiled at her. "Sorry we're so rushed, but it's a weekday, and around here we get up early in order to get to school on time. Wouldn't do for the teacher to be late, you know."

Nicki smiled at the boy and girl watching her closely.

Meg proceeded to introduce her to the two children. She told her the girl's name was Kerry Beth, and the boy's, Tad. Nicki Sue took a place on the narrow bench beside the little girl. She couldn't help but wonder where Jesse was.

"Ma's the best teacher ever," the little girl beamed at Nicki. "You should come to school with us, ma'am; you'd agree, I betcha."

"I'm sure you're right," Nicki agreed.

"Wouldn't you like to come with us?" Kerry Beth persisted.

"That's enough, Kerry Beth," Meg admonished, waving her spoon in the child's direction. "I'm certain Nicki has better things to do with her time. Now, finish up, child, so that we can leave."

Meg put a steaming bowl of mush before Nicki, and noticed the way that Nicki's eyes kept straying now and again to the door.

"He's out tending the animals for me."

Nicki Sue's eyes flew to the woman standing beside her. She was embarrassed to realize she'd been so obvious.

"He'll be in directly," Meg said, then she went back to the hearth to remove the big pot from over the fire. There was only the sound of the kettle hissing steam on the grate for several seconds, then she added, "When you've finished eating, I have a gown that should fit you. Mind you, it isn't anything fancy like I expect you're used to wearing, but it's clean and neat."

"Anything will be fine, and thank you," Nicki replied, picking up her spoon.

Meg was watching her closely. Nicki hesitated, knowing there was something else on the woman's mind.

"He told me . . . what happened on the train," Meg said hesitantly. "I rather expected you to hold hard feelings, but it doesn't seem like you do."

Nicki could feel her cheeks grow warm. Her eyes turned resolutely to the doorway. "I honestly don't know how I feel about him at this moment."

"I know that too."

"I wish he would have never come into my life." Nicki sighed deeply. "Now everything is all mixed up . . . and I'm the only one on that train who knows what he looks like."

"It's a difficult situation," Meg said.

"Mama . . . what sit — situation are you talking about?" Kerry Beth chimed in.

Meg shot her a disapproving look. "This doesn't concern you, daughter, so mind your manners."

Tad tugged teasingly on one of Kerry Beth's golden braids. "Finish your breakfast, freckle face — it's getting late."

"Don't call me that!" Kerry Beth scowled.

"That's enough, children," Meg warned. "You'd better begin gathering your things; it's almost time to leave." Her gaze returned to Nicki Sue's distressed face. "I'm sure Jesse thought you might have been shot if he hadn't acted quickly."

"Whatever his reasoning, I can't condone his methods," Nicki said.

Tad spoke carefully. "Are you going to help them catch him after you're free?"

Nicki trembled at his words. She looked over at him. "I . . . really can't say what I will do."

"I hope not. We sure do need his help around here, ma'am," Tad stated solemnly. "You see, Pa was killed a while back, and Jesse . . . he helps us out whenever he can."

"Tad," Meg interrupted. "You and Kerry Beth go wait for me in the wagon."

"Yes, ma'am," Tad replied softly, taking his sister by the hand.

At mention of her father, Kerry Beth bowed her head and sniffled. "My pa was a good man, and those awful men . . . shot him."

"I'm so sorry," Nicki told the little girl, her expression one of compassion.

"Come along, Kerry Beth," Tad murmured.

Meg waited for the children to leave the house, then she said, "My daughter was really too young to remember how Reed died. She was just a toddler when it happened. But she's heard us talk about it, and of course there have been questions I thought should be answered. It's been hard on the children." The teakettle began whistling and she retrieved it from the fire and brought it to the table to pour hot tea into Nicki's cup. "We try not to talk about it too much. It doesn't do any good to reflect on the past, seeing's how you can't change it."

Bits and pieces of the conversation she'd overheard last night between Jesse and Meg came to Nicki's mind now. She took a sip of tea, then waited expectantly for Meg to continue.

Gathering up the children's dirty dishes, Meg went on. "Jesse has a good side of him. I know it's hard for you to believe that right now. But if you'd think about how you might have been killed in that shootout, you realize that he was truly worried about your safety. I expect most men wouldn't have cared about anything but dodging those bullets. But then, that's not his way."

"How was your husband killed?" Nicki asked.

Meg shook her head sadly. "It's a difficult story, but maybe it will help you to understand better. My husband was a mining engineer. We came from New York when the talk of gold was drawing everyone to the California goldfields. We met Jess shortly after we settled here. He had folks that were planning to move to Sacramento from Reno. He talked about them a lot. They were a close bunch. Reed and Jess got along real well." She beamed proudly. "My Reed was a smart man. He picked a place near Sacramento to settle, certain that there was gold on the property. There were those who called us squatters, and wanted our land for their own reasons. Jess shared the claim with my husband." She paused to swallow painfully. "They were both young, and a bit wild at times, but I loved Reed . . . and was fond of Jess, too. Together the two of them thought they could take a stance against anyone threatening. But Jess was a wanderer even then. He couldn't settle in one place for very long. He was in and out of our lives, but he always came back. One day he turned up by surprise — he did that a lot, just came and went like a summer breeze. He told us he knew someone who was willing to back our mining operation. He said he'd met a man when he'd been back East. He told Reed that all he had to do was give him the okay and they'd make plans. Well, of course we were ecstatic, since our money was running real low and we didn't want to give up. They made plans, and it looked like we all were going to be rich one day soon." Her eyes darkened with pain. "And then . . . ." Her words trailed off and she shook her head as if to ward off painful memories. "And then . . . nothing was ever the same again."

Nicki Sue stared up at her, surprised. "I can hardly believe we're talking about the same man."

Meg nodded. "Jesse was different back then . . . before that awful man came, and everything went crazy around us." Realizing that she'd revealed more than she'd actually intended, she clamped her lips tightly together and untied her apron. "That's enough of that, but just you remember — sometimes outlawing isn't simply in a man's blood. Sometimes there are reasons behind it."

"Tell me more . . . please," Nicki urged.

Meg quickly collected her hat and began gathering up her books. The room was still. Nicki waited. Meg started for the door.

"Meg?" Nicki murmured, softly pleading.

"Jesse might come back at any moment and hear us, and the kids are waiting. I can't tell you any more right now. I'm sorry, Nicki." She left the house, and Nicki stared after her.

After Meg had gone, Nicki sat contemplating what she had told her. There was so much about Jesse that

134

she didn't know. Somehow, she hadn't imagined him leading any other life besides that of an outlaw. Meg's startling disclosure had left her stunned. She found herself comparing the cold, harsh man she knew to the picture Meg had painted of him. More than ever, she could not help wondering what made a man like Jesse go bad.

Chapter Six

After Meg left, Nicki straightened the cabin and then changed into the clean gown that Meg had provided for her. It was a light yellow-sprigged muslin and, surprisingly, fit her very well. She went outside to draw some fresh water from the well, and it was then that she heard it.

Nicki was drawn away from the well toward the river that ran behind the cabin by the wavering, melodious notes of a harmonica. It was a beautiful sound, and she found herself wondering who it was playing the instrument. It was a short walk, a brief stroll through the trees and over a slight hill, and she saw him. Jesse was sitting with his back against a wide tree trunk, appearing lost in his thoughts and the music he was creating. She had not seen him like this and, like the night before, felt herself drawn to him for some inexplicable reason. He was an enigma, totally opposite from everything she believed should be appealing in a man, yet undeniably fascinating in a way that she did not understand.

Nicki realized then that she hadn't thought of escaping him one time his morning. Not even when Meg and the children had left, and she was alone in the cabin. But then she surmised that even if she did manage to get away, she would never be able to escape

Jesse. He would come after her, and catch her, and she feared then he might chose to never let her go. She was his captive, and yet . . . he'd taken care of her, and had brought her here because she'd been injured and needed a safe place to recuperate. Could he really have taken another man's life without regret when he had tended her with such care? It was a question that had plagued her often the past few days.

He looked up to see her standing there and withdrew the harmonica from his mouth. She searched those deep blue eyes for some sign that he remembered last night. As usual, she saw only what he wished her to see. This morning his gaze was coolly impersonal. She was suddenly angry at herself for allowing him to unleash such conflicting emotions inside her.

"Good morning; feeling better?" she heard him ask.

She swept an errant strand of hair back from her forehead. "Yes, I am. Whatever you put on my injury made the difference."

He smiled. "Glad to hear it."

"You should do that more often," she said unthinking.

He appeared puzzled. "Do what?"

"Smile." Her eyes danced merrily despite her firm resolve not to show her emotions.

Jesse studied her silently in the bright sunshine. She reached impulsively for a butterfly skimming over her head. She appeared so unassuming and at ease with him this morning. He watched her innocent gesture with heavy-lidded eyes, taking in everything about her. She was completely unaware how at ease she was with him at the moment. Her hair was blowing in the warm breeze about her shoulders: wispy tendrils of dusky brown unhindered by pins, making him recall how good it felt crushed between his fingers, and how sweet the smell of her. Her eyes were slightly puffy from lack of sleep, but he had noticed their tawny depths were bright and clear. Want, desire, suddenly flowing red-hot and lusty through his veins, made him turn his gaze elsewhere and resume playing the harmonica. There wasn't a minute that passed by when he didn't think about what she'd given him last night. And he couldn't deny there was now a constant hunger for her inside him, gnawing at his reason and driving him mad with visions of her lovely body and the remembered expressions of her exquisite passion. She was sweet torture and, he must remember, very dangerous to his freedom.

Nicki sat down nearby to gaze at him. He seemed oblivious to her presence now, completely absorbed by the music he was creating and some deep inner thoughts that took him far from her. She felt a warm stirring deep inside her as her eyes lingered on those full, carnal lips pressed almost intimately to the instrument. His long fingers curled around it, took possession as though it were a woman's body—and he, determined to woo pleasure from it. She knew the tiny pulse at the base of her throat was fluttering wildly, and she trembled with the knowledge that all he had to do was glance over at her and he'd see how her body was betraying her. She wanted him again—wanted him to take her in his arms and caress her body with those knowing hands and lips. Like last night—he had made her forget everything. And even though she damned her traitorous soul for the thought, she did not deny her need.

When he stopped playing, Nicki could only breathe softly. "That was lovely, Jesse."

He looked over at her, then said, "Nicki, I think there is something you should know. I'll be leaving soon. In fact, in a couple of days."

"And what about me—will I be free to go, too?" she asked with hope in her eyes.

"Soon, Nicki. Just try and be patient awhile longer."

She swept him with a contemptuous glance. "I guess I have little to say in the matter."

He never blinked an eyelash before replying. "What happened last night hasn't changed things between us, if that's what you were bargaining on. You didn't buy your freedom any quicker."

Her cheeks flaming now, Nicki fought back humiliating tears. "You'll never change, Jesse. You'll always be despicable and cruel."

"I never claimed to be anything other that what I am. And I never made you any promises last night."

Seething with pent-up frustration and feeling suddenly degraded, Nicki got to her feet and began walking back to the house. In her heart she was trying hard not to remember the heat his eyes ignited in her body when he looked at her, and the memory of hungry kisses shared the night before.

They spent the remainder of the day keeping a measurable distance between them. Jesse avoided the cabin and spent the afternoon working outdoors, yet always close enough that he could easily call out to Nicki and hear her answer. At this, Nicki smiled, knowing that he really wasn't so sure of her after all.

Even though Jesse worked his body hard for hours beneath the hot sun, until the sweat poured off him and his muscles ached, Nicki was still lingering there in his thoughts. She seemed to unwittingly be offering herself to him with the promise to let him lose himself in the silken prison of her arms and forget. But damn it! He couldn't forget! He owed that much to Allison's memory.

It was late afternoon when he came inside, his shirt tossed carelessly over one broad shoulder, droplets of water clinging to his bronzed skin and black hair. She'd been watching him through the open door from her place at the table. He had washed up at the outside pump. She hadn't been able to stop staring at him until she'd suddenly noticed he was finished and now heading in the direction of the cabin. She concentrated on cutting up the apples she had discovered in a basket next to the hearth. They were big, juicy red apples, and she thought what a delicious pie they'd make, and how it would be nice for Meg to come home after a long day to find a hot meal waiting. Nicki had the makings of a thick stew bubbling in the black pot over the fire and the crust for the pie draped in a pie tin. The cabin was filled with delightful food smells, and she didn't fail to notice that Jesse breathed a satisfied sigh upon first entering.

"You sure are full of surprises," he said, his eyes watching her closely.

Nicki refused to look up at him. "Seems like you're making a habit of saying that."

"Yeah, I guess I am at that. But it is true, you know. I would have never thought a woman like you would take to domestic life so fast."

One dainty eyebrow arched upward. "Are we back to that again?" she inquired icily. She glared at him as he pulled out a chair, and turning it around, he straddled it and rested his arms on the high back.

"You're all claws again, I see."

Her eyes narrowed. "I suggest you stay clear of them, too."

He could not help grinning as he reached for a chunk of apple. Nicki automatically smacked at his hand. Then realizing what she'd done, she slowly drew back her fingers.

"You don't have to fear me, Nicki," he said, tossing the piece of apple into his mouth.

She worked moodily over the apples, ignoring his statement, but knowing that he would not leave it alone as she wished he would.

"In fact, I'd like to get a few things cleared up between us. I've truly never meant you any harm. You must realize that by now. Let's not spoil it and go back to testing one another." She felt that inscrutable gaze searing her and was drawn to look over at him. His voice continued low and husky. "Come on—what do you say we part friends, at least?"

"You have some nerve!" she shot back tartly. "The one thing that we'll never be is friends. I take no delight in my situation, or your condescending attitude. And just because things got a little out of hand last night does not mean that you've managed to bend my spirit to your will." She met his hard gaze levelly, refusing to back down even an inch.

His hand snaked forward to grab hold of her wrist and pull her forward into his lap so fast that the knife she was holding clattered to the floor and the unpeeled apples in her lap tumbled about at their feet.

Nicki knew even before his lips closed over hers that he was going to kiss her, and her lips parted of their own accord. She tried telling herself it was unwise of her to allow him to kiss her whenever he wanted, but she knew that no matter how much she might protest, he would do what he damn well pleased anyway. Trying hard not to feel any warmth from his passionate assault on her mouth, Nicki soon knew it was useless. His mouth moved persuasively over hers, just as hot and hungry as she'd longed for it to.

When he finally ended the embrace, his head drew back and he peered down at her kiss-ravaged lips with a triumphant smile.

"Haven't I?" he drawled, and she felt a tearing jolt as tentative doubts whirled through her.

Refusing to let him defeat her, Nicki smiled her most devastating smile. "No," she replied evenly, her chin held high, "you have not."

Jesse threw back his dark head and laughed, and Nicki shot off of his lap to gather up the scattered apples. Damn him . . . damn him . . . she was raging to herself. He is the most arrogant man I've ever met in my life. His incipient attitude was almost too much to bear at the moment, and she took several fortifying gulps of air before returning to the table to put the finishing touches on the pie. She did her best to act as though his kiss had not affected her, but it had, and she had to struggle to dispel painful truths.

Feeling his eyes roaming over her body, she almost turned and flung the apples at him. What a fool she'd been last night. He'd used her, taken advantage of her confusion and desperation. And she hated him for it. His voice interrupted her silent chastisement.

"Don't be too hard on yourself, Nicki. You're young and vital, and what happened was entirely natural. Two people don't have to love each other to enjoy a night together."

Nicki's eyes narrowed. "I don't even like you, Jesse — so how can you explain that?"

For once, the train robber was at a loss for words. Sunlight played about the thick, dark curls that framed cynical features, and she found herself wishing that last night had not taken place. And until she was free of him, she had to somehow remain indifferent to the lusty yearnings he'd awakened. He exuded an animal magnetism that was difficult to resist, and it seemed all that he had to do was come near her and she was lost in a paradox of emotions that threatened everything she'd once believed in.

142

The remainder of the day passed without further incident. Nicki was vastly relieved when Jesse had left the cabin and managed to stay away until Meg and the children returned.

Supper was pleasant enough, and if Nicki was unusually quiet, no one noticed as the youngsters kept up a constant chatter about the day's activities. Kerry Beth was clearly enthralled with everything about Jesse. She sat next to him at the table and barely touched her food.

"Kerry, if you don't finish your supper, you won't be having any dessert," Meg warned.

Jesse pushed his empty plate aside and raised one dark brow questioningly. "Apple pie, Kerry? You don't want to miss out on that?"

Kerry shook her golden head and promptly began eating her stew.

"That's a good girl, Jesse praised, and the child beamed.

"You spoil her," Meg told him.

He looked over at her, then back at Kerry, who had picked up her blue-checked napkin and was dabbing primly at her mouth, trying hard to appear as grown-up in his eyes as possible.

"It's hard not to with such a little charmer."

Tad sat back in his chair with a disgruntled snort and mumbled under his breath. "You wouldn't say that so fast if you had to live with her for very long."

"That's enough." Meg leaned over to whisper sternly in Tad's ear, and then excused herself from the table to fetch the pie from the warming oven. The evening was passing much too slowly for her. It was a trial to sit and listen to the congenial chatter when she was desperate to find some time to talk with Jesse alone. She reached into the cupboard and retrieved a thick chunk of yellow cheese, then gathered the dessert plates and clean utensils. Placing everything on a tray, she set it before Nicki Sue.

"Thought you should have the honor of serving it, since you went to so much trouble to make such a delicious dessert."

Nicki glanced up at her and smiled appreciatively. "Thank you — however, it was the least I could do seeing as how you were kind enough to let me stay here."

"It sure smells delicious," Tad said.

"Can I have the biggest piece, Mama?" Kerry chimed in, her dimples flashing charmingly as she smiled.

Tad glared at her.

"Everyone will get their equal share, Kerry," Meg said firmly.

Kerry dropped her head guiltily.

Tad did his best to stifle a smile.

Jesse sipped his coffee and watched them over the rim of the cup. It had been a long time since he'd eaten a meal as good as the one Nicki had prepared, and enjoyed female company and children's good-natured rivalry. A curious peacefulness had settled over him since he'd been here, seeming to have assuaged the bitterness that had been so much a part of him for so long that it was ingrained in his soul. Nicki handed him a generous slice of pie topped by a thick sliver of cheese. His fingers brushed hers and he could not help but notice the fire in her eyes.

Tad took a bite of pie, then told Nicki, "I'd say someone who knew a lot about fine cooking taught you real well, ma'am."

"Where did you learn to cook, Nicki?" Jesse prompted.

Nicki picked up her fork and shrugged. "I don't know . . . just taught myself, I guess. My mother died

144

when I was young, and after having to eat Pa's food for a while, I decided I'd best try my hand at it or be satisfied with beans and bacon at every meal." She caught Jesse's gaze, and added, "It's my turn to pry. Where did you learn to take care of a ranch so proficiently? I am astonished by the things you accomplished with such ease today."

He set down his fork and considered her closely before replying. "I didn't always depend on a gun to make a living."

"I know," Nicki Sue replied quietly without realizing what she'd revealed.

Silence settled in the room.

Meg coughed uneasily and quickly began gathering up the dirty dishes. She motioned for the children to excuse themselves. They did so and went immediately to the loft. It came to Nicki then what she'd said, and after finishing her dessert, she excused herself and left the room. Meg waited until she'd closed the bedroom door before turning to Jesse.

"That wasn't fair, Jess. You're too hard on her sometimes."

He glared at her. "What have you two been talking about? Are you siding against me, too?"

"Don't pull that stuff with me, Jesse Kardel," she huffed. "We've been through too much together, and you have no call to say such a thing."

He put his hand out to her, but she ignored him and turned away to begin clearing the table.

Meg carried the dishes to the sink, then suddenly blurted, "Just how well do you know her?"

He didn't answer her immediately because he simply had been caught unawares; dealing with two women at the same time was hard on a man, and particularly when they both were intelligent and appeared determined to give him a difficult time.

Meg's hands stilled but she did not turn around. "I guess by your silence I'm to take it that means — quite well."

Jesse was suddenly weary of defending himself. He got up from the table and came up behind Meg. "She doesn't mean anything to me. You know there was only one woman in my life, and there won't be another to take her place."

Meg didn't know whether he even knew himself how he truly felt, but at the moment she decided it was best not to reply. And she had something else pressing to discuss with him.

"I think I should tell you what I heard from Minnie Wilkes when she came to pick up her son today."

Jesse turned her around to face him. "I suspected you had something on your mind during supper."

Meg nodded over the lump in her throat. "Yes, I did."

"Then let's hear what it is."

"There is talk of a train robbery that took place a few days ago over in the next county . . . and of the woman the bandits took hostage."

He kept his voice even. "Does anyone have any idea who the bandits are?"

"No," Meg answered simply, "but that's not what I thought you should know." She hesitated, then said, "It's . . . it's Nicki. I don't think you know who she really is."

"For chrissake — just say it, Meg."

"All right," Meg continued in a rush. "She was married . . . to a man by the name of Patrick Ryan. He was killed during the train holdup. I don't know whether she knows he's dead yet, but I have a hunch she does, or I think you would know all of this already." She hesitated when she saw the dark fury in his eyes and the tense slant to his mouth. "I think she's afraid what you might do to her if you discover she knows you're the one . . ." She gnawed at her lip.

"Go on — finish it!" Jesse snarled. "The one who killed her husband."

"Oh God, Jess," Meg sobbed, "is it true? Did you kill someone in cold blood?"

Jesse was stunned by her disclosure, but even more so that Meg should doubt him. And how could Nicki have been that man's wife when she'd been a virgin? His thoughts were jumbled. What sort of man had Patrick Ryan been? He must have been either blind or an absolute idiot to not have found a woman like Nicki fascinating, and remembering her uninhibited passion the night before, he felt his groin tighten at the memory. He sensed Meg watching him closely and glanced down at her.

"I didn't kill him, and I don't think any of my men did either."

Meg was visibly upset. "But you did rob that train and take Nicki as your hostage. And everyone is blaming you for the killing."

"Damn the fools," he snarled harshly. "Can't they see it was Evanson again? It all fits now. He was playing her husband for all he could get. . . . That's why she was in his private car. I've got to leave, Meg. I don't want you involved any more than you are already."

"I'm not going to let you face this alone! This is serious, and could mean your life if they catch you."

"They won't catch me," Jesse stated with finality.

"Forget this thing with Evanson, please . . . before they kill you."

There was a brief pause, then Jesse's mouth tightened to a terse line. "I told you that I would catch up with him one day and make him pay for everything that he did to us. Well . . . the time has come — and he's just begun to pay."

Meg grabbed hold of his arm. "No! Allison wouldn't have wanted you to do this—to waste your life trying to even a score."

"I'm not only doing this for Allison; I'm doing it for Reed, too. Allison didn't deserve to die the way that she did—like a hunted animal." His voice was grim with pain. "Neither of them should have had to face death in the manner they did. And if it wouldn't have been for Evanson trying to steal their land because of his godforsaken greed, they'd all be alive today. Allison . . . Reed . . . perhaps even Nicki's husband."

Meg buried her face in the curve of his shoulder. "You can't bring them back, Jess. You mean so much to me. . . . I don't know what the kids and I will do if something should happen to you. We couldn't make it on our own here." She exhaled raggedly. "But I hate to think that we're part of the reason you are doing this."

Jesse hugged her to him and whispered soothingly. "No, Meg—Evanson is solely responsible for what I do."

"We love you so," Meg murmured, wrapping her arms about him.

"And I love all of you," Jesse replied softly, but Meg knew he didn't mean it in the same way she did.

Shortly after that, he told her he was going for a walk to think over some things before calling it a night. When she asked him when he was leaving, he didn't give her an answer. But she knew it would be soon.

Much later, Nicki lay in her bed listening to the night sounds all around her, and found to her distress that she could not stop thinking about Jesse. Over

148

and over in her mind she recalled every intimate detail of their passion the night before. Her hands clenched together on her stomach as warmth drifted lazily through her body, then centered between her legs. She groaned softly. How she wanted him there, his flesh filling her so completely, she ached sweetly from it. She desperately longed for that breathless starburst of ecstasy that would release her and allow her to sleep peacefully without dreams. Her ears strained to hear any sounds coming from the next room. There was only the crackling of the fire. No doubt Jesse was fast asleep, thoughts of her far from his mind. Why, then, didn't she do the same? Humiliation made Nicki toss angrily on the tangled sheets. She'd never known a man like Jesse, one who could torment her until she felt half-crazy, yet satisfy her cravings of passion so completely. Yes she admitted in frustration, she wanted him! But tonight he could care less about her. Sleep came with great difficulty, and was filled with the same nightmares. She heard someone sobbing raggedly, deep, heartrending sobs that broke through her dreams.

"Nicki, wake up, you're having a bad dream."

Nicki opened her heavy-lidded eyes to see Jesse leaning over her, a hand on either side of her shoulders. Confused and still half-asleep, she unconsciously struck out at him with one clenched fist. He wasn't expecting her reaction and only stared narrow-eyed when her small fist connected with the solid muscle of his arm. He shook her roughly and her eyes grew wide and comprehending.

"Damn it, I'm not going to hurt you, I was simply trying to keep you from waking the entire household," he growled in obvious disgust.

"Let me go! You have no right to be in here!" she hissed, bristling when she saw his lips twist in sneering contempt.

"I'll leave just as soon as you settle down."

Nicki fought to twist away from him, but his fingers held her pinned. Suddenly he jerked her forward, bringing her face within inches of his. His eyes flared like silver fire.

"Why do you always force me to get rough with you?"

She came fully awake now, angry and bristling like a cat. "I'm sick of you always blaming me for your detestable behavior! It's because of you that I've lost everything. I hate you. . . . Leave me alone!"

To her open-mouthed surprise, she saw his lips curve upward into a nasty grin. He pushed her back onto the mattress and held her still beneath him. "You little hypocrite. How easy it is for you to blame me. Maybe if you would have been a little more willing with your husband, baby, he might have been with you the night he was killed instead of roaming around looking for some way to idle his time."

Her mouth formed a silent denial that died in her throat. If he'd slapped her, it would have hurt less. She stared back at him with a stricken look in her eyes that almost made him wish he could take back the words. But then, she'd been asking for it. Almost as if she'd been deliberately goading him to cause her pain.

"Don't bother to deny it; I know all about him," he snarled. He turned abruptly away from her and crossed over the floor to stare out of the window. Hell, why not sever everything clean and permanent between them right now? She was big trouble for him, and the only one who could, and perhaps would, see a noose around his neck if she thought she could get by with it. Suddenly more than ready to end things between them, he whirled, and as she watched him with a stunned expression, he retrieved a wad of bills from his pocket and walked over to toss them on the bed beside her.

"What . . . is that for?" she asked tremulously.

"It's payoff time, Mrs. Ryan," he replied without a flicker of compassion in his eyes.

Nicki Sue gasped at his cynical words.

He smiled coldly. "It's not what you think. I'm buying your silence, not paying for services rendered. But if I should find out that you tell anyone about me, I'm going to come looking for you. Do I make myself perfectly clear?"

She could only nod numbly, shocked that he would think she would betray him after what had transpired between them. She had thought she was beginning to understand him somewhat after having talked with Meg, but she didn't think that even Meg knew this side of him. Without a backward glance he walked out of the room, leaving Nicki Sue to wonder how far he would truly go to make sure she kept quiet.

Chapter Seven

By morning Jesse had made up his mind to leave very soon. There was really no reason for him to stay, and with stories of the train robbery already circulating in Sandy Creek, it wasn't safe for Meg and the children with him here. He hadn't seen Nicki since breakfast and knew she was deliberately avoiding him. Just thinking about how she'd hidden the fact that she was married prompted his jaw to clench in renewed anger, and unable to stop himself, he strode out of the house in search of her. By God, she wasn't going to get off so easy! She owed him a decent explanation after all that he'd risked to save her life.

Nicki was sitting by the river beneath the spreading branches of a tree, enjoying the cool breeze and trying not to delve into her inner thoughts and conjure up Jesse. She did not hear his approach and looked up startled when he jackknifed his long legs to sit next to her. What he was thinking must have shown in his midnight-blue eyes, or in the way he held himself so rigidly distant from her, and Nicki instinctively drew back. Both terrified and entranced by his presence, she could only stare numbly at him as he stated gruffly, "Before I go, I want you to answer a few questions for me."

She watched him warily. "I think we've already said

all there is to say."

His hand came forward to grip her chin between relentless fingers. "Not quite everything."

She remained immobile, sensing his anger barely kept in check. He took her left hand and held it up before her eyes.

"There's been something I've been wanting to know."

"What's that?" she breathed, hardly daring to speak.

His voice turned sneering. "Your wedding ring—did you just conveniently toss it away as easily as you did your virtue?"

Nicki paled. "Jesse . . . I . . . I . . . don't know why you persist in this."

His hand slid downward, his fingers encircling her neck, slowly splaying over the fluttering pulse in her throat.

"The hell you don't." Face harsh and cold, he glared at her. "You played me so easily with your innocent act. But it will never happen again, lady."

"How did you hear of my marriage?"

He laughed shortly. "You're news, baby—even in these parts."

"Meg . . . ," Nicki breathed slowly. "Of course! Word of a train robbery would set everyone talking. Meg heard talk of it in town, didn't she?"

"Yes, she did."

Her eyes suddenly gleamed hopefully. "They're looking for me . . . I know they are."

"But they won't find you until I want them to," Jesse stated. Suddenly his face darkened and his eyes narrowed. "Why in the hell didn't you have the decency to tell me before . . .?" his words trailed off as her eyes glittered with fury.

"You have a lot of nerve talking about decency—

and if I would have told you I was a virgin, would that have stopped you from taking what you wanted, Jesse?" She refused to back down from the telltale anger in his gaze.

"Despite what you might think of me, I don't make it a habit to make love to other men's wives."

"It was something that should not have happened . . . but I was frightened . . . and you were all there was to keep danger away."

He shook his head slowly, his mouth curling in a contemptible smile. "You sure are something, Mrs. Ryan. You sure fooled me with your fancy airs. But it's really all an act, isn't it?"

She was stung by his cruel words, but faced him with cool defiance. "I did not take off my ring because of you. I had removed it on the train. My husband had surprised me with it earlier that day at our wedding . . . It was big on my finger and I was afraid it might slip off, so I put it in my bag that night for safekeeping." Her words became terse. "Of course, you can choose to believe that or not; I really don't care anymore."

If what she'd told him was true, then the night he'd discovered her in Evanson's car . . . must have been her wedding night. That would explain her virginity. She was staring at him with eyes bright as bits of glass. Could she be telling him the truth?

"You know he's dead, don't you?" He knew by her expression that she did.

The question was so forthright and blunt that Nicki's eyes filled with tears. She blinked them back and faced him down. "I would never have let you touch me if I'd had any hope that Patrick was still alive. I overheard one of your men talking about the man who'd fallen from the train when you came upon me in the public coach. He . . . he mentioned the man's red hair. . . . I knew it was Patrick then. I was hoping to go to my husband's aid when you effectively blocked my path."

"You would be dead by now if I hadn't grabbed you!"

"Yes . . . I know," she stated coolly, as though death might have been preferable to being with him.

He laughed deep in his throat, a cold, harsh sound. "I'd say you were of an entirely different mind a couple of nights ago."

"Stop reminding me of that awful mistake!" she ground out from between clenched teeth. He had a way of sending her emotions spinning out of control with just a certain tone of voice. "It was the wine . . . and I . . . needed someone." Her voice faltered. "Of course, you wouldn't have the faintest idea what it's like to *need* anyone, would you, Jesse?" She could not stop the torrent of words once they started. She wanted desperately to make him feel hurt — make him feel anything! "You use people to suit your needs — you don't care about anyone!"

He gripped her shoulders tightly. "You're probably right about that — I don't allow myself to feel things the way that other people do. Life is a whole lot easier when it's not clouded by unnecessary emotions." Suddenly he yanked her close to him, his lips almost touching hers. "But there is one emotion you manage to stir in me, Mrs. Ryan. And I think the feeling's mutual."

"No!" she gasped, recognizing the glitter of desire in his eyes.

"You're like a fire raging through me every time I'm near you, and there seems to be only one way to put it out." His hands moved teasingly up and down her arms.

His words made her struggle violently in his arms.

155

"Not this way . . . don't make me hate you any more!"

He ignored her plea, his fingers stroking boldly over her, stroking, possessing, until she moaned under her breath.

"You want me to touch you . . . here . . . and . . . here," he stated huskily, luring her toward surrender with those knowing fingers, watching her with an undefinable expression in his eyes.

"No . . . leave me alone." But even to her own ears her voice sounded breathless and yearning. Desperate, she did the only thing she could to shatter the moment; one hand instinctively swinging outward to catch him along the side of his face with a force that shocked them both. She froze in motion, not certain what his response might be.

He viewed her through narrowed eyes, his lips suddenly twitching in a mocking smile. "There's no sense fighting, beautiful; you know how easily I can make you change your mind."

There was a veiled menace in his husky voice that prompted Nicki to almost panic. How could he have been such a tender lover just the night before, and today turn into some savage stranger who could threaten her life? She saw his eyes change suddenly, become heavy-lidded with desire.

"You'll not have me by force," she stated firmly.

She stiffened when his hand skimmed over the creamy expanse of flesh above the décolletage of her gown.

"I don't think it will take force to have you." His smile was self-assured. His hand slipped inside her gown to cup her breast, long fingers closing around the trembling globe, felt the nipple pulse beneath his palm. He moved his hand in a slow circular motion, and it rose eagerly in welcome. Nicki's eyelids fluttered closed as her emotions went wild.

156

"Damn you . . . Jesse," she murmured, her mind resisting, but her young body more than willing.

"Oh . . . yes . . . ," he whispered silkily, "that's more like the Nicki I've come to know."

Nicki writhed sensually against him, overwhelmed by desire and the hard, masculine feel of him against her. She didn't know if she had the strength to resist the sensual magic he weaved so well, but she was certain that if she didn't get away from him immediately, she would be lost to him. She simply could not allow him to treat her as if she were his plaything who would eagerly share his carnal appetites whenever he desired. Her nerves taut, she flung herself from his arms and hurried as fast as her injured leg would permit toward a mountain path.

The uphill flight was difficult, but she made it to the first plateau and darted through a narrow fissure, and heard the distinct sound of water tumbling across rocks. I must find someplace where I can hide, she thought frantically. She did not stop to think that perhaps he wasn't worried in the least about hurrying to find her.

Jesse took his time following the obvious trail she'd left behind. The ground beneath his feet was soft, scattered intermittently with moss, and left a clear imprint of her footprints, which would lead him directly to her.

Nicki slumped to the ground and tried to catch her breath. She was hiding behind a boulder perched high on a mountain ledge that overlooked the valley below. Before her, jutting rocks reached toward the sky, seeming to blot out the sun. Scattered throughout gaping crevices, bright wildflowers blanketed their harsh lines. She didn't notice the beauty around her; all that she was thinking was that she had nowhere else to run.

That was the way that Jesse found her, appearing like some half-wild she-cat cornered on that ledge with hatred gleaming in her eyes and white teeth bared in a soft snarl of warning.

"Don't come any closer."

He didn't heed her words, but walked slowly toward her until she jumped to her feet, her arms outstretched as if to stave him off, her stance wary. "Stay away from me, you bastard."

"Come here," he ordered quietly.

Nicki Sue shook her head.

He moved so fast to grab her to him that she didn't have a chance to react. Recovering her senses, she hit at him with her fists and struggled violently. And then they were both tumbling to the moss-covered ground, Jesse managing to straddle her and pinion her wrists back over her head. She bit her lip as she read the intent in his gaze.

There was contempt in her eyes, but Jesse knew those golden tiger eyes would soon reveal more, much more. The longing to feel her body writhing beneath his again hurled him into a dark void of passion where desire ruled all senses.

His lips came down on hers to steal her breath away. With ease he inflamed her, caressed the warm, inviting hollows of her mouth with his tongue. Nicki felt a weakening of her will as desire strove to blot out all resistance. She whimpered beneath his skillful manipulation, but knew it was useless to try and pull away. As his hands explored her lush curves, her body eagerly arched to meet his touch, and Nicki became lost to the demands of her young body that he alone had awakened.

He pulled the dampened gown off her shoulder to reveal pearl-white breasts and satin-smooth skin moistened by a fine sheen of sweat. Her breasts quiv-

158

ered, the dusky rose buds growing hard with her mounting passion. With trembling fingers Nicki reached to unbutton his shirt and slide her hands across his bare chest, bury her fingers in the thick mat of crisp black hair. He drew her into his arms, and without forethought she rubbed her fevered breasts against his furred chest. He sucked in his breath, a caressing hand moving down between her legs. His mouth, those ofttimes hard, cynical lips, were now warm and coaxing as they moved downward over her body, stealing away the last of her doubts. He took a rigid nipple between his teeth and played with it gently, nipping softly, savoring it upon his tongue.

When his fingers moved to lift her skirts around her hips, tear offending garments aside, Nicki did not protest. She couldn't, for he had awakened urges in her vital young body that ruled her will. The sun danced warmly across her naked flesh, prickly pinpoints of sensual heat that thirsted upon her moistened skin and made her feel delightfully wicked. She would never have thought that making love in broad daylight could be so uninhibiting and delicious. Nicki arched her hips against his, urging him to touch her there where she burned the hottest. His fingers found her, one long finger moving in such a skillful way into delicate folds that Nicki sobbed that she could stand it no longer.

"I'll show you how much better it can be. . . . Lie still now . . . let me taste all of you," he murmured thickly.

On his knees between her slender legs, he lowered his head to kiss the smooth, flat plane of her belly, his hands moving beneath her hips, lifting her to the touch of his lips. He nipped lightly along her thighs, between her legs where the flesh was as exquisite as silk, and finally kissed the dusky brown pelt that only he had claimed. Her fingers caught in his hair, holding him against her. Her pulse went wild, and she felt as if she were being swept away on a tide of desire. She felt his tongue darting hotly around the throbbing center at the apex of her womanhood. Around and around the hard bud, driving her mindless with desire, wringing soft cries of ecstasy from her that were at last absorbed by the crush of his lips on hers.

The ground was no longer hard against her back, and all sounds except their whispered exchanges faded and became nothing. Only pleasure existed for Nicki now. She wanted to feel him bury himself within her, experience once again the ecstasy they'd shared once before. She unfastened his belt and tugged impatiently at his trousers. And then, because her fingers were shaking too badly to finish undressing him, he brushed her hands aside and finished the task.

He caught her trembling body to him, passion-glittering eyes holding hers. The warm woman scent of her filled his nostrils and heightened his desire. He wanted to watch her face when he eased inside her. Her lips were slightly parted and her eyelids were heavy with desire as her hands moved over him, tantalized his rigid flesh until at last he gave her what she wanted. He penetrated her slowly, filling her completely. Soft little moans escaped her as her liquid heat wrapped tightly around him, drew him deeper and set him afire. She did not want him gentle this time, and she told him. Her words were barely audible, but he heard, and gave her what she wanted.

She wrapped long, lithe legs around his hips and writhed mindlessly against him, matching his hard, driving rhythm. He was hard and almost rough, as if he sought to exorcise his desire for her once and for all. But Nicki was his match in every way. She met his thrusts, equaled his passion, and wove her magic as well.

When it was over and she lay exhausted in his arms, Nicki drowsed contentedly, oblivious to his eyes watching her, and the icy calm that once again glinted in their depths.

Within the town of Bodie, California, there was excitement all along the boardwalk. Dust blew in puffs around the main street and under the swinging doors of the Gilded Lily saloon. Leroy Culpepper swished his broom across the floor for the tenth time that morning and then headed back behind the bar.

"Gonna be a dry summer," he said to the men sipping beer at the bar. "Dust is already startin' to get on my nerves." He swiped a towel over the top of the wood bar.

"For chrissake, Leroy," one of the men growled, "will you just serve drinks and forget about keeping the place spotless? You make me nervous when you do that—reminds me too much of my missus."

Leroy scowled. "If you don't like the way I run this place, Floyd, you can always get off your rump and see if you can get that worthless sheriff to go after the Ryan woman."

"She . . . eet," one old timer guffawed. "That tub of lard ain't gonna do nothing unless that Evanson fella tells him to."

"We all got families, Leroy," Floyd said. "There ain't no way you're gonna catch any of us dodging them train robber's bullets. Besides, that Pinkerton man is here to track them boys down, and I hear tell it's none other than Charlie Star hisself."

A murmur of voices rippled through the saloon.

"I heard about him," the man standing next to Floyd said as he tilted his mug of beer to his lips.

Leroy leaned over the bar. "You heard right, boys," he told the patrons who were hanging on his every word. Enjoying being the center of attention, he eagerly continued. "Mr. Star was in here this morning having his breakfast — had two eggs over easy and bacon, and washed it all down with two whiskeys — "

"We don't want to hear about what he et, Leroy!" a disgruntled customer hollered. "Tell us what he said about them train robbers!"

Leroy went back to wiping the bar. "Well . . . he couldn't say too much, you see . . . reckon he doesn't want to jeopardize his case by letting on too soon what he knows. But I could just tell by the look in his eyes that he won't let them devils get away with the loot and poor Mrs. Ryan."

"Does anyone know what these hombres look like, Leroy?" Floyd asked.

Leroy shook his brawny head. "Nope; they had on masks — all except one of them. But I did hear tell that one was an Injun fella. And you know how it is with Injuns." He started laughing and so did everyone else.

Floyd scratched his beard. "Ain't Charlie Star the one they say done in ole Joaquin Murieta?"

"Yeah! He was the one, all right!" several excited voices exclaimed in unison.

Drinks were ordered by all, and Leroy beamed. It always was a profitable day when you gave the customers something to jaw about.

The patrons of the Golden Lily spent the better part of the day swapping stories about the infamous Charlie Star, and Joaquin Murieta, who had troubled the peace of the California countryside in the days of the mother lode. There had been none worse than the deadly, romantic, charming Joaquin Murieta and his bloody lieutenant, Three-Fingered Jack. And it had been Charlie Star who had tracked them down, and had reportedly struck Joaquin down.

Joaquin had been labeled a Robin Hood of sorts by the people who had never made his acquaintance. Robbed from the rich to give to the poor, they said. But after he was beheaded by Love's bravos, it was discovered that his acclaimed chivalrous deeds were questionable. Some Californians swore that the outlaw still lived, and the raid and gory offering the rangers had submitted as proof to collect the governor's reward had been a setup job. But all traces of Joaquin vanished. Most people agreed the bandit had been killed.

Charlie Star knew for certain—but no one ever questioned Charlie.

Charlie Star walked down the boardwalk, and people respectfully stepped aside. He grinned wryly to himself, this type of reception always bringing to his mind the scene were Moses parted the Red Sea. He liked the respect his notoriety commanded. It had not always been this way; the Joaquin Murieta victory had done much to further his image. He'd been a young man of twenty then, full of vigor and just as ruthless as the men he sought. Harry Love had taught him well. What he had not, Charlie had picked up on his own. Now at thirty-nine, he was in his prime, and on top, and he intended to stay there. He was the best the Pinkerton agency had to offer, and it was a case like the train robbery when he could show off his talents. Charlie tossed a coin at a hawking newsboy and then quickly scanned the front page before turning into the lobby of the town's only boardinghouse. It was a nice place, and he generally preferred the homelike atmosphere of such establishments.

For all his tough reputation, he had one weakness:

a longing for family life that he'd never had. He'd been orphaned when he was ten, and had spent most of his young life drifting from one rough-and-tumble town to the other, careful to hide the fact that his father had been a quarter Apache. Charlie had no love of the Indians, and put from his mind the fact that he had Apache in his blood. It was this unknown truth that made him the best manhunter of his time.

"Good afternoon, Mr. Star," came the voice of Sugar Drucell, the proprietor of the clapboard two-story residence that was Charlie's temporary home.

"Afternoon, ma'am," Charlie responded over the top of his paper.

"How are your accommodations?"

"Right nice, ma'am. Just like home."

Sugar beamed. "I do try my best."

"Well, you do a right good job." Charlie started to walk onward.

Sugar hurried after him before he disappeared up the enclosed stairway.

"Oh, Mr. Star!" she called forth in a melodious voice. "I just wanted to make certain that you knew I'm serving chicken and dumplings for supper this evening!"

Charlie halted and turned around, his sharp eyes automatically sweeping over her cherub's face and plumb figure. "I didn't know that, Miss Drucell, but thanks for informing me. Chicken and dumplings is one of my favorites." He smiled cordially at the beaming spinster.

"Why, isn't that a coincidence?" she gushed.

"Certainly a nice one."

Her round face crinkled beneath a smile. "Supper's at six — can we expect you then?"

Charlie tipped his hat. "Yes, ma'am, you surely can."

"Oh, that's wonderful," she gushed. "The rest of my boarders will be thrilled. They'll have something to talk about for weeks, you know." Her eyes bore a dreamy expression. "Imagine . . . Charlie Star having supper at my table."

"I'll be looking forward to it," Charlie responded graciously, and continued on his way.

He climbed the stairs and strode down the hallway to his room at a rear corner. He had requested a private location, and the charming smile he had added along with it had ensured his request. Sugar Drucell had eagerly shown him her very best room, which she said just happened to have been vacated earlier that morning. It was a nice room, with plenty of sun and a bed that wasn't ticky. He turned the key in the lock and entered.

After tossing his hat on a peg on the wall and removing his guns, Charlie seated himself before the sunny window that overlooked Sugar's flower garden and read the paper. He carefully went over each page looking for an article telling of the train robbery. He found it buried on the next to the last page, a few brief sentences devoid of facts. A frown marred the bronze smoothness of his brow as he scanned the skimpy column. There wasn't enough being circulated about the train robbery, and it was puzzling him. Such a daring deed, and a hostage taken off the train to boot, should have commanded front-page coverage for days. Charlie pondered this for a moment, one great hand rubbing his square jaw. His gray eyes narrowed. There was no doubt about it. Someone didn't want a whole lot told about the robbery. Of course it was reasonable to think it might be because of the bad reputation that would tag the short line; or perhaps fear for Nicole Ryan's life if too much was revealed about the outlaws involved? He pondered the possibility of both, popping a root-beer-flavored candy in his mouth as he did so.

"Something just isn't right about this whole thing," he murmured aloud.

He'd gone over every inch at the scene of Ryan's murder, and on board the PGC. There weren't many facts to go on, but one thing was perfectly clear: the job had been admirably professional, and the leader, from all reports, was a hell of a disciplined man. One of the passengers had overheard him tell his men that he didn't want there to be any casualties. But there had been one. Had they been responsible for Patrick Ryan's death? By all accounts, it seemed highly likely. But if that was true, why had the leader cared about the crew and passengers' lives so much that he'd saved the one woman's life who definitely recognized him? It would have simply been easier to let her bolt from that car and allow the Indian to shoot her. Charlie was indeed puzzled for the first time in his career. He thought he'd talk to the newspaper reporter who'd written the article, then he'd go straight to the source.

"Guess there's really only one way to find the real truth," he murmured. "Find them boys pulled that job and ask them face-to-face."

Chapter Eight

Patrick Ryan had been found dead beside the tracks.

It was assumed that the same outlaws who'd kidnapped his bride were also responsible for his murder. An operative for the Pinkerton agency had been snooping around the site of the train robbery, and had searched the train and the area where Patrick had met his death. One of Lars's men reported back to him that the Pinkerton was a real manhunter, an ornery old cuss who dug deeply for the facts. Lars was not happy to hear this. He'd been careful about publicity regarding the robbery. And most important, he'd managed to steer clear of that bloodhound agent. Lars thought it best to start a rumor and send the man in a different direction. He had his conductor spread the word that clearly indicated the leader of the train robbers had killed Patrick Ryan over Ryan's young bride. Lars hoped the agent would go sniffing elsewhere. And after the word got around to Sugar Drucell and Betty Lou, the town gossips who spread it far and wide, that agent took off in a different direction, and at last Lars smiled.

The good citizens of Bodie, California, all turned out for Patrick Ryan's funeral. He had been well liked and respected. They traveled the thirty miles to the Ryan ranch to pay their respects and to offer their condolences to the people who worked for him, and who had learned to care for the good-hearted Irishman. He had been one of them, and they had liked and respected him.

Early on that gray, blustery morning the wagons and carriages began to assemble in the grit-whipped front yard of the Ryan homestead. It was an extremely warm day in late spring, and hinted of rain. People brought offerings of food and jugs of spirits, and the womenfolk laid out a bountiful table beneath a shade tree, where it would stay cool until after the services. They all could be heard discussing the tragic circumstances that had led to their friend's untimely death.

Maria Lopez, Patrick's faithful housekeeper, bustled about seeing to everyone's needs just as she had done for so long here at Los Paraiso. She was a plump, matronly woman with gray-streaked hair that she kept in a tight knot on top her head, and rosy-red cheeks. Her smile was usually quick and bright, and she loved to talk on any subject. But today she wore somber black and fought back hot, bitter tears. Her dear friend, Patrick Ryan, now lay in a pine coffin in the front parlor, and Maria's heart felt heavy in her breast. Patrick had been good to her after her Pepito had died, leaving her penniless and alone. She'd come to work here and had never once thought about leaving. But now . . . ? And her dark eyes fell upon the boyishly handsome Lars Evanson, who had arrived early this morning with *that woman* and had begun issuing orders as if he had the right, and she felt fear clutch her in its wake. Would this man tell her that she had to leave? She didn't think he had the authority to do so, but then, no one so far had protested Evanson's involvement. Who would dare, considering the rumors abounding of his wealth and power? She clutched at the folds of her crisp white apron and prayed silently for strength.

There were two citizens of Bodie who were visibly surprised to arrive at Los Paraiso and find Lars Evanson apparently in charge of the funeral proceedings. The pretty matron turned to her banker husband and raised a dubious eyebrow.

"Did you have any idea that Lars Evanson would be here today?"

"Never heard a word about it," her husband replied as he halted the team of matched bays beside the other conveyances. "I am as astounded as you, my dear. Although I've heard rumors that Evanson and Ryan were playing cards together right before Ryan was killed. Maybe Evanson feels some responsibility since Patrick met his death on the PGC."

The raven-haired woman sat quietly for a moment, then said, "I suppose that may be true; however, with the elusive Mr. Evanson, I am beginning to suspect it's more than that. Perhaps he will at last consent to an interview."

The distinguished-looking banker smiled at his wife's determined expression. "You've been after an interview for months, Elizabeth, and he deftly avoids you. I strongly suspect he'll continue to do so. He doesn't talk freely about his interests."

"As if anyone had even the slightest notion what his interests are," Elizabeth scoffed. "But I know how to handle his kind." One perfectly shaped eyebrow raised once again. "He may just change his mind when he discovers that I was able to talk with his porter—and learned a few interesting things about that fateful night."

The banker frowned. "Don't make Evanson your enemy, Liz. He's fast becoming a powerful man."

"I'm not frightened by his sort — and you should know that."

"Yes, I do. And that is precisely why the warning. I know there are many of us who are interested in hearing more about the train robbery; however, Evanson has given all of his people fair warning to keep their mouths shut."

"But there are ways of getting information without being obvious about it."

He gazed at her measuringly. "You have a special interest in this story?"

"I would like to see Evanson's version of the robbery in print. The people who travel on board his train should be made aware of the facts. And I'm going to do everything in my power to get them."

"I don't like to think about you under Evanson's close scrutiny."

"You may be my husband, and I respect your opinion; however, you of all people should know why I have to discover the absolute truth."

Vincent's green eyes met his wife's piercing blue gaze. "I always did say Jesse took after you. Proudly defiant, a rebel who did things his own way no matter the consequences."

Elizabeth's eyes grew misty at mention of her eldest son, who had been brutally murdered. "I almost found myself comparing the description of the train robbers to — "

"Do you know what you're insinuating?" Vincent cut in, astounded.

She nodded slowly, painfully. "The description of the leader: tall, with black hair and deep blue eyes — and then, the Indian that was with him . . ." She bit her lip. "Can you blame me for wondering?"

Vincent stared back at her. "Jesse is dead, Liz. And that is why we left the Valley, to begin again and forget the painful memories."

"Perhaps he wants us to think he is," Elizabeth Kardel said brokenly, sorrow etched deeply into her face. "A mother could learn to accept anything . . . but not the death of her child . . . and then . . . never certain if the body that was buried was truly him because it was burned beyond recognition. It is too awful to bear at times."

Vincent didn't wish to recall that horrible morning when they'd been informed of their son's murder, and he had been told that most of the bodies had been horribly burned, or badly mauled by wild animals. No one could positively identify any of the remains as Jesse's, but their son had not returned to his ranch, and had never been heard from again. Everyone had assumed he'd been killed, except his mother, who always hoped.

"You're also thinking that the Indian involved in the train robbery was Dakotah, our daughter's husband," Vincent stated incredulously, then shook himself free of a wild surge of hope. "No, it's preposterous. Do you think Doris wouldn't rush to tell us if she knew that her brother was alive?" He ran his fingers through his crisp hair. "My God . . . ," he sighed, "how could such a thing be possible, and us not know? And Bo? Would he be a party to something so awful?"

Elizabeth closed her eyes and said quietly, "I believe that's entirely possible. If I know anything about my children, they'll stick together hard and fast if they believe they must. And we know that Bo idolized his older brother. And our children would do what they had to to keep us from becoming involved."

Vincent suddenly had a strange look in his eyes. "It . . . could be true. Jesse certainly had good reason to go after Evanson."

"And to allow everyone to still believe that he is dead."

"I don't know how he could have survived that massacre, but I pray to God that you're right."

"We must send word to Doris," Elizabeth said in a rush.

Vincent took a deep breath. "We have to go slowly, Liz. If what you say is true, then our son wants us to think he is dead for a good reason. He would never have subjected us to such pain if he didn't think that he had to."

Elizabeth squeezed her husband's arm. "We'll quietly move heaven and earth until we get the answers we want—the answers we need."

"Yes!" Vincent replied firmly. "That's exactly what we'll do."

They sat there for a moment longer to compose themselves, as they looked at the gracious log house that Patrick Ryan had built with honest money and hard work. Elizabeth glanced up first to observe a solemn-faced Lars Evanson step off the veranda to greet them.

"Mr. and Mrs. Kardel, how kind of you to make the long drive." He shook hands with Vincent, his eyes assessing the slim, attractive woman at his side. He was well aware that Elizabeth Kardel was a reporter for the *Bodie Free Press*, and had earned a notable reputation among the mining town's fifteen thousand citizens. She was an ardent pursuer of facts, and could uncover revelations that the ordinary investigation failed to turn up. He afforded her his most charming smile. "I am honored to have at last made your acquaintance, Mrs. Kardel. From everything

172

that I've heard, you should be commended for your work on behalf of frontier justice, and your efforts to improve Bodie's tumultuous image."

Elizabeth extended a gloved hand to Lars, her blue eyes sweeping over him. "I try my best," she replied with honest candor. "And Mr. Ryan was a good friend, sir. Vincent and I wanted to be here today to pay our last respects."

Lars noted that her hand did not merely rest in his palm. Her slender fingers closed firmly around his.

"I would like to interview you, Mr. Evanson," she continued with her usual straightforwardness.

"Me, dear lady?" Lars appeared surprised.

"Yes," Elizabeth nodded crisply.

"An interview?" Lars pondered aloud. "What about?"

"The train robbery was the most daring of its kind, you know. My readers deserve to know the facts surrounding that night. Everyone seems unwilling to discuss any of the events. And particularly Mrs. Ryan's kidnapping."

Lars led the way into the house, commenting as they went, "I'm certain they fear retaliation from the train robbers. And no one wants to say anything that might jeopardize poor Mrs. Ryan's life."

"But that's precisely the reason I feel we should get to the heart of things," Elizabeth urged.

"I have to agree with Elizabeth," Vincent said, squeezing her elbow reassuringly.

"Perhaps . . . ," Lars said as they entered the quiet parlor and he observed Krystal King approaching them. "But we all must be very careful what we say, and print, ma'am. After all, a young woman's life hangs in the balance, and these outlaws are cold-blooded killers who would think nothing of murdering her in the same heartless fashion that they killed

Patrick." He shuddered. "News spreads like wildfire in these parts. If you run a story on these men . . . well, God only knows what they might do to her."

Krystal came to him and touched his hand briefly before greeting Vincent and Elizabeth. "I am pleased to meet you both. You are woman after my own heart, Mrs. Kardel," she said, her sensuous lips parting in a smile to reveal even white teeth. "I've read many of your articles since coming to Bodie. And I must say you don't waste time mincing words when you have an opinion about something, or someone, do you?"

Vincent could feel his wife go still next to him. Krystal King was a very beautiful woman. She was tall, with a shapely slenderness that lent curves to all of the right places. Her hair was a lustrous raven black; caught now in the diffused light streaming in the bay window, it fairly glowed with golden highlights. Her almond-shaped violet eyes met his intrigued gaze, and Vincent had the impression that he had just been intimately caressed without having been physically touched. He quickly glanced over at his wife, who was trying her best to conceal her emotions, but Vincent knew her too well, and that she did not find Krystal King to her liking.

Vincent was also an extremely good judge of character. In his line of work he had to be, for it wouldn't do well for him to lend money to someone who had no intention of repaying him. Over the years he'd trained himself to note all details of manner and expression. He concluded that Krystal and Lars were two people whom a person could not afford to misjudge. They were consummate actors, with chameleonlike personalities they easily changed to suit a given situation. What situation do we have at the moment? he wondered, then hastened to move the scenario along.

"Miss King, correct?" he inquired politely, and Krystal nodded. "If you have been able to judge anything from my wife's careful reports, you must realize that she adamantly seeks the truth in all cases. There are so many written works of cheap fiction on the gunmen of the West, and particularly of crimes here in Bodie, that Elizabeth sees it as her journalistic duty to write the absolute facts, not some mythical version that the dime novels take delight in printing."

"That is why I wish to get on this story just as soon as possible, Mr. Evanson," Elizabeth added. "Train robberies, and kidnappings, are newsworthy items in themselves. The fact that both took place on your train is something I would have imagined you would want to comment on. And as yet, you've only given a brief statement to the press and, from what I've heard, refused additional comments."

Lars felt the journalist's eyes watching him closely. He cleared his throat. "I have only sought to protect the late Mr. Ryan's memory by doing so. This whole thing could turn rather sordid, you know. And if Mrs. Ryan is still alive, I would think it our duty to protect her. The gossips are already whispering about her, and what she undoubtedly is going through at the hands of those villains. Imagine what she will have to face when she returns as it is."

"I sympathize with Mrs. Ryan's plight," Elizabeth interjected. "And that is precisely why I think I owe it to her, as a woman and a journalist, to make public what happened before the tale carriers spread their own version far and wide. The glory seekers will write any tidbit they're able to pick up. Many stories have already begun to circulate."

"It already appears that Mrs. Ryan's reputation isn't being considered in the least," Vincent stated grimly.

Krystal King stood back in thoughtful silence, then spoke up quietly. "I think they should be made aware of one other thing, Lars." Their gazes met. "Go on . . . tell them," she urged.

Lars sighed deeply. "I seriously doubt if Mrs. Ryan knows the details of her husband's murder, or even that he was killed." He shook his head. "She was traveling here as Patrick's new bride and, when she returns, will be his widow. I have been trying to keep the papers from printing all of the lurid details, for you can imagine how awful it would be if she read them before someone was able to explain what happened."

"It is tragic," Elizabeth agreed, "however, I doubt whether Mrs. Ryan would want us to sit on this story simply to protect her from the horrid details. If I were in her position, I'd want as much publicity as possible. It could do a lot to ensure her safe return."

"Well, I know I wouldn't," Krystal drawled throatily.

"I believe in good old male logic," Lars offered, "and mine tells me that if you print this story right now, you'll be doing Mrs. Ryan more harm than good. So as far as I'm concerned, there is no comment until we have news of her. And I can only pray that it comes soon, and is positive."

Elizabeth knew when she was being manipulated, but at the moment felt there was very little that she could do. After all, this was a memorial service for their friend Patrick. The matter of his death, and his wife's kidnapping, would have to be dealt with in an unassuming manner until she had something firm to go on.

"Very well, have it your way . . . for now," she told Lars Evanson.

Elizabeth said very little after that, just listened with half interest to her husband and Lars make small talk. She felt certain that there was something calculating about Lars Evanson and his mistress. And she vowed silently to immediately seek answers to a good many things. And what of her son Jesse? She had managed to talk to one man who'd been a passenger on board the PGC when it had been robbed. He had told her that there was an Indian who'd been sitting next to him who had later held them at gunpoint while his train robber friends robbed them. And he spoke of the dark-haired, blue-eyed leader who'd taken the Ryan woman with him. Could the leader be her son? Her heart quickened at the possibility.

At last the minister motioned for everyone to take their seats.

Lars found his mind preoccupied with the Kardels. They were a most persistent pair, and greatly respected here in their hometown. He knew if he allowed it, they could stir up sympathy for the Ryan woman's plight, and bring pressure on the sheriff of Bodie to search diligently for her. Lars wished she'd stay lost forever, or better yet, envisioned how easy his task would be if she was dead. Patrick's lawyer held a will naming Nicki Sue Ryan as sole heir of his entire estate. It hadn't taken much of a bribe to pry the information from him. He could not let anyone interfere with his plans now. He'd worked too long for this. His mind drifted back to how it had all begun.

He had come from Norway to America during its earliest boom days, a poor young man in search of a better life. Penniless and alone, the prosperous California mining towns beckoned him. Lars took a job under an assumed name riding shotgun messenger on a bullion wagon over the Sonora Pass road from the Bodie diggings to the San Francisco mint.

Bodie was being touted as "Greater than the Comstock," and with the hysteria of gold fever running rampant, a cunning and astute man like Lars stood the chance of extracting a stake to invest in his own fortune without even having to turn a pick. He waited, and formed a plan.

He knew that holdups over the Sonora road were of such frequent occurrence that it was expected with each run. It just so happened that Lars had become acquainted with a couple of lawless desperadoes in Suzie Wong's Oriental Saloon who were also looking to turn a fast dollar and then be on their way.

At that first meeting it was decided that the two hombres, Smith and Hood, would lay in wait for the bullion wagon the next time it made a run with Lars riding guard. The plan was laid down, and went without a hitch.

Smith and Hood pulled off a surprise attack, held up the wagon for seven thousand dollars in minted double eagles, and spirited the shotgun messenger (Lars) away with them as their hostage. The threesome laid low in a mountain cabin for several months, then went their separate ways, each weighted down with gold coin. Lars returned to Bodie and invested his stolen funds in several leases, and soon they accumulated more than he had paid for them. He reinvested his profit in a gambling house in San Francisco.

Not surprisingly, within a year he was bored and felt stifled by the confines of the city. It was then he began to dream of bigger things, of building his own narrow-gauge railroad to carry the bullion from the diggings in the Mono Lake region to Austin, Nevada, and a connection with the Central Pacific. He was certain it would succeed. And over the years he began realizing that dream. He began building his short line;

and nothing, and no one, stood in his way.

Lars was satisfied that he could handle the Widow Ryan, but after having encountered the pertinacious Mrs. Kardel, he knew that she was of a special concern. Yet there wasn't a female born whom he had not been able to handle. And he was confident now that Elizabeth Kardel would prove no exception.

Chapter Nine

It was a quiet evening. A gentle rain was pattering against the windowpanes, and a cooling breeze drifted through the open front door. Supper was over, the dishes washed and put back in the cupboard, and Nicki Sue sat in a cane rocker before the hearth helping Meg with the mending. She'd eagerly offered her assistance, but had forgotten that without her spectacles, she wouldn't be able to see clearly. Ordinarily she was a good seamstress; however, tonight she was finding she had to concentrate very hard to make her stitches tiny and neat.

"Darn! I can't seem to sew a straight seam!" She examined the droplet of blood on her finger.

Meg, who was sitting in a chair beside her, paused in her mending and looked up. "Are you all right?"

Nicki nodded. "Yes, just exasperated."

Jesse glanced silently over at Nicki from the table where he sat with Meg's children, and one of his dark brows quirked upward. He was whittling a toy horse for Kerry Beth out of a piece of wood, and both children were watching him intently. Kerry Beth was enraptured by his every move, and Tad was doing his best to whittle a horse similar to Jesse's version from his own piece of wood. Everyone in this household viewed him with such affection, and Nicki had to

Nicki could still feel Jesse watching her, and she had to concentrate on her sewing or risk having her blood race like quicksilver through her veins if she met his gaze. She immediately felt her insecurities surfacing. No! she told herself — it makes no difference what he thinks.

Jesse resumed whittling, but he could not stop the images that flitted through his mind. He found himself envisioning what Nicki looked like in spectacles, and he could easily imagine delicate wire rims on that cute turned-up nose. Inwardly, he smiled. Nicki was not like any other woman he'd ever known. She was naive, yet seductive, and completely innocent of her allure. Even with his eyes closed, he could recount her features inside his head with ease.

Tawny-gold eyes like topaz fire, lustrous hair, like strands of silk, sleek and firm body with legs that took his breath away. Innocent temptress, luring him without ever being aware, always so distant and mysterious. Christ — she was becoming like a drug on his senses. He shook himself free of the haunting visions, for he wanted no part of what she represented. He'd tried respectability once, and it had led to tragedy and grief.

Putting the last touches on the miniature wooden horse, Jesse handed it to a delighted Kerry Beth, and then went to bed down the animals for the night.

Meg put the children to bed and returned to the main room. She observed Nicki closely, noticed the way her eyes kept darting to the door every few minutes. She could see by the hopelessly lost expression in her eyes every time she looked at Jesse that there was more between them than she would have liked. Being a kind person, Meg could not begrudge Nicki her infatuation with the enigmatic Jesse. Women always did find Jesse irresistible, and Meg knew that she was no exception. But she was wise enough to know there could be no future with Jesse until he'd exorcised all of his personal demons.

Hoping she wasn't prying into Nicki's private life too deeply, Meg decided she just had to warn Nicki to spare her unnecessary pain. She liked the young woman very much, and they did have widowhood in common. Meg knew only too well that Nicki Sue's loneliness had just begun. She didn't realize yet what she had to face when she arrived at her husband's ranch and was confronted with the reality of Patrick Ryan's death.

"Nicki," she began softly, returning to the rocker before the fireplace, "I don't want you to think I've been judging you in any way, but I feel I'd best explain a few things about Jesse." Her voice was kind. "He isn't a man a woman should fall in love with."

Nicki missed a stitch, and her hands began to shake. "I . . . don't think this is something I wish to discuss," she said tremulously.

"We have to, honey," Meg persisted gently. Nicki's needle paused.

"It's plain as the nose on your face what you and Jesse have shared," the older woman said kindly.

"I . . . really don't think you can truly know what it's like for Jesse and me," Nicki said, her glance lifting briefly.

"I'm a woman, Nicki — I know when two people are attracted to one another."

"It isn't like that at all," Nicki stated, her tone hardening. "There has been no sharing between Jesse and me. And we hate each other. He doesn't know the meaning of sharing." Her eyes gleamed. "Sometimes I think I hate him enough to . . ." She sighed. "And then he comes near me and . . ."

Meg smiled in understanding. "That doesn't sound

at all like hate to me."

Nicki's eyes widened, and she looked shaken. "I despise what he's done, what he is—and I can't wait to get as far away from him as possible."

Meg wished she could believe what Nicki said, but she knew the young woman was trying hard to deny any emotional ties to Jesse because she could not accept him as he was. "Don't judge him too harshly, Nicki," she said, her eyes kind. "Or yourself."

"I know so little about him." Nicki suddenly turned hopeful eyes toward Meg. "I wish I could understand him. . . . Won't you finish what you started the other day?"

Meg looked sympathetic, but wary. "I don't know, dcar. Jesse would be furious if he knew I'd told you as much as I have already."

"Please . . . I know you can tell me why he does what he does . . . why he's an outlaw."

"Not an outlaw—not in the way you mean," Meg stated quickly. "He was driven to it."

Nicki looked skeptical. "Jesse doesn't appear the type of man who could be driven to do anything he didn't choose on his own."

"Oh yes, he can . . . and was," Meg said softly. "It was because of Allison—and the way she was murdered."

"Who . . . was Allison?" Nicki felt her heartbeat quicken.

"A young woman he cared for."

"He loved her . . . you mean."

Meg nodded. "Yes. He loved her very much. They were engaged to be married."

Nicki appeared visibly shaken, and Meg laid a comforting hand on her arm. "She was killed by some horrible men who were at war with the Simmonses. They rode in on horseback, stampeding through Jesse and Allison's engagement party, shooting anyone who got in their way. The entire Simmons family was killed, as well as a good many of the guests who had stayed late. Jesse was the only one who survived, and if not for his brother and Dakotah finding him the next day, he would have succumbed to his wounds. I remember my husband saying how it had been a blessing that Jesse's family had not been able to attend at the last minute because his little sister came down with pox and they had had to stay home. . . ." She hesitated, appearing doubtful once again.

"Go on, Meg—don't stop now," Nicki urged.

Meg nodded, hoping she was doing the right thing, but sensing that Nicki cared for Jesse more than she was willing to admit, she continued. "It isn't a pretty story, but it happened, and it's that incident that changed his life. Jesse believes the men may be the same ones who killed my husband over our land. You see, several families in the Valley had an ongoing war with a man who was seeking to take over their lands for his railroad. All of the killings took place within several years of each other."

"Railroad?" Nicki pondered aloud.

It seemed that once Meg got to talking, she was eager to continue, and Nicki found herself an enraptured listener.

"Yes. Jesse suspects it may be Lars Evanson. There are rumors that some of the men who work for him are actually hired guns."

"And you think Jesse's reasons justify more killings?"

"No, I don't," Meg replied grimly. "But try telling that to Jesse. He hasn't been the same man since this all began. I only hope he doesn't get killed in the process."

Nicki could not help but shudder at Meg's words.

Absolute silence prevailed as the two women each reflected on their own thoughts.

Nicki went to bed soon after, leaving Meg waiting alone for Jesse.

Nicki found herself thinking what a nice wife Meg would be for Jesse. Perhaps she could help him work through the awful rage he was keeping inside him. Meg seemed to understand him better than anyone, certainly better than she did. She imagined Jesse, Meg, and the children living here together, spending their nights like this before the hearth . . . and then, much to her dismay, Jesse and Meg in this bed in each other's arms. With a cry of denial, Nicki lay there until almost dawn before she finally quieted enough to fall asleep.

When Meg woke her the next morning, Nicki knew instantly that something was amiss. There was no cheerfulness about Meg when she entered the main room and took her place at the table. Kerry Beth was fighting back tears as she held on to her wooden horse, and Tad was unusually quiet as he ate his breakfast.

Meg handed her a cup of coffee, meeting her eyes. "Jesse left late last night. He told me to give him enough time, then see that you got into town and on your way."

Nicki felt her stomach muscles quiver, and she had to force her hand not to tremble as she reached for the cup. "I see," is all that she could manage to mumble.

"Since it's Saturday and there is no school, I'll take you in myself." Meg was fighting hard for control. Jesse's abrupt departure hurt her terribly. She longed for him to stay, but knew that was impossible.

"No," Nicki said. "You mustn't be seen with me, Meg!"

Meg assessed her closely. "I wouldn't have thought

you'd care as long as you were getting your freedom."

"That isn't fair," Nicki told her softly.

Meg sighed. "No, it isn't. Please forgive me, I'm just cranky this morning."

"I care very much about you and the children. I don't want to cause you any trouble, for you've been very kind to me." Nicki Sue drew a shaky breath. "But I won't forget how my husband died. And there will be trouble for the person responsible for his death."

"It wasn't Jesse," Meg stated levelly before returning to the hearth to tend the scrambled eggs she was cooking for Nicki. She worked as efficiently as ever, frying thick slices of bacon as she talked. "Believe me, he wouldn't kill your Patrick for no reason."

"That's not to say he didn't have a reason," Nicki was quick to respond.

"No! I won't believe it," Meg stated with finality.

"I just don't know what to believe," Nicki said as Meg placed the hot food before her. And recalling what she and Jesse had shared, she could only hope that Meg was right. For she didn't know how she could live with herself if she found out differently. But the things Meg had told her about his past still plagued her. Could Jesse have killed Patrick by mistake, thinking somehow that he was one of the men involved with Evanson who was responsible for Allison's death? She didn't even like to imagine it might be true, but knew it was a distinct possibility.

By the time Jesse reached Hawk Point, he was feeling a whole lot better. His mind was clear, his thinking back on target. The men were all gathered at the tiny cantina in the outlaw village, watching with keen interest the newest saloon girl, who had arrived yesterday with two drifters who'd known the way.

188

Deidre McCain had been on the run before she had arrived—but not from the law. She'd seen a means to escape a drunken, abusive husband who had kept her under lock and key in Abilene, Kansas, and she'd wasted no time in taking it. Her husband had been drunker than usual and had forgotten to lock her door before he'd gone off for the day. She'd fled with only the clothes on her back and had taken up with the friendly drifters, who'd been only too happy to take her along with them. She'd had no money, no prospects, and needed a place where she could hide from her husband should he decide to search for her. The threesome made a jovial trio, each with their own secrets and nightmares they wished to escape.

When Jesse walked through the swinging doors, the sultry beauty paused in her frenzied dance in the center of the tabletop and smiled invitingly at him. Then with a swirl of red skirts and a flash of slim brown legs, she leapt through the air to pounce in a graceful landing at his feet. Her white teeth flashed in a welcoming smile as she threw her head back and tossed long red hair back from wide green eyes.

"Would you like to buy me a drink, handsome?" she asked in a throaty voice.

Jesse grinned slowly. "I'd say after that sort of welcome, I just can't refuse." He took hold of her elbow and guided her toward the crowded bar. Every eye in the place followed them.

Robert Bodine leaned over to snicker in Dakotah's ear. "I knew that Irish wildcat would take to Jesse first thing. Sometimes I wonder what my brother has that I don't." He truly looked puzzled thinking on that, and Dakotah burst out laughing.

"Women always want what they think they can't have. And Jesse doesn't really give a damn about them—so they want him."

189

"That doesn't make a lick of sense," Robert Bodine said disgustedly.

"What woman ever does?" Dakotah hooted, downing his shot of whiskey.

"Surely none of the ones after my brother. He hasn't truly cared about anyone since Allison."

"No, he hasn't," Dakotah agreed, his expression becoming somber. "Sometimes, Bo, I wish he could find him some gal to turn him around . . . before it's too late."

"Aw, shoot, don't go spouting off that Mojave intuition stuff of yours again," Robert Bodine said.

"It isn't only my dreams." Dakotah quickly sought to defend himself. "Your own sister is saying the very same thing."

"Probably 'cause she's married to you and has to listen to you so much, she just finds it easier to agree than argue," Robert Bodine snickered.

Dakotah shrugged. "Maybe, but somehow I don't think so. I believe it's about time I talk to Jess about leaving these parts for a while and going to the Mojave encampment. He's got something eating at him, and I don't like the chances he's been taking."

"You can try—but I don't think you'll be able to do it."

"I hope I can," Dakotah said. "Maybe Doris can talk to him, make him see he's walking on too narrow an edge of late."

"The only thing that is going to change Jess is destroying Evanson and everything that he stands for," Robert Bodine stated assuredly.

The redhead's throaty laughter reached them. They watched as Jesse caught her to his side and ordered up a bottle from the bartender. With the bottle in one hand and the redhead firmly in tow, Jesse climbed the worn stairway that led upstairs to the private rooms.

Robert Bodine turned to Dakotah with a snort. "It doesn't look like he plans on being lonely tonight."

"More'n I can say for some of us," Dakotah drawled.

Robert Bodine poured them two more drinks. "Wrong, son — more'n I can say for you." He gulped his whiskey and pushed back his chair with a meaningful grin. "This here boy intends to find him some other companionship right quick. Not that you're not a good sort and all, partner," he hurriedly added at Dakotah's scowl, "just not what I had in mind for this night."

"Go on! Leave me here to drink this bottle by myself," Dakotah yelled after him, but his eyes were crinkled watching Robert Bodine approach a saloon girl who was smiling encouragingly at him.

"What's your name anyway?" Jesse said, unbuckling his gun belt and untying the holster at his thigh.

The lithe, perfectly formed female lying on top of the rumpled sheets stretched lazily and moistened her lips with the tip of her tongue. "Deidre McCain."

"Well, Miss McCain, you are exactly the sort of welcome I needed tonight. You're new around here, aren't you?" He watched her green eyes glitter when he stripped off his shirt. Yes, he thought, you're exactly what I need to forget that golden temptress, and come morning, I won't even be able to recall what there was about her that had me so enthralled.

"I've been here a week . . . mmmmm. . . . Let's quit talking, honey."

Deidre welcomed him with hands and lips eager to please. She rolled on top of him and nipped along his chest to his belly. Jesse lay back and closed his eyes, allowing his thoughts to center on the pleasure she gave him. She was a skilled lover, and there wasn't anything she didn't know about arousing a man. Her hands were all over him, and her lips, wet and hungry.

When the sharp knock came at the door, Deidre swore just as skillfully. Jesse could not help but grin. One thing about a woman like Deidre: a man knew exactly how she thought and reacted. He wondered if maybe he wouldn't have been bored after all.

"What is it?" he called out.

"Something you oughta know, Jess," he heard Smiley say.

There was a pause, then Jesse swung his legs over the side of the bed. "I'll be right out," he said, and Deidre flopped on her backside with a hurt pout.

"Where're you going, handsome?" she inquired with mournful eyes. "I thought you and me was gonna have us some fun."

"Maybe later, baby," Jesse flung back over his shoulder as he buttoned up his shirt and grabbed up his gun. She was gone from his mind just as soon as he closed the door.

Smiley looked sheepish. "Sorry . . . uh . . . about disturbing you and all, but this is something you'd better know."

"It's okay; you weren't disturbing anything special." Jesse caught the worried expression in his eyes. "Something's on your mind, Smiley—why don't you just tell me about it?"

Smiley nodded. "Let's go to Lil's office, where we can talk in private."

When they were seated in the proprietor's office, Smiley said, "I heard news that a Pinkerton man turned up in Bodie."

"Damn," Jesse swore softly. "I was hoping for a bit more time."

"I knew you wouldn't like it none. I hear tell he's

taken up residence at Sugar's." Smiley snorted. "She's even taking to feeding him chicken and dumplings."

Jesse's eyes narrowed. "What's his name?"

Smiley shook his head. "You're not going to like it one bit."

"Just tell me," Jesse gritted.

"Charlie Star."

"Should have known a train robbery would attract the best."

"What do you intend to do about it?"

Jesse's grin was self-assured once again. "Guess I'm going to have to make certain we don't make any mistakes."

Smiley rubbed his grizzled jaw. "Sounds to me like you intend to keep right on robbing Evanson's train."

"I do."

Smiley grinned then too. "Seems there isn't anyone who can stop you from getting whatever it is you're after."

"It's a lot like counting coup," Jesse said.

"What's that?" Smiley snorted.

Jesse smiled indulgently. "Dakotah's people have a true test of bravery in battle that is said to reveal the real strength of a man's courage. In the heat of the conflict he will throw away his weapons and shield and charge at his enemy with only his coupstick. If he is able to inflict a wound on him and still manages to escape with his own life, then he has been successful, and will be honored by all that know him. The only thing a man has to be careful about is knowing for certain who the enemy is." His gaze appeared thoughtful. "In this case, my enemy is quite clear."

"Guess there's nothing more to be said then." Smiley paused with his hand on the doorknob. "Thought you might like to know your pa and ma are doing well." He knew better than to wait for a reply;

there wasn't ever any discussion when it came to Jesse's folks. Smiley closed the door behind him, leaving Jesse to his own private thoughts.

Patrick's attorney, Walter Page, was waiting for Nicki Sue when her stage arrived in Bodie. He introduced himself and bid her welcome. Nicki had sent a telegram ahead to Patrick's ranch to inform the people there that she was safe, and on her way to her new home. She looked around at the bustling town, remembering the articles she'd read in the San Francisco papers proclaiming the Bodie diggings as being "Greater than the Comstock." The town itself did not look as big as its reputation. In fact, it was quite small in comparison to San Francisco. Around her, miners trudged by with their heavily laden pack mules, obviously on their way to the mines to begin their day's work. Townfolk strolled up and down the wooden boardwalk, pausing to chat with those they knew along the way. Nicki recalled several of her aunt's rich friends having invested vast sums of money in Bodie's mining operations, hoping they'd reap the benefits and add to their wealth.

Nicki Sue could not believe that this was the place she'd heard so much about. Fast, loose, and a town where it was hard to grow old, she'd heard time and again. As if on cue, there came the sound of gunfire from one of the beer parlors across the street.

Walter Page was immediately at her elbow.

"I suggest we go to my office and talk over Patrick's wishes, Mrs. Ryan. It isn't safe to dally when evening's coming on."

"Very well, sir," Nicki agreed, turning to follow him down the street. "But I hope it won't take awfully long; I am tired from my trip and anxious to get to the ranch."

"You'll be on your way in no time," Walter assured her as they walked along. "Patrick left everything to you. I just want to make certain you realize what that entails."

Their conversation was interrupted by someone shouting at them.

"Oh, Señora Ryan!" a Spanish-accented voice called forth, and Nicki turned around to see a short, round man of Mexican descent hurrying toward her. "I'm sorry I'm late. It's a long drive from the ranch."

Nicki smiled at his look of concern. "And you are . . .?"

He swiped his hat from his head and smiled back. "Pablo, señora; I have come to see you safely home."

"How thoughtful of you to come and meet me," she replied.

"It is what Señor Ryan would have wanted," Pablo returned, his dark eyes gleaming.

"However did you know me?" Nicki inquired, trusting the little man immediately.

"Señor Ryan sent us a newspaper clipping of your engagement announcement. It was a very nice picture of the two of you." Suddenly he beamed at her. "There could be no mistake—I knew it was you."

"Well, it's very nice to meet you, Pablo, and we'll leave just as soon as Mr. Page and I have concluded some business. I can't wait to see the ranch."

Pablo left them, telling Nicki he would wait in front of the hotel for her.

Soon after, Nicki Sue was seated in the attorney's small office overlooking the main street while he informed her of her holdings, which, as it turned out, were really very little.

"Is that all that there is?" she asked, white-faced upon realizing there was barely any money and few assets.

Mr. Page appeared contrite. "I am sorry. Patrick saw something in that place but for the life of me . . . I have no idea what it could have been." He considered her stricken expression and added, "Of course, there are the Arabian horses he raised. It is possible you might continue with that and manage to derive an income."

Nicki averted her eyes in embarrassment. "Yes . . . but I know very little about blooded horses . . . or their upkeep." She took a deep breath. "There has to be something more. . . ." She was thinking of Patrick's shining face when he'd informed her of the surprise waiting for her that would ensure their future.

"Oh! there is one more thing I almost forgot about," the attorney exclaimed. Pushing quickly away from his desk and going to a wall of deep shelves, he retrieved a good-size box and set it before Nicki. "Patrick told me that if anything should prevent him from returning, I should see his next of kin receives this. He left further instructions that the box is to be opened in private. You may take it with you — you are his next of kin, madam."

Nicki Sue stared at the wooden box in astonishment. "I'll . . . have Pablo drive by on our way out of town so that we can pick it up." She met the attorney's kind eyes. "Do . . . you think this is some sort of joke on Patrick's part?"

"No, it's something quite serious," came the reply, "for he was adamant that no one else should see the contents but the person who inherited it."

The sheriff of Bodie was waiting for Nicki Sue when she stepped from the attorney's office. He made no pretense of formalities, just began at once to ask her questions. She did not like his approach, or his gleaming eyes. He made it a point to tell her how they'd scoured the countryside in search of her and had come back every day in frustration because they had found nothing to go on.

Nicki didn't know why, but she didn't believe him. Her eyes flickered over him. He was thick-waisted and heavy-jowled, and appeared the kind of man who was just putting in the last of his time until he could retire.

"Well, I'm here now, Sheriff, so you can call off your ardent search," she told him with a trace of sarcasm in her voice.

"When you're feeling up to it, I'd like to talk with you about the men who kidnapped you," he continued, ignoring her statement.

"There isn't much I can tell you," Nicki was quick to reply, knowing she would never tell this man anything about Jesse until she was certain of a few more facts herself.

The stodgy sheriff puffed on a thick cigar. "There may be more than you think. At least you can give me a description of them fellas, can't you?"

"That's quite impossible," Nicki returned coolly.

The sheriff glowered. "You trying to be difficult about this?"

"No — I was blindfolded," Nicki stated, almost smiling at the quick lie. Jesse would have been proud of her boldness with this man.

"I see," the sheriff muttered, obviously distressed by his news. His gout was bothering him, and the last thing he wanted to do was stand here trying to outwit this uppity little bitch. He sliced a glance at the well-dressed man coming down the boardwalk toward them, and his beefy face turned even uglier. "Guess we'll just have to continue this another time — perhaps when you feel more like talking."

"Welcome back," came a man's deep voice, and Nicki glanced over to see Lars Evanson approach her.

He met her cool gaze and tipped his hat.

"I'm happy to see that you are alive and well."

Nicki had to force herself to reply evenly. "Yes— quite well, as a matter of fact."

He stood before her, his face unreadable. "I must say I'm surprised to see you here in Bodie."

"And where else would I go?" she reiterated.

"I would have thought back to San Francisco."

Nicki shook her head. "There is nothing for me there."

"You'll forgive me—but what is *here* for you?"

"My husband's ranch; I intend to live there and continue on with his plans."

Lars kept his features perfectly controlled, but he was in a rage. More obstacles! More delays! And now, more killings.

"You know what those plans are, then?" he asked nonchalantly.

"Of course—Patrick and I shared everything."

Nicki was testing Evanson. She was watching him closely, but could not decipher a thing behind those Nordic good looks.

"I'm surprised at you, Mrs. Ryan. That ranch is no place for a woman of your discriminating taste."

"My husband thought so," she reminded him with a haughty toss of her head.

"You'll forgive me—but Patrick did not always make the wisest decisions."

Nicki held her chin high. "Oh—but this time he did."

Lars appeared contrite. "My apologies, madam. You should know, of course."

Nicki whirled away from both men, calling over her

shoulder. "I really must be going, gentlemen. There are people waiting at the ranch for me, and I have a long drive ahead." She could feel their eyes on her as she approached the buggy and allowed Pablo to help her into the conveyance. She fixed her gaze on a point in the distance and said, "We must drop by Mr. Page's office to pick up a box first, Pablo. And then we'll go home — I've been waiting a long time for this day."

Pablo kept up a steady conversation on the tiring journey to the ranch.

"Señor Evanson was very kind to take care of the funeral arrangements," he surprised her by saying after she'd asked him if he knew Evanson. "He was at the house for a long time that day. He said he felt it was the only thing that he could do to make up for Señor Ryan falling to his death from his train."

"I wonder if that was the only reason he was there," Nicki murmured, and Pablo favored her with a strange look.

"He seemed very kind that day," Pablo said.

"Yes, well, looks can be very deceiving."

Nicki fell silent after that, and Pablo felt it was his duty to keep up a steady stream of conversation to ease her distress. He told her how he'd first come to the ranch and of the early trials they'd had. He thought he might have said too much when she frowned upon hearing how the ranch never did produce a crop that turned a profit.

"But why did Patrick have such high hopes for the place, then?" she thought to ask him.

"I do not know, for it is as barren as the day he bought it. But he loved it very much, and he did have great plans — I know this too. He spent many hours riding the land — almost as if he were just waiting for the right time to tell everyone of his news."

Nicki appeared crestfallen. "But I don't have any idea what he saw there, Pablo — he never told me. Whatever will I do?"

Pablo felt sorry for her and hurried to reply. "Marty and I will help you. We'll manage somehow."

For the remainder of the journey, Nicki was quiet. She had very little money, no definite plans for the future, and now she'd just learned her ranch was virtually scrubland. Staring out at the dismal land before her, she tried to bolster her flagging spirits. Well — she couldn't turn back now. All there was in San Francisco was Aunt Lorna and her ridicule, and loneliness. At least here, she stood a slim chance at making her own happiness.

Chapter Ten

Nicki's inheritance was certainly not what she had hoped it would be. It was a mystery to her what Patrick had seen in the place. Acres of dry wasteland stretched for miles around the house. And although it was a comfortable, spacious-looking home, it did not lessen her unease. She simply had not been prepared for this. Surely Patrick's glowing descriptions could not have been about here? She had not been prepared for such a shock, and suddenly it all seemed too much to bear. If not for Pablo sitting beside her, watching her with sad eyes, she knew she would have broken down right there and cried until she had no more tears. And then there was the housekeeper, Maria, hurrying from the house to greet them and clucking over Nicki Sue like a mother hen.

"Poor little one, you have been through so much." She wrapped a comforting arm around Nicki's shoulders after Pablo helped her from the buggy, and guided her steps toward the house. "Come inside and let Maria take care of you. Some warm milk and a nice supper and you'll feel better."

"Yes . . . yes . . . that would be nice," Nicki heard herself reply in a faint voice.

Pablo had called after them. "Marty and I will see you in the morning, señora—it will all look brighter then, you'll see."

She remembered nodding numbly and allowing Maria to lead her through the house to a comfortable bedroom that the woman said she'd prepared just for Nicki's arrival.

"I will bring you something to eat right away," she said. "You rest for a while; I'll not be long."

Later, after Nicki had eaten the delicious meal Maria had prepared and lay soaking in a hot tub of scented water, she allowed herself to vent some of the tumultuous emotions raging inside her. Hot, bitter tears streamed down her face as the full realization of her situation descended like a cloak of doom about her. There was at last something so final about it all. Patrick was gone from her life, and once again she had no one but herself. With an unhappy sniff, she decided she just might have to return to San Francisco after all. The ranch didn't appear to hold any great promise for the future. The house was lovely — large and airy, and filled with nice pieces of furniture — but the land! It was pitiful.

She recalled the particular morning that Patrick had taken her to Cliff House on the bay. It was shortly after they had met, and he was very attentive. She had enjoyed spending time with him very much. He was an interesting conversationalist, and she, an enraptured listener. She'd always thought of herself as rather dull and with little to offer that would be of interest to most men, so she usually allowed her escort to do most of the talking. Patrick was far from dull, and she had marveled at the colorful tales he could tell about his Irish homeland and the relatives he'd left behind there five years ago. They'd had a leisurely breakfast by the windows, laughing as they'd watched the seals frolic on the jutting rocks. He had told her in a sober moment how he had carefully planned his future, and the generations of his family that would follow. Surely he was referring to something other than this wretched land. She wondered if perhaps he'd had a suspicion there was gold here . . . or knew there was gold here! With growing excitement she remembered he had mentioned an old, abandoned mine somewhere on the property. She knew she must begin searching for answers.

In the morning, after a troubled sleep, as she stood staring out the parlor window at the monotonous countryside, she thought the same thing all over again. It was so desolate, and she was accustomed to living in a bustling city. But did she really wish to return there? At least here she was free of her aunt's censure, and able to make her own decisions. Her thoughts were interrupted by a knock on the front door. Maria called out that she would answer it and moments later, showed Pablo and another man into the parlor.

"Good morning, señora," Pablo greeted her warmly. He turned to the man beside him. "This is Marty Collins. He was the señor's horse trainer."

Marty Collins was a small, wiry-looking man with sharp eyes and an easy smile. "It's a pleasure, Mrs. Ryan," he said.

"Nice to meet you," Nicki replied.

Marty stood there after that rather hesitantly, his fingers plucking nervously at the wide-brimmed hat he held in his hand.

Nicki Sue sensed there was something on the man's mind and asked, "Is there something that you wish to discuss, Mr. Collins?"

"Yes, ma'am, there is," he answered. His eyes met hers. "I know it's awful soon after your husband's death and all . . . but . . ." He sighed. "There just ain't no other way to put it, I'm afraid. We got us a problem soon if we don't complete the Arabians' training and have them ready for sale."

Nicki appeared very confused. "I'm sorry, but my husband never mentioned any of his plans to me. Are you telling me that Patrick was intending to sell his horses upon his return?"

"He has some of the finest in the territory," Marty was quick to reply. "And he always made a nice profit off of them too. In fact, the Arabians keep this place from going under."

Nicki Sue smiled for the first time since her arrival. "I think we'll manage to do just fine," she assured them with more bravado than she felt. And in thinking about it, perhaps things weren't really as bad as they had first seemed. She had a lovely home, and now at least she had a way to provide herself with an income.

"Mind you, it ain't much," Marty hurriedly added. "So don't get your hopes up too high. But after I heard Pablo here speak of how down you were when you first saw the place, I felt I should come right over and tell you that things aren't as bleak as they seem." His gaze softened as it beheld her animated features. He couldn't get over the change in her. She was actually a very pretty woman when she smiled, not at all plain like he'd thought when he'd first walked in the room. "We can get by, Mrs. Ryan, don't give up on us too soon."

"Marty . . . do you have any idea what future plans my husband had for the ranch?" She watched him hopefully.

"No, ma'am, I don't. But I can tell you he wouldn't give this place up for anything. He believed in it, and whatever his dreams for the future, he appeared determined to see them through."

"Yes . . . he did," Nicki commented softly. "It's

204

just too bad that none of us knows what those secret dreams were so that we could continue onward with them for Patrick."

"We were hoping that he had told you," Pablo said.

Nicki shook her head. "I wish he had, but he did not."

It was then Nicki remembered the box that she'd had Pablo put in the study yesterday. There could be something important there. I'd almost forgotten, she thought, and was suddenly anxious for Pablo and Marty to leave so that she might see what the mysterious box held. She glanced up at Marty. "I want to be involved in every facet of this ranch on a day-by-day basis. I think the answer is here somewhere, and I am beginning to suspect that if I involve myself in the daily activities, perhaps even get to know every inch of the land, I just might discover what hopes Patrick had for the future of the ranch."

Marty and Pablo looked vastly relieved.

"You both thought I was going to turn around and go back to San Francisco, didn't you?"

The two men appeared rather sheepish.

"Don't feel badly about it," she told them. "Until just a few moments ago I was beginning to suspect I should do just that. I'm glad you were so frank, gentlemen. And now, if you'll excuse me . . . I think it's time I begin."

The men left, Marty promising to show Nicki Sue around the stables later that day. As soon as she closed the door behind them, she whirled around and directed her steps toward the study. Stepping over the threshold, she called out to Maria, who was busy in the kitchen.

"I don't wish to be disturbed, Maria! If anyone comes by, just tell them I'll see them later!"

With trembling fingers she unbound the rope from

around the box and pried off the lid. There at the bottom lay a scaled-down model of a train. No . . . she thought as she lifted it out of the box . . . not just a train set, but an entire town, complete with a water tower, a lake, and numerous little buildings scattered intermittently before the tiny train tracks. A hill overlooking the scene contained a castlelike mansion, and Nicki found herself staring in disbelief.

His words rang inside her head. *"You'll love my surprise when you see it. I can't wait to see your face when I tell you what it will mean to us in the near future. It shall be my wedding present to my bride."*

This was what Patrick had thought important enough to leave with his attorney for his heir? A toy! He must have had it since he'd been a youngster, and it held some sentimental value. It was heavy, and she hurriedly carried it to a place on a side table that stood before an expanse of wide windows. As she stood there, perplexed, staring down, the sun beamed through the sparking glass and she noticed the lake appear to gleam silver. Peering closer, she noticed that the imaginary lake was actually a mirror. Patrick had gone to a great deal of trouble to add realistic touches. The train cars were all painted; the engine, a bright yellow with tiny letters etched on the side. Nicki shook her head in bewilderment. This entire disclosure was perplexing. She decided she would learn nothing here, and with a shrug, she left the study to go and ask Maria if all of her trunks had been delivered. She hoped to find her spectacles in one of them. She was weary of not being able to read what lay before her eyes.

When Marty had warned her that the horses barely met the expenses, he had not been exaggerating. The half dozen Arabian horses they were training would hopefully provide them with enough of a profit to see them through the remainder of the year. Their care and feed cost a great deal, and even though Marty and Pablo demanded very little other than room and board and a few coins for their own expenses, Nicki was beginning to wonder how she could manage in the years to come without something else to fall back on. There just wasn't enough of a market in Bodie. She needed to take them someplace where there was more of a demand. A big city perhaps? But how in the world would she get them there safely? The thought haunted her much of the time. She stayed busy, and she was so exhausted by nightfall that she slept soundly, and rarely dreamed of the blue-eyed outlaw.

On one particularly hot, cloudless morning Nicki decided to go for a ride and check out other sections of her land that she had not yet seen.

She had been surprised to learn that Patrick had bought a silver Arabian mare just for her and had Marty train her. Her name was Kyra, and the first time that Nicki Sue saw her, her eyes had filled with tears. How like Patrick to have been so thoughtful. She could not stop herself from thinking how his concern for her had led to his death. If he had not been worried about easing her mind on their wedding night, he would have been with her inside the car, and alive today.

Pushing dark thoughts to the back of her mind, she'd quickly taken Kyra's reins and allowed Marty to assist her onto the mare.

Dressed in a leather riding skirt and lilac shirt with her ash-brown hair pulled back severely from her face in a chignon, Nicki rode to the south section, reined Kyra beside a scraggly pine that provided skimpy shade, and allowed her eyes to search the area. She rode the land frequently, patiently covering every square mile in hopes of seeking an answer to the mystery that haunted her day and night.

"Patrick . . . what was it you saw here that no one else has been able to find?" she posed quietly, her only answer the wind's sigh. And then that same sense of unease, of warning, and she froze, certain she was being watched. Carefully she looked around, but there was nothing but tumbling dried sagebrush caught in the breeze and endless bleak range wrinkled only by dry washes.

The man who watched Nicki Ryan from a ridge overlooking the Ryan land did so with diamond-hard eyes, in sharp contrast to his golden-bronze face carved in smoothly chiseled lines. He was dressed in impeccable clothing and wore polished leather knee boots; even the woman waiting in the carriage behind him appeared extracted from the same mold.

She was growing increasingly restless, her distress evident by the manner in which she kept tapping one dainty slipper up and down.

Krystal King was not accustomed to being ignored, not even for a minute. She knew she was beautiful and turned heads wherever she went. Her figure was perfection: tall, buxom, with a tiny waist and gently rounded hips. She had a wealth of black curls and pouting pink lips. She'd brought her pair of thoroughbred horses from San Francisco along with her expensively designed carriage because the jet-black geldings complemented her image. As if understanding their mistress's distress, the horses shook their regal heads impatiently, their silver-trimmed harness jingling, signaling their impatience as well.

Krystal pursed her full lips and swept gracefully down from the elegant conveyance to snap open a ruffled parasol. Stepping carefully over the uneven ground in her white kid slippers, Krystal King went after her man.

"Lars, I do declare I am getting jealous of that female. You spend more time thinking about that woman lately than you do me."

Lars continued to peer though his field glasses at Nicki, who had dismounted and disappeared inside an abandoned mine shaft. He wondered what she found so intriguing about it that she'd taken to coming here at least twice a week. He waved a hand impatiently behind him.

"Get back, Krystal, and quit that harping. You have nothing to worry about, I assure you." And then, knowing exactly what would soothe her, he added, "Any man who finds a woman like Nicole Ryan attractive needs to have his thinking readjusted. She doesn't hold a candle to you when it comes to looks."

Krystal dabbed at her moist brow with a lace hanky. "You're right, of course, but I still resent you coming out here so often just to watch her flit about." She glanced around her at the barren land. "This place distresses me—and this awful sun is going to ruin my complexion." Her lips tightened to a thin line when Lars didn't respond instantly. "As if you care . . . but I do. . . ."

"You've made your point," Lars cast back over his shoulder. Disgruntled, but knowing he couldn't afford to anger Krystal further, he joined her. With a solicitous smile, he added, "You know I don't enjoy coming out here, but we must follow the Ryan woman's activities. She's up to something, and I intend to discover what it is."

Krystal settled herself in the carriage once again and snapped her parasol closed. "So you keep telling me. But I am no fool, Lars. You would sell your soul to the devil to have the land you need to continue laying track for the PGC. And you'd love nothing better than to get to know Nicki Ryan better . . . a great deal better."

Lars picked up the reins and set the team in motion. "Only because she has something I want."

Krystal made a pretense out of examining her nails. "You know, darling . . . I've been hearing talk that the railroad business is getting riskier, that there are more roads coming into operation every day and the chances of succeeding are becoming slimmer with each new road."

Lars shrugged lightly. "Maybe that's true up East, and even in the Midwest. Too many imbecile politicians got their fingers in the pot. But out here — it's an entirely different story. Gold is king. And everybody is too busy searching for it to worry over the progress of the PGC."

Krystal smiled. "You are such a shark, Lars," she purred. "Perhaps that is why I find you so intriguing" — she leaned toward him, her full breasts pressing against his arm — "and keep investing in your road."

Lars placed an arm around her shoulders and pulled her near. "And since you've brought that subject up, sweet . . ."

She made a face. "More money?"

Lars kissed the lobe of her ear. "Only a small sum."

"I have this exchange memorized."

"I only ask for what I truly need — you know that," Lars attempted to soothe her. "Unless, of course . . . you prefer I ask someone else."

Krystal's face darkened. "And who would that be?"

"Oh . . . there are certain persons who might be interested in a surefire investment like the PGC."

"That won't be necessary," she relented hurriedly,

then added just for spite, "You know as much as I wish to see you succeed, darling, I think soon I am going to go broke if I continue investing in PGC when it has yet to show a profit."

Lars forced a smile on his face he did not feel. "It's totally your decision, love. I wouldn't dream of infringing on our friendship by badgering you for money." His eyes beheld hers. "But you know how important this is to me . . . how I cannot let anyone hold me back."

"Yes . . . I do," Krystal murmured softly, wondering if he meant she would be dead weight around his neck if she didn't continue to prove useful in a monetary sense. She searched his face for some sign that he was only teasing her, and would smile reassuringly at her in that way of his that turned her bones to jelly. But he did not, and Krystal felt a chill tingle along her spine. Although she knew deep down that Lars related everything, including friendships, in terms of dollars, she had had no idea until now that she was included in that list as well. It was a most sobering realization—one that made her shockingly aware who actually controlled their relationship. She sat back against the plush leather cushions to gather her wits and decide just what she was to do. One thing she knew for certain: Nicki Sue Ryan was not going to get a chance to snare Lars away.

Lars clucked to the spirited team and they surged forward on command. He was thinking, with an inner smile, how soon, Krystal would respond in much the same way.

Nicki Sue was to learn that widowhood in the wide open mining town of Bodie was viewed quite differently than in San Francisco. This far-removed society of people could waste no time on widows' weeds and grief. Life here was precarious—if not downright dangerous — and an individual lived for the moment, sometimes giving little thought to anything other than day-to-day survival. Bodie was indeed a "shooter's town," with a rightful reputation. Tumult and unpredictable violence became a matter of course each day. Nicki was glad the ranch lay thirty miles outside of town. It afforded her the peace and tranquility she needed, but was still close enough to allow her to drive in for supplies each month, visit the dressmaker's, or have lunch with her newfound friend, Cathleen Kramer, who worked as a bookkeeper for the Gilded Lily Saloon. Few people knew what she was about, for she kept her private life to herself and made certain that she didn't cross paths with Sugar Drucell and Betty Lou Walsh. Nevertheless, she heard their tales about her: how she'd taken over her late husband's ranch just as if she'd planned to do so all along. They said things that hurt Nicki, but she tried not to let it show.

She recalled with a smile the last time she'd been to town and had been in Karen Mitchell's dress shop for a fitting. Hearing a ruckus just outside the establishment, she and Karen had looked out the wide window to see little Sarah Marie Tuttle's mother racing down the boardwalk behind Betty Lou's boy, who was thirteen, swatting the luckless youth on his rear with a buggy whip.

She cornered him at last in front of the Wells Fargo office. She was in a terrible rage. Her face was crimson, her petticoats swirling about her ankles as she shouted that if the arrogant tough ever again dared to make her young daughter an indecent proposal, she would box his ears for him so soundly, they'd be ringing for weeks. It was difficult not to laugh when the malefactor dashed screaming into the countinghouse, pursued by the avenging Mrs. Tuttle. Through the open door the two women watched as the manager, when Mrs. Tuttle apparently informed him of the young man's dastardly deed, picked up a ledger and banged him soundly over the head. Mrs. Tuttle, looking satisfied he'd received proper punishment for his actions swept from the establishment with head held high, and was last seen retreating down the boardwalk, the crowd that had gathered in front of their stores applauding her tenacity.

Nicki had returned home later that day to discover she'd received a dinner invitation to the Mendlesons' party on the weekend. She had told Maria she simply could not attend, but then Cathleen had paid her an unexpected visit later that afternoon. They were sitting in the light, airy parlor sipping lemonade, and Nicki happened to mention the invitation to her friend.

"That's wonderful—you're going, of course."

"I can't possibly," Nicki returned firmly.

"The folks here don't stand on formality," Cathleen hurriedly said. "Bodie is considered rather a precarious place to live most of the time—I guess with so many rowdies about, they've learned to live each day to the fullest. No one is going to look down on you if you go."

Nicki shook her head. "Patrick hasn't even been dead a year, Cathleen."

"And you haven't been out formally in public since you came here. I want you to start getting out more. . . . It's time. The Mendlesons are very nice people; you'll enjoy yourself." She smiled encouragingly. "And I'm going."

Aware of the speculative whispers she'd had occasion to overhear, Nicki Sue stated sullenly, "Maybe they are only inviting me hoping to hear all of the lurid details of my kidnapping."

"Phooey! The Mendlesons aren't like some of the others. I'm certain they simply wish to meet you and prove to you that not all of the citizens of Bodie are like Betty Lou and Sugar."

"You've heard, then?" Nicki questioned, sounding dismayed.

"They have vipers' tongues — no one ever believes anything they say."

"Yes . . . some do." Nicki dropped her gaze.

"Those biddies have nothing better to do than gossip. They even talk behind each other's back."

"I know what they're saying, Cathleen — how they hint to everyone that I'm partly responsible for Patrick's death. They're all wondering why he wasn't in our car with me. . . ." Her eyes held a bleak expression. "Aunt Lorna sent a wire shortly after she received my telegram informing her of my safe return and decision to stay on here that said the very same thing."

"Oh, for God's sake," Cathleen said, exasperated. "You *have* been out here too long by yourself when you start worrying about what your Aunt Lorna thinks." She rose from the settee and took hold of Nicki's arm. "Come with me, dear girl. You and I are going to do what's needed to banish those doldrums. Why, if I let you go on much longer living like a recluse, you'll simply withdraw completely and become exactly what your Aunt Lorna predicted — a spinster."

Nicki had been so certain that everyone in Bodie viewed her scornfully that she'd purposely avoided socializing. But now after listening to Cathleen, perhaps it was time she put the past behind her and stepped out. She felt close enough to Cathleen to trust her judgment, and she really had grown weary of the long evenings spent all alone.

"You really want me to attend, don't you?"

"Yes, very much."

Nicki smiled. "Then come help me find something to wear."

Ten minutes later the young women were happily tearing through Nicki's clothes in search of a suitable gown. Nicki was looking for something befitting a woman who was in mourning. She quickly shook her head when Cathleen held up a fetching silk in forest green trimmed in rich black lace. There was a black Irish lace shawl and fan to accompany it.

"This is exquisite, and quite appropriate, I think," Cathleen said, tossing the dress at Nicki. "Wear it."

"But . . . don't you think perhaps something all black, or even navy, would be more appropriate?"

Cathleen remained stubborn. "No—I do not. This will do just fine. The color is sedate, yet will look fetching with your eyes and skin tone. Trust me, Nicki. . . ."

"Even if I do decide to go," Nicki ventured, "I have no one to escort me. How will it look, my going alone?"

"You won't be coming alone," Cathleen told her. "Jake and I will be with you." At Nicki's expression of surprise, she added with an encouraging smile, "You can stay with me at my place. It will be fun—you'll see."

Nicki smiled affectionately at her friend. "You just aren't going to take no for an answer, are you?"

"You're right, I'm not."

"All right, then," Nicki relented at last.

Cathleen hugged her. "Good! It's just what you need."

The day of the party dawned bright and clear, and after packing her things, Nicki drove her buggy over into town to Cathleen's little house on Overton Street.

The two women spent the day talking and preparing for the coming evening. They washed their hair, manicured each other's nails, and gabbed incessantly on every possible subject. They spent an enjoyable afternoon together, and Nicki Sue was glad that she had come.

Nicki had to agree, after she soaked in a hot scented-oil bath and dressed with care, that Cathleen had been right. Her spirits were lifted, and her heart felt lighter for the first time in a long while. She *had* been spending too much time alone, without giving thought to her appearance or mood. She surveyed her image in the mirror. She hadn't worn this gown in a long time, and even though she had lost weight over the months, it still looked becoming on her. The neckline was gracefully rounded and edged in delicate lace, and after a quick alteration, the waistline nipped in snugly to accentuate her slender form.

Cathleen had taken great pains to fashion Nicki's riotous hair in a becoming coronet of curls entwined with black velvet ribbon. An extraordinary necklace of jet-black stones graced her throat, glittering flecks of fire gold sparkling when she moved, enhancing their gleaming beauty. Her skin was no longer creamy white as it had been in San Francisco, but golden, from days spent beneath the hot sun. Yes, she thought, with confidence restored, Cathleen had been right to insist she attend the dinner. It would be good for her.

But later, as the two women, escorted by Jake Moran, a ruggedly handsome man who operated the assay office in town, were shown into the Mendelsons' lovely home at the end of town, Nicki Sue began to have doubts as to her decision. There were more people in attendance than she would have imagined. And in looking around, she saw that Lars Evanson and his companion, Krystal King, had been invited also. Of course, the Mendlesons would have had no idea how she'd managed to carefully avoid the railroad man until now.

His gaze caught hers, and Nicki stared at him coolly. He'd sent countless messages to the ranch requesting her permission to call. She had promptly sent a return message that stated it just was not possible at this time. She didn't allow her gaze to linger long on his countenance, and vowed she'd see they never had a moment alone.

Carol and Tony Mendleson were gracious hosts, and seemed genuinely pleased that Nicki had accepted their invitation. They made certain she felt welcome. She had circled the room of people at Mrs. Mendleson's side, smiling warmly as the woman introduced her to each guest.

Lars Evanson was the only one to make her feel uncomfortable when he took her hand in his, bringing her fingertips in contact with his lips. "It's nice to see you again, Mrs. Ryan. I hope you are finding life here to your liking."

"Yes, I am," Nicki replied calmly, but distantly. "And I intend to make my home here, see to building up my late husband's ranch."

A portly man standing to one side of them spoke up. "Don't know how you plan to scratch a living out of sand and rock." To which Lars added, "Never did know what Patrick was thinking of when he settled there and staked out his claim."

Nicki faced them with a cool smile. "Why, he was thinking of the future, gentlemen."

"Future!" the man chortled. "My dear woman, that place has little to offer for your future. If I were you, I'd sell it to the highest bidder and take me a nice house here in town."

"Mr. Thornburg makes good sense, Mrs. Ryan," Lars hurriedly agreed. "A place as desolate as that is no way for a woman to spend her days. You should be near other women your age, attend social functions — perhaps even meet a man who can give you the nice things a woman like you deserves — " He hesitated when a gentle voice interrupted.

"I think Mrs. Ryan is the sort of woman who likes to design her own course of life, gentlemen."

They glanced over to see Elizabeth Kardel now standing beside Nicki. Lars was the first to speak.

"A woman after your own heart, Mrs. Kardel?"

Elizabeth met his gaze without wavering. "Yes, I think that she is."

She smiled at Nicki. "If these gentlemen will excuse you, I'd like for you to meet my husband."

Lars inclined his head. "By all means . . . it was a pleasure, ladies."

Nicki was never more relieved in her life than to follow Elizabeth Kardel to a quiet corner, where Vincent Kardel stood with a drink in his hand.

"I see my wife effectively spirited you away from the charming Mr. Evanson," Vincent proclaimed with a knowing grin. "When we first glimpsed you talking with him, we thought it best to send Liz to the rescue."

"He is just a tad overbearing at times," Nicki found herself commenting.

"All of the time, actually," Elizabeth responded.

"You sound as if you aren't overly fond of Mr. Evanson," Nicki inquired of Elizabeth with a bemused expression.

"I believe my wife feels our Mr. Evanson would be best suited to selling snake oil," Vincent drawled with twinkling eyes.

Elizabeth didn't deny it. "I'm certain that is exactly

what that man must have done before he got into the railroad business."

"I'm afraid there isn't enough profit in snake oil, my dear, to have acquired a railroad empire," Vincent exclaimed drolly.

"Oh, but we all know where he gets his backing," Elizabeth was quick to add.

"I'm afraid I don't," Nicki admitted quietly.

"Time enough for that later," Vincent said as their host held up his hand for the guests' attention.

Dinner was announced at that moment and Vincent took Nicki Sue's arm. "My wife is a bit of a crusader, Mrs. Ryan," he murmured wryly, "and our railroad entrepreneur seems to have captured her inquisitive nature. She will tell you all about it at dinner, I'm sure."

Nicki took an immediate liking to the Kardels, and was delighted to find herself seated with them at dinner. Vincent and Elizabeth Kardel were the sort of people one felt comfortable with from the start. Vincent became engaged in conversation with a man to his left. Nicki Sue and Elizabeth talked through dinner.

"Your job sounds so exciting," Nicki told Elizabeth Kardel after listening to the lovely woman tell about her profession and the satisfaction she derived from her job as the town's only female journalist. "I'm envious," she added with a smile.

"Oh, my dear, it certainly isn't as glamorous as it sounds."

"But so exciting and challenging." Nicki's face revealed her genuine interest.

"Well . . . it can be at times, I suppose—and I do manage to get all of the news firsthand."

Nicki wondered then what Elizabeth had heard about her abduction, unaware that her thoughts were revealed in her eyes. "I suppose that's important in your line of work."

Elizabeth studied the refreshing young woman closely for a moment, and then she said, "Nicki, I like you very much. I don't want you to think that I've been cultivating you to get a story. I have not."

"I know that," Nicki replied solemnly.

Elizabeth observed her closely. "But when you feel the need to discuss it, please come to me first. I'd like to talk with you about the night the PGC was robbed—and about the man who abducted you."

Nicki tried to keep her voice from shaking, but trembled as she said, "I don't like talking about that terrible night."

Their eyes met. Elizabeth's were filled with compassion. "I understand, Nicki—and I promise not to pry where the memories are still too painful. Is that agreeable with you?"

Nicki studied her quietly for a moment. There appeared no malicious intent about the kind woman. "What is your interest in this, Mrs. Kardel?"

"You haven't heard, then."

"Heard what?"

"I'm really not surprised since Evanson is doing his best to keep it quiet because he fears bad press. There's been another train holdup about twenty miles west of here."

Nicki could not hide her shock. "Oh—that's terrible news. However, I . . . don't know what that has to do with me."

"These could be the very same men who are responsible for your husband's death."

"I am not really certain the men who kidnapped me are responsible for Patrick's death," Nicki found herself murmuring.

Elizabeth leaned closer. "That Pinkerton man

seems pretty certain. He's already on his way to the location of the latest robbery. He hopes to pick up a fresh trail."

"I see," Nicki said softly, but inwardly her thoughts were racing. There was talk all over town about Charlie Star. If anyone might catch Jesse, it was him.

Elizabeth sat quietly studying the myriad of emotions on Nicki's face. She was never more certain that Nicki Ryan was hiding something, or—by the expression on her face—could be protecting someone. But why? And even more importantly—who? Could Jesse be alive and the leader of the train robbers? It was possible this young woman could provide her with a clue that would locate him.

Elizabeth hadn't heard from her daughter, Doris, or her younger son, Robert Bodine, in months. She knew her children, remembered very well how as youngsters they'd been very loyal to one another and would take punishment upon themselves before saying anything that might incriminate the other. Yes, they'd help their older brother without question if he'd come to them and ask. They would have been so happy to learn that he was alive! Her eyes misted just thinking about the possibility. God—she knew exactly how they must have felt. And she knew her children would do everything in their power not to involve their parents. She prayed she was doing the right thing by involving this lovely woman, but she knew that she really had very little choice. Jesse was her eldest son; so many of her hopes and dreams had died when she'd been told of his brutal murder. Nicki's voice interrupted her thoughts.

"Are you all right?"

Elizabeth nodded, then cleared her throat. "I need your help. It's important that the right man is captured, for they will undoubtedly charge him with

Patrick's murder as well as the train robberies . . . and for certain, he'll hang if he's proven guilty."

Nicki shivered. "Yes . . . I know." She took a deep breath and clutched her trembling hands in her lap. "Very well; when would you like to meet, Mrs. Kardel?"

"I'll send word to you. I'll be away for a while visiting my daughter. I'm not really sure how long I will be gone, but I will contact you when I return."

"That's fine," Nicki returned softly. "I'll be waiting."

Unwillingly, Jesse's face swam before Nicki's eyes. She tried desperately not to think of him, or recall those dark days when he'd been her captor, her lover, and had come very near to destroying her. Nicki had heard there were several men in Bodie who longed to pay her court just as soon as she would allow them. But she didn't want anyone to come courting. She'd known two men in her life — one had been kind and good, but still manipulative. The other had been all dominating, had consumed her soul and had broken her heart. For now, she wanted no part of another relationship with a man. The past had taught her too much already.

Although Nicki Sue made certain all evening that she stayed on the opposite side of the room from Lars Evanson, he finally managed a word with her just as the guests were gathering their wraps to leave.

"Lovely party, wasn't it?" he inquired, standing next to her as she waited for Cathleen and Jake outside on the wide veranda.

"Yes, it was," she returned without hint of a smile.

He was watching her with a predatory gleam in his eyes. "It's good to see you're getting into the social whirl; perhaps now you'll consent to my calling on you?"

Nicki liked him less with each passing minute. "We really have nothing in common, Mr. Evanson. And you must know it is still too soon for me to receive gentlemen callers."

"If you think it is, then I must agree. But surely I can drop in on you from time to time to pay my respects."

Nicki stared at him. "That you agree is surprising."

"I am not a ogre, Mrs. Ryan. And I wish only for us to become friends. I feel bad about your husband's death." His eyes swept boldly over her face. "I hope you believe that."

"To tell you the truth, sir, I don't know what to believe. But I fully intend to discover how Patrick fell that night."

"You've only to ask and I'll be happy to tell you."

Nicki tried not to sound eager. "Then I am asking."

Lars made her wait for agonizing minutes before replying. "I saw the leader of those bandits struggling with Patrick on the platform near my private coach. Before I had time to react, the man had shoved him over the side." He shook his head. "It was awful . . . simply awful."

Nicki began to tremble and she was very near tears. She didn't know whether she could believe Lars Evanson or not, but his version of that night was the same as everyone's. She felt him watching her closely and managed a weak reply.

"I . . . thank you for telling me. I suppose there is nothing more to be said."

Lars saw his chance and stepped forward to place a comforting hand on her shoulder. "I didn't wish to ever put you through that. But you asked, and you certainly had a right to know how your husband died."

It was then Krystal King came through the door

and slipped her arm through Lars's. She favored Nicki Sue with a sugary smile. "You look distressed, my dear. Are you feeling well?"

"Yes . . . I am fine," Nicki Sue replied, although she felt far from it.

"Well, I am sorry we didn't get to say more than a few words to each other all night. It seems as though we just never were in the same place at the same time. But I see you managed a few minutes alone with Lars."

Recovering her composure, Nicki replied in a most refined drawl, "Think nothing of it, Miss King; I don't." She moved away alone to Jake's buggy, feeling a measure of satisfaction when she heard Krystal's sharp intake of breath.

Krystal turned to Lars with a catty smile. "It seems she doesn't like us, darling. Such a spiteful little bitch, isn't she?"

"Oh, shut up for once, will you, Krystal?" Lars said, his face as dark as a thundercloud.

"Well! What's gotten into you?" Krystal pouted.

"I think — you," Lars said, and hurried her down the stairs and into his waiting conveyance. Why was it Nicki Ryan could act furious and still manage to look refined, and Krystal, for all her wealth and good breeding, always managed to give the appearance of a spitting alley cat? Lars had certainly been impressed with the Ryan woman's friend too.

Yes, Cathleen Kramer was a beautiful, desirable woman, and if he wasn't mistaken, he thought she'd deliberately brushed her leg against his a few times as she sat next to him at the dinner table. Now, there was a woman to his liking. He decided he just might drop by the Butterfly Saloon tomorrow afternoon and talk with Miss Kramer.

And what of Krystal? He would have to carefully

maintain his relationship with her, for she was the one who held the purse strings.

As if she could read his thoughts, the alluring Krystal pressed closer to him, her gaze, when it caught his, burning seductively out at him from behind night-black lashes. Her lips formed into a sulky pout.

"Don't be mad, lover. I didn't mean to say those things; it's just that I can't bear it when you even speak to another woman."

Lars picked up the reins and urged the black team forward. "I am growing weary of trying to convince you that you have a secure place in my life, my dear." His eyes darkened on her face, and he saw her shiver.

She took one of his hands and brought it to her lips to kiss it softly. Looking up at him with eyes that now shone with desperate desire, she said huskily, "Words aren't needed between us, darling; you know that. There are far better ways to express ourselves. . . . Don't you agree?"

Ever the seductress, Krystal slipped his hand inside the bodice of her gown and placed it against her full breast. His fingers instinctively sought out the sensitive nipple and rolled it slowly between his thumb and forefinger.

"Ohhh . . . yes . . . now, isn't it so much better when we are communicating like this?" Her own fingers reached out to him, caressed him until she felt him pulse and harden beneath her touch, the cloth of his trousers stretching tighter as she manipulated him.

A low growl rumbled in his throat. "If you keep that up much longer, you will find yourself stretched out in this buggy like a common trollop, my lovely."

She sucked in her breath. "Yes . . . do it, Lars," she taunted hoarsely. "Take me that way, now."

Needing no further urging, Lars jerked the team to

a halt on the side of the dark road and tumbled the breathless Krystal onto her back. Their hands were all over each other, seeking, stroking, igniting fires within that burned to a fever pitch. His mouth possessed hers hungrily, and she eagerly met the hot thrust of his tongue with her own. She suckled teasingly on it, drawing it deep into her throat and squeezing gently. His hands tore at the fastenings of her gown, her silken undergarments, and bared her creamy flesh to his seeking lips. Greedily he captured a round nipple between his teeth and nibbled until she was squirming, eyes closed dreamily.

"Oh my . . . oh my . . . oh my," she gasped repeatedly, until he almost smiled.

And then all thoughts save desire left him as she stroked him faster and faster.

He was burning with the need to assuage the searing heat in his loins. She knew so many little ways to excite him and send all thoughts of anything else but possessing her out of his head. There was no cloth between them now. She grasped his near-bursting manhood with her skilled hands and moved her hips against the velvet softness, slowly allowing him closer with each gyrating thrust.

"Damn you, Krystal, you are driving me mad," he gasped, bucking his hips against the imprisonment of her fingers. "Share your honey with me, pretty lady."

Creamy white thighs slowly parted, and Lars groaned in relief. He drove into her with a fury that made her cry out in rapture. Again and again his hard manhood sought her warm sweetness, until at last he felt his release bursting from him. And at the very peak, he imagined he was holding silver-blond Cathleen, and he cried out lustily, head thrown back to meet the night.

* * *

Nicki sat within Jake's buggy and had watched the stylish vehicle until it disappeared in the bend of the road. There was something about Lars Evanson that made her uneasy, had always made her feel that way — even on that very first night when Patrick had introduced them on the train.

She made an effort to compose herself, and tried not to think about how careful she must be where Lars Evanson was concerned. She did not know what his concerns for her were. But he seemed overly interested in too many things regarding her that were none of his business. She knew she would cultivate his interest in her, but also that she would have to be very careful not to encourage him to the point where he began to get suspicious. He was clever, but then, so was she.

Chapter Eleven

"Jesse's been shot!"

The urgent cry was almost lost in the thundering hooves of the galloping horses as the Kardel gang raced across the rocky terrain. Only moments before they had halted Evanson's train and had been in the process of relieving the PGC of the gold it was carrying when a disturbing sound had alerted Jesse to possible trouble. It was the unmistakable sound of horses' hooves thundering through the wind. He whirled out of the express car, carrying a half sack of gold coins, and yelled to his men to mount up at once. It was only his keen sense and quick thinking that had saved them from catastrophe.

Without protest the men obeyed, and it was seconds later that they saw the heavily armed horsemen galloping toward them from around the back of the caboose. A barrage of gunfire was exchanged before Jesse and his men could make good an escape. Jesse had trailed his men, firing over his shoulder at the formidable group of riders in hot pursuit. Their rifles appeared to Jesse as if they were all trained singly upon him. Shots rang out. He barely felt the bullet that caught him as they charged through a narrow mountain pass, but he saw the men who'd cut away from the main body of riders to charge upward and along the rim of the steep drop above them. But there just wasn't time to worry about it now. The air was thick with dust and fear. Bullets zinged past so close that at times the men were forced to duck low over their mounts' necks.

Swinging his blue roan's head around, Robert Bodine glanced back and saw with relief that Jesse was still in the saddle. Smiley had fallen back to ride alongside of him. His face was grim as he viewed the blood streaming from the ugly gunshot wound in Jesse's arm. It looked bad, but the men knew they couldn't afford to turn and take a stand until they found decent cover. They were outnumbered, and whoever it was back there, they had come well armed: they'd been dodging bullets for over an hour. They raced across flatland that gradually sloped upward into rugged, mountainous territory where the narrow paths were flagged on both sides by enormous boulders.

"Keep riding!" Jesse ground out from between clenched teeth. One hand was hanging useless, and the other tightly gripped the reins. "The only chance we stand is to keep as far ahead of them as possible!"

"Who in the blue blazes are they?" Robert Bodine snarled over his shoulder.

"Don't know—and don't aim to find out!" Dakotah growled as he reined his horse in next to Robert Bodine. "But they'd like to see us dead—that much is certain."

"Jess looks pretty bad to me," Robert Bodine stated.

Dakotah's mouth was set in a terse line. "I know it.

But if I know him, he's so damned riled that those guys caught us on that mountain pass that he'll hang on just to spite them. I never even knew they were riding over us until they opened fire. How did they manage to surprise us like that?"

"I knew everything was going too smooth!" Robert Bodine yelled. "I bet those men were planted on board the PGC."

"It's a possibility," Dakotah replied.

"Did you get a close look at them?"

"If I had, one of *them* would be sporting lead in him instead of Jesse," Dakotah shot back with ill-disguised disgust.

They rode on in silence for several more miles, and finally Jesse looked back to see there was no sign of riders dogging them. He called out to the men to slow their mounts to an easier pace. They reined the horses to a canter, their faces a contrast of intense emotions. Their taut nerves eased and the men began to voice their concerns.

"We're wearing out the horses, Jess; we can't keep riding them this hard much longer or they're going to fall in their tracks," Smiley, the caretaker of the horses, warned.

"We may have outrun that chase party for now, but we haven't lost them," Jesse was quick to reply.

Smiley kneed his mount to catch up with the big fellow leading the pack. "Hey, Turkey! Don't you come from around these parts?"

The man had a shock of bright red hair beneath his sombrero and an Adam's apple that protruded from his long neck much like his namesake. "Sure do — born and raised just over them mountains yonder. My ma still lives in the same house." He sliced a quick smile at Smiley. "What's on your mind?"

"We can't outdistance them boys much longer. We

have to come up with a plan."

Jesse rode in beside the two men. "Already got one. We're splitting up! Turkey, you and Smiley head for your ma's—stay there until things cool down, then head for the hideaway. We'll meet you there as soon as we can."

"You need that arm doctored—come along with us," Turkey proclaimed.

Jesse shook his head. "Can't do that. We have to split up here. Dakotah, Bo, and I will lay back and draw their attention so they'll leave you alone and follow us. You and Smiley get going—and don't look back."

"You're not going to last another hour in the saddle with that wound!" Smiley protested.

"I'll last," Jesse gritted. "Now, ride!"

Knowing better than to argue further, the two men did as they were told, leaving Jesse and his companions to cover their tracks. Dakotah swung around after he completed his task, and heard Jesse yell.

"Let's move fast; they've gained on us!"

Glancing back over his shoulder, Dakotah saw that their pursuers were spread out and angling in for a sweep.

Jesse waved his arm toward a mass of large boulders that banked up to a solid wall of towering rocks. The men nodded, understanding. They vaulted from their horses and darted toward the boulders just as the first flank of riders charged directly at them. Rifle fire exploded, the bullets splintering pieces of shale from the cliffs down upon the three fugitives as they dove for cover. Surrounded by their rock fortress, they began returning the fire. They were in a good position, but Jesse knew they didn't have enough ammunition to hold out for very long. The sound of gunfire echoed through the canyon for an agonizingly long time, it seemed, but Jesse knew, in reality, it hadn't been over twenty minutes since the first shot had been fired. He had never been more tired, but at least he'd lasted long enough to help two of his men escape.

Concentrating fully on his own survival now, he no longer felt the pain in his wounded arm. He focused his attention on the riders — who it appeared were taking turns, charging from different directions. It was a siege, and the smells of gunpowder, blood and sweat were thick in the air.

Three of their pursuers had fallen wounded when at last there came a command for them to disperse. They regrouped in a distant covering of trees, and Jesse caught his first glimpse of the man he knew had to be their leader. He was none other than Charlie Star. Jesse had seen and read enough about the man to know him in an instant.

"Where have I seen that fella before?" Dakotah growled, watching from afar as the leader regrouped his men and issued further orders.

"It appears that we have the distinct privilege of joining the Pinkerton's wanted list." Jesse's answer was terse. "That's Star leading those men. I've heard he gathers an elite group of men to ride with him when he needs assistance. I suppose we should feel honored. They're rumored to come from various backgrounds: Indian scouts, a retired ranger — a hell of a bunch to find yourself up against. I'm sure it's who we're dealing with. No one else is that good."

"Can't say I appreciate the honor," Robert Bodine quipped sardonically.

"Me neither," Dakotah was quick to add.

Jesse glanced upward. The day was waning. Soon night would be closing in, and they might make good an escape. There was a reckless excitement in his eyes when he turned to his companions.

"All we have to do is hold them off until sundown and then we can get out of here. Remember, we're damned good too. I'm confident we can shake them off our tail in the dark."

"They're moving out!" Robert Bodine declared, clearly astonished. "Can you figure that?"

The threesome watched Charlie Star lead his men away.

Jesse's sudden grin was approving. "I think that's just what that Pinkerton man wants us to believe."

"What are you saying exactly?" Dakotah inquired with a puzzled look.

Jesse indicated a narrow trail leading into a rock divide. "It's my guess, unless he's mellowed some, that he's taking his men through that pass to mislead us. If I'm not mistaken, just about the time we think he's pulling out and make a run for our horses, his men will have taken a hidden trail that only Star knows about and come charging out at us from behind those rocks." He pointed to a stretch of dry wash where the rocks formed a barrier that blocked their view. Their horses were grouped near there nibbling on wild grass growing sporadically alongside the wash. "He's noticed the light is fading fast, and he knows we've got to pass through that wash to reach the open trail on the other side of that divide. He's trying to lure us there while it's still light."

"He's damn well trying to trick us!" Dakotah exclaimed, disgruntled, but sobered on realizing that Star's plan might have worked if not for Jesse.

"Oh yeah," Jesse drawled. "Charlie Star doesn't give up that easy. He's just using a different strategy."

"And just what is on *your* mind, Jess?" Robert Bodine cut in.

Jesse's wound was throbbing worse than ever. He cradled it with his right arm, while still gripping his gun tightly in his good hand. "We are going to beat him at his own game. I'm going to yell for Max. If Smiley has all the horses trained proper, they'll come at a whistle. Then we'll get mounted before Charlie leads his men all the way through that divide and out into the wash. If we can do that, we stand a good chance of getting a real head start on them. And we need it." His gaze fell on his brother and Dakotah. "What do you say we give it a try?"

Dakotah stared back at him. "Yeah! let's do it," he declared with a daredevil smile. "And then just let them boys try and catch up to us."

Robert Bodine agreed. Jesse whistled shrilly, and within minutes Max trotted over a sandy rise with the other two horses loping behind him.

Dakotah grinned broadly at Jesse and Bo. "Always did say Smiley had to have some Indian blood. No white man can understand horses the way he does."

Jesse sprinted to his feet and snatched up Max's trailing reins.

"Time enough for discussing Smiley's pedigree when we're cross-country from here. Let's get going!"

Once they cleared the divide and were racing wildly across the rough terrain, they breathed easier. It was then Jesse could feel his strength ebbing and, glancing down, saw that his shirt was soaked with blood. He was tired and every muscle in his body ached. In a few hours he knew the chills would set in. And after that, he knew he would be aware of very little. With difficulty he turned in the saddle to face his brother.

"I'm going to be slowing you down pretty soon. When that happens, you two go on ahead. I don't want any of my men facing a lynch mob because of me."

"We're going to make it together!" Robert Bodine shouted back.

"Don't argue with me, Bo!" Jesse snarled.

"Then I won't," Robert Bodine flung back at him. "I'll just wait until you pass out and do what I damn well please!"

Swearing under his breath, Jesse swung back around. Determined, he dug his toes firmly into the stirrups and gripped Max's sides with his knees. But by nightfall he was hard put to keep his head up.

It was very late. Unable to sleep, Nicki Sue had been out riding for several hours. She was riding back to the barn when she thought she caught sight of a man darting behind the stables and approaching the well. Cautiously she guided Kyra past the corral and around the barn. She placed her rifle across the pommel, gripping the stock tightly. There came a noise like someone was drawing the bucket up from the well. Without hesitation, Nicki called forth.

"Stop right there and don't make another move, and if you do, you won't be needing any of that water."

The man immediately obeyed. "You sure gave me a start." He spoke slowly and carefully, and when he noticed she had the rifle positioned for quick fire, added, "Hold on there, Mrs. Ryan. I guess I wasn't all that thirsty after all." He stepped into the path of the moon. He looked like he'd just ridden in from the depths of hell. His long duster was travel-stained, as was his hat, and his face when he tilted his head to stare up at her was flaked with dried mud.

"What are you doing here, mister?"

He cautiously moved toward her, and halted in his tracks upon hearing the click of the hammer.

"Please—I . . . need your help. I came here because it was the only place I could bring him." His eyes were pleading with her now, and Nicki grew even more uneasy.

She kept the rifle pointed at him. He was of medium height, but wide of shoulder and dangerous-looking. A dark handlebar mustache added to the sinister effect.

"Who are you — and how do you know my name?" she queried.

"First answer me this. Are you Nicki Sue Ryan?" Robert Bodine sought her absolute confirmation to that fact even though he was almost certain.

"Yes. And you're trespassing. Now you'd better tell me just who *you* are."

"My name isn't all that important to you . . . but I expect Jesse's might be." Robert Bodine heard her indrawn breath. He breathed easier. He saw her expression was immediately one of concern. Thank God, he thought, someone who will help us. They had separated from Dakotah earlier that day when it became evident, at the watering place they'd stopped at, that Jesse was not going to make it much farther. He was slumped astride his horse, barely able to hang on to the pommel. Dakotah said he would do his best to draw anyone who might be on their trail away from them. It was agreed they'd regroup once again at the hideaway. But there had been grave concern in his eyes when he'd bid Jesse good luck. Robert Bodine knew Dakotah doubted whether Jesse would make it back to the hideout alive. But damn it! He would! He wasn't going to let his brother die.

"How do you know Jesse?" she was asking him, and he didn't hesitate in replying quietly.

"He's my brother — he's been shot bad, ma'am. If you turn us away . . . he'll die."

Without another word exchanged, Nicki shoved the rifle back in the saddle scabbard. She nodded crisply and Robert Bodine vaulted on his mount's back.

"I left him in an abandoned mine not far from here. Do you know where I'm talking about?"

"Yes, I know the way."

"Bring some bandages and whiskey. We're going to need them."

They was only three feet separating them now. He was watching her with a hawklike gaze so much like Jesse's, it sent an ache through her. He had that same look deep in his blue eyes that prompted you to do as he asked without really knowing why. It was a powerful lure. She remembered it all too well.

"I sure hope Jesse was right about trusting you," he said, suddenly appearing uncertain of his decision to place their lives in her hands.

"You can trust me," she replied in an even voice.

"Then I'll meet you there. Bring anything you've got to treat a gunshot wound. And some water. We ran low this morning."

"He's real bad?" Her eyes were filled with sudden fear and her voice trembled.

Robert Bodine nodded. "Yes, ma'am. He lost more blood than a man oughta." He didn't add that he thought Jesse would have been dead by now. If it had been any other man, he was certain he would have been.

Nicki fought back rising hysteria.

"Hurry!" was all that he added before jerking his horse around and thundering in the direction of the mine.

"Can you hear me, Jesse?" Nicki bent over the still form lying on the pallet, her hands immediately reaching out to touch him. He appeared not to have heard her, but then his eyes blinked momentarily.

"He's been unconscious for several hours," Robert Bodine informed her.

"Why didn't you seek my help sooner?" she shot back at him, peering over the top of her spectacles, which were perched on her nose.

He favored her with a reproachful glare. "Right — I should have just walked up to your front door and have asked your housekeeper if the lady of the house was at home. I took a big enough gamble speaking out like I did."

"I'm sorry," she breathed. "Of course you did the only thing possible. Hold that lantern higher, please." She was quickly all business once again.

Jesse groaned when she took a knife and slit his shirt to peel it off. Robert Bodine noticed that her movements were as gentle as possible, but even her slight touch appeared to cause Jesse agonizing pain. His body trembled repeatedly, and a fine sheen of moisture lay on his skin.

"He's burning up with fever," Nicki murmured, then demanded, "Get some of those cloths I brought and pour some water from the canteen on one. I've got to clean some of this grime off his arm so that I can see what I'm doing."

When she had managed to wipe off a good deal of the grit and dried blood, she saw that the wound was already beginning to fester. A sickly smell was faintly evident, and she knew if not tended, it would only get worse. If the flesh was to heal, the bullet had to come out now and the wound be cleansed and cauterized. Gently she felt the arm to detect the possibility of any broken bones. To her relief, there didn't appear to be any.

"He's lucky at least there are no fractures," she told the anxious-looking young man. "By the way, what do I call you?"

"Most folks call me Bo," he replied, his voice tight, hinting of the turbulent emotions churning inside of him.

"Are you his only brother?"

"Yes, we have a sister. She's married. . . . She'll be awfully upset if he should . . ." his voice trailed off.

"Don't say it—or even think it," Nicki gritted.

She swallowed back nausea as the wound in Jesse's arm began to bleed again from the movement, and said, "He's lucky to have a brother like you. Most folks wouldn't have taken the chance that you did tonight."

Pain flickered across his face. "Our family is close-knit. . . . At least, at one time we all were. Now . . . well . . . circumstances kind of prevent us from being that way. But hopefully, that will all come to pass real soon."

"It's up to you and me to save his life. Together I think we can do it." Their eyes met and held.

"Damn! But nothing like this has ever happened before!" he suddenly swore in frustrated anger.

Nicki laid a comforting hand on his arm. "You had to have known you couldn't keep robbing the PGC and not face this one day. I'd say you've been lucky until now."

"I reckon so." He sighed raggedly, then set the lantern down on a rock next to them. "Did you bring any whiskey?"

"Yes, a full bottle."

"I'll hold his head still and you pour as much as you can down his throat. Maybe we can get him so drunk he won't feel any more pain."

Nicki retrieved the whiskey bottle from her saddle pack and uncorked it. Tilting the bottle to Jesse's mouth, she couldn't help but shiver. She didn't want to tell his brother, but she didn't believe Jesse was

239

going to live through the night. He'd lost too much blood to survive.

By dawn the deed was done. The deadly bullet had been removed, the wound tended and bound with clean strips of cloth. Nicki was exhausted and lay half-asleep curled next to Jesse. Robert Bodine was dozing fitfully with his back against the wall just inside the mine entrance. He clutched his rifle in his hand.

Although they had done everything they could for Jesse, he was still far from out of danger. There was the possibility that the infection would get worse. They had discussed that, and the only means of saving his life if that happened. Robert Bodine had told her Jesse wouldn't want to live if they had to amputate his arm. Nicki had reminded him that it wouldn't make him less of a man, and at least he *would* be alive. They had parted without resolving their difference of opinion, deciding to sleep on it and discuss it later if it appeared they must.

They'd done everything that they could; they could only hope it had been enough.

When the sun crested the mountains, Robert Bodine opened his eyes. He got slowly to his feet and walked back into the cavern to check on his brother. He stood staring down at the two figures sleeping together on the bedroll. Nicki was resting on her side, one arm tucked beneath her head. Her spectacles had come unattached from one ear and lay at a crooked angle on her face. In sleep she looked like a small child. It was a deceptive pose, he knew. She was one tough lady when the need was there.

Jesse was quiet and pale, but breathing evenly. He never did appear to Robert Bodine the fierce outlaw that the entire state was spinning tales about. Yes, they were some pair. Nicki Sue Ryan had just as much spirit as Jesse, and didn't react like most females when confronted with a life-and-death situation. She'd been something to watch last night. He'd make it a point to tell Jess all about it when he was feeling better.

"And you *will* get better." He forced the words out even though his throat felt tight.

When Nicki Sue woke a half hour later, she immediately checked Jesse's vital signs. His pulse was weak, but he was still fighting. Wearily she stood up and looked around for Bo. At first she didn't see him, and when she heard the crunch of shale beneath booted feet, she instinctively lunged for her rifle. It was aimed at his middle when he came around the bend in the wall.

"Hold it there, gal, it's me!" he blurted in a rush, hands spread out wide in front of him. "You sure took me by surprise again. You sure are the quickest draw for a woman I ever did see."

Nicki chose to ignore the intended compliment. She was half-awake and rattled. "Let me know who you are next time!" she snapped testily, then apologized for sounding so harsh when he appeared contrite. "Don't pay any attention—I guess I'm jumpy, but we have to be cautious."

He lowered his hands to his sides and grinned appreciatively. "I will remember your warning. You know . . . I sure never expected you to stick it out here. The first time I saw you, you were half-scared to death. I swore then you were a gal who would be on the next train back to the big city just as soon as you were able."

Nicki propped the rifle against the cavern wall. "I have to admit, those first days with Jesse, I thought of little else. But after we parted and I cam back here to live, I found that the time Jesse and I had spent together had taught me a great deal about endurance. In many ways I don't think the experience was all bad. Without it, I wouldn't have developed the strength necessary to have faced the hardships here."

"Has it been hard for you?" He knelt down beside Jesse and studied him intently.

"Very hard," she admitted unhesitatingly. "At first it was so difficult, I wondered each morning whether I could stand it another day." She shrugged. "But I did — and I'm not sorry."

He glanced up at her. "*I'm* sorry you were put through so much. I don't think Jesse meant to cause you such grief. He forced you to go with us because he was certain Evanson posed a threat to your life."

"I want to believe that. I don't like wondering about who killed my husband, and why."

Robert Bodine sat back on his heels. "My brother has never taken a man's life without reason."

"He certainly does have his share of admirers." She couldn't help the sarcastic edge to her voice. Turning away, she began gathering up the articles scattered around her. She picked up the whiskey bottle. There were only a few good drinks left. "I expect he'll have some headache when he wakes up."

"I think you're right. It always did take a powerful lot of liquor to get him so drunk he'd pass out."

"Who shot Jesse?" she asked.

He didn't know how much he should tell her, but then he realized they might need her should Star manage to track them here. Although he knew he'd been careful to cover their tracks, he wasn't as talented at it as Dakotah. Several times they'd ridden into streams, doubling back to ride through the water for a time, then crossing to the other side and back into the stream again. But with Star, a man could never be certain. He was as cunning as a wolf and could track a man just as good as an Indian.

"I think it may have been one of Charlie Star's men."

Her face paled. "We have got big trouble."

Hearing her include herself in their dilemma, Robert Bodine was finally convinced that she was on their side.

After Nicki Sue repacked her saddlebags, she slung them over her shoulder. "I have to be going now. If I don't show up at breakfast, Maria will send the men looking for me. We don't want them getting suspicious."

"I'm glad he told me how to find you," he declared, and watched her eyes widen in amazement.

"*He* asked you to bring him here?"

"Sure did. Said you would help us. Guess he knew what he was talking about for a change." He grinned wryly at her.

His declaration had brought her up short. She left after that, calling back that she'd return later with some supplies and food.

What a strange man Jesse Kardel was, she thought as she rode back toward the house with the sun already high in the sky. It was going to be another hot day. At least in the dark, cool mine, Jesse could rest comfortably. And for now, it was the safest place.

It wasn't until she thought of how and what she would bring the two men to eat that she began to realize she would soon have an entirely different set of circumstances to worry about.

How was she going to slip food and supplies from beneath Maria's ever-inquisitive nose? The woman knew every item that was in her kitchen, and became downright indignant if you intruded upon her territory without first asking her permission. And the horses would need grain. Nicki Sue figured if there was a will, she would undoubtedly succeed in finding a way.

Chapter Twelve

Charlie Star was sitting in her kitchen drinking a cup of coffee when Nicki Sue walked through the back door. Even though they had never met before, she just knew who he was. She realized a moment of panic, but forced herself to remain calm when she thought of Jesse lying so gravely wounded and dependent on her cool nerve. She was glad that she'd had the forethought to leave the saddle packs in the barn to be retrieved later. Nicki cast him a scant glance as she removed her hat and hung it on a wall peg.

"Something I can do for you?"

Star pulled a watch from his vest and checked the hour. "I hope so. Guess you know who I am."

She deliberately allowed her gaze to study his face. "Hmmm, I'm sorry, but I don't recall when we've been introduced."

His expression was droll. "Don't reckon we have been—"

"Oh, yes—now I remember you," she cut him off with a too sweet smile. "I've seen you squiring Sugar Drucell about town, haven't I?" She was feeling suddenly like a cat who'd just discovered sharp claws.

The Pinkerton man appeared amused, then once again pondered the hands of the watch. "Reckon you may have a time or two."

Nicki stood several feet away from him and dared not even conjure up Jesse in her mind lest her face reveal what she was thinking to this sly fox.

Finally, after a long silence, Star abruptly snapped the watch cover closed and peered up at her. "My name is Charlie Star, ma'am. I just thought perhaps you might have heard about me from the townfolk . . . or maybe even from somebody else." The expression in his eyes was manic.

"No, I haven't," she answered carefully.

His probing gaze flickered over her. "You're Mrs. Ryan; I know that. I've had a difficult time catching up with you, ma'am. Either you weren't receiving callers or I was working elsewhere."

"I'm still not receiving callers," she said through stiff lips.

Star appeared contrite. Nicki Sue thought he played his part very well.

"I know, and I apologize for coming here so early in the morning, but I need for you to answer an important question for me."

"Very well, what is it?" she relented calmly.

Her control was almost shattered when he extended his hand and allowed the watch to dangle by its gold chain. "Ever seen this before?"

Oh Lord, she groaned to herself, it was Jesse's watch! A vision of him retrieving it from his pocket and checking the hour as they'd tried to stay ahead of the law danced in her mind's eye. Her gaze was drawn to stare at it, and then catching herself, she glanced away.

"I don't believe I have . . . no," she managed evenly.

She walked nonchalantly past him, and remembering the splattering of blood that she'd hastily wiped off the front of her shirt before entering the house, knew that he must have seen it. How stupid of her not to have remembered, but she'd been so tired! She paused before the dry sink to gather up several fresh eggs and then walked over to stand before the stove. Swallowing, she replied in what she prayed was a convincing voice.

"It's a very nice timepiece. Is it a family heirloom?"

"You're absolutely certain you've never seen it before?" he persisted.

She cracked the eggs one by one into the frying pan. "Oh, I'm certain all right. Who does it belong to, Mr. Star?"

"There was another train robbery not far from here. The leader of the bandits lost it when he vaulted on his horse. It's the first piece of evidence I've been able to come up with." There followed a timely pause, and then she heard him chuckle. "Now, don't that beat all! Would you just look at these initials . . . and an inscription too."

Nicki imagined him staring down at the watch and felt her mouth go dry. She knew he damn well had noticed the inscription before now! He was a clever bastard, but he wasn't going to get Jesse from her!

"What are the initials?" she dared to ask.

"Let's see here, I have to get my specs out." Another nerve-wracking delay, and them, "To J.K. — with love, Mother."

Nicki could not stop the shiver that raced down her spine. *J.K. — Jesse . . . ?* Almost immediately the name Kardel flashed through her mind. *Dear God! Could Jesse be Vincent and Elizabeth Kardel's son?*

Star's voice cut into her frantic thoughts. "I sure wish I could put a name with those initials," he was saying as thought totally perplexed. "You have any ideas there, Mrs. Ryan?"

Shaking her head, she managed to respond. "I wouldn't have the faintest notion, sir. I'm sorry, but I'm afraid I can't help you."

But Star would not give up that easily. He knew two of the bandits had to be nearby, and Mrs. Ryan just hadn't been cooperating with the law since her return — at least, he thought, the way a normal kidnap victim would. He'd followed the telltale trail of blood to a point just east of her land. The trail had stopped at the river. He assumed the outlaws had forded the river, and he had begun to get suspicious when he tried to reason why the hunted men would come near Ryan land. Especially when the little lady could so easily put a noose around their necks. Unless, of course, they knew she wouldn't turn them in. He was almost sorry she'd shown up in Bodie after the gang had turned her loose. At least they would have had one description to give the marshals in the surrounding counties. As it was, they really had very little to go on except for a scattering of conflicting statements. His irritation began to surface.

"I intend to catch those outlaws. And I prefer to

bring them in standing up, not lying down."

She felt like shrieking at him, was he through trying to badger her? But she did not. Instead she inquired in a tightly controlled voice, "Have any luck yet?"

"As a matter of fact, yes," he replied smugly. "I think I'm close on their trail. I expect it won't be much longer now."

Nicki felt Maria's eyes upon her as she flinched at Star's words and almost burned her hand on the hot skillet.

"Then you have reason to believe that they're nearby?"

"Yes, I do," came Star's confident answer.

Maria was glancing sullenly from out of the corner of her eye. She knew the woman was wondering why she'd suddenly decided she needed to intervene on her precious territory, but at the moment, the housekeeper's grumpy pout was less intimidating than the formidable Star. Her thoughts raced to stay ahead of his; and she desperately wished she had never laid eyes on Jesse, or felt the need to shield him from the law.

"You always get up and out early, Mrs. Ryan?" came the next abrupt question.

Lifting a lid on a skillet and sniffing appreciatively, Nicki responded lightly. "I'm a very busy woman; I can't afford to waste a single minute of the day." She half turned in his direction, then remembering the stain, thought better of it and quickly picked up a spoon to stir the simmering oatmeal. "You're out awfully early today yourself — you *must* be certain of catching that gang soon."

Charlie Star never took his eyes off of Nicki Sue.

He studied her like she was prey. After scrutinizing her closely for several long seconds, he replied. "I'm close. Been hunting them for two days. They made off with a hefty sack of gold coins on that last heist. I'm determined to get them this time. Almost had them too—cornered them in a canyon, where it should have been all over. But I made a costly error; I underestimated their leader."

"And he got away," Nicki finished for him, feeling smug within.

"But he'll pay when I catch him for trying to outfox me." He sounded mean and vindictive, and certain he'd run Jesse down.

Nicki did not turn around, but concentrated her best efforts on removing the lumps from the oatmeal. Maria still looked very disgruntled.

"Do you have *any* idea who the men are?" Nicki asked.

"Never have seen them up close or learned their names—they're doing their best to steer clear of me. But we'll meet face-to-face soon. You just can't keep robbing trains and expect to remain unknown."

"Well, I'll be glad when you catch them; I certainly shudder to think that they might be nearby."

"Don't worry, we'll get them, all right. I've never lost a man yet that I've hunted. And since they went and robbed a bank in the next town the other day, I expect they'll have even more men out looking for them."

Nicki swallowed. "They held up a bank too?"

"Sure did. Over in Middleton."

She barely heard his next words, she was in such a state of shock. Had Jesse gone completely bad? Perhaps he'd been living on the edge of the law for so long now that it had been easy to slip completely over to the other side.

"Oh, by the way," he added as if it were an afterthought, "you'd better wash out that splotch on your shirt before the stain sets."

Nicki blanched, then recovering quickly, addressed Maria. "Oh, I almost forgot. I picked some wild berries for you. I thought they would make a delicious pie. Except I went and left them in the barn. I'll get them for you in a little while." Before Maria had time to respond, Nicki was going on about anticipating a scrumptious dessert for supper. Then she turned around and forced a smile. "It won't be necessary for you to stop by and check on us again, Mr. Star. We're fine, as you can see. And I really doubt that those men would be so foolish enough to come here."

Charlie Star did not look happy. His face appeared haggard and his eyes held a burning fire deep in their depths. He wanted Jesse desperately. But he wasn't going to get him with her help.

Star glared at her. "I'm not so certain about that."

"I am," Nicki stated firmly.

"I hope for your sake that you're right," he reiterated.

The Pinkerton man slid his chair back and got slowly to his feet. He appeared tired and worn, not at all the bold legend that Nicki Sue had heard so many tales about.

"If you happen to see anything at all suspicious, contact me. I'm going to be staying around these parts for a while." His piercing eyes met Nicki's. "One of my men is certain he wounded the leader.

251

He won't be able to keep riding forever with a bullet in him. And maybe with a bit of luck, he'll die of lead poisoning."

She tried not to flinch at his cold declaration. "Yes, of course I will, and thank you for looking in on us," she added, even though she knew very well that their welfare had not been the primary motive behind his unexpected visit.

After Charlie Star left, there was breakfast to get through. Marty and Pablo came in and were in a talkative mood this morning, what with the excitement of the train robbers in the area. No one appeared to notice that Nicki Sue had other things on her mind. She said little. Her single thought was on returning to the mine and warning Bo that Star was not giving up the chase.

Just as soon as the two ranch hands left, Maria promptly cleared the dirty dishes from the table and left the kitchen to go make up the beds. Nicki waited to make certain that Maria did not return before she began gathering food to take to Jesse and Bo. She wrapped up half of a ham, some cheese, and a loaf of freshly baked bread. She added to that several apples and a jug of hot coffee. She'd simply explain to Maria that she was going out to check on some of the horses they'd turned out in the far pasture. It wasn't unusual for her to do so, and she could only hope it didn't appear any different today.

Robert Bodine stood just inside the entrance to the mine and watched her ride up on the white Arabian mare. He had to smile appreciatively. She had certainly learned how to ride, and handled the spirited horse with admirable skill. His eyes widened when she dismounted and he saw that she was dressed in snug-fitting boy's trousers and a faded blue shirt. Her hair lay in a single braid down her back, and she wore a light gray Stetson on her head. In her arm she carried a bulging saddle pack, obviously laden with supplies. He hurried forward and relieved her of her cumbersome burden.

"Hope you brought something good to eat."

"I'm afraid it isn't very much this time. I didn't want to make Maria suspicious, especially after the visitor we had this morning."

They walked side by side to the main body of the mine. She saw that Jesse hadn't moved since she'd left.

"What visitor?"

She knelt down to examine Jesse. "Charlie Star was at the house when I got back this morning."

Robert Bodine was visibly shaken. "He has a nose on him like a bloodhound. I could have sworn we lost him."

"Obviously not. He asked a lot of questions. Even said you were responsible for a bank robbery over in Middleton."

"Middleton is over fifty miles away!" Robert Bodine snarled. "I guess Missouri has the James boys and California is going to have the—" He bit off the last word when he realized what he had almost revealed.

She wanted very much to believe they had not robbed that bank. Taking a deep breath, she said, "Star showed me Jesse's watch—he dropped it at the train site."

"Damn!" Then quickly, "Does he know who Jesse is?"

She lifted her chin. "He didn't learn anything from me, if that's what you mean. But he's very good at what he does. He suspects you're hiding nearby."

"Any other bad news?" he inquired bitterly.

She bowed her head. "They're getting close, Bo. And now that they know you're in the area . . . it can only be a matter of time." She decided to say nothing to him about her suspicions regarding their last name being Kardel. He looked so tired, and she knew he was upset enough already.

She knelt down to examine Jesse and was distressed to notice he didn't appear any better. "How does Jesse look to you?"

"It's too soon for any change," Robert Bodine stated wearily, then smiled apologetically. "I'm sorry for growling at you. I didn't mean for it to sound like you'd turn us in to Star. I'm just sick of everything right now. All I want is for Jesse to get better so that we can head someplace where it's safe."

Nicki knew he meant every word. She dropped her eyes and began searching through the packs he'd laid beside her. "I brought some laudanum." Her fingers closed around the bottle and she held it up to the light.

The purplish liquid looked unhealthy to Robert Bodine. "That stuff looks awful. You sure it will help him?"

"I'm sure," she stated patiently. "I'll give him a spoonful now, and you give him another in a few hours." She put on her spectacles to measure the correct amount into the spoon. "It will kill his pain, and I've been told the opium in it gives one interesting dreams. So if he talks out of his head sometimes, don't be alarmed."

"Maybe he'll wake up with some insight as to how we're going to get out of this mess," Robert Bodine quipped dryly. Catching her gaze upon him, he looked over at her. "You know, I *never* did enjoy tearing around the countryside robbing Evanson's train."

"Then why do you continue? Surely you realize the law is closing in on you . . . and that soon . . ."

The tension inside him had to be released, and he said viciously, "I can't abandon him. But I do wish to hell it would all end. Of course, it won't be soon—not until Jesse has done what he set out to do."

Nicki Sue stared thoughtfully at him, but said nothing. In both of their minds they were thinking the same thing. Jesse wouldn't give up until he had destroyed Evanson. Finally, Nicki asked quietly, "Why don't you get out if you hate it so?"

"Because we're brothers—and I would never forgive myself if I let him do this alone and he was killed." His expression was one of anguish. "I almost lost him once. I swore then I'd be there if he ever needed me again." He followed this with a quirky smile. "And here I am."

Jesse stirred restlessly and moaned. Nicki motioned for Robert Bodine to hold his head still so that she could spoon the laudanum into his mouth. When the foul-tasting medicine met his taste buds, Jesse's eyes fluttered open. Nicki saw at once their depths were still bright with fever. She tucked the blanket snugly around his bare chest. He was mumbling incoherently. She pretended she had not heard what he had said. But Robert Bodine knew by the pained expression on her face that she had heard his brother call for Allison. He left her in private and went to the back of the mine to tend the horses.

Two days later Jesse was still burning with fever, and to make matters worse, an angry red line zigzagged along his arm.

"I wish Dakotah were here; he'd have some herbs for the fever and would know what to put on the wound to draw out the infection," Robert Bodine said.

"Jesse put some awful-looking moss on my leg when I fell and injured it," Nicki remembered now and told Bo. "Do you know what it was?"

"If it's the same thing Jesse used on my horse once after he cut his leg on a piece of wire, I'd say I could find some."

"You mean he uses that stuff on horses! He told me it was an old Indian remedy!"

"Jess must have known what he was doing. . . ." His words trailed off when he saw her eyebrow quirk upward. "Well, it worked, didn't it? And sometimes we have to make do."

"Yes, it worked," she was forced to admit. "Can you find any around here?"

"It grows wild in these parts, looks just like an ordinary weed. But if you soak it in water, it expands and can draw out an infection quicker than anything I've seen."

"Well, if it didn't hurt me, or your horse, I sup-

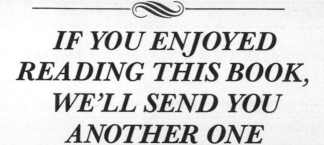

ACCEPT YOUR **FREE GIFT** AND EXPERIENCE MORE OF THE PASSION AND ADVENTURE YOU LIKE IN A HISTORICAL ROMANCE

Zebra Romances are the finest novels of their kind and are written with the adult woman in mind. All of our books are written by authors who really know how to weave tales of romantic adventure in the historical settings you love.

Because our readers tell us these books sell out very fast in the stores, Zebra has made arrangements for you to receive at home the four newest titles published each month. You'll never miss a title and home delivery is so convenient. With your first shipment we'll even send you a FREE Zebra Historical Romance as our gift just for trying our home subscription service. No obligation.

BIG SAVINGS AND **FREE** HOME DELIVERY

Each month, the Zebra Home Subscription Service will send you the four newest titles as soon as they are published. (We ship these books to our subscribers even before we send them to the stores.) You may preview them *Free* for 10 days. If you like them as much as we think you will, you'll pay just $3.50 each and *save $1.80 each month* off the cover price. *AND you'll also get FREE HOME DELIVERY.* There is never a charge for shipping, handling or postage and there is no minimum you must buy. If you decide not to keep any shipment, simply return it within 10 days, no questions asked, and owe nothing.

pose it's all right to use on your brother," she quipped dryly.

Robert Bodine appeared sheepish. "I hope you aren't offended. I know Jesse was concerned for you or he wouldn't have resorted to trying it."

"Just go quickly and fetch the wretched weed," Nicki muttered under her breath.

He nodded and retrieved his horse from the roped corral they'd constructed in the back of the mine.

As he was getting ready to ride out, he turned his head to see Nicki standing at the mine entrance wearing a pensive expression.

"Be careful, Bo; Star's men could be around. Jesse would never forgive himself if anything should happen to you."

He grinned. "I'll be back in no time. Just stay with him."

Sticking to a cover of towering rock and pines, he rode off.

Nicki returned to Jesse's side. The rasping sound of his breathing alarmed her. Kneeling down, she felt his forehead. It was hotter than the last time she'd checked, and even in the diffused lantern light she could see that his skin bore a fever flush. His face and upper body glistened with a moist sheen of sweat.

Quickly while he lay quiet for a moment, she snatched up a clean linen cloth and the leather water pouch. After she dampened the cloth, she turned to him and wiped off his face, arms, and across his thickly muscled chest. He was a handsomely formed man, and even the dark, stubbled beard did not detract from his bold good looks.

257

Her fingers paused when she felt his heart beating steady and strong. She felt a glad quickening of her pulse, and on impulse she leaned forward to brush her lips across his. If she could, she would summon the strength for him to live.

"You aren't going to die on me, Jesse. I have too many questions I need answers to." This was murmured near his ear and he seemed to sigh as if he'd heard.

Throughout the long wait Jesse thrashed about in his delirium, and it was difficult for her to hold him down. She continued to tell him other reasons why he must fight to live, and realized that much of what she said had come straight from her heart. The exhausting struggle took a toll on Nicki too. And hearing Jesse moaning Allison's name when she had touched his forehead a moment ago did not help her frame of mind. Still, she did what she could to soothe him, and finally he seemed less restless and slept soundly until at last Robert Bodine returned.

By evening they had opened and drained the wound. After applying the moist poultice to Jesse's wound, Nicki rebandaged it with clean strips of a cotton petticoat. They had done all that was humanly possible.

Robert Bodine sat back with a sigh of relief. "I guess now we wait."

"Yes, we've done everything we can." She met his eyes. "Of course, we could always fetch Doc Samuel."

"No, we cannot!" came the terse reply.

"But he still might lose the arm . . . or die," Nicki Sue persisted.

"He will *not* lose his arm — or die — I just won't believe it," Robert Bodine ground out from between clenched teeth, then added, "Besides, if you bring a doctor here, you might as well bring a noose right along with you."

"Yes, I suppose you're right." She sighed despondently.

When it was time for her to leave, she hesitated, but Bo insisted that she must get some rest, and promised her that if Jesse's condition changed, he would come for her.

Without realizing what she was doing, Nicki reached up and hugged him. He held her close and they drew courage from each other.

Chapter Thirteen

Within twenty-four hours the red line on Jesse's arm was fading and the flesh wound appeared healthier. It was a definite sign the infection was clearing up. Both Bo and Nicki Sue felt like celebrating; however, they knew it was still too soon for that. Jesse still had a long way to go before he was well again.

It was a full week before they were certain that Jesse would actually survive. During that time either Nicki Sue or Robert Bodine was at his side. She became quite fond of Jesse's younger brother. She thought he and Jesse must have been very much alike at one time, before the terrible tragedy that had turned Jesse into the cold man he was today. Bo was sweet and gentle to her, and with clean clothes, minus the long, sinister duster, he no longer appeared as disreputable. Nicki Sue was laughing at one of the hilarious stories that Bo frequently related to her when she happened to glance over at Jesse, as she often did to check on him, and saw that his eyes were open and watching them. For a moment she suspected he was still delirious, but then she saw him blink, and a hard gleam fixed upon her. His face darkened.

"What in the hell are you doing here?" he growled, clearly unhappy to awaken and find her present.

Words failed her—she was stunned speechless.

"She saved your life, you ungrateful jackass," Robert Bodine was quick to answer for her. "And you should be thanking her for letting us stay here instead of jumping down her throat."

Jesse's clouded gaze sliced to his brother. "Fine! And now we're getting out of here."

"You're in no shape to go anywhere, so just forget it!" Robert Bodine snarled right back.

Jesse attempted to raise his head and realized his mistake. He wasn't able to summon the strength to move a muscle. He swore angrily under his breath, then grumbled, "Stay away from here, Nicki. I have enough people to worry about without adding one more."

There was a moment of strained silence, then Nicki Sue rose quietly, drawing her dignity around her. She hadn't been expecting his hostility, although she knew she should have been prepared. He had caught her off guard. She had felt relaxed and easy with Bo's company, and now to be faced so abruptly with Jesse's abrasiveness was just too overwhelming. Things would never change between them. Hurt, fighting tears, she turned and walked away without a word.

Jesse swore softly, then said, "Nicki . . . I . . . didn't mean to growl at you."

He watched her hesitate, then stand motionless. Yet she did not turn around, but stood all stiff-necked like he was so used to seeing her, silently demanding an apology from him. He felt like a herd of buffalo had been stomping all over his body, and his throat was so dry it hurt to talk, but he knew she was furious with him and would expect it. Aw, hell! What would it hurt, he thought, and forced the words to come even though it galled him to do it.

"I'm sorry, for chrissake—come back here, Tiger Eyes."

Realizing that was an acceptable apology by Jesse's standards, Nicki Sue turned around and stared narrow-eyed at him.

"I will forgive your rude behavior this time, Jesse, because you've been a very sick man. But I swear by all that's holy, if you ever talk to me in that fashion again, I'll walk away and never come back." Then she calmly came to his side and sat next to him on the bedroll.

They stared at each other: tawny gold eyes glittering challengingly at midnight blue.

"I think I'll take a short walk," Robert Bodine informed the couple, although he doubted if they even knew he was there any longer. He strode away to allow them a private moment together.

She was so close to him that Jesse could not resist reaching out to touch her, run his hand along her arm. His breath left him. It was always this way when he was near her.

At that moment it no longer mattered about their differences, or who made the first move. Suddenly she was bending over him and he was drawing her against him. The smell of her had tantalized him even through his delirium. He sighed deeply.

"I knew it was you by my side," he surprised her

by admitting. "The smell of apple blossoms seemed to soothe me and draw me back even when I felt myself drifting away."

Her throat tightened and she could not speak. He traced a finger along her smooth cheek. "I wouldn't have blamed you if you would have just walked out of here and not have come back."

"I'm just glad you're better," she was finally able to whisper against his lips. "But I mean the last . . . I will keep going if you try that high-handed stuff with me again."

He grinned crookedly. "Yeah, I think you would at that." Then with a low growl he drew her head downward.

Their lips met in a passionate kiss. Desire threatened rational thinking, but Nicki knew only in his mind would he make love to her; he was still far too ill to physically do so. He clung to her almost desperately, as if in saving his life she had somehow become a part of him. When she finally was able to pull gently back from him, she was shaking with emotion. He reached for her again, but she remained firm.

"No, you'll open up your wound if you persist." She ran her fingers through his shaggy black hair. "I've been doing my best to keep you respectable-looking, but I'm afraid you resisted all of my efforts."

"You're taking a big risk by letting us stay here. I do appreciate it." He smiled slowly at her, and she thought she had never seen a more beautiful sight. It was the first time since she'd known him that he had truly smiled at her. Always before, his lips had lifted in a mocking, cynical fashion that had been insulting, as well as blatantly insinuating.

And later, after he'd drunk some hot coffee and nibbled on some bread and cheese, they began talking. She was lying with her head on his shoulder. Before she could stop herself, the words were out. "Tell me about Allison, who she was and what she meant to you."

There was a strained silence, and then he said, "She's dead—there isn't anything else to tell."

"I have to know more, Jess," she pleaded even though she hated herself for doing so.

He closed his eyes tiredly for a moment, then opened them to stare blankly upward into the darkness. "It all happened such a long time ago that sometimes I have a hard time recalling exactly how it was between Allison and me."

The disclosure stunned Nicki. "Try and remember what it was about her that makes you call out to her even now."

His head jerked sideways to slant her an inquiring glare. "What?"

"It's true, Jess. You called for her several times while you were delirious."

"I'm not saying it isn't. I dream about her a lot." He sighed. "I can't seem to stop."

"Oh," was all that Nicki could manage to say.

"But then I guess it's not all that unusual; we were engaged."

She didn't turn away, but replied with a catch in her voice, "You miss her terribly, don't you?"

"I miss her. But not in the way that you think," he stated softly. He sighed. "Allison was taken away from all the wonderful things that life promises those who are young. She was full of dreams and goodwill, counting on doing so much in the years ahead. And she depended on me to see that nothing bad came along to shatter her dreams." His voice became hoarse. "And I failed her."

"Stop blaming yourself," she pleaded, her eyes filled with compassion.

"I'm the one he was really after that night. I had told Lars after Reed was killed that I'd find a way to stop his railroad. I swore to see him ruined. He saw a way to eliminate me and have the Simmons's land. He sent his men to watch us without our being aware, and when the time was right, they made their move. They wiped out the entire Simmons family — except for one child who was away at college — and left me wishing I would die. It took me a long time to come to grips with myself."

"Bo helped you then, too, didn't he?" she probed gently.

He nodded. "Yes. He was with my brother-in-law when they found me. They feared the killers would come back and finish the job if they found out I wasn't dead, so without telling anyone I was alive, they took me to my sister's."

"And where was that?" she asked when he hesitated.

"She lives in the Mojave Desert on the Colorado River."

"But I've heard that only the Indians live there."

"That's true. Doris is married to a Mojave Indian. You've sort of met him."

She recalled the Indian on the train who would have shot her if not for Jesse's intervention. "That awful man is your brother-in-law," she gasped.

"He was only going to shoot you because he

265

thought you were a threat," he pointed out irritably.

"Oh! And I suppose that excuses his actions then!"

"No—it does not," he ground out impatiently, "but you could have gotten a lot of people killed if you would have dashed from that car screaming your lungs out. You were hysterical, and those other passengers were on the verge. He was just seeking to prevent further bloodshed."

Her lips pressed firmly together as she stared stonily at him.

"Should I continue? Or have you decided you've heard enough?"

"Continue," she stated stiffly.

He nodded. "It was there, living among the Mojaves, that I slowly healed, and planned my revenge. They taught me their ways and their methods of warfare. And my sister's relatives treated me as one of their own." She was looking at him differently now, and his mouth curled upward in a caricature of a smile. "Does that offend you to think you've made love with a man who has lived side by side with the Indians?"

"No . . . that isn't it." She fell silent and he pressed his lips to her temple.

"Tell me, Tiger Eyes, what is on your mind?"

"I was just wondering . . . well, after the things I'd heard about the beautiful Indian maidens . . . well, why you didn't chose another woman to help you get over losing Allison."

He took a deep breath, and then said, "There *were* other women—but none of them special. I didn't need anyone back then; my hatred was enough."

Her eyes were wide in her face. "And now?"

"I can't," he replied thickly, "for I have nothing to offer a woman."

She tried not to show him how much his declaration had affected her and hurriedly changed the subject less she hasten to tell him how wrong he was. "What about your mother and father?"

"What about them?"

"I know . . . about your family, Jess. Star has a watch that you dropped at the site of the last train robbery. The inscription reads—"

"I know what it reads!" he cut her off with a snarl.

Nicki fought to keep her voice even. "I think Vincent and Elizabeth would want very much to know you are alive," she stated with bated breath.

"Enough about my parents. I particularly do not want them involved. Once your enemies know you have family and ties, then they have something to hold over your head. I severed all ties with my mother and father because I heard what the Pinkertons did to the Norton brothers' family. They surrounded the house, thinking the brothers were there, and threw some sort of explosive through the window. They claim it was only supposed to smoke them out. Well, it killed five of the Norton kin, and the mother lost an arm."

Nicki was too horrified to comment. His eyes were heavy-lidded when they met hers.

"Do you understand now why no one must know?"

She nodded. "A pact then?" she posed huskily, tears in her eyes.

"Yes, a pact," he agreed.

They glanced up when Robert Bodine walked into view. He grinned, having heard the last of their words. "Welcome to the Kardel gang, Nicki Sue. I'd say we're damn lucky to have you." He was watching her with a wry smile.

"Don't go giving her any ideas, Bo," Jesse quickly reminded him. "Or next she'll be wanting to ride with us."

Nicki Sue appeared affronted. "I can ride and shoot just as good as any of your men," she stated with an assured nod.

"Yes, sweetheart, I'm sure you can," Jesse replied soothingly. "Now, why don't you be a good girl and let me get some sleep. We'll talk more later."

Nicki left soon after so that he could rest. She had to agree that for now, Jesse was right. The fewer people who knew he was alive, the better off they were. But she was rather miffed that he still thought of her as a tenderfoot.

Jesse was becoming stronger every day, and Nicki Sue could tell he was anxious to leave. She spent as much time with him as she could now. He had insisted that Robert Bodine go on ahead to Hawk Point and let everyone know Jesse was alive and would be there soon. She had been there when Jesse had informed his brother of his decision.

Bo did not want to leave Jesse to ride back alone, and the two brothers had argued about it, until at last Jesse had convinced him it would be easier for them both if they traveled their separate ways back to the hideout.

"It will attract less attention. People are keeping

their eyes open for a group of riders, not just one man. You have to get to Hawk Point and let the men know that I'm all right. They'll be worried if we don't show up in a few days."

Without further argument, Robert Bodine began gathering his gear.

Nicki Sue had watched him with a bleak expression.

When night fell, he was ready to leave; he stood with legs braced apart, his rifle gripped tightly in his hand, and faced them. "Guess this is adios for now, Jess. I don't like leaving you, but I can understand your reasoning." He grinned crookedly at Nicki Sue. "Thank you for your hospitality, ma'am, and don't let that brother of mine give you a rough time."

A lump had formed in Nicki's throat and she blinked back tears. She was going to miss him terribly. *Vaya con Dios,* Bo," she stated softly.

"I'll join you at Hawk Point in another week," Jesse told him. "Follow the old cattle trail; it's the safest route. And keep to yourself — you don't know when you might ride into an enemy camp."

Robert Bodine was grinning as he walked away. "I'll be real careful, big brother. You just make certain you do the same."

After he mounted up and rode out of the mine, there was an uncomfortable moment when they both realized at the same time that from now on it would be just the two of them. She was sitting beside Jesse on the bedroll. He was lying back smoking a cheroot, the pungent smoke tantalizing her nostrils. Nicki rose to her feet and began putting together the makings of a meal. She felt his

269

eyes watch her every movement.

"I'll have this stew cooked in no time. I know you must be famished. It won't be much longer." She knew she was babbling, but she felt she had to keep talking or find herself wrapped in his arms.

"I'm not going to touch you, Nicki," he stated softly, surprising her.

She turned to stare wide-eyed at him. "Wha-what did you say?"

"You heard me. I said you don't have to worry that I will take advantage of our situation. I know it's been on your mind since Bo left."

I'm not worried about you, she was thinking as she met his eyes. *I'm struggling with my desires, my need of you.* However, she said, "I don't think in your present condition that I have anything to concern myself over."

He didn't answer that. Already he was envisioning her without any clothes straddling his hips, and him impaled deeply inside of her. At that, the buttons on his pants threatened to burst.

Nicki poured two cups of steaming hot coffee and handed him one. "I've been considering the fact that you might like to try and get some exercise tomorrow. I think it should be all right. We'll wait until nightfall and then we'll take a walk."

"I can manage to get around on my own now," he replied testily, suddenly weary of depending on others to do things for him, and the urgent need to make passionate love to her. His confinement was coming to an abrupt end, he thought. It was time to get on with his plans.

Her eyes rounded. "You don't have to bite my head off! I was only considering your well-being."

270

"Well, stop it," he grumbled. "I'll see to my own needs from now on."

She began furiously stirring the stew bubbling over the fire. "If I thought that you could, I'd be happy to let you," she retorted flippantly.

"You've been getting awfully bossy, lady." His voice had turned teasing once again.

"Someone has to keep you in line," she replied, but her tone had lost its sass.

Jesse's midnight-blue eyes lingered on the soft thrust of her breasts straining against the constricting material. He gave considerable thought to surprising her and tumbling her back onto the bedroll with him, but he had second thoughts about her reaction. He might prove to her too well that he didn't need her coming around. And he wasn't real certain he wanted things to go that far. So he simply let the thought slip from his mind, and instead dragged deeply on the cheroot and let the fragrant smoke trail through his nostrils. He closed his eyes and savored the moment. There was nothing like a good smoke and a willing woman to make a man forget all of his cares. He had a damn good smoke . . . and then, half opening his eyes to stare at Nicki Sue while she worked . . . but as for the rest of it? No, he wouldn't make the first move, and then afterward have her blame him for taking unfair advantage again. She would have to come to him this time. He groaned inwardly as he felt his loins tighten until they ached. It had been too long since he'd made love to her. And it seemed lately there was no other woman except Nicki whom he truly desired.

Nicki had no idea what Jesse was thinking. She

271

was innocent in many ways, and in passion, particularly so. Her body felt flushed, and she had an awful gnawing feeling inside of her that was a hunger of another kind. But she refused to acknowledge, even to herself, how to assuage it and be at peace.

He ate the stew she served him, and they drank coffee together. It was growing late, and she knew that she must leave him soon. She didn't want to go. Her blood was racing like quicksilver through her veins, and all manner of images kept tantalizing her brain. His bare chest, covered with that mat of dark hair, drew her eyes time and again. She was so close to him now that all she would have to do is reach out her fingers to touch him. She started when an owl hooted outside.

Jesse laughed lightly. "You sure are jumpy tonight, Tiger Eyes."

Nicki got quickly to her feet. "I'm . . . just tired, I guess. I think I'd better say goodnight."

"Will I see you in the morning then?"

"Of course; why wouldn't you?" She was watching him with a puzzled frown.

Those deep blue eyes were hooded to her.

"No special reason—just wanted to know, that's all."

"I see. Well, goodnight."

Jesse watched her walk away from him and, with a disgruntled snort, tossed the remains of the cheroot into the fire. "Why I went and let that woman get under my skin when I could have half a dozen others, I don't know," he growled to himself.

Nicki Sue's thinking was the same as Jesse's as she waited outside beneath her bedroom window for

272

Maria's light to go out in her own room. She'd taken to climbing in and out of the window each night after telling the housekeeper that she was going to bed. It saved a lot of explaining as to why she went out without fail just as soon as the sun went down.

Once she was back in her room, Nicki Sue sat for hours and thought about how she would feel when Jesse left her to rejoin his men. Despite her desperate efforts to remain immune to his charm, she knew that she had failed. Just thinking of his leaving her again made her ache inside. She had not been lonely once since he'd been here.

The rest of the night was spent in even greater frustration.

Chapter Fourteen

The man called Waco didn't hesitate to wake Lars Evanson, even though it was very late. He had important news that he was certain he would want to hear.

Lars left his bed, slipped on a robe, and went to answer the knock at the coach door. When he opened the door and saw Waco, he frowned. He glanced over his shoulder at Krystal, and was relieved to see that she was still sleeping soundly. Of course, she'd drunk enough champagne at dinner to keep her out of his hair until late tomorrow.

"What are you doing here at this time of night?" He fixed his gaze on the man before him.

Waco grinned slyly, revealing several missing teeth. "Brung you some good news."

"It better be," Lars responded with an angry scowl, stepping onto the platform and closing the door gently behind him. "Well—speak up, man."

"Me and a few of the men been keepin' an eye on the Ryan place, like you said. We spotted a stranger riding near her spread, so we followed him. He sure looked like he was in a hurry to get out of there without anyone seeing him."

"Are you certain it wasn't one of those Pinkerton men?"

"I'm sure." He grinned triumphantly. "We had one of the girls over at the Butterfly start a rumor that she'd heard from a reliable customer that the train robbers were holed up over in Middleton caves. Guess the Pinkerton and his men are riding hard to get there by now."

Lars's interest was evident. "Did you recognize this man?"

"Too dark for that. But he was wearing a duster just like them fellas who robbed the PGC. I sent the boys on ahead to plan a little surprise for him. Figured you'd be pleased about that."

"Yes, I am very pleased," Lars drawled. His expression was thoughtful for a moment, then he added, "I want to do something real special for our clever hombre."

"I figured you would, so I told Shawnee not to rough him up too bad. I thought you might like to head over and meet them. After all, you've been waiting for this a long time."

Lars's eyes glittered with a hard, piercing light. "Yes, I'll get dressed and be right with you." He suddenly swore heatedly. "I knew she was lying to everyone, the self-righteous bitch. I bet she's had a thing for that outlaw since he held her captive. That explains why she was so tight-lipped about the time she spent with him. She's been protecting him all along."

"Your idea to keep watch on her place was a good one. Now that we've managed to catch the leader, maybe they'll leave the PGC alone."

"*If* this man is indeed their leader. How can we

be certain when he's always kept his face concealed by a mask?"

"Guess we'll just have to persuade him to tell us."

Lars grinned sardonically. "We're going to set a real good example with that outlaw. We'll show them all what happens to those who cross me."

Waco licked his dry lips. Evanson made him nervous talking about making known their vigilante-style justice. He'd been anxious to come tell Evanson that they'd finally gotten a lead on the gang who had been robbing his train. Now he wasn't so sure. He didn't mind hanging the outlaw and leaving him strung up for passers-by to see, and remember. But letting everyone know you were the ones responsible was inviting trouble that they did not need. That wild bunch could outride and outshoot any of his men. Evanson may be able to buy the sheriff's cooperation, but possibly having to face down that gang of outlaws made him more than uneasy.

"I . . . don't know about that, boss," Waco summoned the courage to say.

Evanson grabbed his shirtfront in his fist. "Don't you dare think of backing out now, Waco," he growled. "No one cuts out on Lars Evanson and lives to regret it!"

"Lars honey, what's going on out there?" Krystal called groggily from inside the coach.

Lars released his grip on Waco's shirt. "Get out of here — I've got to take care of Krystal. I think it's time to persuade her to leave town for a while." He watched Waco hurry away, already thinking of how he needed to send Krystal back to Denver to enlist additional funds. With that gang soon behind bars,

276

or better yet, dead, he knew he could go ahead now and expand the PGC without fear of their destroying his efforts. It wasn't too late to redeem the reputation of his railroad. But he needed more money to pay the crews their back wages and to pay construction costs.

Dear Krystal better not fail him, for he was becoming increasingly bored with her of late. If she wasn't able to secure funds for him, then he would soon kiss her good-bye and send her on her way.

Robert Bodine remembered his brother's warning and kept to the side trails. The night was quiet, with a bright silver moon to light his way. He was five miles from Nicki's ranch when the ambush came.

They just rode out of the thick fir trees that banked the uneven trail, and before he could fire off a shot, they were surrounding him. One rider spurred his horse forward and carefully assessed Robert Bodine. He was an ugly cuss with a bearded face and a patch covering one eye. Bo would have liked to call him out. But he knew when the odds weren't in your favor, it was best to just watch and listen.

"Something I can do for you?" he called out, his manner appearing relaxed, but his gun hand was poised and ready.

"Think you'd better give us a name and destination, mister," the ugly man told him, his intentions obvious by the nervous twitch of his gun hand.

Robert Bodine didn't like anybody telling him what to do. His eyes narrowed and his lips turned upward in a sneer. "I really don't think that's anybody's business but mine."

The man laughed jeeringly and leaned forward in the saddle. "That's not the answer I want, boy; now, why don't you just give it another try."

"Why don't you go straight to hell," Robert Bodine drawled. He already knew what was going to happen—he watched the man's eyes, saw the look of death staring back at him. Unless a miracle occurred, it was all going to be over in a matter of minutes. That murderous gleam was all too familiar, the scenario one that had haunted his dreams. He'd seen that particular look before when he'd had to face down gunslingers who thought they were faster on the draw and certain of staying alive. He was the hunted, and they were anticipating the thrill of the kill. But the devil take him if he was going to just let them take him down. He just wasn't ready to die.

With a bloodcurling yell he drew his pistol and began firing into their midst, hoping to either hit a few or scatter them. An anguished scream pierced the air as one of his bullets found its mark. His horse reared back on his hind legs on command, sending the riders in front of him scrambling to get out of the way of deadly sharp hooves.

"Get the son of a bitch!" one of them yelled.

The scene was one of complete chaos; no one knew what to do, or dared to try anything.

In that moment, Robert Bodine was riding. Behind him there came the sound of rifle fire. They had regrouped and were racing after him. He knew he had only gained a few seconds time, but considering the alternative, it was enough. For now, he

"Don't worry, you ain't gonna die that easy. We're just gonna make sure when we get where we're going that you're more of a mind to talk," the brute hissed as he looped one end of the rope under Bo's arms and tied it across his chest.

They secured the rope tightly around his saddle-horn. He knew then what they were going to do even before Lars Evanson gave the command.

"Drag him along behind us, boys. And not too fast — just at a steady pace so he understands we aren't going to play games with him when we get back."

Jesse lay in the cabin on the cliff overlooking the peaceful lake and listened to the wind beating a loose window shutter back and forth. Nicki had helped him move here last night. He had thought that with Star snooping around, it might be a good idea to be in a place where there was more than one way in and out. He'd be too easily trapped in the mine. And it was comfortable here and had a panoramic view. The little cabin was perched on the edge of the cliff and surrounded by trees. It also provided him an excellent vantage point from which to peruse the area.

Jesse tossed restlessly on the bed. For some reason he was worried about his brother. He just had this gut feeling that all wasn't as it should be. He knew it was time for him to leave. His arm was almost healed; every day he'd been exercising the muscles, and they were responding very well. He'd been practicing drawing his gun too, and was relieved he could still clear leather almost as fast as before he'd been shot. Then get on with it, he told himself. There is still Evanson, and your vendetta. He was disgusted when he couldn't summon the familiar bitter hatred that fed his drive for revenge. Nicki was everywhere in his thoughts, and that should not be.

Shaking his head to clear his thoughts of her, he resolved to quit considering Nicki more than his responsibility to his men. He'd known there was never going to be any future with her when they'd first come together. And since Nicki, he'd thought of Allison's murder less. He was beginning to forget what he was about, and why. And he knew he could not do that—not even for Nicki.

He wiped the back of his arm across his damp brow. The morning had dawned unbearably hot, and already the cabin was stifling. He was more comfortable with a soft bed to sleep in, but the cave had been cool, and right now he missed that terribly. Nicki had left him before dawn with a promise to return as soon as she could. She said she was scheduled to train some of the horses. Jesse didn't know if he could stand staying inside the cabin all day. Since he'd begun to heal, he had grown increasingly restless. He wasn't accustomed to inactivity, and it made him tense. The day was going to be long until she came.

He thought again of Bo, and hoped he'd made it to the cattle trail all right. Suddenly weary and sick of worrying about everyone, he got up and walked over to the open door. Outside in the dirt yard, a warm breeze was blowing the dust around in front of the cabin. He stared out over the lake and, on impulse, retrieved his field glasses. He stepped out onto the front porch and sat down on the stairs. Training the glasses on the horizon, he scanned the area carefully.

At first when he saw the cloud of dust far off in the distance, he froze, thinking it was riders scouring the area for him. But when it appeared the cloud remained almost steadily in the same area, he knew it had to be something else. The whirl of dust cleared for a few minutes, and he sucked in his breath.

The men were driving spikes into rails stretching as far as the eye could see. They were laying track for the PGC, and they didn't have far to go before they reached Ryan land.

He sat there for the remainder of the morning and watched them slowly progress toward Nicki's property. And looking out over the lake toward the newly laid tracks, it came to him then why. The water, of course. Her lake was the only water in miles. And a steam locomotive couldn't go very far without water. Evanson had probably figured it out too. But then, not before Jesse. He knew Nicki Sue stood to gain a lot if the railroad laid track along the edge of her land. Jesse had known of whole towns that had sprung up around a water tower and a depot. She'd be rich one day. Hell, she'd have her own town! He knew beyond any doubt why Patrick Ryan had held on to this land.

Soon Nicki would too.

"You'll never reach your destination, Evanson," he vowed under his breath. And even though he knew what this discovery could mean to Nicki, he would go ahead with his plans to stop the growth of the PGC. He had in mind another railroad to lay track across her land. She would never have to fear that it would seek to wipe her out and take her prize away from her. Greed was not the sole motive behind the growth of the K.K. Railroad. But Lars Evanson's greed had helped finance its rapid progress through the mountains, and onward to compete for this territory. Soon Evanson would know the K.K. was not building according to the original plan, and that they were intending to beat him. Jesse wanted to see the look on his face.

"Easy, Storm, you're fighting me again." Nicki held tightly to the end of the rein as the night-black stallion attempted to rear up on his hind legs. He was the most valuable Arabian in their stable, but until Nicki Sue had taken over his handling, there had not been anyone who could work with him.

Marty stood on the opposite side of the fence looking on proudly. He'd taught Mrs. Ryan everything that he knew, and she'd grasped it all very quickly. He couldn't believe that this was the same woman who had arrived appearing so uncertain about her future, and her place here. It had not been easy for her. Even with her firm resolve, the transition had been difficult. Marty knew people were talking behind her back about a good many things. Mrs. Ryan didn't care much for socializing, and she'd riled a few of Bodie's matrons when she'd refused invitations to attend their teas and social events. That had set their tongues to wagging even more. Marty didn't think she would have been comfortable with that sniping bunch of cats anyway, and he was happy that she'd taken a liking to Cathleen Kramer.

Miss Kramer was a nice young woman and appeared to sincerely enjoy Mrs. Ryan's company. They'd had lunch together just last week. When Mrs. Ryan had returned, she'd been happier than he'd ever seen her.

"Put him through his paces now, ma'am," Marty suggested. "He'll behave for you."

Nicki had trained him thoroughly, and he changed from one gait to the next with ease. She kept his body between the reach of her outstretched hands, encouraging him with a gentle voice and a long whip that was used only to set his timing. She waved it slowly in her right hand, careful not to frighten him, while holding the lead in her left. When Storm changed gaits and cantered around the perimeter of the corral with his neck arched regally and his nostrils flared wide, Marty applauded the feat.

"Takes good hands to get a horse to do that," he praised with open admiration in his eyes.

Nicki smiled gratefully at him. "It took him a while to come to terms with who was boss, but I think he actually enjoys showing off."

"He sure looks like it."

"I'm going to keep him, I think, Marty. He could become invaluable as a stud in a few years." She brought Storm to a slow walk in order to cool him down.

"I think that's a right smart idea," Marty agreed. "We could charge to stud him out—probably bring in a lot of money too."

"Patrick knew what he was doing when he

bought this champion as a foal. He just didn't know he would prove so difficult."

"Can't believe how easily he obeys you. I hope soon he'll be that way for all of us."

Nicki brought the stallion to a halt, then approached to pat his silky neck. He nuzzled her shirt pocket. She sliced a quick glance at Marty. He was grinning knowingly.

"Been bribing that fella, have you?"

"Just a little bit." Nicki reached in her shirt pocket and withdrew a chunk of carrot. Storm took it from her open palm with careful regard.

Later, after Nicki had finished with the Arabian's training for the day and had changed into a pale peach dress before going to the cabin to see Jesse, she thought about the inevitability of his leaving once again. She could no longer deny the fact that she cared what happened to him with all of her heart. She had never known another man like Jesse. He was the most exciting man that she had ever known, and the only man who could stretch her tolerance to its limits. When she wasn't with him, she longed to be, and when she was, she fought madly not to succumb to her fatal attraction for him.

She had just spun about quickly to pick up a light shawl for later when the first wave of dizziness hit her. Nicki grabbed hold of the tall bedpost to keep from falling. For a week now she'd been experiencing nausea in the mornings, and now dizzy spells. There were other changes going on in her body, and she was terrified of what it all might indicate. Even though she suspected she might be pregnant, she refused to acknowledge it. For she was well aware that if she bore Jesse's child early next spring, there was a distinct possibility that her child's father would not live to see his son or daughter born.

It was dark by the time she reached the cabin. There was no sign that he was there, but then, he had told her he couldn't risk lighting a lamp at night. With quick steps she hurried onto the porch and pushed the door inward. She stepped over the threshold and her eyes widened in surprise. He wasn't there! She called out to him, but only her own words came back at her. As she threw aside the saddlebags laden with supplies, Nicki's thoughts raced. Could someone have discovered him — or had he left without telling her good-bye?

"Jess! Jess, where are you?" Frantically, she spun around and ran back out onto the porch. It was dark, but the moon was full, and as she reached the edge of the cliff and looked out over the lake, she instinctively knew where she would find him.

She made her way down the winding trail and to the cove that lay cupped in a shelter of trees. There was no immediate sign of Jesse, but then, she didn't expect he'd be that easy to find. And then she walked through the tall cottonwoods beside a deep cove and saw Jesse's horse. Relief surged through her. She walked over to Max, who was grazing on thick shoots of grass bordering the water. He whickered softly in greeting, and she patted him on his sleek neck.

"Where's Jesse, boy?"

Glancing around the perimeter of the lake, Nicki

still did not see him. She had just turned to start off in another direction when a hard-muscled arm slid around her waist and pulled her back against him.

"Were you looking for me, sweetheart?" Jesse drawled over her shoulder, prompting her to spin around and favor him with a reproachful glare.

"What kind of games are you playing now, Jesse Kardel?" she flung back at him. She saw that he was dressed only in trousers and his boots. His hair was longer now, curling softly about his ears and lying damp against his forehead. The moon glinted off of his wide bronze chest and drew her eyes. He'd removed the bulky bandage from his shoulder, as he'd been threatening to do for days. The wound was healing nicely; she knew he couldn't tolerate having limitations placed on him of any kind. No other man could capture her gaze so completely or stir desire within her so easily. It was a tremendous relief to see that he was all right. She knew she would be furious with him for leaving the cabin and frightening her so, but it was difficult to summon anger when she felt a different mood altogether.

He was grinning at her as if he could read her mind. "Guess I got cabin fever. It's cool and peaceful here, and a man can think easier."

"You had me terribly worried," she scolded in mock severity.

Deep in the fringe of brush and trees the water Nicki thought she caught sight of a man sitting on a trunk of a fallen tree that lay half in the water. Jesse saw her stiffen in alarm and quickly sought to reassure her.

"It's okay—he's a friend."

Her eyes flew to his, but he didn't offer any further explanation.

"Why is he here?" she questioned with a frown.

"I've been getting stronger every day; there isn't any reason why I need to stay around much longer." The answer was quiet.

She felt sudden hot tears but stubbornly blinked them back. "I see. Well, I suppose that is your way of telling me you'll be rejoining your men soon." She was never a woman who could tolerate lies, but would rather face the truth no matter how much the pain. For the first time she was almost ready to accept what was less than the truth from Jesse.

"You knew that I would; it was just a matter of time."

She couldn't help clinging to him. "When are you leaving? Where are you going?"

He held her against him for a moment, and then he gently pulled back from her, placing a finger against her lips. "No questions. I don't want you to know anything that might put you in jeopardy."

Nicki knew there was something troubling him. But it was clear to her that he did not intend to share it with her.

"Wait for me here; I'll just be a short while. My friend and I have a few things left to discuss," he told her.

Any other time she would have argued with him and demand he tell her what the two of them were up to. But not this time, for she knew he was brooding deeply about his men, and that other part of his life that she could not share. There was something decidedly familiar about the man waiting in the shadows. He moved as surefootedly as any

289

night creature, his footsteps silent, barely allowing her to catch a glimpse of him. She wished she could see him clearly.

Jesse went over to talk with him. They appeared engaged in a serious discussion, but they kept their voices low so that she could not hear them. She strolled nonchalantly down to the edge of the water and stood there. She could still see them out of the corner of her eye. At last she saw the man turn away and slip off into the night. He had slipped stealthily away, as if he were accustomed to doing so and could easily elude anyone who tried to follow him. His abilities reminded her very much of Jesse's. And then she knew who it was, and the unbidden memory surfaced. The man had been the Indian, Dakotah. Why had he come? Nicki wasn't certain she wanted to face the answer that was in the back of her mind, but it surfaced regardless. Dakotah had come for Jesse.

"Am I ever going to see you again?" she had to ask him when he had rejoined her.

"It's better if you forget about me, Nicki. I'll be out of your life for good soon, and that's how it has to be."

Lifting her chin, she forced herself to reply calmly. "You're right, of course. We have our own lives to resume."

He walked away from her toward the lake, leaving her to her silent misery.

She was shaken from her troubled thoughts by the sight of Jesse hunkering down to splash cool water over his bare arms and chest. He had retrieved a soap and towel from his saddlebags; she saw them lying on the ground beside him.

"Are you certain your arm is healed enough for that?" she asked out of concern.

Sluicing water through his hair, he shook his dark head of excess moisture and turned his head to meet her eyes. His hair appeared like wet sable, it was so black and sleek in the moonlight.

"My arm is fine, and I'm going to have a bath," he told her in a voice that brooked no denial. "You can stay, or you can go on back to the cabin. But there isn't going to be any argument about it."

"But . . . what if someone is around?" she couldn't help protesting, feeling her heart already thudding faster as she stared mesmerized while he unbuttoned his tight pants, carelessly kicking off his boots before tossing the pants aside.

"I'm just going into the cove. No one can see me as long as I stay near shore under the trees."

There was no denying he had other things on his mind when her eyes traveled the length of him and fixed upon the part of him jutting outward with desire. She had seen him without clothes before, but this was the first time she had actually let her eyes feast upon him. He stood there unmoving, allowing her eyes to linger over him without a flicker of emotion visible in his gaze. But she knew what she was doing to him; there was no way for him to hide the proof of it from her. He picked up the bar of soap and with proud arrogance walked into the water until it lapped gently about his waist. With one hand he splashed water over his body, sighing with enjoyment. He glanced at her.

"Care to join me?" The husky timbre of his voice left no doubt in her mind what he was suggesting.

"I . . . I . . . don't know if I should," she stammered.

He shrugged. "Suit yourself, but you have no idea what you are missing."

Now, what was that supposed to mean! she wondered. She lifted her chin in answer to his challenge, and he stared back at her fully aware that she would not be able to resist the dare. His eyes widened appreciatively when he saw her remove her shoes and begin to unfasten the front of her dress.

With methodical grace she slid the dress off her shoulders, then stepped out of it. Her ivory shift fell in a soft flutter about her slim ankles, and she stood before him in stockings held up by ruffled peach garters.

The creamy smoothness of her full, ripe breasts and long legs drew his heated gaze, leaving Nicki flushed with desire and hungry for his kisses. It had been so long, and nothing else mattered at this moment but her need of him. She slid the garters and stockings from her legs and heard him call softly.

"Come here, Tiger Eyes." His eyes were smoldering as they caressed her perfect form.

She went to him then without hesitation, walking into the water and his arms. He gathered her close and her lips nuzzled his shoulder, along his neck, then moved upward over his unshaven chin to capture his mouth. She ran her fingers through the hair on his chest, over the firm muscles along his arms, and caressed the hard ridges of his belly.

"Will it be all right?" she asked softly, her fingers touching the fresh scar on his shoulder.

"I'm fine, and you'd better not stop now," he replied huskily.

When her fingers closed around his hard shaft,

he groaned low in his throat. Her tongue teased the inner softness of his bottom lip before thrusting boldly into his mouth.

Jesse was on fire for her and excited by her initiative to make love to him. It had been so long since he'd made love to her that he only hoped he could endure her sweet torture of his senses and prolong this ecstasy.

Her lips skimmed lightly downward, trailing heatedly along his chest to the tight indentation of his navel. Warm, wet strokes of her tongue there brought his hands forward to lace his fingers through her hair.

"I want to make love to you," he murmured thickly.

"And you shall," she responded in a throaty whisper, "but first, that bath you wanted so badly." She took the bar of soap from him, and lathering her hands, she proceeded to bathe him.

Wantonly, she did things to him with her soaped hands that even the most experienced courtesan would not have thought of. Slippery, sleek fingers pleasured him, caressing hair-roughened muscles that rippled and tightened beneath her touch. After she had cleansed him and rinsed the film of soap from his body with rivulets of cool water, Nicki pressed her warm lips to his chilled flesh. His hands clenched in her hair as she allowed her instincts to lead her path. When her lips closed around him to pleasure him, Jesse caught his breath in his throat.

"Damn it, Nicki . . . that's enough," he groaned pulling her head back when he felt his control slip away to hold her there motionless on her knees. He stared down at her, his breathing ragged. "You are something, you know that?"

She didn't acknowledge his praise. She had acted on blind instinct, her love for him guiding her passion. But she could not say what she longed to — it would be the last thing he would want to hear. Her eyes were half-closed and seductive, long, dusky lashes shadowing her innermost thoughts from him as she proceeded to kneed the tight muscles along his thighs. "I bet you've never had a bath like this before."

"Never," he breathed huskily, reaching down to cup one of her full breasts in his hand. He rolled the silky crest between his fingers until it grew pebble-hard and she sighed softly.

"You'll never get your bath completed like this."

"Perhaps I could think of something else more pleasurable to take its place," he hinted with a wicked gleam in his eyes.

She drew back her head to smile seductively. "Just what did you have in mind?"

His white teeth flashed in his sun-brown face as he reached down to take the bar of soap from her hand. "I'll bathe you." He drew her up to stand before him and slowly caressed the curve of her shoulder with the satiny bar of soap, then trailed a path to her breast and drew it around and around the quivering globe.

Her lips parted and her eyelids fell closed. She surrendered to the magic of his touch and felt the hot spiral of desire curl within her.

First one, then the other breast became slick and softly scented with soap and then abandoned to quiver in protest. Jesse's fingers kept her in an agony of mindless desire as they stroked and teased a path to down-soft curls. She cried out when he swept his hand quickly over her feminine charms to glide smoothly down one slender thigh, and dip between her legs. Before his fingers sought her warmth, he quickly sluiced them through the water.

"Open your legs, love," he said softly, and when she complied, he slipped one finger inside of her. She was sleek and warm, and very aroused. It sent his usual firm control reeling, but he fought to regain it and woo her slowly.

"Jesse . . . ," she pleaded, but he stilled her words with his kiss, wanting to prolong her pleasure as long as possible.

Her legs were trembling with need, her body screaming for release. At last he took her hand, and together they waded to the shore. As he led her toward a secluded spot in the cove that was thick with soft pine needles, he grabbed up the towel and draped it around her damp shoulders.

She spread the towel on the cushion of pine needles and turned into his arms. He drew her against him and slowly they came to their knees, his mouth possessing her at the same time he claimed her body.

He entered her immediately, his hand cupping her from behind to impale himself as deeply as possible. A soft sigh escaped her lips and he captured it in his mouth. Their tongues met in a passionate dance.

Vaguely she thought again about his injured shoulder, but it evaporated almost immediately when she felt the strength of him against her. He was strong and vital, as wild and indomitable as the stallion, Storm. She entwined her legs in his, trying as best she could not to give him her heart as he claimed her passion.

Over and over she murmured his name inside her head as he made love to her with such sweet, tortuous strokes that Nicki was certain she would never get enough of him. Her hands clutched his taut buttocks as he paced himself slowly, teasingly, each thrust claiming a tiny bit more of her soul.

Their fulfillment came in a glorious rush, and they clung to each other in a shattering release. And afterward, resting with her cheek against his sweat-slick belly, she was lulled into slumber by the even sound of his breathing and soothed by the knowledge that no matter what happened after this night, she carried a part of him beneath her heart.

The cabin was so empty and quiet after she left. They had ridden double on Max up the mountainside. Nicki had wanted to come inside with him, and as soon as they shut the door behind them, he swept her up into his arms and carried her to the bed. They made love again. And for the first time, dozed peacefully content, wrapped in each other's arms.

Now Jesse lay awake with the knowledge that he was going to have to leave her. He had not wanted to involve her further, so he had not told her that Dakotah had come to tell him his brother had not returned to Hawk Point yet. And Charlie Star was getting closer all the time. His men were everywhere, and only the outlaw's keen knowledge of the countryside saved them from certain capture. Jesse was to meet Dakotah just before daybreak to search the trail that Robert Bodine was supposed to have traveled back to the hideout. Damn it! Why did he think more about Nicki at this moment than his own flesh and blood? But he already knew the answer. Here in their own private world the weight of his problems had somehow become bearable, because of her. It was the first time since Allison's death that he had thought about not going back. But Dakotah had come, and he knew that he must, and that he was ready to return.

He thought perhaps he should have told her good-bye, but then he knew that it would be easier for her this way. She would have asked a lot of questions he didn't want to answer. As it was, she knew nothing, and was safer that way.

Chapter Fifteen

The following day summer arrived in Bodie with a vengeance. It was already ninety-one in the shade and it wasn't even noon yet. Morris Skiles, Sheriff Will's deputy, knew that meant the miners would be especially rambunctious tonight. Bodie's cavernous mines supported a population of fifteen thousand miners, who, in their off time, played fast and drank themselves into a drunken stupor. Drinking establishments such as the Butterfly and the Gilded Lily did a land-office business amidst unending rowdiness that went on far into the steaming nights.

Shootings, which had always been frequent, became a daily occurrence, and more than one scuffle on the hundred-foot-wide main street ended with the presence of the town's luxurious hearse.

The town's prominent and genteel citizens could be heard complaining about the sheriff, who, more often than not, was off on official business, leaving poor Morris to single-handedly keep the peace. This was no easy feat, but the deputy gave it his best.

If the good citizens had known that Sheriff Will could actually be found relaxing with a cool beer in Lars Evanson's private railroad car on the tracks that came to a halt just on the edge of town, they would have realized why there never seemed to be any peace of late. As it was, only the deputy had any inkling where the sheriff really went, and that was because he had a good source of information.

It just so happened that the sheriff and Morris shared the same taste in women. They liked them plump of hip and firm of bosom, and Ruby Rose, from the Gilded Lily, had those exact attributes. She didn't know that she babbled a lot in her sleep, and one night she let it slip, when Morris was lying awake next to her, where Sheriff Will spent most of his time. And that after Morris had had a run-in earlier with a few rowdies who were drunk and giving the bartender a rough time. He sure was getting sick of covering up for the sheriff and was about ready to tell him a thing or two.

The crowd in the saloon had been arguing over the words to a ditty they were trying to write about the train robbers and the PGC. It was common knowledge that the Butterfly Saloon had come up with a ballad for its patrons to sing about while in their cups. The Gilded Lily was not to be outdone. Business was booming in the "watering holes" since the train robberies, and only a few of the miners' wives could be heard expressing concern for their children's safety. Everyone else was too busy spinning yarns about the train robbers. But when these particular wives got something stuck in their craw, they could nag a man to death and make the time he was at home pretty miserable. So the miners had taken to hanging around the bars after work for as long as possible.

And they drank until their ears buzzed and they no longer heard the little lady's words ringing in their heads. One of the burly miners slammed his foaming mug of beer on the table and growled in a bearlike voice, "Should be writing a song about our lazy-ass sheriff and his chickenhearted deputy! They're the ones my ole lady keeps haggling me about every night when I get home. Gettin' so I'd rather just sleep here than spend another night listening to the wife nag me about moving where they've got some law and order!"

"Oh, pipe down, Milton! We're havin' us a good time here!" one of his comrades roared, tired of hearing the same complaint every night.

"Yeah! Pipe down, Milt!" a dozen of his comrades agreed.

Milton favored them all with a mean, drunken leer, and then, filled with pent-up rage, abruptly hurled his empty mug right over Leroy Culpepper's head.

There followed a chorus of audible gasps as the mug sailed through the air and crashed smack-dab into the voluptuous, bare-breasted goddess etched on the glass. As Leroy stood behind the bar with a sick feeling washing over him, she splintered into a thousand tiny pieces and fell around his feet.

Leroy's face turned a mottled shade of red, then purple, then he grabbed up a broomstick and promptly rapped it over the smirking miner's head. The drunken man swayed, stupefied, on his feet for several seconds, then toppled forward like a felled oak tree onto the hard plank floor. The impact sent a cloud of sawdust swirling upward, and when the last bit settled, the first punch was thrown, and caught Leroy squarely on the chin.

A fistfight broke out that soon spread into a regular brawl.

Ruby Rose wasted little time and sashayed right

on over to the jail house to fetch the law.

When she got there, the only law there was Morris. She convinced him to come back with her and put a stop to the brawling before they tore the Gilded Lily apart and she found herself out of a job.

Morris didn't want to go, but he knew he had to for Ruby Rose. He arrived on the scene and tried to persuade the miners to all go on home and sleep it off. He almost had them settled down when Leroy Culpepper spoke out and demanded payment from the man who had smashed his Venus of love. He received another sound right to his person, and the peace was once again broken.

One of the miners gave Morris a swift boot on his bony rump and sent him flying through the saloon doors into the street. Ruby Rose peeked over the top and inquired in a concerned voice, "Oh, Morris . . . did those roughnecks hurt you? Do you need me to kiss it, boopsy, and make it all better?"

Morris picked himself up and snarled back at her, "Get yourself back inside, woman! I'm fine—and I'll take care of this my own way!"

He decided it was time to lay things on the line with Sheriff Will. He had been pushed around long enough in this lousy town while the sheriff collected a salary for sitting on his backside and doing Evanson's bidding.

Riding over to Evanson's private coach, Morris dismounted and climbed the stairs to knock on the door. He paused on the platform upon hearing Sheriff Will and Evanson engaged in a conversation. Curious by nature, he stood there and listened intently to what they were saying.

"I have tried everything, Evanson, and I can't get

the outlaw to tell me anything," Sheriff Will was saying. "If you don't let up on him for a while, you're going to kill him, and then we'll never learn where the rest of them are."

"I wonder about his being the leader of that bunch," came Lars's voice.

"Why do you say that?"

"I thought you said the leader had been wounded in a fracas with Star."

"That's what Star claims."

"Well, from what Waco told me, there aren't any scars on him to indicate that he was recently shot."

"What do you want me to do?"

"Leave him to my boys. We'll get the truth out of him," was Lars's blunt reply. "That freight car must be like an oven today. Maybe the heat will help loosen up his tongue."

Sheriff Will laughed coldly. "I sure am glad you and I are on the same side, Evanson. I guess you'll be going after the Widow Ryan next?"

"Yes, all of my hindrances are not out of the way yet. And my crews are fast approaching her land. The Widow Ryan doesn't seem to have any idea of the gold mine she has in her possession. I want her run out of here before she does."

"You want the Widow Ryan off that land?" the sheriff posed.

"I wouldn't ever come right out and suggest such a thing." He thought about that for a minute and smiled coldly. "But then, she never really did belong there. So perhaps someone should provide her with some incentive to do so."

"She takes great store in those Arabians of hers," Sheriff Will said meditatively. "And if something should happen to them, she might just decide to

302

give it all up."

"Now, *that* is a thought, Sheriff."

"I know she needs the money from their sale to keep her ranch going. What do you think she would do if a terrible tragedy befell them?"

Lars's eyes already gleamed triumphantly. "She's a female, isn't she? She'd probably cry her eyes out, admit defeat, put the ranch up for sale, and go back to San Francisco, where her kind belongs."

"You seem pretty sure about that."

"I know women, Sheriff," Lars drawled confidently. "She may have everyone else fooled, but not me. If you dispose of those horses and she finds herself without any means of an income, she'll crumble under the pressure and leave Bodie."

Sheriff Will scowled. "Now, wait a minute, Evanson. I don't mind turning my head whenever you need to eliminate another one of those 'obstacles' of yours—but damn it, I'm not putting my head on the chopping block. So you'd better get one of those hired guns of yours to do your piece of dirty work for you."

His triumphant grin warned Sheriff Will that Evanson had no intention of having anyone do this piece of dirty work but him.

"No . . . they've been getting a bit too much exposure of late. You *will* do it for me, Sheriff," Lars said, his expression smug. "Because if you don't, when election time comes around next month, you may just find one of my boys running for sheriff against you." He paused to allow the distraught man to absorb the full import of his words. "And you know I have ways of making certain that the candidate of my choice wins." He didn't think the sheriff realized that he wanted Will directly involved and not just as a sideline observer. Lars always made certain he had something on each of his people, and his victims, in his file that he could blackmail them with if the need ever arose. In his line of business, one had to constantly keep track of accomplishments and eliminations.

"All right! You've made your point," the sheriff growled. "I'll take care of your little problem for you. But this is the only time I'm getting my hands dirty."

"I knew I could count on you—and there'll be an added bonus for you when the deed is completed."

"You know, I've been curious about that land," the sheriff stated, thinking now that he had a right to know a few more details. "Why did Ryan hold on to that worthless place? God knows it couldn't be worth a plug cent."

"Oh, but you are so wrong, Sheriff," Lars stated assuredly.

Morris was so engrossed in their conversation that he failed to see the brute of a man creeping stealthily up behind him.

Inside, Lars was assessing Sheriff Will closely. "You rode over with me yesterday to see how far the railroad crew had progressed. Did you happen to notice the scenery?"

"There wasn't nothing special, 'cept maybe that nice lake in the distance."

Lars's smile was cunning. "That lake—is actually a gold mine. It would have made Patrick Ryan a rich man. He knew it—I didn't suspect until my crews were working near the area."

"You mean there's gold somewhere in that lake?" for water   Lars's sharp bark of laughter prompted the sheriff's face to fuse scarlet.

"What's so damned funny about that?" he asked.

Outside, Morris had to cover his mouth with his hand to suppress a hoot of laughter. Even *he* knew that land didn't contain any gold.

Lars went on to explain, and Morris pressed his ear to the door.

"My railroad is going to need that lake for the steam locomotives. Ryan knew that his place has the only water for miles. And that a railroad stop draws people . . . and people come and settle . . . and pretty soon what do you have?"

"A town," Morris murmured to himself, then stiffened in shock when he felt cold iron jab him in the back and heard a jeering voice over his shoulder.

"What ya doing here, Deputy? Ain't them town boys keeping you busy enough?"

Morris's bony knees shook so hard he thought they were going to give out beneath him. "Ah . . . I . . . was just waitin' around until the sheriff and Mr. Evanson were finished talkin' before I knocked."

Waco's face darkened angrily. He spun Morris around and backhanded him across the mouth. "Don't lie to me, boy. I know what you were doin'! You heard every word they said—and that's too bad."

Morris shook his head back and forth. " 'Twasn't . . . didn't hear a word . . ."

"I say you're lyin'!" Waco snarled, before knocking on the door. When it was drawn inward, he shoved Morris over the threshold ahead of him.

Morris felt like he was walking into a pit of rattlers when he glanced around the plush car and saw Lars Evanson favor him with a merciless look that made his blood run cold.

"You got real trouble now, you stupid fool!" Sheriff Will said.

Waco reached out and grabbed Morris by his collar to throw him into a chair.

"Not here, you idiot!" Lars yelled. "Take him someplace else. Then when they find him, there'll be no way to trace us to the murder."

The following day Nicki Sue was buying grain at the feed store when Sheriff Will walked in the door and approached her.

"Saw you come into town and I thought this was as good a time as any to speak with you."

She moved around him and picked up her bill for the grain off the counter. "I really don't think we have anything to say to one another unless you have something more on my husband's murderer."

His eyes turned dark and bore an ugly light. "Just come over to my office when you've finished here. Unless you'd rather I come out to your place."

"No—that won't be necessary," Nicki Sue said stiffly. "I'll be there just as soon as I take care of my bill."

The sheriff viewed Nicki Sue with an implacable expression as she walked through the jail house door. His bulky form was squeezed into a swivel chair behind his desk.

"Why don't you just have a seat and make yourself at home."

"Thank you, I'll stand," Nicki replied. "I'm sure whatever we have to discuss won't take that long." She was doing her best to hide her unease, but in the back of her mind she was fearful this meeting might have something to do with Jesse. She was well aware that the citizens were all talking about the latest train robbery. And Charlie Star had stirred up a lot of excitement with his gang of manhunters. There was even a rumor going around that he was fast closing in on the outlaws.

He leaned back in his chair and regarded her closely. "You know a woman like you shouldn't be living way out there on that isolated ranch. The law can't protect you when you're out of reach. Kind of leaves you at the mercy of any hombre that might come along."

"I feel secure there," Nicki Sue was quick to reply. "And I can take care of myself just fine."

"Yeah, well — I don't have any help around here no more. So if something happens, don't you come crying about it to me. I warned you — just you remember — and I won't have time to listen to you then."

"I've never asked for your help before, Sheriff Will. And if I have any complaints, I'll take them to your deputy . . . since he seems the only one truly concerned for law and order in Bodie."

He began to think he just might enjoy seeing her pack them bags and leave town. She had brought him nothing but trouble since she'd come to town. It was time somebody brought the snooty little bitch down a peg or two. And he was going to do just that, later tonight.

"I don't have a deputy anymore to help me out. That bumble butt Morris up and took off on me without nary a word. Puts the whole load on me now. And of course I'm going to be looking out first for the people who show me the most respect."

"Morris is gone?" Nicki couldn't believe what

she'd just heard. The little deputy was devoted to his job; she knew he wouldn't just quit. "Don't you think your deputy's abrupt departure a bit odd?"

"Not considering who we're talking about. He always was a bit touched in the head."

"I would think you'd be out searching for him, Sheriff. Perhaps he met with foul play."

"Don't have the time or the manpower. Everybody is too scared to do anything. They blame every mishap on them train robbers. Some folks think Morris may have run into one of them bandits and come to a bad end. You did hear all about them robbing the PGC again and tangling with Charlie Star not too far from your place?"

"I did hear something to that effect."

Sheriff Will narrowed his eyes. "Guess you never saw hide nor hair of them, though, or you would have come told me about it first thing, right, missy?"

"No, I did not see them," she replied coolly.

"Well, just remember if you do—I'm the one that needs to know about it first. Stay away from that Charlie Star; he's nothing but a troublemaker and couldn't even catch a grasshopper, much less some gang of criminals."

"But you just told me you couldn't be bothered with me," Nicki was bold enough to remind him.

The sheriff sat forward and began fussing with a stack of papers on his desk. He controlled his anger with a great deal of effort. "There's a reward being offered for any information on them, and double if they're captured. It could be split two ways and still leave both parties with a tidy sum."

"I don't need any blood money on my conscience," Nicki told him.

308

He viewed her with an implacable expression. "Money can help ease a lot of misery."

"But I'm not miserable, Sheriff," she was quick to respond. Without a backward glance she turned and marched out of his office.

"Not yet," Sheriff Will grinned cheekily. "But I bet you soon will be."

The sheriff had been thinking about the reward money since Morris was killed. Evanson was beginning to make him nervous with his quest for power and his casual attitude toward murder. The sheriff had never thought of himself as a coward, but after he'd learned what Lars had ordered done to poor Morris, he'd felt a rising fear. He was now an accomplice to a murder. Yet he couldn't have protested killing Morris or Evanson might have seen fit to murder him too. If he was to get out of town and away from Evanson, he had to make it look like he had just disappeared. He could go away somewhere and start over; he'd be free of Evanson. The railroad man's reputation was getting too big; Sheriff Will didn't think he was a good man to be associated with any longer.

At the sound of the door, he glanced up. A tall, imposing man stepped into the room. The sheriff almost groaned aloud. What in the devil did Charlie Star want now?

"Just get back in town?" Sheriff Will inquired evenly.

"About an hour ago," Star replied, allowing his gaze to sweep the room. "Lost valuable time on a wild-goose chase. Heard a rumor the trains robbers were hiding out in Middleton caves, so I had to go check it out."

The slow, thoughtful look that Charlie Star cast

his way made the sheriff's hands begin twitching. He was glad they were in his lap because he had a feeling ole Star didn't miss much of anything.

"Anything I can do for you, Mr. Star?" Sheriff Will inquired.

"Maybe."

"I'll be happy to help; just tell me what it is you need."

Those piercing gray eyes lingered on the sheriff. "Wondered if you'd heard anything about those men jumping some fella last night over by South Pass. Roughed him up real good too—in fact, he's as good as dead, I would say."

Sheriff Will felt his pulse leap, but he tried to reply evenly. "Can't say that I did. My deputy usually fills me in on what's been happening each morning, but he's not around any longer."

"One of my men was riding past that area last night and thought he saw a group of riders dragging a man behind his horse. He fired off several shots, but by the time he had made it down the mountainside, they had disappeared. All he saw was a train pulling away in the distance."

"Ain't that just awful," the sheriff said in mock despair. "Did your man have any idea who the hombres were?"

Charlie Star fixed an obsidian eye on Sheriff Will. "No. That's why I came to you. I thought maybe you might have an idea."

Sheriff Will shook his head. "Sorry to say, I don't."

"If you should happen to hear anything about last night—or, for that matter, who those men tangled with—let me know."

"I certainly will, Mr. Star."

310

Those ice-cold eyes flickered over him with disdain in their depths. "I'm not so sure about that anymore, Will. I'm staying over at Miss Drucell's boardinghouse. Send word — I'll come to you." Just before he left, he added, "Oh, one other thing. If you see Evanson, tell him I'm watching him real close. I don't know why — but I have this gnawing feeling in my belly about that man. There are just too many things that happen when he is around. And I'm not the only one who feels that way. I'll be watching you too, and when you or Evanson make a wrong move, and you will, I'll be there waiting."

"I hardly know the man — hell! His kind don't mingle with town sheriffs."

Charlie was already walking out the door when he suddenly paused and turned to favor the sheriff with a benign smile. "You ride a spotted gelding, don't you, Will?"

"Well . . . yeah . . . most of the time."

Charlie grinned wider. "Thought I seen it a time or two tied up out front of Evanson's private car. Could that have been you?"

The sheriff mumbled some inane response as Star continued onward without waiting to hear his reply. The son of a bitch was on to him! There was no doubt in his mind.

Will sat gazing off into space for a long time recalling the picture that had run in all of the newspapers after Love's bravos captured the outlaw Joaquin Murieta. His hand crept to his neck without his being aware. And unbidden, the gruesome image of Murieta's remains at the mercy of those primitive men taunted him vividly. He made a promise to himself at that moment to do what he must to save his life. He would do the job for

Evanson, and then he was leaving town!

Charlie Star crossed the street from the jail and entered Wong Le's laundry. He didn't hesitate, but walked around the counter past the Orientals bending over steaming vats scrubbing clothes. Wong Le glanced up and, seeing it was Star, indicated with a crisp nod that the person he'd come to meet was already in the supply room waiting.

When Star stepped in the cubicle, which was crowded with barrels of soaps and freshly laundered clothes, the woman greeted him with an anxious look in her eyes. He removed his wide-brimmed hat and took a seat on an empty crate across from her.

Elizabeth Kardel was the first to speak. "Did you learn anything over at Middleton?"

"It was a setup. No one had been in those caves in a long while."

She was relieved, yet disappointed. She had agreed to help this man with his case, but for her own reasons. Elizabeth wanted to learn more about the bandits, and bring an end to Evanson's reign of terror.

Star had been surprised when she'd approached him several days ago and had offered to help him obtain information to solve his case. Normally, Star would have scoffed at the idea of a woman tracking down information for him, but this was no ordinary situation he was dealing with. He was beginning to suspect that the bandit who kept robbing the PGC had a reason, other than gold, to continue to plague Evanson's railroad. And after checking out the description of the men who had robbed the bank at Middleton with some eyewitnesses, Star knew they were not the men he was assigned to capture. The gang he was tracking was good—very good, as a matter of fact—although he hated to admit it even to himself. For the first time in his career, he was beginning to wonder if he would catch them. He fixed his silvery gaze on Elizabeth.

"You know, ma'am, I'm beginning to think there is something more to this bunch of train robbers than ordinary greed. And after sending out some inquiries, I've found out the gang has never robbed anyone else. They only go after Evanson's train. Don't you find that strange?"

"I've done a bit of investigating myself, Mr. Star. And that is why I wanted to speak with you in private. I am beginning to suspect, as you, that the leader may have a vendetta to settle with Evanson. I was able to locate several of the PGC's passengers, and they all agreed that the bandits didn't take a thing from any of them. Most of those reports were instigated by Evanson. It seems he's not beyond bribing people to say what he wishes the public to believe."

Charlie nodded. "I know it. That's the same response I've been getting from some of the passengers. That gang may have started out terrifying the countryside, but now they're turning into regular folk heroes. The gamblers are even placing bets on whether they'll wipe Evanson out before he gets his track laid to the end of the line." He almost smiled, then caught himself. "One of the boys over at the Butterfly Saloon has even written a song and titled it 'The Ballad of the Last-Chance Railroad.' "

"Oh my, I bet Mr. Evanson isn't too happy about that. I know he goes in there a lot to see Cathleen Kramer."

"Never did figure what a woman of her character sees in the likes of him. Maybe it's his money?" Charlie pondered aloud, somewhat disgruntled. He'd had his eye on the charming Miss Kramer since he'd arrive in Bodie, but she wouldn't give him two minutes of her time. Funny, but he was certain he had recognized her from Chicago. Although when he'd asked her, she'd quickly denied ever having been there. He sliced a glance at Mrs. Kardel.

Elizabeth had fallen silent, and Star watched her closely.

"Anything bothering you, ma'am, that you'd like to talk about?"

"No," she replied softly, meeting his eyes. "I just have this feeling that, in the end, Evanson is going to be the man you'll be pursuing for breaking the law."

Charlie sighed deeply. "It's getting more likely every day, ma'am," he admitted.

"One other thing," Elizabeth said. "I want you to know that I'll be leaving town for a while. I'm going to make a few inquiries into Evanson's background, perhaps visit some of the areas where his railroad has expanded."

"Do be careful, ma'am," Star warned. "There is a whole lot about that man I don't trust."

"I will," she assured him as she prepared to leave, then almost lost her calm when she heard him ask bluntly, "Forgive me, ma'am, but I've had something on my mind all day."

"What's that, Mr. Star?"

"You wouldn't be doing this because your last name is Kardel, would you?"

Elizabeth managed to maintain her composure.

"Why would you even suggest such a thing?" she returned.

Star withdrew a timepiece from his vest pocket and made a pretense out of winding it. He extended his hand and held the watch before her. "The bandit leader dropped this at the site of one of the robberies. Nice-looking watch, isn't it?"

"Yes, it is," she replied carefully.

"There are initials inside — J.K. It seems his mother must have cared for him an awful lot to have given him such a fine watch."

She didn't blink an eyelash as she stared the agent right in the eyes. "What mother doesn't love her son, no matter what side of the law he is on?"

Chapter Sixteen

When Nicki first woke and smelled the smoke, she lay there for a moment confused. And when she padded from the bed to the window and saw that it was not yet morning, but that there was a bright glow in the distance, she was even more puzzled. She was rousted from her languid state when one word flashed through her thoughts—fire!

Her only thought was to save the horses stabled there; grabbing up a robe, she pulled it on and went running from her room into the hallway, screaming for Maria. Pounding on the woman's door, she yelled.

"Wake up, Maria! I need your help!"

The woman threw open her door, her expression one of concern as she tied the sash around her robe. "What is the matter?"

"The stable's on fire! Hurry, Maria, we have to see if we can put it out!"

By the time the two women were dashing out the front door, Pablo was hurrying to meet them. His face was ashen, and he was shaking all over. Nicki Sue grabbed hold of his arms.

"Where's Marty? We need everyone's help."

"He's already there, Señora—he went inside the

stable to try and save some of the horses. I thought I'd better come wake you. . . . We may not be able to save them all," he finished with an anguished sob.

"Oh, this is terrible," Maria moaned, and stood with her hands clenched before her.

Nicki was immediately catapulted into action.

"Grab up those buckets at the trough," she ordered both of them. "We can't just stand here without doing something!"

By the time that they reached the stable with the buckets of water, it was already a raging inferno. It was too late to try and save anything but the horses.

"Give me your shawl," she told Maria, then added that she wanted Pablo and Maria to wait outside and try and guide the horses that she and Marty were able to save into the nearby corral. She threw a bucket of water on the shawl and, pushing her tumbled hair back off her forehead, draped it over her head. "They'll be spooked, but try and manage them as best as you can. If they head for the open range, they might keep running until they drop."

"*Sí*, I will do what I can," Maria promised.

"Please be careful," Pablo added, his expression one of grave concern.

They could hear the roaring flames devouring the dry structure, and the crashing of lumber as it fell to the floor. The screams of the horses were chilling, and Nicki didn't think she would ever forget the sound of their terror.

Pablo reached out and took hold of Nicki's hand. "I will go instead, señora; you should not go in there."

"No, I can't ask you to do that. It's hard enough to think that Marty is in there and may not come out, without my worrying about anyone else. I want the horses saved, but not at the expense of human lives."

She had moved away from him and was running into the blazing structure before Pablo could say anything else. Maria was sobbing softly behind them. All they could do now was pray.

Jesse was just riding away from the cabin when he caught a glimpse of a man on horseback racing across Ryan land, his mustang stretched out in a full gallop. And even though it was still not daybreak, Jesse knew by his form who it was.

"What is Sheriff Will doing out here on Nicki's land?" he murmured to himself, and then wondered why the man looked as if the hounds of hell were after him. His gaze skimming past the sheriff, Jesse saw that there wasn't anyone following him.

Something told him to go after him, that Sheriff Will had not been at Los Paraiso paying a social call. He urged Max into a gallop and was quickly in pursuit. Max's long legs covered the distance between them in no time.

Too late, the sheriff glanced back over his shoulder and saw the rider gaining on him. he didn't know who the man was, but he knew if he caught up with him, he was in a lot of trouble. For what explanation could he give for being here, and the stable that was on fire at this moment? Terrified, he whipped out his six-shooter and fired off several wild shots in rapid succession.

Angered by the unprovoked attack, Jesse withdrew his rifle from his saddle scabbard and fired two shots over the sheriff's head. He didn't want to hit him; he just wanted to warn him that he could if he chose to.

Sheriff Will heard nothing but the bullets zinging over his head and the sound of his own heart pounding with fright in his chest. It was miserable terrain to ride through. The rising sun was just cresting the rough, boulder-strewn mountain when he cut his horse to the right and up a narrow trail — and then cursed the fates when he saw where it had led him. A dead end! Nothing but a yawning gap of sky about fifteen feet across and the flat mountaintop on the other side. He sawed at his horse's reins and brought him to a jerking halt.

The spotted mustang pranced restlessly beneath him, seeming to sense the urgency of the moment. He was winded, and his coat lathered with sweat. The sheriff swung his head around, caught a quick glimpse of the horse and rider coming up the trail and the sunlight glinting off the barrel of his rifle. He had no choice but to turn and take a stand. He jerked his horse about to face the approaching rider with drawn gun.

Jesse rode Max in slowly, his rifle cocked and ready in his hand. He was tense and expecting anything. "Don't make me kill you, Sheriff," he said sharply, able now to make out the scared light in Will's eyes, and never certain when a man was this far gone just what he might do.

"What are you going to do?" the sheriff demanded in a tremulous voice. He had assumed that Jesse was one of the Ryan ranch hands.

Jesse kept the rifle at his hip aimed and ready to fire. "Something tells me you've been up to no good. I think we'll just go over to the ranch house and see if everything checks out all right."

"I . . . never started that fire. . . . It wasn't me," the sheriff suddenly began babbling, a mad expression in his gaze.

Jesse's eyes slitted like a stalking puma. "Mister, you'd better get that horse moving in the direction of the ranch or I just might go and lose my temper—and I don't think you want me to do that."

Sheriff Will froze, his hand on the grip. If he pulled the trigger, he knew he'd be a dead man, for he could see it in the stranger's eyes. But he'd be a dead man anyway if they brought him in and Lars Evanson was informed.

"Drop the gun," Jesse said fiercely.

"Come get it!" Will growled, and lifted his gun to take aim.

Jesse's reflexes were smooth and lightning-fast. He fired the rifle from the hip, and the bullet sent the sheriff's gun cartwheeling crazily over the side of the mountain.

The sheriff, realizing his error too late, clutched his bleeding hand, his face a mask of pain. "I won't come with you. . . . I can't," he screamed, and before Jesse could move to stop him, he'd spurred his horse toward the open chasm before them.

"No! You stupid fool!" Jesse yelled as he watched the spotted mustang leap through the air in a valiant attempt to clear the gaping distance and land safely on the other side.

The horse screamed almost in outrage as he cleared the distance but caught one of his back hooves on a twisted root protruding from the mountainside. It upset his balance, throwing his weight to one side and unseating the sheriff.

Sheriff Will did his best to stay in the saddle, but his bulky weight was too much for the cinch to endure, and it snapped, sending the screaming man plunging through empty space, his hands grasping at thin air.

Without the burdensome weight, the mustang was able to scramble to safety, and the last Jesse saw of him, he was grazing peacefully on lush mountain grass. All thoughts of leaving Nicki were forgotten. Spurring forward, Jesse sent Max galloping down the mountain trail and in the direction of the ranch.

Inside the stable it was a hellish scene. Marty had managed to get the last two horses out of their stalls and, coughing violently, his eyes burning from the acrid smoke, had led them safely out of the stable. They had been fortunate that the worst flames were centered in the back hayloft. But Marty was certain that at any minute the entire upper structure would come tumbling down. He had caught a glimpse of Nicki struggling with the stallion Storm, and knew that he had to go back inside and help her. Hearing Maria give a sharp cry, he looked up to see half the roof crashing inward in voluminous, billowing flames.

"Take the horses!" he screamed to Pablo over the roar of the blaze. "I've got to try and save her!"

Pablo grabbed the terrified animal by the halter, doing his best to stay out of the way of his sharp, prancing hooves. Maria rushed to grab the mare Kyra as she leaped to safety over the flames raging in the doorway. The horses were frightened, but they'd been saved. Without a word, Marty plunged back into the stable to do his best to help Nicki

When Jesse arrived upon the scene and saw the stable enveloped in flames and Pablo holding a sobbing Maria in his arms, with Nicki Sue nowhere to be seen, his first thought was that she had been killed in the fire.

Pablo didn't ask him who he was or where he had come from; he just began begging for Jesse to help the señora and Marty, who as yet had not come out of the stable.

Jesse swung fluidly from the saddle, grabbed his duster from his gear, and hurriedly swept it through the water trough before he put it over himself and ran toward the burning structure sending black smoke billowing into the pink morning sky. He had never really been scared before in his life, not even the night Allison had been killed, because everything had happened so quickly. But he'd ridden back here knowing somehow what he would find. He'd thought of Nicki trying to save her horses and losing her life instead, and every muscle in his body had urged Max onward to a faster pace. He ran blindly through the searing, raging flames, knowing once he was inside, his chances weren't very good of coming out alive. But he had to save her!

The intense heat and smoke almost drove him back, it was so overwhelming. Only the thought of Nicki Sue lying trapped and helpless as the flames crept toward her made him forge ahead. He heard a feeble cry for help; and his body quivered in reaction. She was alive! She was alive!

"Over here . . . help us . . . help us . . . ," Nicki cried from where she lay helplessly pinned beneath

322

a fallen beam.

Jesse had barely heard her above the deafening roar of the blistering flames. He knew he had to hurry before the rest of the top floor caved in upon them.

Marty was beside her, doing his best to keep the stallion from accidentally trampling Nicki, who appeared injured and barely conscious.

"Thank God, someone to help us," Marty cried. His face was burned and blackened by the smoke, but his only concern at the moment was for Nicki Sue.

"I'm here, sweetheart. You'll be fine; just hang on," Jesse told her as he worked quickly to save her.

"Don't let me die, Jess . . . please—not like this," she pleaded.

"Sh . . . nobody is going to die," he reassured her.

Jesse saw that an overhead beam was blocking the door of the stall and also lay partially across Nicki, who had been hurled by its force into a corner of the stall. She knew her situation was critical, and her eyes beseeched him for help. He went a little crazy thinking that she might be burned alive in this inferno. Not even realizing what he did, he grasped the fiery end of the beam and threw it aside. He had freed her! Turning quickly to Marty, he yelled, "I will take Nicki; you get the stallion to safety!"

Marty nodded and grasping Nicki's shawl, managed to secure it over the terrified animal's eyes. It was still not easy, but finally he was able to lead the stallion from the stall. Behind him, Jesse was carrying Nicki Sue in his arms.

She clung tightly to him as cramplike pains

wracked her body. There had not been time to think about it before — everything had happened too fast, and she'd only done what she knew she had to. But now, feeling the roiling waves of pain centered in her abdomen, she knew the child she carried was in jeopardy.

"Jesse . . . I think I might be losing the baby," she gasped, biting down on her bottom lip.

He hadn't even suspected that she was pregnant! Nicki was carrying his child, and now might lose it. Why had she gone into the burning stable if she had suspected she was pregnant?

"We're almost at the house, Nicki, and then you'll be fine." He tried to offer her what encouragement he could, but he didn't know about these matters. A doctor! She needed medical attention. Noticing Maria hurrying along beside them, he cast her a harried look.

"She needs a doctor; do you know of one?

Maria was crying openly, for she'd heard the señora's anguished plea for her unborn child's life and knew there wasn't a doctor in miles. "There is no doctor, señor. The only one in a hundred miles is in Bodie. And that would take hours."

"You're right, there isn't time. I'm going to need your help," he told Maria. "Get hot water and clean cloths and bring them to her room."

Jesse carried Nicki through the front door of the house and took her to the bedroom that Maria had indicated before she'd bustled toward the kitchen.

Nicki was barely conscious when he gently laid her on the bed. Her face was drawn in severe pain, and her arms immediately grasped her abdomen. She moaned, and sweat rolled down her face as she grimaced with intense pain.

"Don't let me lose the baby, Jesse. . . . Please help me." Her small hand reached for his.

"I'll do everything I can," Jesse murmured encouragingly, taking her fingers within his and squeezing them reassuringly.

She was dazed and afraid, but her eyes continually held his, as though she took strength from his being near her.

If the housekeeper thought it strange that Nicki moaned Jesse's name throughout her ordeal and clung to his hand, refusing to let him leave the room, the kindly woman chose to keep her opinions to herself. She did not know who the stranger was, but there was no doubt he had been the father of the señora's child. It puzzled Maria, but being a woman of many years and experiences, she put it from her mind, for she knew the señora must love this man very much to want their child so badly.

Jesse, with Maria's help, did everything that he could to prevent Nicki from losing the child. He had sent Maria to fetch his saddlebags, then withdrew a small pouch and handed it to her.

"Boil the herbs with some tea and then bring it to me."

When Maria had glanced suspiciously at the elaborately beaded buckskin pouch of Mojave design, he had sternly reminded her that time was of the essence now. She'd hurried from the room to do his bidding.

Jesse had held Nicki's head and tried to spoon as much of the tea in her mouth as she would allow. Half-delirious with pain, she lashed out at him with her hands, and finally he'd gotten Maria to hold on to her arms. He was skeptical about saving the baby, but at least the herbs would help prevent her from hemorrhaging, which was what he was most concerned about now.

The next few hours were critical, and during that time Jesse and Maria did all that was humanly possible to save Nicki and her unborn child. But when it was over, only Nicki could be saved. Maria tenderly bathed Nicki and dressed her in a clean gown before removing the soiled bedclothes.

"You'd better let me take care of your burns, señor," she offered, smiling gently at the man slumped in a chair beside the bed.

He did not even look up at her, but kept his eyes trained anxiously on Nicki, who was sleeping.

"I'll take care of it later; thanks anyway, ma'am."

"Sí, I will leave you now," she replied.

Maria had given Nicki some laudanum at the last, to ease her pain and help her to rest, for she had been through a terrible ordeal, and only sleep could help her to recover now. She offered now to sit with Nicki so that he could rest too, but he shook his head.

"No, I'll be just fine here. When she wakes up . . . she's going to ask questions, and I want to be the one to answer them for her."

Maria could see he was dreading the moment. And also that Nicki would be inconsolable when she learned that she had miscarried. Maria knew what that was like; she had lost her first child when she had been four months pregnant. Sighing sadly, she told the man Nicki had called Jesse that she would be in the kitchen if he should need anything.

Just as soon as Maria stepped out into the hallway, Jesse could hear her explaining to a desperately concerned Marty that Mrs. Ryan would recover from her injuries. She said nothing about Nicki's miscarriage, and if Marty had overheard Nicki's earlier words to Jesse, he did not mention it now.

He watched Nicki closely, studying the small, helpless figure lying beneath the covers, her face streaked with burns and her eyes swollen from crying. He could understand why she had gone into the burning stable to try and save the horses, but why hadn't she told him three nights ago, when they had been so close, that she thought she was carrying his child? Had she assumed he would be angry with her? Did she think their child would not matter to him? Or was it that she thought it would not matter to him more than his shadowy past and the restless spirit within him that drove him to wander? He would have taken great pride in their child, and even now in thinking about what might have been, felt like cursing the ghosts of the past that were certain to take him away from her once again.

It was late at night when Nicki stirred and moaned softly. Immediately Jesse was by her side reaching for her hand.

"I . . . lost . . . our baby . . . didn't I?" she asked, her eyes searching his as she tried to fight back the tears.

Her lips were bloodless and her words barely audible, but he had heard, and knew he must answer her. He wished he could wipe out the agony he knew she was feeling in her heart, but he had forgotten how to comfort, he had lived so long with his own bitter hatred. He would never forget his terror at seeing her trapped in that burning stable, or hearing her sob pitifully when she knew she was losing the baby. It brought back the memories of his helplessness the night Allison had cried out for his help, and him watching, powerless, as she died in his arms. And the same thing might have occurred again tonight. He shuddered just thinking about it.

"Yes . . . but you're going to be fine." He kissed her fingertips, then sat down on the bed next to her.

She was reaching for him then, wanting to be cradled in the security of his arms and have him banish the hurt away. He held her against him and allowed her to draw the strength she needed. At last she breathed a ragged sigh and drew away to lie back and stare up at him.

"I'm sorry. . . . I wanted to give you a child . . . to make up for . . . the past." A sob escaped her. "But now . . . that won't happen."

He knew she could have no idea that even a child of their flesh could not completely heal the wounds of the past. They had cut too deeply.

"Shhh," he soothed, "what happened wasn't your fault." Within him he felt as if he had somehow failed Nicki in the same way that he had Allison. He should have killed Evanson a long time ago, quickly, cleanly, without dragging out his agony to satisfy his own need for revenge.

"Jesse . . . please don't leave. . . . Say you will stay?" She tried hard to keep her eyes from closing before she received his answer, but she was so tired from her ordeal, and the laudanum, that she drifted off before his hoarse reply.

"This has to be good-bye, Tiger Eyes. I'm no good for you, and the sooner you forget me, the better off you'll be."

When he first heard the throated call of the crow, he was reaching for his guns where he'd tossed them into a chair earlier, and was strapping them on. His head came up and his nostrils flared wide. He waited, holding his breath, and the same call repeated itself. It was Dakotah, and the message must be urgent for him to have come back. He left the chair, boots scraping softly across the plank floor as he crossed the room and stood by the bed, considering the woman lying there.

For a long moment he studied her every feature, as if putting them to memory, where he might draw upon them in the months to come. Leaning over her, he lowered his head and kissed her on the lips. When he straightened, his face had settled into the familiar hard, cold mask.

Dakotah was waiting in back of the house near the corrals. He saw Jesse step off the porch and came out from behind the corncrib.

"It's good to see you. I didn't know what to think when I saw the burned-out stable." He met Jesse's frown. "I'm glad I found you."

"Why did you come back?" Jesse asked.

"It's Bo. I think some of Evanson's men jumped him after he left here. I found evidence of a struggle along the trail you told your brother to follow."

"I didn't think he would go that far," Jesse growled. "But then, I never figured he'd have the sheriff try and burn Nicki out either."

"Is that what happened to the stable?"

"Yes." Jesse briefly explained how he'd chased the sheriff down on Nicki's land and how the man had met his death. "So you see, there are a lot of lives at stake, and it's up to us to stop Evanson before any more people are killed."

Dakotah looked grim, but determined. "I think we should start looking at Evanson's private coach.

It's not too far from here." His eyes locked with Jesse's. "Will your woman be all right without you to look after her?"

"She has some good people here to take care of her. It's better this way, and I always did hate good-byes." His eyes fired with the usual dark glitter of hatred whenever he thought of Evanson. "My brother is the one who needs me the most right now. It's time for me to think like your people, Dakotah, and to exact my revenge in the same way."

They were to find out, when they went to the train tracks where they had last sighted the PGC, that it had left. There were no work crews laying new rails, not a sign of any progress that day to be seen. The driving hammers and iron spikes lay beside the heavy wooden beams used to support the rail sections.

"What do you make of it?" Dakotah asked Jesse as they viewed the deserted work area.

Jesse's face was clouded with indecision. What should he do now? He realized then there could only be one way to save Bo. "The bastard! Somehow he knew we'd be coming after him!"

"I suspect the sheriff's horse must have returned to the stables and caused quite a stir. Evanson had enough time to get out of town before we could stop him."

Frustrated anger prompted Jesse to whirl, whip his gun from the holster and with lightning speed, and empty the chamber into the massive railroad beams. Then, holstering his pistol, he snarled angrily. "I'll find him, Dakotah, and when I do, he'll have no place left to run."

Cathleen Kramer heard the rumor that Sheriff Will had been on the take before most of the good citizens. Leroy Culpepper had come bustling in to work after having just visited with Bones Benton, the town undertaker. Leroy was out of wind and desperate to tell his news. He took several fortifying gulps of air and motioned for Cathleen to leave her bookwork and join him at the bar.

Cathleen had been sitting by the front window, enjoying the morning breeze drifting under the swinging doors and thinking about the dinner engagement she had tonight with Lars Evanson. He had invited her to dine with him in his private car, and this had surprised her since he'd never done that before. Of course, he couldn't have with Krystal King underfoot so much. Cathleen could only assume that at least for tonight, she would not be around.

"My goodness, Leroy, you're going to choke to death if you don't take a minute to calm down," she commented, walking over to stand before the bar.

"You aren't gonna believe this," he blurted excitedly, "but it's the God's truth. Sheriff Will is layin' dead on a slab over at Bones's place. Tumbled over a mountain ledge into Devil's Canyon." He clucked to himself, then rambled. "Flatter than a flapjack — must have broke every bone in his body."

Leroy's vivid description made Cathleen shudder. "That's awful! Of course, we all figured something horrible might have happened when his horse came back to the stable without him."

"Bones said some miner found the sheriff's body at the bottom of Devil's Canyon. I wouldn't doubt if they don't find that poor fool Morris dead somewhere too."

"Do they have any idea how Sheriff Will fell?"

"No, guess they're just gonna scratch it up as an accident. Bones is overworked as it is. He just decks 'em out and plants 'em under. This here town is the fightin'est, dyin'est place you'd ever want to see. I don't know who we're gonna get for sheriff now."

Cathleen didn't know either, but she felt certain that Lars Evanson would find someone to take the job.

It was then she decided she must speed up her fact gathering before Lars Evanson quite literally raped this town like he had the others and went on to gain another victory. Cathleen knew she wasn't going to allow that to happen. She was trained to examine the facts, sum them up, and derive conclusions. Until several years ago, she had been content with the knowledge that she would graduate from law school, reside in Chicago, and set up her practice. But of course, all of that had changed because of Evanson, although he had no way of knowing that — or knowing of the past that linked their lives.

Her dreams of a law practice had been set aside, for her tutelage as a criminal attorney must be used in a different way now. She began a mind file: gathering, sorting, and documenting. And soon she would begin Lar Evanson's trial.

Chapter Seventeen

Nicki Sue's recovery was rapid and uneventful. Ten days after Jesse had walked out of her life, she was ready to resume some of her activities. Although Maria was doing all that she could to keep Nicki confined to the house and away from the grim ruins of the stable, Nicki had felt a need for some fresh air and insisted she was going outside.

Maria fussed like a mother hen, for she knew that Marty and Pablo were presently tearing down what remained of the stable, and she felt a need to shelter Nicki from the sight of the destruction.

"Why don't you stay inside. I'll make us some tea and we can add another square to the quilt you've been working on," Maria encouraged persuasively.

"I'm *going* outside," Nicki insisted. "I can't run away from my problems, Maria." Nor can I forget the way he held me so tenderly when I was hurt and needed him to keep the heartache away. But obviously Jesse can. He left me without even saying good-bye.

"Then at least let me fix a place for you where you can sit in the yard beneath the shade tree," Maria coaxed.

"That would be nice, thank you," Nicki Sue replied with a brief smile.

With the cool evening breeze blowing across her face, Nicki sat and observed Marty and Pablo tear down the shell of the burned-out stable. Watching them, viewing the charred lumber and the remains of the stable, she felt an anger building within her. Thinking back over all the events, she knew now beyond any doubt that Lars Evanson was the force behind the fire, and Patrick's murder. There was no doubt in her mind any longer. Even Meg had tried to warn her that he would stop at nothing to see his railroad completed. He wanted her land for his own gains, his own town, and the power he would realize. He didn't care how many lives he had to destroy to obtain it.

Nicki Sue was more determined than ever to stay and fight him. And she would do so in the only way he understood. Staring at the devasation, she vowed with fierce determination to survive by his rules.

"I'll make you regret having tried to defeat me."

She was utterly drained of emotions and no longer wished to think about the past. Physically, she knew she would recover—the discreet physician who had come to examine her had assured her she would be fine: the burns were healing nicely and would not leave any scars, and she would be able to bear other children—however, emotionally, Nicki didn't think she would ever again be the same. She had allowed Jesse to invade her life, trample her heart, and use her to satisfy his own needs; then he had left her without a care to resume his outlaw ways.

Nicki instinctively knew that Jesse was involved in the sheriff's death. She could only assume that he had been leaving that night when he had discovered the sheriff fleeing the scene of the fire and had chased him into Devil's Canyon. The fact that Jesse had come back to help her, and had saved her life, never entered into her reasoning. She no longer deluded herself about Jesse. He hated Evanson with such consuming intensity that there was no room in his heart for any other emotion.

When night fell, Marty and Pablo came over to join her. Maria brought them glasses of chilled cider, and they discussed rebuilding the stable.

"You've done a fine job running the ranch," Nicki praised both men. "I can't thank you enough. I'll always remember your loyalty."

"I wish we could have done more," Pablo said, staring remorsefully into his glass.

"Hey! you aren't trying to tell me and Pablo adios, are you?" Marty favored her with a mock glare.

"Well, there isn't going to be any money for a while." Nicki thought she'd tell them straight out how things stood.

"Marty and I won't leave you, señora," Pablo stated firmly.

"We did manage to save all the horses," Marty reminded her, "and they should bring in enough money to begin building a new stable."

"If I can get them to market as soon as possible," Nicki said. "There's no sense deluding ourselves. That isn't going to be easy. And I don't have any money to ship them to Sacramento in order to obtain the best price."

Marty grunted. "That is a problem, but maybe we should just see if we can find a buyer in Bodie. We might have to take a bit of a loss, but at least there'll be cash available right away."

Nicki answered quickly and with a tired sigh. "I can't afford to absorb any more losses. I'll sleep on it." She rose from her chair and turned to the two men with a grateful smile. "I can't tell you how much you both mean to me. I'll see you in the morning."

It was while she was rummaging through her bureau drawer for her nightgown that she happened to turn suddenly, feeling as if someone was watching her, and gasped when she saw the Indian staring in at her through the open window, his brown face in startling contrast to the lacy curtains fluttering at the window. Her heart began a hammering beat. He stared at her for several seconds without trying to communicate, and then he seemed to vanish into the dark night. She had no idea who he was, but she knew without a doubt why he had come. Jesse had sent him. She did not even consider the fact that he might be concerned about her. Nothing could ease the bitterness she felt for him now.

Faithful Maria had told Cathleen when she'd met her at church that Sunday that Señora Ryan had been injured in the stable fire when she'd been trying to save her beautiful horses.

"I am worried that the señora will lose the ranch if she is not able to sell the horses soon," she had gone on to tell Nicki's concerned friend. "And now with no shelter for them, she must sell them right away. Poor little one, that will probably mean she will not get as much money for them as she had hoped."

Cathleen had gone to the town hall meeting that night and explained Nicki Ryan's circumstances. It was unanimously agreed that they would have a barn raising at the Ryan ranch just as soon as it could be organized. After much discussion it was enthusiastically agreed that they would all gather at the Ryan ranch that very weekend. Everyone would bring food and items to sell for chance, they'd have music, and there was even a committee appointed to solicit materials from area merchants.

Sugar Drucell announced that the Bodie ladies' quilting circle would donate their quilts to be sold for chances to raise additional funds. Everyone was surprised by Sugar's generosity, but there were a few who knew she'd do anything to have the opportunity to snoop around Mrs. Ryan's ranch. She was the type of woman who never did anything for anyone unless she stood to gain something in return. And the idea of an entire day of gossiping with her neighbors always warmed her heart.

"I'd like to be the one to tell Mrs. Ryan, if that's all right," Cathleen Kramer had stood up and said. She thought it would be best if Nicki heard the news from her. She didn't add that she suspected there was more troubling her friend than the loss of her stable. She'd gone out to the ranch the day after she'd heard the news about the fire, but was told that Mrs. Ryan wasn't up to receiving visitors yet. And when she'd stopped to chat with Pablo beside the charred remains of the corral, he'd indicated that he also thought there was something more troubling Mrs. Ryan.

"I have never seen her like this," he had explained. "She is different somehow, not like the same woman."

"How do you mean?" Cathleen had probed.

He'd stood there thinking and then he'd replied.

337

"She is very bitter over the fire. We know it could not have been an accident, and the man who was here that night helping us agreed."

"A man was here? Who was he?"

Pablo tossed a blackened post into the back of the wagon. "Some stranger, although I wondered about that because he seemed to know the señora very well. He saved her life, you know. Pulled her out of the burning rubble, stayed until she was out of danger, and then rode off." He shrugged. "I never thought much about who he was; I was just glad he showed up when he did."

"Yes, I suppose that is the important thing." But Cathleen could not put Pablo's disclosure out of her mind. There were too many unanswered questions concerning many things. And now a mysterious fire that had almost killed Nicki.

When Cathleen came to the ranch with the news of the barn raising, Maria convinced Nicki Sue to see her. She thought it would help lift the young woman's spirits.

When they were seated in the parlor, Cathleen began to explain what had been suggested at the town hall meeting and was taken aback when Nicki blurted heatedly,

"Why are they offering to do this?"

"I . . . suppose because they care about you and wish to help," Cathleen explained perplexed; then, frowning, she asked, "What is wrong?"

"What do you mean?"

"You're upset over more than the loss of the stable, I can feel it." She viewed Nicki silently, then added, "Is there anything you'd like to talk about?"

Nicki opened her mouth to speak, then shook her head. "No . . . there isn't a thing. And if everyone would like to help rebuild the stable, then that's fine with me. However, I will not take charity. If each merchant will keep an accounting, I'll pay them just as soon as I sell some of my horses."

"You are a stubborn woman, Nicki Ryan," Cathleen said calmly.

"Yes, I am," Nicki replied as pleasantly as possible. "But I have to be, don't you see? It's all I have left to hold on to." A hint of bitterness had crept into her voice, but Cathleen did not appear to have noticed.

He wasn't dead, but Robert Bodine was beginning to wonder why he had fought so hard to stay alive. For the past weeks — or was it days? . . . he didn't know anymore — he had been a prisoner in this cattle car. Evanson's thugs had dumped him here after they'd finished with him.

How he'd survived the torture of being dragged behind his horse for so many miles, he did not know. There had been times when he'd blacked out, awakening when unbearable pain seeped through his unconscious state. Several of his ribs had been cracked, and his face swelled up so badly that he couldn't eat for days.

Evanson had him beaten regularly, seeking the location of the other gang members and exacting his own revenge. Robert Bodine refused to tell them anything, but they were determined he would. Evanson only stopped short of killing him because they weren't ready to let him die just yet. Besides the brutality inflicted upon him, the stench and the heat had been unbearable in the beginning; and the previous four-legged occupants had left reminders of their stay that made the accommodations less than desirable.

His tormentors believed he was the leader of the train robbers, and he hadn't bothered to tell them any different. He figured just as soon as Jesse showed up, they were in for a real surprise; he didn't want to spoil it, and just thinking about it kept him from going mad.

Last night they'd dragged him from a sound sleep out into the cool darkness. He'd felt revived until they'd looped rawhide around his wrists and strung him up beneath a tree. There was no escaping the blows they pounded into him. Blessedly, he had passed out, and fearing they had killed him, the men quickly cut him down.

"He can't die until he tells us who he is and where we can find the rest of his men, and the gold they've stolen from me," he heard Evanson growl. "Throw him back in the car, and don't go near him unless I instruct you to."

"If we keep him around here much longer, boss, somebody is going to discover him." Waco was anxious to get as far away from Bodie as he possibly could. He didn't want to be around if that gang showed up and found this man in the shape he was in. And Lars's current lady was getting mighty snoopy when the boss wasn't around. He hadn't said anything about it to Lars yet, but Waco had caught her going through the boss's desk yesterday when she'd thought no one was around. She had quickly shut the drawer when he'd come into the car, but her eyes had revealed her guilt. What had she been looking for?

Evanson's lips lifted in a jeering smile. "Getting nervous, Waco? Well, you can breath easier. I've decided we are going to put our friend where he won't be found. He can die there, for all I give a damn. Just get some names out of him first."

Robert Bodine awoke in the morning to the movement of the train and the blood pounding through his ears. His entire body exploded in pain when he moved. God, how much more of this could he take? They were traveling to another destination again. He lay there in the filthy straw and stared through the cracks of the boards. A cool, sweet morning breeze with the scent of wildflowers taunted his nostrils as the train picked up speed. And it rumbled on throughout the long, blistering day, stopping at last when the air he breathed was thin and the sun was setting behind the towering mountains. Sitting up, he wrapped his arms around his knees and bowed his head. It was then he heard the sharp sound of a car being uncoupled, and the roar of the engine as it gained speed and pulled away.

They were leaving him here! Scrambling on hands and knees, he pressed his face against the rough, weathered boards to look through the cracks again. There were three men left to stand guard. The man he'd come to know as Waco, and two others who were free with their fists. Waco was telling them to get a fire going and put on some coffee. He sat back on his bedroll and watched them work.

Frustrated, Robert Bodine hit his fist against the wall. Damn Evanson! How was Jesse going to find him?

* * *

The Mojaves were accustomed to traveling great distances to make war on their enemies. They endured the hardships of these journeys without complaint because for generations their people had eagerly conducted expeditions across country simply to satisfy their sense of curiosity about unknown lands and people.

Dakotah Smith and his people generally made their home along the lower Colorado River in California. There weren't very many of them left to roam the land anymore. Most of the Mojaves lived on the Fort Mojave or Fort Yuma reservation. Although they had a strong sense of tribal identity and a reputation for ferocity, there had not been any direct attacks on white settlers in many years. The old ones said the way of battle and fighting that had made the Mojaves feared from the Rio Grande to the sea would be no more. Civilization had come to the West.

Yet this small tribe of fifty would once again make war on their enemy. They were patient as they waited for the time to pick up their bows and war arrows. Their attack would be silent, but no less deadly.

Doris Smith stood with her youngest child in her arms in the doorway of the brush wickiup and watched her husband tie a war bridle on the jaw of his pony. She had dark hair and blue eyes, and was quick with a sunny smile. But today her face bore an expression of concern and frustration. For days they had been scouring the countryside around Bodie and in the mountains along the tracks for a sign of Lars Evanson's train. Today one of their scouts had returned to relay a message from her brother, Jesse, that had given them their first lead.

342

The PGC had returned to Bodie, and they assumed work would resume on the rails again.

The men who would ride with Dakotah were a distinct class of warriors the Mojaves called Kwanamis. Their specialty was warfare, and Dakotah shared this special title with them. The Mojave raiding party was divided into three classes: archers, clubbers, and stickmen (who carried feathered lances).

"We ride at dawn," Dakotah had told the others. "Our brother will be waiting for us to join him."

Doris shared mixed feelings about this. She had heard enough about Evanson through the years to know he was the deadliest of enemies. But they had come too far to turn back now. Every second lost now meant her brother's life might end at any moment. She'd put away the lovely watch her mother had given her last Christmas, for she didn't wish to constantly be reminded of the minutes ticking past.

"Where are you going to meet Jesse and the others?" she asked her husband.

He slung a bow across his back and stuck several lethal-looking arrows into his bow quiver. "By the old stamp mill just after dark. He'll be taking the ore trail down from the mountains."

"I will ride to meet you after you have rescued my brother," Doris stated with quiet firmness.

Dakotah didn't respond immediately, but stood with his back to her, adjusting the gear on his pony's back. Then he said, "I suppose you have that right. Be ready in three days. We will be home by sundown."

"I'll be ready," she said.

He swung up onto his mount.

"Be careful, my husband," she said, her eyes fixing him with a burning intensity that he understood.

Few words needed to be spoken between them; she knew he always understood how she felt, although she never got used to having to conceal her emotions in front of the others. She was a warm, loving woman whose life revolved around her husband and family. But Dakotah would not appreciate any open sign of affection from her now. He was getting ready to ride into battle with a raiding party of braves whose influence among their fellow tribesmen was unequaled. The wife of a Kwanamis warrior was content with her prestigious place in the Indian society. She tended their home, raised the children, and helped farm the land. And when her warrior went off to battle, she was there to see him off with quiet dignity.

After Dakotah and the others had ridden off, Doris gathered her two young children close and sat before the fire to recite the prayers her mother had taught her years ago. In that, she had not changed. She was still her mother's daughter.

"It's good to see you again, Brave Eagle," Jesse told the chief of the Mojave raiding party. Dakotah had brought his tribesmen to the old stamp mill as he had promised.

The fierce-looking party of braves was garbed in narrow breechclouts and moccasins. White-tipped feathers dangled from their scalp locks, and colorful tattoos were etched on their bronze arms and legs. They were a handsome group of twenty warriors, whom Jesse had ridden with many times in the past. But that had been years earlier, before he began riding the outlaw trails. They sat around the campfire just watching for the moon to rise high in the black sky. There was food prepared and eaten, and conversation in quiet voices.

"It has been too long, my friend," Brave Eagle returned, his black eyes searching Jesse's face carefully. "I asked your brother, Dakotah, if our people had offended you in any way that would keep you from visiting our village."

"No, your people are not to blame for my absence," Jesse was quick to explain. "I have been fulfilling a promise to someone made long ago."

The two men spoke at length as people do who have not seen each other in some time. Finally the chief set down his pipe and turned to Jesse.

"What can Brave Eagle and his people do to help you?" he inquired unhesitatingly.

"The man I have been chasing for many years has taken my brother prisoner. I don't even know if he is alive or not. I can only hope that he is." Jesse nodded his head in the direction of the vast mountain range that stretched for miles before them. Kneeling in the dust beside the firelight, he drew a finger along the line he'd drawn for railroad tracks. "This is the place where I believe my brother is being held captive. I was searching the area higher up when I saw the smoke from a campfire. Looking below the ledge I was on, I saw three armed men standing guard in front of a railroad car. I have a strong suspicion my brother is in that car. I know if I don't get the drop on all three of them at the same time, they'll kill my brother before I can get to him."

"We will go to this place," Brave Eagle assured him. "We will surround these men so swiftly and

345

silently that they will have not time to strike back."

Jesse clasped hands with Brave Eagle in a sign of comradeship. He had no doubt of the chief's words. They *would* successfully rescue his brother.

It was early morning, and Waco eased the hunger pangs in his belly by chewing on a piece of jerky. He'd kept guard for the past four hours and now he was ready to get some sleep.

"Hey, Tim, wake up. It's your turn to keep a look out."

Tim rolled over on his bedroll and favored Waco with a grumpy scowl. "I sure will be glad when Evanson decides what he's going to do with that bastard. I don't know why he just don't turn him in to the law and collect the reward money. He's been bellyaching for days about how he needs money to pay the railroad crews."

"He can't turn him in, you fool! He might talk too much about Evanson." Waco stretched his arms back over his head. "He sure likes to make folks suffer before they die. I think he gets a kick out of other folks' misery. If he has a particularly frustrating day, he just makes a trip out here and takes it out on that fella in there." He shook his head slowly. "Likes to watch people and things die slowly."

"Well, I sure feel a helluva lot better stuck up here than keeping that fella so close to town," Tim said.

Waco glanced nervously around before replying. "I reckon we're safe here . . . don't ya think?"

"Sure we are," Tim replied confidently. "Who could track us over all that rock?"

But Lars Evanson had underestimated his phantomlike enemy. There wasn't any place he could run, or hide, where Jesse would not eventually find him. All of his primitive instincts were concentrated solely on this one man. Hidden on the edge of a ridge, Jesse watched the men below. Yes, he'd taunt Evanson even more, rob from him, and then he'd kill him. And he would even take another kind of revenge.

Most of the money that he had stolen off the PGC he was giving to those families whom Lars had victimized for his railroad's passage. And some of it he'd invested (under an assumed name) in the Bank of Bodie, the newspaper, and several area mines. And of course there was the enterprise he was fast developing with amazing speed. When this was all over, he'd have enough money to build up his ranch, which he'd been forced to abandon years ago. He might even get rich.

With quick, silent footsteps, Jesse, his face and hands smeared black, crept toward the men around the campfire, his Mojave brothers behind him.

Tim had just sat up and tilted his head back to let the water from his pouch flow down his throat when the first arrow struck the leather with a dull thud and froze him in motion.

"Indians! Grab your rifles!" one of his companions yelled.

War whoops and chilling cries were all around them, but they could not see their enemy. A knife swooped past Waco's arm, slashing downward and bringing an anguished scream from him. Tim and the other man were running for a shelter of rocks, where they hoped to turn and fire their rifles. Arrows hissed over their heads, one of them embedding in Tim's leg. Still, he kept struggling to make to to the rock formations.

The three men had little chance to make good an escape; they had run for any cover that they could find, but their efforts were futile. The arrows had claimed one man's life and had wounded Tim. Waco knew if he was to escape, he'd have to make a run for it now.

Waco could not see the enemy, but he heard their guttural war whoops and knew by the feathered tips of their arrows that they were of the Mojave tribe. Everyone knew of the Kwanamis warriors' skill at warfare and the agonizing tortures they inflicted upon their enemies.

Before his horror-stricken eyes a brave leaped lithely across the rock Tim was crouched behind holding his wounded leg, and pulled a knife. When he saw the knife plunge downward, Waco went crazy with fear. He heard Tim's high-pitched scream, and bile rose in his throat.

"Damn you, Evanson! I'm not gonna die for you!" Jumping to his feet, Waco ran blindly through the surrounding woods. he didn't hear anyone following him, and he was beginning to think that perhaps he just might get away from them. And then the man stepped out of the trees before his path.

"There's no place to run; it's come down to you and me," Jesse gritted from between clenched teeth.

Waco could see that the man was not an Indian, but he was dressed in much the same fashion. He had on a buckskin shirt and leggings, and his face was streaked with gruesome black charcoal. And those midnight-blue eyes staring at him with such hatred . . . where had he seen them before? Knowing he was looking at his own executioner, Waco began to plead for his life.

"Don't kill me . . . please. . . . Just tell me what you want and it's yours!" He fell to his knees, his hands clasped before him imploringly. Scurrying across the damp earth on his knees, he beseeched Jesse with his eyes to spare his life.

"You don't remember me, do you?" Jesse asked jeeringly. "No — I guess you wouldn't expect me to still be alive. But I remember you real good, Waco."

"Who . . . are . . . you?" Waco stammered, then, "God . . . the Simmons ranch! . . . The man with the yellow-haired girl."

Jesse stared down into the face of the man he had dreamed about for many years. Every nightmare surfaced; the anguished voices from the past echoed inside him. A vision of Allison running toward her slain father.

Murderers! Filthy animals! Leave us alone!

The sound of the gunfire, the screams of the dying, and Allison tumbling, mortally wounded, to the ground.

It was this man who had taken her life. There was no mercy in the eyes that beheld Waco.

"You've been living on borrowed time, Waco. Today you even got to see the sun come up one last time."

Jesse pulled the trigger.

Chapter Eighteen

Nicki Sue went riding on Storm that night. She was the only person whom the stallion would allow on his neck, and they were a beautiful sight as they streaked through the moon-kissed shadows.

She really didn't know where she was going, so she allowed Storm his head, and he showed his appreciation by giving her the ride of her life. He was sleek and fast, and his gait was so smooth that Nicki Sue relaxed and just enjoyed herself.

She never saw the other rider until he came over the top of a rise and appeared to consider her carefully from afar; then she glimpsed him out of the corner of her eye sending his mount forward to catch her. He was an excellent horseman and had a fast mount too, but she knew Storm could outrun any horse in the area.

"Come on then, mister; show me exactly what you can do." She leaned over Storm's back and whispered her special words in his ear. "Show 'em your heels, fella."

The mountain trails were just ahead, and having tired of leading the race, Nicki sought to lose her opponent. She reined Storm to the right, and he charged like a powerful machine up the steep incline. Leaves and branches caught at her tangled hair, but Nicki Sue did not care. Suddenly she was wondering who this man was. And why was he following her? Her hand whipped her rifle from the scabbard and gripped the stock.

After having traveled at least a mile of winding, narrow paths, she was certain they must have lost him, for she heard nothing behind her now. She had just shoved the rifle back in the scabbard when a man slipped out of the shadows on a rock above her and grabbed her out of the saddle. His hand covered her mouth as she kicked and tried to bite him. She sensed a certain savage urgency about him that turned her bravado to fear.

"Shut up, little wildcat," came the silky growl, and she knew then who it was who had her. He removed his hand from her mouth, and she scrambled around to glare accusingly at him.

"Jesse! What are you doing here?" Her mouth twisted bitterly. "Surely you cannot have come back because you feel bad for leaving me like you did!"

He grabbed her roughly and jerked her to him. There was something in his eyes that she had not seen before: a glitter of death that he seemed almost desperate to banish. He was dressed in buckskin and not at all like the same man. Even his face was garishly streaked in black. Nicki could feel the coiled tightness in his muscles, the sweat that beaded his skin, and the raging blood lust that threatened to overpower him.

She did not know where he had been, but she was certain it was something that he would not share with her. He wanted her because she was warm, and vital, and far removed from where he had come from.

351

The heat from his body seared her, lured her arms around his neck and her lips to his. He laid her back on the cold, hard stone and stretched out over her. He drew back his head and murmured thickly, "I need you, baby . . . I need the spirit of life that burns so hotly inside you."

"What have you done, Jesse? . . . Where did you go today?"

But he didn't answer, and then it was too late for anything else but the feel of his bare skin next to hers.

"Is it too soon?" he whispered, poised above her, yet concern for her now in his eyes.

She knew he meant because of the miscarriage. "The doctor said I am fine," she said softly.

His body joined with hers in one smooth thrust, and Nicki Sue cried out her pleasure and shivered in his arms. He ravaged her, loved her, and drank deeply of the source of life she gave him so willingly. She gloried in his possession, matching the fever of his passion and the explosive release he brought them to. Their mating was as untamed and wild as the darkness that surrounded them. And when their bodies quivered and trembled, and then were still, Jesse lay quietly with his head in the curve of her shoulder, and one hand covering her breast.

"Will you leave again?" she could not help but ask.

"Yes," he whispered near her ear, "you know I have to."

He sat up a few minutes later and began to draw on his clothes. He turned to view her silently, then helped her to dress and walked her back to her horse.

She looked down at him from Storm's back. "If this is all there is ever going to be for us, then don't come back, Jesse," she told him with a deep sigh. "There's nothing here for you anymore."

He didn't answer. Putting her heels to Storm's sides, Nicki Sue rode for the ranch as fast as she could.

Doris Kardel Smith did not show surprise when her six-year-old son entered their wickiup to tell his mother that his grandmother Kardel had been seen by the lookout approaching the clustered village.

He was a miniature replica of his father, with ebony hair and eyes, and a sturdy body that was packed with boundless energy.

"Well, go welcome her, Swift Wolf. She will be amazed to see how much you have grown."

Swift Wolf smiled, revealing two missing front teeth. "And also that I don't have these anymore," he stated proudly.

"I'm sure she'll want to hear all about how you finally lost those teeth," Doris told him. She had been after him for a week to let her pull the two baby teeth that were loose, but he had refused, telling her that he'd rather just let them fall out on their own. His pony had accomplished the task when it had been frightened by a rabbit that had darted across its path and, throwing back its head, had struck Swift Wolf in the mouth. The dad was done, and mother and son were both relieved.

Doris watched her son dart back outside and heard his excited chatter as he announced to his friends that he was going to welcome his grandmother to the Mojave village.

353

Doris tended the fire and considered the reason for her mother's visit. She knew Elizabeth Kardel well enough to realize something must be on her mind or she would not have made the arduous trek through the mountains alone. Placing her young daughter in the arms of her sister-in-law, Morning Flower, Doris began to tidy the wickiup.

Morning Flower grinned. "It is the same with mothers and daughters everywhere, is it not? When my mother comes to visit from Arizona, I find myself doing the same."

"I haven't seen my mother in many months," Doris murmured. "It will be good to visit together." But she did not like to think that her mother would undoubtedly ask questions. Doris knew the Kardel gang's daring robberies were the talk of the area. And her mother would have begun gathering facts—it was just her nature—and she would have begun to wonder, even though she would have argued with herself that it was impossible.

Morning Flower detected a slight nervousness about Doris. She watched as she fluttered about the enclosure, snatching up a colorful blanket and folding it to place it to one side. "You are worried that your mother has picked this time to visit for a special reason?"

Doris sank back down on the pallet before the fire. "Terribly worried. I told my brother Jesse that Mother would be the first to suspect that he was still alive, and that he should go to her and explain his reasoning, but he never would. I know it's because he wanted to protect our parents, but if Mother has found out . . . who is going to protect me?" She uttered the last with a light laugh, but already she was thinking furiously of what she should say if her mother was to ask that *one* question.

Elizabeth returned from visiting her daughter and grandchildren satisfied that she now had the facts she needed to begin her campaign against Lars Evanson. She would meet with Charlie Star and tell him of her discovery in the backwater towns she had visited where the PGC tracks ran.

It was time to put an end to the death and violence, and the misery that Evanson seemed to take such delight in wreaking. She would agree to help Star. Perhaps she might help Jesse's cause if she could expose Lars Evanson as the man behind the vicious murders through the years. But first she had to tell her husband of her discovery, and seek his silence.

Her visit with her daughter had gone well. Doris Kardel Smith had appeared very happy to see her mother, since their visits were few and far between, but Elizabeth would never forget the look in her daughter's eyes when she'd asked her in a quiet moment if she'd heard from her brother Jesse.

Doris's voice had been soft and hesitant when she'd replied, and her blue eyes had rounded with apprehension. "You've found out, haven't you, Mother?" She had not thought to deny it; she knew no good would come of it. Their mother was a determined woman. If she thought they were keeping something important from her, she'd persist until she would uncover what it was. And Doris knew that they could not risk exposure of any kind. So she'd instinctively known it was time to let their mother know that her son had never been killed.

She explained as best she could Jesse's reasoning. But still, it hurt her to see her mother's pain. She'd been through so much already.

Elizabeth had felt her face turn ashen, and she hugged her tiny granddaughter tighter in her arms at Doris's words. Anger, then hurt at all of her children, swept briefly through her. How could they have kept Jesse's survival from them?

"Jesse is alive, isn't he?"

"Yes . . . he is," Doris had replied softly.

"How could you, my own daughter, have kept the truth from me?"

"I didn't want to, Mother," Doris had stated gently. "It was what Jesse wanted. And he had a sound reason. He begged us not to tell anyone."

"And why would he ask this of you and your brother?"

"You know the answer to that, dear. He didn't want you or Father involved. You're prominent citizens in Bodie. What would people think if it had been discovered that your sons had been labeled outlaws?" Doris had not mentioned the fact that Jesse feared they might be killed or injured. Her mother did not need to know of that.

"I want to see him. And I want to see him right away." And by the stubborn look in her mother's eyes, which was so much like Jesse's, Doris knew she must do what she could to persuade her brother it was time. Elizabeth had trembled with emotion, and Doris had taken her in her arms. "My son is alive . . . I knew it. . . . I knew he would come back to us someday."

"I'll talk to him, but I agree with Jesse it's far too dangerous for you to see him yet. There is still much to do first," Doris explained as compassionately as she could.

Elizabeth had regained her composure. "Yes, there is. And I intend to help." When she saw that Doris was about to protest, she held up one hand. "Nothing any of you can say will persuade me otherwise. I have experienced the worst that a mother can feel—nothing can be as terrible as that. Now, you tell your brothers the next time that you see them that their father and I will not be sheltered any longer. We'll do as they ask and not insist upon seeing them—for a while. But not forever, dear. Soon . . . I want to hold him, tell him how much he is loved." She smiled brilliantly through moist eyes. "Or they will be in big trouble with me if they ignore their parents much longer."

And now what was she to do? Elizabeth mused silently on the long journey home. She concluded that there was no better time than the present to begin the series of articles she'd been considering writing about the PGC railroad, and the train robbers. She had done her homework while she'd been away, and with Doris's encouragement, she'd interviewed many of the families who'd tangled with Evanson in other towns, and had lost relatives and homes in the undeclared war. Elizabeth was determined to let everyone in Bodie know about the horrible wake of violence that seemed to trail behind the long, winding path of the PGC's rails.

When the first article appeared in the Bodie newspaper, Lars Evanson managed to view it with indifference. Everyone knew Elizabeth Kardel was quick with a pen, and an opinion. He was confident that the citizens would consider the source and pay little heed to the glaring innuendos that hinted at the PGC obtaining much of their grants and properties by methods that were questionable. But when he'd gone to the Gilded Lily Saloon to meet Cathleen Kramer for lunch, he'd found the place in a stir. His poker-playing buddies had bid him a cool greeting, and the bartender seemed a little bit slower in fetching him his usual drink. Lars had not been pleased by the reception, but then Cathleen had emerged from her small office with a warm smile, and all else was forgotten. She commanded his full attention. What did the small folk matter anyway? he'd surmised, taking her arm and directing her outside to his waiting carriage. This gorgeous creature was the only person whose opinion he was concerned about at the moment.

And when they were seated within the plush interior of the carriage and she snuggled close in his arms, Lars forgot about everything but the afternoon he had planned in his private coach.

For Lars Evanson this was the closest he had been to loving anyone since his mother had abandoned him in a shabby town on the border of Mexico. Inga Evanson had sailed with her young son to America from Norway after his father had been killed aboard his fishing boat. His mother had been very beautiful. And the hot-blooded men in the rough border town found her cool blond looks and tall, slender body a delectable sight compared to the dark-eyed señoritas they were accustomed to. And Inga liked them too. She had a different lover every night, until at last she became bored with all of them. When a prosperous gunrunner asked her to come live with him in Mexico, she accepted. And when he informed her that he hated children and she would have to leave Lars behind, she had agreed to this also. At the tender age of nine, Lars Evanson was on his own.

Cathleen interrupted his musings when she strolled out of the dressing room wearing nothing but a whisper of silken undergarments and stockings with lacy garters. Lars dismissed painful memories without another thought. Her slender hips swayed provocatively as she crossed the floor and joined him on the bed. He tumbled her into his arms and rolled her onto her back. Resting his weight on his hands, he peered heatedly down at her.

"Damn it woman, but you excite the hell out of me," he growled. He sucked in his breath when her hand slipped inside his satin smoking jacket and caressed his smooth, muscular chest.

"I'm glad," she purred, her caresses becoming bolder. "I want to ignite a passion inside of you so fierce that you'll never again think of making love to anyone but me."

His eyes glazed with desire as she began to remove his clothes. "I think you are well on your way to realizing your wish, my love," he said hoarsely.

When he was naked and lying over her once again, she wound her fingers in his gleaming blond hair and drew his head downward.

"You are as naughty as I am, aren't you?" she murmured in his ear. She felt the hard throb of him against her bare thigh and whispered other things that she knew from experience would soon have him writhing in uncontrollable passion.

Lars hungrily kissed her face, her closed eyelids, and her luscious, pouting lips. His teeth nibbled the ripe, succulent fruit of her breasts while his hands stroked the moist softness between her legs. God, she was ready for him already! Her tight muscles tantalized him, and Lars felt just like a schoolboy his first time. He wanted to tear off her undergarments and take her swiftly and with no further preliminaries. She excited him unbearably with the allure of the innocent, cool beauty, where lay dormant in her soul a sultry vixen with carnal appetites to surpass his own. And even the fact that he had not been the first to introduce her to desire didn't bother him. It was enough that he had her now. The things she whispered to a man while he thrust in and out of her inviting body sent raw passion ripping through him so intense that Lars feared at such times that he was completely captivated by her. He had never known a woman, even the best of whores, who could put him in such a frenzy.

"Kiss me here," she beckoned him huskily, and drew his head downward until his lips were eagerly sucking the honey sweetness he was mad to possess.

Her musky woman scent intermingled with the rosewater perfume she always wore, tantalized his flared nostrils and sent his thoughts swirling. He could think of nothing but her at that moment: how good she looked and smelled, and the taste of her on his tongue. He gripped her firm buttocks so tightly that he knew she would bear bruises later, but she didn't seem to feel it, or care, for she only laughed, a sultry sort of gurgle that lingered deep in her throat.

"Yes . . . like that . . . oh my, you're really very exciting, you know."

He rubbed his throbbing staff against her leg, glancing upward into her eyes with a lusty grin. "Is that more to your liking, pet?" He kissed her lightly there again. "Can you feel how badly I want you?" He knew he was too excited and his rational thinking jeopardized, but he couldn't resist her charms. She was his beautiful wild rose, and he would have sold his soul at that moment if she had demanded it of him.

Cathleen drew him upward to capture his lips with her own. Her long legs locked about his waist in a grip so tight she took the breath from his lungs. He slid into her welcoming sheath in one smooth thrust, and she groaned in pleasure, her head falling back as panting gasps escaped her. Her hips moved in sensual rhythms against his own, her hands grasping his tight buttocks to hold him to her.

Lars reacted like a man possessed, nipping at her lips, her tongue, and the graceful arch of her neck. He was like a mighty stallion seeking to conquer a mare. Again and again he drove into her, the sweat pouring off of his smooth golden body and mingling with hers. She received all that he gave her, and bit his shoulder for more. His body trembled and shook, his face contorted with his effort. Beneath him, Cathleen urged him onward to higher crests. Lars responded, taking them both to another peak, then another, until at last the world exploded around him and he felt her body react in kind, shuddering against his again and again.

Lars lay half upon her, his breathing slowly returning to normal, but knowing that his life would never be so again. This passionate creature was the woman of his dreams! He wanted her exclusively for his. He gazed upon her flushed features, her white-blond hair lying tangled about her bare breasts. She was so perfect, so beautiful in every way. He knew that Krystal would turn into a screaming shrew when he told her of his decision, but that was the least of his worries, actually. It seemed to him as if his empire was beginning to crumble. And now those newspaper articles. His eyes ran over the creamy swells and valleys of Cathleen's body. Was it true what he'd heard about being enraptured of only one woman? Did it weaken a man, make him vulnerable and indecisive?

Gazing upon her soft beauty prompted him to ignore any of the warnings inside his head. Even the fact that she had not come to him a virgin did not matter. He did wonder of her past, where she had come from, but he knew a few discreet inquiries could answer that. At the moment, nothing mattered as much as possessing this woman, body and soul. He lowered his head and kissed her lips.

"You were absolutely wonderful. How do you feel?"

Cathleen half opened her eyes to view him through thick wheat-colored lashes. She stretched her lithe body lazily, affording him a fine view of her lovely charms. "It was marvelous, darling. When can we do it again?"

He laughed with delight and grasped her tiny waist to pull her over on top of him. She could feel his desire rising, pulsing between her thighs like a searing hot brand.

"I think . . . right now would suit me just fine," he murmured against her seeking mouth, and drew her legs up on either side of him.

"Oh my, but you truly are the virile stallion, aren't you?" she breathed throatily as she bent her head to capture his lips.

It was later, while they were having dinner and

watching a glorious sunset from the window, that she happened to mention the story that Elizabeth Kardel had written up in the newspaper that morning.

"Where does that woman come up with her wild ideas?" she stated with glaring disapproval.

Lars stirred cream into his coffee. "She is a woman who became quite bored with her dull life, and sought to add excitement to it by calling herself a newspaper reporter and writing about any absurd notion that popped into her head. There is no truth to the story, and if the editor isn't careful about what he allows that woman to print, I just may have to see what I can do to put a stop to it."

Cathleen regarded him curiously. "And just how can you do that? There is freedom of the press, you know."

"Yes, there is," Lars drawled before sipping his coffee. Then, staring at her over the rim, he added, "But I have my rights too . . . and ways of seeing that they are not infringed upon more than once."

"You mean . . . you have a means of eliminating any problems that might shed an unfavorable light on you and the PGC?" she inquired with an innocent light in her eyes.

Lars set his coffee cup down and reached across the snow-white tablecloth to enfold her hand in his. "I am not without some power, my lovely wild rose. I usually have things my way. Sometimes peacefully, and other times with a bit of persuasion."

"I hope I never meet with your disapproval, darling," she stated in a soft voice, glancing out of the window at the men who were never far from Lars's side.

"You have nothing to fear from them, sweetheart—or from me, ever. They only do what I tell them to. And you know I would never think of hurting you."

Her anxious eyes met his. "They appear so ruthless, and they carry such deadly looking weapons."

"I know," he responded in gentle tones. "A man in my business has a lot of enemies. I need the men around to discourage anyone who might be thinking of crossing me. But you needn't worry; the men follow my orders implicitly. They're really very stupid fellows, actually. They wouldn't know how to act on their own plans."

"Why would anyone disapprove of your actions when all that you're seeking to do is complete passage of your railroad?" Her smooth brow furrowed slightly. "I simply don't understand."

Lars patted her hand indulgently. "Now, now, my pet. Why confuse yourself further with these complicated matters? Just let me worry about business and taking care of you from now on." His expression intensified. "I want you to quit your job at the saloon, and let me take care of you."

"You mean you wish to keep me." It was stated without hint of her inner feelings.

"I could give you everything," he hurriedly added, kissing the tips of her fingers.

She lowered her lashes. "I will never completely belong to anyone, Lars. I like my freedom, and the fact that I answer to no one but myself."

"And I am accustomed to getting what I want."

"What is it that you seek so earnestly?" she asked him.

"Everything that life has to offer, except marriage," he replied with a wolfish smile.

One pale blond brow arched upward. "You think

you would find it dull with me one day?" she posed in a husky voice.

"No, not dull, never! But confining. I suppose it's the same way *you* feel about becoming my mistress."

Cathleen left her chair and was in his arms before he could catch his breath. She kissed him passionately, her hands knowing just where to touch him to make his heart pound out of control. Drawing back from him, she said, "I think you would change your mind about marriage if the right woman came along."

"Just be satisfied that I want you like I've never wanted another woman," he said hoarsely.

With a snarl of raging desire, Lars swept her up into his arms and carried her to the bed. Just as he lowered his body over hers, she heard him say, "I'll never desire another, my wild rose, in the way that I do you."

"No," she murmured, "you won't . . . I'm certain of that."

But he hadn't heard, for already he was thinking of another path he must follow. It seemed the only way for him to realize his dream now. He couldn't marry Cathleen Kramer, for there was another woman he must marry. He was going to marry Nicki Ryan. She would resist, of course, but he figured he could convince her. All that he had to do was issue a threat here and there, tell her if she wanted to keep her friends safe from harm, she'd have to do what he asked. Of course, the fire hadn't shaken her. But there were better ways.

He'd marry her and show everyone how much he loved his little bride. That would go a long way toward salvaging his reputation, and his dreams.

Krystal had sent him a wire stating she was having an impossible time of it securing funds for the PGC. Even in Denver the stories about him were beginning to make themselves known. Damn that newspaperwoman! If she wasn't careful, he just might have to shut her up for good too!

Satisfied that he had a promising means to secure his future, he kissed Cathleen good-bye and went outside to give orders to the crews in the yard.

While he was gone, Cathleen swiftly covered every inch of the coach, searching for the one piece of evidence she might find that would prove to everyone he was a murderer.

"I can't believe it!" Jake Moran growled to Nicki Sue as he paced back and forth in her parlor.

"Nor can I," Nicki Sue replied. She was doing her best to console Jake after he heard the news that Cathleen had been seeing Lars Evanson. He was stunned the day that Cathleen came to the assay office to tell him that she had to postpone their luncheon engagement because something had come up.

"She just strolled right in my office with a smile on her face like she always does—and them bam! She tells me we'll have to quit seeing each other so often, that there was someone else she was going out with too." His face was rigid with anger. "What can that woman be thinking about? Doesn't she know that man is dangerous?"

Nicki sat in a chair, her expression bleak. "I never thought she was the sort who was impressed with money and power, but perhaps that explains it better than anything."

"She's been spending a lot of time with him alone—in his private coach." Jake snarled the end of his words, pounding his fist into his open palm. "I don't think they're just holding hands either."

"This is not like her at all," Nicki mused aloud. "We had many in-depth discussions about a good many things. She's such a hard worker, Jake. I never thought she appeared the sort who was impressed by people with money and power. And she even told me once to watch out for Lars Evanson, that she thought he was an odd sort who trouble seemed to follow wherever he went."

A tense, awkward silence fell between them as each became lost in their own thoughts. Then Jake spoke softly.

"Did Cathleen ever tell you anything about herself?"

"Oh sure, we talked a great deal about our childhood, our hopes and dreams—" Nicki paused suddenly.

"What is it?" Jake urged.

"Or at least, I talked a lot about those things."

"Cathleen never did, you mean?"

"Yes, but never much about the past. She spoke more about the future, and there was one particular thing that she said she had yet to accomplish."

Their eyes met.

"Did she ever tell you what that was?"

Nicki Sue chewed on her bottom lip, then shook her head. "Now that you mention it . . . no, not a word."

"The same here. She discussed a great deal with me, too. And I tried to get her to open up about herself, tell me where she came from and something of her past. It was useless. She would immediately seek to change the subject."

Curious, they studied each other.

Perplexed and feeling dejected, Jake sat in a chair next to her. "Maybe neither of us knew her as well as we thought we did," he said.

Nicki Sue cast him a sympathetic look. "Cathleen is decent and good. That much I do know. She'll come to her senses soon and realize what sort of man Lars Evanson really is."

"I don't know what to believe anymore," Jake exclaimed. "I thought she was the woman for me, and that she was interested in me too. We never put our feelings into words, but a man knows when a woman enjoys his company and thinks of him as her friend." He sighed despondently. "Maybe that was my trouble — I wasn't forceful enough, like him."

Nicki knew his spirits had hit rock bottom, and that if anyone needed a friend at the moment, it was Jake. He had been kind to her since she'd arrived in Bodie, it was time for her to return some of that goodwill. "Then do something about it."

"What do you suggest I do? Try and compete with him?" His tone was sarcastic. "Heck, she only let *me* kiss her once. And I've heard how she's been spending all that time with Evanson in his private coach."

"No doubt from our tongue-wagging neighbors, Sugar and Betty Lou?" Nicki drawled.

"Facts are facts, Nicki Sue, no matter who you hear them from."

"Jake, there is something Cathleen isn't telling us. I don't know what it is, but I just sense it. You *must* get her away from Evanson before it is too late."

Jake's brow furrowed. "Why do you always make it sound like that man is as deadly as a snake? Do you think those articles in the newspaper could really be about him?"

"Without a doubt," Nicki replied quickly. "But don't concern yourself with that; just do your best to persuade her you're the better man—and you are."

Jake stared at her in complete bafflement. "And just how am I to find time with her when Evanson isn't around?"

"You'll think of a way," Nicki told him.

Suddenly his terse lips lifted in a smile. "I will! I'm not going to let him spoil things. She's mine, and I intend to reclaim her."

Nicki Sue beamed. "Good, for I hate thinking of her with that awful man."

"I'll find a way to have her to myself this Saturday at the barn raising. She's been helping organize everything with Vincent Kardel." He gazed down at Nicki. "And I happen to know what her quilt looks like. I'm betting that Evanson hasn't even seen it—that gives me an edge."

"You plan to buy Cathleen's quilt, don't you?"

"Yep, I sure do. And spend a few hours alone with her too."

Nicki Sue looked pleased. "That's the way I like to hear you talk. And I know the best man *will* win."

Chapter Nineteen

Saturday dawned bright and sunny. Everyone at Los Paraiso rose early to have breakfast together. Marty and Pablo told the women they should be ready within the hour, as the workers would be arriving soon to begin rebuilding the stable. This sent the housekeeper into a flurry of motion. She began clearing the table. Marty hurriedly grabbed a piece of bacon from his plate as she swiped it away.

"I wasn't even done yet," he complained good-naturedly.

Maria told him in Spanish that, as far as she was concerned, he was.

Nicki and Pablo took the hint and left the kitchen to Maria. Marty was braver. He lingered over his cup of coffee while she hovered at his elbow, her foot tapping impatiently on the tile floor.

He cast her an indulgent look, and at last handed her his cup.

"All right, woman, I'm agoing," he stated with mock gruffness.

By eight o'clock Nicki Sue was standing outside in the yard greeting the first of the arrivals.

"Morning, Hal, Cid—nice of you to come and help out."

"Howdy, ma'am!" Cid returned with a wide grin. "Tell Maria to brew up a powerful lot of coffee—there are a whole bunch of fellas that were on the road behind us."

"We'll have you a new stable before you know it, Mrs. Ryan!" Hal called out to Nicki as he jumped down from the wagon filled with supplies.

"What time are your womenfolk due to arrive?" Nicki asked them, having walked over to offer her assistance in carrying the nail bucket.

"Mine said around ten," Cid replied. "She was frying up the last of the chicken she's bringing. She's riding out with Miss Drucell."

"Oh? I thought Mr. Star might be escorting her," Nicki asked nonchalantly.

"No. He ain't been around lately," Cid informed her.

Nicki set the bucket down next to the lumber that the two men were stacking neatly near the proposed site for the new stable, and could not help but wonder if Star had learned Jesse's whereabouts. No matter how much she told herself she didn't care what happened to him, she could not manage to banish him from her thoughts.

"Mrs. Ryan?" Pablo was standing next to her, his coppery face set in tense lines. "Did you hear me?"

Nicki glanced over at him. "I'm sorry . . . what were you saying?"

"Mr. Evanson is here," he told her. "He said he'd like to speak with you in private."

Her eyes narrowed. "I'm very busy; would you just take a message for me, please?"

"I would like to, señora, but he told me this is a very important matter."

"All right," Nicki relented, moving away from

371

Cid and Hal, who were still busy unloading the lumber. "I'll speak with him. Where is he?"

"Waiting on the front veranda," Pablo said.

She nodded and strode off in that direction.

Lars watched her approach. His eyes were gleaming with intent and his emotions were in a turmoil. He felt as if he was fast losing a grip on his future. He'd ridden out early in the morning to check on the imprisoned outlaw, and ask his men if they'd obtained any information from him as yet, only to find his prisoner gone and his men killed by Indians. He could only hope that the savages had taken the outlaw their prisoner and would finish him off, thereby eliminating the concern that the man might yet return to once again stalk him. It was then he knew he'd have to put pressure on Nicki Ryan immediately. There wasn't a minute to waste. He devised a scheme to convince her that she must marry him at once. Without her, he stood a chance of losing the land. If he had her and the wealth she represented, no one would dare challenge him again.

"You wished to speak to me?" Nicki Sue favored Lars Evanson with an inquiring look.

"Yes." His eyes roamed over her face. "I heard from Miss Kramer about your misfortune. I thought now would be a good time to come offer you a solution to all of your problems."

Nicki favored him with an assessing look. "Surely you must realize that I would never accept anything from you."

"I think you will when you hear what I have to say."

Her eyes narrowed and she faced him boldly. "I'll give you exactly five minutes."

He smiled at her obvious show of spirit. "That doesn't allow me much time, but since you insist, I'll come right to the point. I believe it's about time you had a man in your life to take care of things for you." He gestured toward the devastated stable, then grinned infuriatingly at her. "Maybe I could even prevent something like this from occurring again."

Nicki Sue had heard enough and cut him off in outrage. "Get out of here! How dare you come to my home and talk to me of my misfortunes when you—*yes,* I do realize that—are the one behind them all!"

"You don't have a lick of proof," he drawled confidently.

"You murdered my husband, and I'll see you pay for that one day," she threatened, staring hard into his face.

"Such outrageous accusations," Lars smirked, reaching out to grasp her arm.

Her golden cat eyes shot daggers at him. "Let go of me before I call my men to throw you off my ranch!"

"I don't think you'd better do that—unless you want them all to hear about the man my boys caught riding off your place the other night." He dropped his hand when he saw her stricken expression. He had gained the upper hand. "That tamed you down a bit; I thought it might."

"You're . . . lying," she gasped weakly.

"He wore a long duster and was heavily armed—had the kind of guns only professionals use." His gaze became intense. "Dark hair, blue eyes. But of course, if you don't care if he dies . . . there's always one of your other friends to take his place. In fact, there may be several."

"Enough!" she rasped. Her face appeared bloodless as she asked the dreaded question. "What do you intend to do to him?"

Lars watched her with an amused expression. "I don't really think I should answer a question like that; it might incriminate me."

"Damn you, answer me or I swear I'll manage to drag you down with me."

There was a moment of unbearable silence, then he said, "He's not dead—yet."

Nicki frowned. She didn't like this conversation one bit. "Just what is all of this leading up to?"

"I'm afraid your dalliance with this man is going to cost you that proud spirit you value so, my dear," he drawled.

"What do you mean?" she asked, but already knew what was on his mind. He had her, and the land, unless she gave him Jesse's life. As much as she had imagined getting her evens with the black-haired devil, she knew she could not allow this horrible man to kill him. God, never had she considered taking Jesse's life. Making him miserable, yes, but only because he had hurt her so by rejecting her when she had needed him.

"I'd say you have no choice but to marry me. If you don't, I'll have your lover killed, slowly . . . and painfully."

Her stomach churned as she said, "I was innocent of many things when I came here. I never fully understood how greed can warp men's minds and souls, but I have seen how firsthand. You will do anything to get what you want. And you want me to marry you so that you can take over my ranch and become a rich man."

"You're also very smart," he told her with a gloating smile. "One day I will be a very important man in this area. You can share in that with me. I'll be very rich just as soon as my railroad is completed — and a town bearing my name is developed around the lake."

She glared at him. "You might not live long enough to see it."

He laughed, but suddenly he didn't appear quite so certain. "I suppose that's your way of trying to tell me that you are threatening to put an end to my life."

"All I can say is, watch your back every minute or something just might happen to prevent our getting married."

Their gazes locked as Lars considered the little hellion before him. She was certainly not easily intimidated. He considered the possibility of breaking down her defenses and truly claiming her for his. What might it be like to take such a woman to his bed? He had never had a female hate him with such intensity as this one. He could feel himself getting excited.

"Well? What's your answer, yes or no?"

"Do I have a choice?" she sneered.

He shrugged. "One always has a choice, but in this case, it depends on how much you want that outlaw to live."

"I'll marry you, Evanson," she said stiffly, her eyes bright with tears of frustration. "But it will be in name only. If you try and lay a finger on me, I'll stick a knife in your gullet just as soon as you go to sleep."

He almost winced, but managed to accept her pronouncement with little expression. "I suppose neither of us has any choice but to agree to one another's demands — for now." His lips lifted in an abrupt half smile that appeared to Nicki Sue like hungry snarl. "You drive a hard bargain. You're really not all that unattractive, and you might have found my lovemaking quite enjoyable."

She tried not to let his words upset her cool composure, and retorted as calmly as possible. "When is the wedding?"

"I have a few matters to attend to first. Oh, one other thing. You'd better tell your friend Mrs. Kardel to stop writing those articles of hers if she knows what's good for her." He took her cold hand within his. "It's a pleasure to do business with you, madam. And I expect you'll be discreet and not let anyone know about our pact, at least until after the ink has dried on the marriage certificate."

"Another stipulation?" She withdrew her hand and brushed it off on her pants. He only smiled benignly at the implication.

"The first of many," he drawled.

Nicki Sue whirled away from him and walked toward the house, where she hoped to regain her composure. God! What had she done? She had sworn to hate Jesse forever, and here she was sacrificing her life to protect him again!

By late afternoon the stable was half-completed and the men called it quits for the day. It was agreed that they would come back several evenings next week and finish the job. The men retired to the bunkhouse to spruce up and change into clean clothes for the night's festivities while the women busied themselves with the last-minute preparations.

Most of the ladies had been working hard all afternoon setting out food, gathering the donated items to be sold, setting up tables, and last but not least, putting the final touches on the prepared food for the late night supper.

Nicki stood on the front veranda. She had changed into a pale blue gown sprigged with tiny daisies and had fashioned a length of satin ribbon through her long tresses. More than one young man who passed favored her with a charming smile. She felt as if her life had been turned into a nightmare, and she didn't know how she was going to get through the rest of the day. Evanson's visit hours earlier seemed so unreal. But it had truly happened, and she told herself that she could do nothing but marry him out of fear for Jesse's life. Afterward, she would make Lars release him or she would find a way to do so herself.

Marty and Pablo strolled past and waved. They were dressed in their Sunday best, their hair slicked back with sweet-smelling pomade. Nicki wondered who they were envisioning dancing with throughout the night.

There were colorfully stitched quilts strung on a line that went clear across the yard. Nicki could see hers from where she stood. It was pale yellow, with several Arabian horses racing across the squares in shades of brown, tan, and gold thread.

Maria had sewn her quilt in the same bright colors as her skirt. She was certain there could be no doubt in a gentleman's mind which of the quilts she had made. She had used careful forethought, and she hoped that Roberto, the town's blacksmith, did the same. She knew he was interested in her, for he always hurried to help her carry her parcels whenever she went shopping in town. She looked lovely dressed in a brightly patterned skirt and white *camisa* with a lace mantilla covering her dark hair. It was obvious she had been looking forward to the evening.

One side of the yard was crowded with buggies and wagons. Beneath a large shade tree, Leroy Culpepper had set up a makeshift bar. It was already crowded. Nicki had no doubt that Leroy would keep everyone's thirst to a minimum.

Nicki glanced around for Cathleen, but there was no sign of her silver-blond head anywhere. Was she with Lars? Did she know of his plan? She stepped off the porch to chat with people whom she knew along the way, and once she even caught herself glancing over her shoulder with a sense of breathless anticipation. A dark-haired man was standing some distance away, but turned into the throngs of people just as soon as she noticed him. She could have sworn when she'd first caught sight of him that he had been watching her closely. He wore a wide-brimmed hat pulled low over his eyes, but what she could see of his features was dark and lean. Even from where she stood, Nicki could sense the devilment in him. She swung her gaze away quickly, then had to glance back again, but he had completely disappeared. A tinge of pink heightened her complexion.

"Is there something wrong, Nicki?" Elizabeth Kardel walked over to stand next to her, her gaze following in the direction that Nicki had been staring.

"Did you see that man with the light blue shirt

378

standing over there?" Nicki asked softly.

"I saw no one," she returned.

Nicki Sue knew she had not imagined seeing him. "He was standing right over there." She pointed to the spot.

Elizabeth's eyes followed the direction she indicated. "There is no one there now," she said.

"But there was," Nicki stated hoarsely. "I know there was."

"I hope you two lovely ladies are looking for me?" Jake Moran quipped as he joined them.

Nicki smiled up at him. "I for one am certainly glad to see you."

"Hello, Jake; it's good to see you again," Elizabeth greeted him.

"And to see you smile again, Nicki Sue," Jake said.

"I think it is the first happy smile I've managed in a long time," Nicki replied, wondering how she could manage to act so unassuming when she was terrified of what lay ahead of her. And she didn't dare say anything to anyone, less Lars make good on his threat.

"I'm glad I make somebody happy," Jake said, an angry expression clouding his eyes. "I've been looking for Cathleen, but I don't see her anywhere. Has she been here today?"

"I haven't seen her. But I must tell you . . . I had a run-in with Evanson earlier. I don't expect him to come back tonight. Perhaps Cathleen will spend the evening with him."

Elizabeth became pensive. "Nicki, you must promise me you will not antagonize that man." She glanced over at Jake's clouded expression. "Either of you." Her eyes captured Nicki's once again.

379

"There are people working behind the scenes to stop him once and for all. Charlie Star will be returning from Chicago soon. I know that when he does, a lot of ugly matters will be exposed, and dealt with."

Jake's lips twisted into a sneer. "Whatever does Cathleen find appealing in Lars Evanson? He's a double-dealing coyote who should be shot."

"He can be very persuasive when he chooses," Nicki found herself saying, and clamped her lips together. She saw Elizabeth watching her oddly.

Jake touched her arm reassuringly and announced he was going to search the crowd for Cathleen one more time before calling it a night.

"Maybe she's here now and we just missed seeing her."

"That's possible." He favored her with a searching look. "Are you all right, Nicki? Did Evanson say anything to upset you?"

She shook her head. "It's nothing . . . and I want you to stop thinking about that man. He's dangerous to have for an enemy; please don't make him yours." He started to say something, but she hurriedly continued. "Go on; I'll be fine. I'm going to help out in the kitchen for a while."

"I'll go with you," Elizabeth said.

When they were in the parlor and she had Nicki momentarily alone, Elizabeth asked her to sit with her for a minute. Nicki agreed and they took two chairs in a relatively quiet corner.

"I can't tell you a great deal, dear," Elizabeth began quickly and in a hushed voice. "But I do want you to know that Mr. Star is well aware of Lars Evanson's crimes. When he returns, he'll undoubtedly place him under arrest for questioning. Through weeks of investigation, and one particularly important witness, whom I am trying to convince to come forward and testify, the railroad man's freewheeling days are soon to end."

Nicki didn't know what to say. If they arrested Evanson before she could find where he was holding Jesse, Lars might have Jesse killed. She had to keep quiet for his sake and manage somehow on her own.

"You have a witness?" she asked.

Elizabeth bent her head closer. "I know I can trust you not to say anything. It's that friend of yours—Cathleen Kramer. She came forward recently and told Mr. Star that she would do everything she could to help, and also to gather evidence of Evanson's misdeeds."

Nicki was astounded, but tried to mask her astonishment. "I . . . I . . . can hardly believe it. Why would she do something so dangerous?"

"I don't know, but I'm glad for her help. Evanson has slipped through one foxhole and another when cornered in the past. But this time the evidence brought against him will stick, and serve to hang him."

Nicki's thoughts were spinning. This entire day had brought startling revelations. Star, Elizabeth, and Cathleen all working furiously to place Lars Evanson behind bars. More than ever she wanted to tell her about Jesse. She was just about to say something when Vincent joined them.

"There you are, darling," he said. "I was looking all over for you. It's about time you spent some time with your husband. The musicians are starting to play." He drew her to her feet. "And I want to make certain I get the first dance with you. You'll excuse us, Mrs. Ryan."

After the Kardels had departed, Nicki was called to the kitchen. But she could not forget what Elizabeth had told her, nor the situation she was in. Dare she go to Cathleen and ask her if she knew anything about Jesse? Pondering this, she entered the kitchen.

The kitchen was a beehive of activity. Most of the women were busy working hard to distribute the platters and bowls of food. They were gathering the assortment of food and placing it on long pine tables just outside the back door underneath the trees, which were strung with lanterns. There were platters of fried chicken and thick slices of smoked ham, huge bowls of potato salad and various other vegetable salads. The spicy scent of baked beans and the fragrant, yeasty aroma of baked bread drifted throughout the house.

Nicki had just finished squeezing lemons for another pitcher of lemonade and was pouring the juice into the container when she heard two women outside below the window mention her name. She knew immediately by the tone of their hushed voices that it was Betty Lou Walsh and Sugar Drucell.

"And I heard it straight from Flora Davis, whose husband Eugene owns the feed store, that her man bought a fresh supply of feed the other day and mentioned that they were thinking about taking the horses to Sacramento," Sugar was saying.

"Do you mean to tell me that woman is going to travel across-country *alone* with those two men?" Betty Lou asked snidely.

"Yes, ladies, that's exactly what I mean," Sugar

was quick to clarify.

"I always thought she didn't like men," Betty Lou stated waspishly. "Heaven knows she never pays them any mind."

"That's because they're all too ordinary and decent for her taste," Sugar drawled. "I think she likes them rough and forceful . . . Remember all the time she spent traveling alone with that wild outlaw." She snorted. "I think he spoiled her tastes for a kind, decent man. Why, look at the way she dresses, and breaks horses — why, it's quite obvious his influence is surfacing."

The third woman gasped in understanding. "You don't mean . . ."

"I do," Sugar returned unhesitatingly.

The three woman clucked their tongues, then Betty Lou said, "I bet that outlaw could tell some things about the widow that would make some of Leroy Culpepper's tales seem tame by comparison."

"Do you think when they catch him . . . that he will?" the third woman asked, sounding very much like she hoped he would.

"We shall come to find out very soon, I would think," Betty Lou said. "My Conner says with the offer of the reward money, those criminals will be behind bars in no time."

"Then we'll see if the Widow Ryan is all that she appears," the woman snorted.

"She may fool some people by acting like a God-fearing woman, attending church every Sunday and looking so prim with those spectacles perched on her nose during hymn singing, but not me." Sugar's voice dripped with sarcasm. "Why, I heard from Charlie Star himself that she was in Evanson's private car on her honeymoon night, and her husband was off playing cards right before he met his death."

"Is that true for sure?" Betty Lou pried breathlessly.

"Told you it was, didn't I?" Sugar snapped, irritated that her friend should question her with another listener present.

Nicki felt hot tears flood her eyes, but she fought to blink them back. As soon as she'd completed her task, she flung off her apron and slipped out the door onto the back veranda. She waited quietly until the women were finished talking, and then she calmly tapped Sugar Drucell on the shoulder.

Sugar turned around, and recognizing Nicki Sue, her jaw went slack.

"My, my, Miss Drucell, don't tell me you of all people find you're at a loss for words." Nicki's eyes were narrowed in angry indignation. She was unaware that there were other women beginning to gather around and that they were frowning at the three tightly huddled women. Her body quaked with the force of her own rising temper. "I have never said an unkind word about any of you. Which is more than I can say for you three ladies. From what *I've* heard, you even talk behind one another's back."

Betty Lou was the first to recover, but her face remained drained of all color. "Why, Mrs. Ryan, we didn't know you were there. You must understand we were only repeating what is being rumored about town."

"You have the nerve to slander me and then say you live by the Golden Rule. I doubt whether you really even know what it is." Nicki Sue stated.

"Of course I do," Sugar proclaimed, having recovered from her shock. "Do unto others as you would have them do unto you." She nodded smugly. "We're all God-fearing women here, madam, and we *live* the Golden Rule."

"As I do!" Nicki was so furious she had to clasp her hands together to still their shaking. "And the ninth commandment states that thou shall not bear false witness against thy neighbors — I suggest you read over them again, ladies, since you've so obviously forgotten a few."

Maria stepped outside to join Nicki Sue, having heard the fuss from the kitchen. The three offenders stood shamefacedly, feeling the scorn of the women gathering to offer their quiet support to Nicki. Several voiced their disapproval out loud, and a few even wagged their fingers before the women.

Betty Lou could bear no more. She suddenly burst into tears and buried her face in her hands.

Finally, unable to bear the disapproving glares any longer, Sugar grasped Betty Lou's arm and they fled down the back stairs into the crowd. The other woman had already vanished.

Nicki Sue released a pent-up sigh, and was amazed when everyone who passed by her gave her a gentle smile and a reassuring pat on the back. She was not surprised to recognize Elizabeth Kardel as one of her supporters.

"That tongue-lashing was well deserved," she said.

"But even so, it wasn't pleasant for me."

"I hope you won't let them ruin your evening. They would love to know that they did."

Nicki smiled weakly. "Even though it's true, I won't let them know."

"I am sorry you had to go through that. And I want you to know that not everyone here shares the opinion of those narrow-minded biddies."

"Oh, I realize that," Nicki said, but she was still shaking. "Most of the people here have been very kind."

"Perhaps that interview we discussed at our first meeting might be just the thing now?" Elizabeth unexpectedly declared. "You did mention your own troubles with Evanson. Perhaps I can help?"

Nicki Sue was embroiled in a quandary then. She longed to make some sort of statement about the horrible things she suspected Evanson was guilty of perpetrating. But what would happen to Jesse? No, she could not say a word and risk his life. Even though she had followed the recent articles in the *Bodie Free Press* regarding a certain successful railroad entrepreneur who literally annihilated anything that stood as a roadblock to his success. Elizabeth used assumed names, but the stereotypes of her characters and the incidents were all too vividly realistic not to have been based on careful research, or even in-depth interviews with persons who may at one time have been victims of this man. Drawing a fortifying breath, she surprised Elizabeth with her reply.

"I've really nothing to say that could be of any help to you; I'm sorry, but I really cannot."

Elizabeth was stunned by Nicki's change of attitude. "I can't believe after what I told you that you would say this. You know better than anyone how Evanson destroys people's lives to further his own gains. That railroad is all he cares about—and you should know how far he'll go to obtain the land he needs."

"Yes, I do know very well, and that is why I cannot risk talking with you again," Nicki said, her expression bleak. She started to walk away, but Elizabeth grasped her arm.

"He's gotten to you too, hasn't he?"

Nicki did not turn around, but replied quietly. "Know that what I do is because I must . . . But I wish . . ." Her voice almost broke and she shook her head. She wanted to tell Jesse's mother that he was alive and being held a prisoner by Lars Evanson, but she knew if she did, it might jeopardize his life even more. There was no one she could turn to. She had to marry Evanson and make certain that he set Jesse free.

"What do you wish?" Elizabeth probed.

"Nothing! Forget I said that. Now I must rejoin my guests."

Elizabeth allowed Nicki to walk away, but her words stayed with her. She had at last been reunited with her son, and she would not lose him now. It had been wonderful to see him the night he had come to the house after dark. His father had almost appeared as if he'd known Jesse had been coming. They'd talked, held each other, and Elizabeth had cried when Jesse had told her what had happened that night long ago that turned her life into a living hell. No, she would not let Lars Evanson take her son away from her again. He had failed the first time, and he would fail this time.

The men had gathered around the beer kegs, where Leroy Culpepper, the Gilded Lily's bartender, kept liquid refreshment flowing freely, along with his opinions. His mouth kept as busy as his hands.

"Charlie Star was hot on their trail when he got called back to Chicago," he was telling the men within earshot. "Told me just before he left that he would be back, though, and resume his investigation."

"You still think he's gonna get them boys?" a man asked.

"Sooner or later," Leroy told them. "We should start building us a gallows right quick." He slid a foaming mug of beer down the bar to a thirsty customer. "There you are, Floyd—this'll wet you down some."

"I figured when Charlie Star came in from Chicago, those boys were as good as caught," one man commented grimly.

Floyd quickly agreed, as did everyone else within earshot.

"To tell you the truth, I'm kind of glad he didn't track them down so easily," a man they knew as Pete said.

"Yeah, me too," Floyd agreed. "We got us our own James gang, just like Missouri. That's something to be proud of."

"Not for long," Leroy Culpepper chimed in. "There's a sum of money being offered for their capture. We'll soon have every roughrider and fast gun riding out looking for them desperadoes." He nodded assuredly. "Yes sir, we better start gathering lumber right quick. We're gonna be needin' us a gallows pretty soon."

"Don't think you need to rush right out and begin," a deep voice interrupted.

All eyes swung to the man who had spoken.

He was very tall and muscular, his dark hair covered by a Stetson, his sharp blue eyes taking in everyone before him in a sweeping glance. In one hand he held a long cheroot; the other rested lightly on the top of the makeshift bar, as if ready for action at any given moment. He had deeply tanned, chiseled features and a commanding air, but the sun was so bright setting over the mountains in back of him that the men couldn't look directly into his face without squinting.

"Why do you say that, mister?" Leroy broke the silence first.

The man dragged deeply on his cigar and exhaled a spiraling cloud of blue smoke before answering. "Because they aren't going to catch the gang."

It was so positive a statement that even Leroy was at a loss for words.

"Think about it," the man said. "They really have nothing to go on. Nobody can identify them; nobody even knows their names. Hell! Those boys could walk right beside you and you wouldn't even know who they were."

That set everybody to talking once again, and when they paused to ask the man another question, he had disappeared from their midst.

Floyd scratched his grizzled chin. "Now, where do you suppose he took off to?"

The sound of Reverend Black announcing the sale of the quilts could be heard.

"Young fella like that don't want to waste his time hanging around with us married men," Leroy snorted. "He's gonna go buy himself a quilt and find him a pretty little gal to go along with it."

Chapter Twenty

Nicki was very glad to glimpse Cathleen Kramer donating her quilt just seconds before the sale began. She had begun to think she was not going to come, and knew that Jake would have been terribly disappointed.

Glancing over at Jake, who was standing near the wooden dance platform with a group of men, she favored him with an encouraging smile. And then she saw Lars Evanson. He whispered something in Cathleen's ear just before he caught sight of Nicki, then he started walking toward her. Cathleen's eyes followed his retreat, a glimmer of concern in their depths. She wanted to help Nicki Sue. Soon, she thought, wishing Nicki could read her thoughts, I'll take care of him forever for you.

Nicki Sue felt like whirling about and running to the safety of her room. But she knew she could not, for even there she was not safe from this man. She stood quietly and pretended interest as Reverend Black offered the first of the quilts for sale.

"Is one of yours for sale?" she heard Lars ask. "Perhaps I should buy it, show all of our neighbors how charming I find you."

She met his amused gaze with slitted eyes. "If you do—I'll burn it."

He laughed softly. "Ah, what fire you possess. I hope you stay that way after you become my bride."

Nicki ignored his remarks and asked, "What are you doing here? I didn't think you'd have the nerve to come back."

"Let's just say I am protecting my interest." He stared at her with a taunting grin. "When do you think we should let everyone know of our plans?"

"How can you talk about letting everyone know you are planning to marry me when you are here with Cathleen?"

"Cathleen is not the sort of woman to be jealous of other women. She understands my relationship with Krystal—she'll also accept my marriage to you." He shrugged. "As for the rest of them—they'll be green with envy, that's all."

"Does Cathleen know about us?"

"Of course. She's more than willing to share. She's very independent, like you. It will be a nice arrangement for all of us."

"And what if *I* should decide to change my mind?"

"Quite simply, the outlaw dies," he replied evenly.

"You are despicable," Nicki choked.

"Hush now, or your friends will hear us disagreeing. We wouldn't want them to think that ours will strictly be a marriage of convenience, now would we?" His eyes bore an ugly light when he noticed her look of distaste. "Don't worry, you don't have to recognize the marriage if you don't want to. All I want is the assurance that I'll have your land. And just as soon as Krystal turns over the funds I need to resume building, I will break the news to her about our forthcoming marriage. She's a bit more temperamental than Cathleen and will take special handling, but when she hears my explanation, she'll understand."

"Where is she?"

"In Denver. Actually, she was beginning to bore me of late, and I felt the need to strike up new acquaintances. I don't think she will be back for a few days yet."

Over her shoulder Nicki Sue glimpsed Jake quickly purchasing Cathleen's quilt before anyone else, and then the two of them picked up a basket of wine and assorted tidbits and began walking toward the moonlit shadows. Lars was so engrossed in taunting her and making her miserable that he had no idea what was going on behind his back.

Nicki could not help but smile. "I hope you weren't planning on spending the evening with Cathleen."

Lars spun around and saw that Cathleen was nowhere to be seen. His fists clenched at his sides, but he said nothing of what he was thinking.

"It must be nice to have a relationship where there are no demands," Nicki said with feigned sweetness. She walked away from him, wondering what in the world she could do to get out of this situation.

Storm was in the far corral, the only one that hadn't been touched by the fire. Nicki had picked up several carrot sticks from the food table and now stood at the corral fence with her hand extended. The musicians were playing a lovely ballad, the melody drifting on the breeze to where she stood. She was feeling lost, and so very alone.

"Come here, Storm; look what I have brought you."

The stallion trotted over to the fence and she patted him on his velvet-soft nose, then fed him one of the carrots.

"Did you bring me anything?" a deep, masculine voice inquired, and Nicki Sue was so startled, she dropped the carrots and whirled toward the sound of his voice.

It was Jesse—here! Lars had either been lying or Jesse had managed to escape. Her heart leaped at the sight of him. She was so glad to see him, but was also very concerned for his safety.

"Jesse! What are you thinking of coming here like this? There are people all over!"

He grinned crookedly. "I know; I've already had the pleasure of talking with a few."

"You *what?*" she gasped, noticing that he had what appeared to be a quilt under his arm.

"Don't worry, those boys were so full of beer and Culpepper's bull—" He smiled apologetically when he realized what he'd almost said. "Anyway, they never even looked twice at me. They were too busy discussing building a gallows."

"Why did you come?" her eyes were wide and luminous in the moonlight.

"Why do you think?"

"Don't, Jess—tell me . . . say it," she whispered with bated breath.

"I came to see you, Nicki. I wanted to explain why I needed you so the other night." He reached out for her and she walked unhesitatingly into his arms. She buried her face in the curve of his shoulder, breathed deeply of his wonderful clean male scent. Tears came, and she cried softly. What he was about to say was forgotten at the sound of her sobbing.

"He . . . told . . . me you were his prisoner . . . and I was so afraid, Jesse."

"Who told you that?" he asked.

She drew back from him and stared up into his narrowed blue eyes. "Evanson came to me and told me he had taken you prisoner, and that if I didn't agree to marry him, he would kill you."

"That rotten bastard," Jesse snarled, "he'd do anything to get hold of your land. He had Bo prisoner for a while, but Dakotah and I managed to rescue him. That was why I had to leave you right after . . ." His gaze softened and he added, "I'm fine, Nicki, and so is Bo. He's recuperating with my sister and Dakotah near here."

Suddenly she was clinging tightly to him. "Jesse, this has all got to stop. I can't watch you die—I won't watch you die."

His lips were against her temple. "Hush . . . let me hold you. I need time with you, baby; I've missed you so damned much."

"You know we shouldn't . . . it's too risky." But already his hand was caressing the curve of her breast and she felt herself weakening.

"I didn't snitch this quilt of yours to have you turn me down."

She was staring up at him, noticing the quilt and debating only seconds before she nodded. "You took my quilt . . . How did you know it was mine?"

Jesse slipped an arm around her and they walked

off into the thick shelter of trees. "The horses — and your crazy stitches."

Her bright golden eyes narrowed. "I did a good job on that quilt."

Jesse grinned. "I was only teasing, Nicki. Try not to take everything I say to heart, for just a little while anyway."

She slapped playfully at him, and he grasped her finger, biting the slender tips, then kissing each one tenderly.

They didn't make it very far before Jesse was tossing the quilt outward to flutter to the ground. He had her in his arms, and somehow their clothes no longer were a hindrance but lying scattered, and Jesse was kissing her as if he couldn't get enough of her.

His hands were everywhere, bringing such exquisite pleasure wherever they touched. His fingers traced lacy patterns over her pretty breasts, then drifted downward, skimming over her sleek stomach and the smoothness of her belly, at last stroking lightly between her legs. Her hips jerked wildly as his hand cupped her womanhood. His fingers entangled in her cascading hair as his lips nibbled at first one breast, then the other, suckling at the trembling rose-tipped nipples until Nicki moaned deeply in her throat.

Jesse kissed the curve of her breasts, along her rib cage, and lathed the indentation of her navel. He wanted to taste all of her, possess her completely in every way. Soft, slender thighs quivered beneath his mouth and parted to receive his intimate kiss. Her fingers laced through his hair, clung tightly as wave after wave of ecstasy took her toward complete satisfaction. But Jesse would not let her go. He smothered her soft cry of protest with his kiss, his body at last thrusting into her welcoming warmth.

Her slender form trembled in shock but eagerly received all of him. He was gentle, and rough, then whispering near her ear how she excited him beyond control. Unable to restrain his desire any longer, he rolled his hips against her in a sensual, heated rhythm that drove her crazy for him. Writhing, gasping, she grasped him to her with long legs and felt his own body convulse with hers. And when the last shuddering peak inside her had quivered and died, she still held his body within her, reluctant to part.

It was the sound of a roaring explosion ripping through the night that tore her from his arms. They dressed hurriedly and she was watching the glitter of excitement in his eyes that was all too familiar. He hadn't come back exclusively to see her! There was another reason! A shudder rippled through her.

"What have you done, Jesse?" she heard herself ask, grimacing as he snatched her arm and was hurrying away from their peaceful shelter, pulling her along behind him.

"I don't have time to explain it all to you now." He was staring down at her, issuing orders in a short, clipped voice that rang in her ears, as did the sounds of excited voices near the house. "I want you to play along with Evanson. Don't let on that you know I'm not his captive or he'll realize how you found out the truth. It's the only way I know to protect you now."

"I only need you!" she was pleading despite her best efforts not to. "Don't leave me again!"

"I'll be back; wait for me—I promise, Nicki Sue."
He kissed her cold lips. "You belong to me. And
Evanson will never have what is mine again."

Nicki grasped at his arms even as he was gently
pushing her away.

"When it's quieted down, look for me. And stay
away from Evanson before you become his next victim."

She was suddenly sick of everything! The thought
came that Jesse didn't intend to come back for her.
He'd been using her tonight just as he'd always
done. Beneath his civilized veneer lurked a deadly
stranger that she did not know. Their moments together would always be like this; they'd never be
able to act like a normal couple. He wouldn't stop
until he either killed Lars Evanson, or was killed
himself.

"No—don't come back! We're finished, Jesse . . .
for good this time!" she sobbed after him, never
certain if he heard her, for he had not looked back
even once.

Suddenly Elizabeth was there, enfolding Nicki in
her arms and allowing her to cry until there were no
more tears.

"I know . . . I know how much it hurts you," she
whispered. "I've had to stay on the sidelines too,
but we must remain strong; he needs that." Nicki
drew back, her eyes widening. "What I suspected is
true, isn't?"

"Yes, Jesse is my son," Elizabeth replied, knowing that Nicki would give her life before she would
betray him.

Nicki regained some semblance of composure and
accepted a hanky from Elizabeth to dab at her
moist eyes. "How can you stand by and let him go

on this way?"

"Because I have no other choice in the matter, Nicki. I love him. And I can only hope this will all be settled soon, and he'll come back to me—as he will come back to you."

"No, you're wrong, Mrs. Kardel. I am beginning to believe he is drawn to me because I have something that Evanson wants desperately. My land. If Jesse has my land before Evanson, he would have a means to taunt the man further. He's like a mountain lion who has his victim beneath his paw, teasing him mercilessly until he's ready to inflict the mortal blow."

"I don't think even your land will help Evanson regain what he's lost tonight. Jesse's men blew up the tracks near the lake."

Nicki Sue was never more aware that if Jesse had her, and her land, he would have the power he dreamed of, and the means to crush Evanson completely. Well, she wouldn't give either man the chance to use her again.

Marty and Pablo came galloping past the corral on their horses, calling out frantically to Nicki Sue. She gave a shudder. The tone of their voices warned her there was more grief yet to come.

"Mrs. Ryan! Are you all right?" Marty blurted, swinging down from his prancing mount.

"We were so worried," Pablo added with obvious relief.

Elizabeth and Nicki Sue stepped out into the bright moonlight.

"I'm fine; I was just showing Storm to Mrs. Kardel," Nicki replied.

"What is going on? We heard a terrible explosion." Still she could not believe what Jesse had done and wanted desperately to hear someone tell her it had been nothing more than an accident.

"Someone blasted Evanson's newly laid track to pieces. By the time we got there, there wasn't much left except smoking track deliberately twisted like a bent hairpin. Heard about some raiders during the war left their calling card that way." Marty cast his eyes downward and his voice became husky. "Morris Skiles's body was found nearby. We think he could have been coming back into town when he came upon the men setting the blast . . . and was killed."

"He never was too bright," Pablo said impulsively, "but the poor man shouldn't have died like that—"

Marty saw the two women looking utterly mortified, and intervened. "Uh, the ladies don't need to hear the details, Pablo."

Everyone began talking at once, it seemed, but Nicki Sue wasn't listening any longer, for her thoughts were elsewhere. No, Jesse, not innocent, dumb-witted Morris, who couldn't shoot straight to save his life, she was pleading silently. Don't let it be true, for how could she live with herself knowing how easily he controlled her traitorous body, and just as easily, killed.

Vincent met them as they were making their way back toward the house. He was visibly shaken, but smiled weakly when he saw his wife.

"I became worried when I couldn't find you. Where did you slip off to so quickly?" When she didn't answer, he just continued. "One minute I was buying your quilt and some nice little cakes to take along with us, and the next, you had disappeared and there came that awful explosion."

Elizabeth patted his arm reassuringly. "Vincent, dear, I'm fine. Please, don't fuss anymore."

Lars Evanson was livid by the time Nicki Sue returned to the social. One of his men had come to report the extent of the damage. Tents, supplies, and irreplaceable equipment. Lars became like a madman.

"You fools!" he roared at his men. "What do I pay you for? You should have killed them . . . all of them dirty back-stabbers!"

People stood and stared at him in stunned disbelief. They had begun to doubt him before this, but now they were certain they did not want this man in their town.

The explosion had dampened everyone's party mood. People were beginning to gather up their things and leave. Nicki knew many of them were beginning to wonder if they should involve themselves further with Lars Evanson. The entire issue of the PGC and Nicki Ryan's land was too volatile even for the citizens of precarious Bodie. If this was what happened when a railroad took over a town, then they wanted no part of it.

Lars was darting from one couple to the other, trying to regain their support. He knew he had lost his temper and had spoken too freely. "Look, Stan, Nancy—things are just a bit out of hand right now. They'll get better. There's no danger to any of you . . . Please, give the PGC a chance to get established here." When he got no response, he spun around to confront two men he played poker with. "Sam . . . Curly . . . you know me; I've put a lot of money into this town, all of your businesses, and I'm going to do even more."

Sam mumbled something about violence following the tracks of the PGC and everyone was getting wise to it. With a snort, he started to walk away. Lars grasped his shoulder and jerked him around. He grabbed Sam by the lapels of his jacket and began shaking him.

"You don't turn your back on Lars Evanson! Nobody does that!"

"Stop it, Evanson," Vincent Kardel spoke out. "Let folks go home peaceably if that's what they have a mind to do."

Lars wasn't listening; he was frantically trying to reestablish his credibility. If he let them get away now, he'd be done in this town.

Everyone was watching. Lars reached Nicki Sue in two steps and snared her wrist between unrelenting fingers.

"Wait! You're all leaving before my surprise announcement!"

Nicki tried to calm him, told him with flashing eyes that this was not the time to announce anything! But he was not listening, nor did he care that she appeared horrified. He leaned close and hissed that she'd better go along with him or he'd see her entire ranch was left nothing but a burned-out shell by morning.

"One order, and there'll be nothing, and no one left alive. Now, smile; you're supposed to look happy."

"You won't get by with these threats much longer," she promised him. "I *will* find a way to stop you."

"We're getting married! Yeah, that's right," he

401

rambled on as everyone stared silently. He raised their entwined hands. "Soon you'll see peace in this valley and my railroad bringing prosperity to each and every one of you. Just give me a chance, folks."

Jake and Cathleen came hurrying over to Nicki Sue.

Cathleen put a comforting arm around Nicki Sue. "It will be all right, I promise you," she whispered. "Don't try and fight him on this . . . trust me."

"He's gone crazy, hasn't he?" Jake asked Nicki.

Nicki could not seem to find her voice to say anything. She wanted to say something to deny his declaration, but she knew now wasn't the time. Suddenly she was overwhelmed by people gathering around her, all of them talking at once, some of them offering their congratulations even as they whispered as they walked away about how unpredictable human nature was.

And Sugar and Betty Lou were right there, ears attuned to every word and opinion. Nicki knew if she said anything now, they would crucify her. No . . . there had to be another quieter, yet effective way, to stop this man.

"Why, what a nice surprise," Sugar said with a tight smile.

"And she never let on at all, did she?" Betty Lou was telling the woman standing next to her. "But whatever do the two of them have in common?"

Head aching and suddenly longing to be alone, Nicki Sue found an opportunity to slip from Lars's side and hurried toward the safe haven of her room.

"Nicki, wait!" Cathleen called after her.

But Nicki couldn't wait, couldn't tolerate another

402

minute of the shattered evening.

Maria was right behind her, a cool compress in her hand, then, without saying a word, helping Nicki to undress and get into bed.

At the moment all that she wanted to do was go to sleep and forget. Forget that only a short time ago Jesse had been holding her in his arms, and the world, for a time, had seemed so far removed.

Chapter Twenty-one

Nicki awoke the next morning feeling like the weight of the world was upon her shoulders. She didn't think she could summon the necessary strength to battle Lars's takeover of her land any longer. There was no one he loved, his greed was all that he needed. And there were too many people whom she cared about. He knew it, and knew how to effectively use it against her. There was nothing she could do to stop him. He was a vile, ruthless man who had killed her husband and unborn child—and would resort to any means to obtain his objective.

What should she do now? She considered her options as she dressed for the day. Somehow she had to keep going, maintain a spark of hope that everything would eventually be fine. If she could just sell the horses, even Storm, at least she would not have to be constantly worried about their well-being. There was a knock on her bedroom door.

"Yes, what is it?"

"There is a man to see you, señora," Maria's voice answered through the door, sounding grim and somehow conveying a warning.

"I'll be there in a minute," Nicki replied, hastily tying her hair back in a ribbon. As an added precaution she strapped on the pearl-handled Colt she had bought right after she had come to live here.

When she stepped into the parlor and saw the man lounging casually in a chair beside the hearth, she felt her temper sizzle. He was one of Evanson's hired guns, crudely dressed and wearing crossed bandoliers and twin guns. He grinned insolently at her and just sat chewing on the stub of a cigar and intermittently sipping coffee from one of her best china cups as if he had every right to be there. His eyes flicked with half interest on the gun that rode low on her slim hip.

Without a word of greeting she crossed the room to stand in front of him, one hand resting on the butt of her gun, and snapped, "What right do you have coming here? I will not stand for it."

Cold eyes like those of a reptile stared back at her, and she had to force herself not to look away.

"Got my orders, and they were to stay here today."

Maria was poised anxiously behind Nicki, scowling as she explained in rapid Spanish that she had told the *pistolero* he would have to wait outside and he had gotten ugly.

"*Madre Dios!* He almost knock me down pushing his way in the door and then he even demand I bring him cup of *café*, with cream and sugar; can you imagine the nerve!"

"Shut up your harping, woman," the man known as Bart growled. "Get back in the kitchen, where you belong, before I give you something to whine about."

That brought a blaze of fury to Nicki's eyes, and if Bart had had the least bit of sense, he would have known never to rile a woman with Nicki's fire and deadly aim. But being the dolt that he was, he decided to taunt the two women further. Rising from the chair, he stated with a leer, "Then again, maybe I'll just join you in the kitchen. I like hot little chili peppers — eat 'em for breakfast every day — and today I didn't get a chance to eat yet." He took a threatening step forward, and Nicki Sue stiffened. Maria cringed behind her.

"You get out of my house," Nicki ordered furiously, shielding the trembling housekeeper with her body.

"Stay out of this, lady," Bart growled with a dark scowl.

Nicki Sue stood her ground, bright spots of color staining her cheeks and battle lights dancing warningly in her eyes. "You take one step closer and you will surely regret it," she threatened.

Being a huge man well over six feet, there was little doubt in Bart's mind that this delicate-looking creature posed no serious threat to him. He swung outward with his arm, intending to knock her aside, when there came a blur of motion before his eyes and he found himself staring down the barrel of her gun. He started to open his mouth to growl, and she pointed it directly at his lips.

"Take one step closer — say another word — and you can forget about ever eating another chili pepper, mister."

Bart did not move, or barely breathe. My God! He'd never known a woman who wielded a gun with the confidence she did. And the steely look in

406

those flashing gold eyes gave him pause. He blinked rapidly and blurted, "Okay, gal, you can put that revolver away . . . I was only funning with the lady." He smiled weakly when her hand never wavered.

"Honest, now, back off before you get shaky and that gun goes off accidentally."

"Look at my hand, mister; does it appear the least bit shaky to you?"

Bart stared at the firm grip she held on the handle of the gun. "No . . . no, ma'am, it doesn't."

"Then you know if this revolver goes off, it won't be by accident."

Bart gulped.

Nicki Sue was enjoying the moment immensely. She was feeling a return of her old self-confidence and was enjoying her obvious control. Her shoulders squared obstinately, and suddenly her melodious laughter echoed through the room. "You don't appear so hungry anymore, mister; I guess I've gone and made you lose your appetite."

"Señora, just tell him to leave," Maria whispered urgently over Nicki's shoulder. "Do not make him angrier than he is. His kind, they never forget."

Nicki realized she was right, and stated softly, "Now, is there going to be any more argument about your leaving?"

Her humiliating treatment of him had Bart in a rage, but he knew that for now, there was nothing he could do to retaliate. But there would come a time, when she least suspected, that he would make her pay dearly for this.

"I'm leaving," he stated coldly. "But I ain't forgettin'—you can try to sleep nights thinkin' about that." He stormed around both women and stalked from the room.

When the front door slammed behind him, Nicki Sue sagged in a chair with a relieved sigh.

Maria was trembling so violently that she had to hug herself to stop from shaking. "That big ox, he mean what he say. He'll never forget. . . Oh, I feel so bad that he will try to get back at you now because you defended me."

"It wasn't your fault, Maria. His kind is always spoiling for a fight." She smiled reassuringly at the beloved housekeeper. "He'll get over it."

"Just the same, do not turn your back on this man."

Nicki Sue sat for a long time thinking about Maria's words after the woman had left the parlor to begin cooking breakfast. Her temper had overruled her caution, and perhaps it had not been wise to ridicule the man the way that she had — but *goodnight!* He had deserved it!

Krystal returned later that day. Lars was sitting nursing a brandy after dinner in his private car when he heard the sound of a carriage outside. At first he hoped it might be Cathleen, and his pulse jumped. But then he heard the distinct sound of Krystal's voice as she told the driver to go on back to the hotel and pick her up in the morning.

Lars was in a particularly black mood. Since the night of the social at the Ryan ranch, Cathleen had deftly avoided him. He didn't know if it was because she feared for her safety in his company, or if she was peeved because of his forthcoming marriage to Nicki Ryan. Hell, she had agreed that they should not just see each other, but go out with other people and enjoy life while they could! He'd sent her flowers, notes explaining why he'd had to make the announcement so abruptly, but she had not responded as yet, and he was getting desperate to hold her in his arms once again. Damn, but she had the kind of face and body that drove a man crazy for her.

Lars glanced up when the door banged inward against the wall and Krystal flounced into the car. He could tell by the heat in her eyes that she had also heard the news. He almost groaned out loud. Women! They were driving him to drink and almost had him entertaining thoughts of becoming a monk!

"You son of a bitch! You send me out to secure monies and supplies for your damned railroad, and while I'm gone, you're bedding one wench and become engaged to marry another!"

"Shut up, Krystal," Lars demanded, his voice harsh.

"Not until you answer me this. Which of us are you brooding over—me, Nicki Ryan, or Cathleen?"

"I'm not in the mood for this—"

She cut off his gruff protest heatedly.

"As if I am! I expected to come back here and find you waiting with open arms—and what do I find waiting for me instead? Your dirty laundry!"

All at once the folly of his actions of late came crashing down on him. He did a brief summary in his head and realized he had not been handling his women, or his railroad, very well. He had allowed that outlaw to shake his belief that he *would* see his railroad completed. It was time to quit licking his wounds and go ahead with his plans. There was talk of another railroad competing for a grant across the same section of California. His scouts were sending back daily reports that the K.K. track layers were moving fast out of White Rock. He was beginning to get very nervous. Surely they were only running a trunk line to the mines in that area!

"So I made a few errors in judgment," he said gruffly, trying to cover his unease. "I've been under a lot of pressure lately."

"Yes, I heard someone dynamited the tracks and destroyed the supplies, stacks of rails and all."

He nodded, feeling the tight feeling in his chest ease somewhat. No matter how she got on his nerves at times, Krystal was really the only woman he could talk with who understood his dreams. Too bad she didn't excite him in bed any longer. He shrugged. "We'll do our best to recover, although they had enough dynamite strung through camp to blow five-hundred-pound steel rails to hell and back."

"Where were your men?"

"They were in the tents, I suppose. None of my men heard anything suspicious until the explosion. But I know it was that damned outlaw and his gang. He's been after me with a vengeance because I almost killed his brother."

"What has been going on since I've been gone?" Krystal inquired, astounded by the rapid turn of events.

Lars set the tumbler of brandy aside and shrugged, perplexed. "I simply did what I had to do to protect the growth of the PGC, and now every-

410

one is turning on me because of a few unfortunate incidents."

"It sounds to me as if you've let things get completely out of hand."

He glared at her. "What should I have done, Krystal dear, just let that outlaw keep helping himself to whatever he wants without trying to stop him?"

Krystal knew better than to push him too hard, for he could very easily explode into violence. She flung her reticule on the settee, her anger dissolving to hurt. She had planned all the way out from town to give him hell for betraying her loyalty so shabbily just as soon as her back was turned. But now, seeing him before her, wanting him so, and hating the tortured look in his eyes, she softened.

"It might have been done a tad more subtly, darling," she drawled. "Really, Lars . . . you married to that Ryan chit?" One eyebrow arched distastefully. She withdrew a folded newspaper from beneath her arm. "Have you seen the Bodie newspaper yet today?"

He was almost afraid to say no. "Why?"

She tossed it in his lap. "You have other concerns besides that outlaw and your woman troubles. Go on, open it."

Lars unfolded the paper and saw immediately the article she wanted him to read.

Supplies arrived by wagon today for the construction of a water tower on the northern section of land at Los Paraiso. This reporter can only speculate that it may be in conjunction with the rumor circulating that there is a railroad construction gang furiously laying track

411

for a spur out of White Rock onward through this area and into Nevada. If this is true, it has been the best-kept secret in the history of rail construction, and the mysterious president of the railroad is said to have generous investors who have bought a staggering amount of stock in his road. The entire town is anxiously awaiting the first sign of the crews and the mystery man behind the K.K. line.

Lars threw down the paper with a roar of outrage. "Whoever this bastard is, he is not going to steal my fortune right out from under me! Why didn't any of my men get me their schedule?"

"I hate to be the one to break the bad news to you, Lars darling," Krystal said a tad smugly, feeling a measure of satisfaction at seeing Lars suffering so, "but it seems the K.K. is going to reach Ryan land first—unless you have some way in mind to stop them?"

"I'll stop them—don't you worry about that." He suddenly remembered why he had specifically sent her out of town, and asked hastily, "Did you get the security I need, Krystal?"

She took a chair beside him and folded her hands in her lap. "Bad news does travel fast, my poor darling. Everyone who purchased bonds before simply refused to offer you additional money."

"Great! I suppose they too have read the stories about that outlaw robbing me blind." he fumed. "They've been going all over the country."

"It doesn't seem like anyone wishes to place money on a lame horse. You're going to have to watch your step, darling; the talk about you is not good.

Lars lunged and grabbed her by the shoulders. She thought he was going to break her neck, he shook her so furiously.

"This is all your fault; I know it! You encouraged everyone to back out. Well, I'll have what I want yet. The Ryan woman *will* marry me . . . she will . . . she will . . ." He had become like a wild man, ranting, pawing all over her, and now his eyes were gleaming with a hungry light.

Pent-up frustrations merged with raw desire, and Krystal found herself eagerly twisting in his arms, a half sob bubbling in her throat.

"It's been so long . . . ," she groaned.

Krystal gasped as he suddenly tumbled her onto the floor and grasped the hem of her gown to yank it up over her hips. His fingers tore at offending undergarments and sought her hidden charms. He invaded her womanhood, seeking her moist warmth, moving his fingers in such a way that Krystal was soon writhing on the floor in ecstacy.

"I'll have you . . . I'll have you . . . ," he was panting, sweat rolling down his contorted face, his eyes glazed with desire.

And she could only wonder as he took her then with an almost urgent need if, while his body was embedded in hers, he was envisioning her face behind closed eyelids, or conquering the woman who held the key to all of his dreams.

After Krystal fell asleep on the couch, her body covered by a thin satin wrapper, Lars went to the safe he kept hidden behind a section of the mirrored wall and opened it. He intended to go through his files — he kept a complete file on the people he had victimized, and those yet to come. And tidbits on politicians that he could use to blackmail them with if necessary. When he swung the door open, he saw that the file was missing.

"I'll break her neck," he snarled; pivoting and reaching Krystal in three strides, he dragged her from the couch.

Her eyes flew open as he raised his fist.

"How long have you had those files? Did you take them with you and sell them to the highest bidder to get even with me?"

She shook her head in denial, but the blow fell anyway.

When he was done with her, he threw her limp body on the bed and stormed out of the coach.

Chapter Twenty-two

Krystal knew she had devised the perfect plan to dispose of Nicki Ryan. She sat in her hotel room at the Fairmont, a look of calm resignation on her beautiful oval face. Bart had just left her room. She smiled remembering their visit, the visit she had precipitated in order to set her scheme into motion.

"It's very simple, dear man," she had explained with infinite patience. "You are one of the few people Lars allows near her ranch. You must try and lure her away from the house. I will be waiting with a wagon. I don't care about anything anymore. And it appears of late all that Lars cares about is his women. He'd rather dally with their charms a bit before he disposes of them." Her smile was sensual. "How about you, Bart honey? "Do you ever dally with the ladies?"

His eyes seemed to have already undressed her.

"Yeah . . . I like 'em any shape or size," he chortled.

She thrust out her breasts, which were full and ripe, almost spilling over the filmy neckline of her lacy wrapper. "I thought you were the sort of man who had a way with the ladies. That's really why I picked you, you know. You're big and strong. . . . I like my men big, everywhere."

Bart grinned proudly. "Then you got yourself the right man, in every way, sweetie. But there's only one thing I want to know."

"What's that?"

"How do I lure her away from the house and then explain her disappearance to Evanson?"

She felt like screeching at him that he was a big, dumb ox that didn't have an ounce of brains! But knowing that he was just the sort that she needed kept her from doing so. "It's really pathetically simple," she chuckled, delighted with her flawless plan. "You just make certain she thinks someone is bothering her horses, and she'll come running real quick. Then she she gets there, grab her and bring her up on the South Ridge trail. I'll be waiting for you there. Just make certain you get the girl. "I'll make Lars believe she ran off with that outlaw. It shouldn't be too difficult, actually. Lars doesn't trust her; he'll fall for it."

Bart grinned. "That sounds easy enough." He was fast losing his ability to reason with Krystal rubbing provocatively against him, promising him all kinds of things with her eyes. Still, he knew Evanson would be furious, and he would have to make certain he was not on guard duty when the girl's absence was discovered.

"I guess I could do it; I owe that little bitch for making me look like a fool once before," he agreed at last. His hands began sliding up and down Krystal's back; she twisted feverishly beneath them. "First, though, I want a little something to whet my

416

appetite."

Krystal allowed him to slip the lacy gown off of her shoulders. She tried not to cringe when he wet his lips with the tip of his tongue. This was something she would try not to think about, just endure. For it would be worth anything to be rid of the Ryan chit for good! She wanted to be the only woman in Lars's life. And with Bart on her side, she would keep Lars's dalliances to a minimum.

Her head fell back as wet lips moved over hers, then slid downward across her arched throat to her heaving breasts. With her eyes closed she could imagine it was Lars's mouth doing such erotic things to her body.

"Oh . . . yes . . . that really is wonderful," she murmured throatily, feeling his tongue swirl around as he took her body. Krystal pretended the rough hands that caressed her belonged to another lover, one she would soon no longer share with anyone.

Nicki imagined in her sleep that she heard the horses whinny nervously. And was that . . . the haunting notes of a harmonica? Or was she only dreaming? She tossed restlessly, the thin cover tangling about her legs and holding them prisoner. In her sleep-drugged mind it was Jesse's legs, Jesse's arms, Jesse's body that was next to hers and setting her afire.

The low, plaintive melody continued, a ballad she discerned even as she slept. Nicki wanted to elude the magic the melody was weaving about her, luring her, it seemed, to abandon her will and surrender.

417

She awoke abruptly to find her brow damp with moisture and her heart beating like a rabbit caught in a trap. She lay there listening, and knew it had only been the sighing of the wind that had penetrated her dream and made her imagine it was something else. But there came Storm's whicker, and she knew that she had not imagined she'd heard the horses. Were they upset about something? Wide awake now, Nicki got out of bed and padded across the dark plank floor to stand before the open window. She wore only a thin cotton gown, but the night was hot as a firecracker, and even the persistent breeze blowing through the floor-to ceiling-casement windows provided little relief. It was quiet again.

The guards were at their usual posts; there were only two tonight. Funny that Bart was not there.

Her eyes trained on a ghostly shaft of moonlight trailing through the window, drawing her gaze to the starlit sky. She stood there quietly thinking, and could not help but wonder where Jesse was at the moment, if he too found it hard to sleep and was perhaps watching the beauty of the night and the full moon. Why did she even care where he was . . . or who he was with? There was every indication that he was responsible for Morris Skiles's murder. Her head ached with conflicting feelings. She wanted Jesse to come back, and yet, she could not face loving someone who could kill without a shred of conscience. Then, remembering how she'd been ready to do the very same thing, she was even more torn with indecision.

Nicki forced herself to think of the ranch, and

Patrick's hope that she would love Los Paraiso as much as he had. She wished there were one man she could share her dreams with, to comfort each other during the awful times when you felt you didn't have a friend in the world and the nights were so lonely. Thinking of Patrick brought to mind the scaled-down model of the train and buildings in his study. Would she ever see the dream realized? Drawing on a robe, she left her room to go to the study.

There was no one stirring. She lit a lamp and crossed the floor to stand and stare thoughtfully at the miniature replica of the train and numerous buildings, and the lake, remembering the night she and Jesse had shared such passion in the cool blue waters. Tears formed in her eyes when she thought of the man who would soon be holding her. She reached a hand forward to touch the water tower next to the tiny track that ran in front of it.

"If only I had some way of getting out of this without anyone being harmed, I could hold on for another year until the railroad fully expands here . . . and then there would be no more worries, ever."

"Señora?"

Nicki whirled to find Maria standing in the doorway.

"My goodness, you scared me," she breathed.

Maria looked contrite. "I'm on my way to the kitchen for a glass of warm milk and I saw the light. I thought perhaps you might like some too?"

"You couldn't sleep either?"

The housekeeper fussed with the sash of her colorful wrapper.

"I . . . I awoke thinking I'd heard . . . someone out by the corrals." She laughed lightly. "But I'm sure now it was only the wind." She hurried forward when she saw Nicki's face go pale. "It was probably only Evanson's men."

"Yes . . . probably so . . . ," Nicki Sue managed to reply, but Maria's words had frightened her. "I think I'll just get my gun and check around."

"Well . . . I'm not certain exactly . . . but it sounded like someone was deliberately trying to frighten them."

Nicki went still. "Maria, go ahead and make me that warm milk, will you? I'll be along in a minute."

"You are certain there is nothing wrong?"

"No . . . everything is fine — go on ahead."

"*Sí*, I'll go right now," Maria agreed, casting Nicki a dubious glance over her shoulder as she left the room. Quickly, Nicki went back to her room and shucked off her nightclothes and drew on a blouse and riding skirt. Then she hurriedly snatched up her rifle (she'd been practicing daily and had become a fairly accurate shot — at least, she could hit what she aimed at if given a big enough target) and left the room.

Maria was sitting in the Spanish-style kitchen sipping a glass of milk when Nicki passed through on her way outside. She cast the young woman a look of disbelief when she saw Nicki was dressed for riding.

"Señora Ryan — where do you think you are going this time of the night? And your milk is almost ready."

Nicki paused. "I'm just going out for a while. Now, don't look at me like that; I'll be just fine." She held up the rifle. "The boys taught me how to use this, although I don't think I've anything to worry about."

"But it is terribly late . . . and those men will not let you out of their sight."

Nicki grinned. "I know every nook and cranny of this place — do you think they can truly stop me if I wish to slip away? And Marty is probably already at the corrals, so stop fussing."

Maria set her glass down to throw her stout arms into the air in exasperation. "Ay! you will do exactly what you wish anyway — I have learned this by now."

"I promise I'll be very careful." She was already going through the open door.

Maria watched her go, mumbling under her breath.

Nicki did just what she told Maria she would. Slipping stealthily through the night and across the yard, she ran quickly toward the far corral. She saw to her relief that the horses were fine, but in the distant shadows a man was running to his horse. Who was it? She had become very adept at saddling Kyra, and she did so now with efficient ease.

Her riding skirt was split down the front and made it easy for her to mount the prancing mare. Once she was up on Kyra's back and galloping into the blanketing night, she could feel her nerves become less tense. She thought about how much she had changed over the past months, how she could

421

ride and shoot, and take full responsibility for her actions.

Marty and Pablo had taught her a great deal about survival here—where sometimes a gun and quick thinking were all that kept you alive—and she had been an eager pupil. Her finely honed skills had made her even more feisty (a term that Marty was fond of using in referring to her self-assurance).

Feeling suddenly full of daring, she leaned low over Kyra's regally arched neck and whispered the command to send her literally skimming over the flat land.

There was nothing but the wind, she told herself, but her ears were straining to detect any unusual sounds. Ahead of her, the faint outline of a horse and rider drew her onward.

Before her lay the cabin on the bluff. There was no sign of the other rider now, but somehow she had instinctively known to come here. Trying hard to stave off her rising excitement, Nicki reined the mare in front of the cabin. It was still now, and the cabin dark. There was no movement around her— no one was here. God! Was she losing her mind? Had he affected her so deeply that she imagined every sigh of the breeze, or shadow in the night, to be Jesse?

She didn't know what she planned to do if she confronted him. Could he have come back to make certain she hadn't talked, or could there be another reason? Rifle clenched firmly in her hand, she walked up to the door and pushed it inward. She knew there was a lantern to her left on the table, but dare she use it? What if someone was truly prowling around?

Making her way slowly across the room, she fumbled on top the hearth for the tin of matches she knew to be there. It was then the door slammed hard behind her. She jumped with fright.

Nicki tried to remain perfectly still, not daring to even breathe. She cocked her head and listened— then, what was that? It might have been the wind that closed the door . . . and then . . . it might not. Then she heard the footsteps: a light, almost soundless tread coming toward her. The back of her neck tingled. Someone had followed *her* here!

"Stay where you are!" she blurted, swinging her rifle in front of her. "I have a rifle, and I'm not afraid to use it."

There was no reply.

She thought she could take a stand, fire blindly and hope to scare whoever was there. And then strong, relentless fingers closed around her neck. She struggled to break away, to take aim with her rifle. A soft cry of rising panic escaped her. Fear was trying hard to overtake her, and she was certain the man before her was counting on it. They were stumbling about in the dark, his bigger body easily encompassing hers. In desperation, she managed to squeeze the trigger, and the rifle shot exploded in the confining room. There was no scream of anguish, but he had let go of her neck and she could breathe. Had she hit him? Oh God, what should she do now?

Her instinct to survive prevailed and Nicki darted to one side, planing on circling around the edge of the room to the door. She had lost complete sense of direction and stumbled over a chair, the rifle flying from her hand as she tumbled hard to the floor. Her head hit the back of the chair, and pain exploded in her skull. A rainbow of color swirled before her, and she remained on the edge of that blind hell for agonizing seconds before she blacked out.

"I knew something awful would happen. . . . I tried to tell her," an almost hysterical Maria was sobbing three hours later to Marty after hearing him relate how he'd discovered Kyra saddled and lathered from a hard run in her stall only minutes earlier.

"Try not to go thinking the worst," Marty told her, his mind already calculating what needed to be done. "I've already told Pablo to saddle our horses, and we're going right out to have us a look see." He rubbed the back of his head. "Somebody sure walloped me good on the head – and Pablo, he drank so much tequila after supper, he slept through the whole thing. We'll probably find her no worse for wear, sitting somewhere waiting for one of us to give her a ride back to the house."

Maria nodded tearfully. "*Sí*, I hope you are right." She chewed on her bottom lip. "The señora did not say where she was going. . . . Oh, this is awful," she wailed louder, then waved her hands at Marty's distressed face. "Go! I'll be fine; you just find the señora."

Pablo was waiting outside by the stable with Marty's bay gelding. Evanson's two guards were also there. Pablo had already explained what had happened, and the two men had agreed to search the eastern section of the ranch.

"Did Maria have any idea what's going on?" Pablo asked Marty.

"Not much. But she did say that Mrs. Ryan snuck out of the house after they heard the horses acting up."

"All by herself?"

Marty swung up into the saddle and picked up the reins. "You know how that little lady is—she gets a notion in her head and she does it, with no thought for the consequences."

Pablo nodded as he reined his horse forward. "Sí—I have never met a woman who seems so determined to stand on her own two feet, and has managed quite well up till . . ."

"Up till now," Marty stated grimly. "She's earned my respect."

"It's too bad Mr. Ryan didn't live to see how well she's taken to the place."

"I had my doubts when she first came," Pablo admitted. "She seemed such a proper lady, and the first time she discovered a callus on her palm, I had to smile at the look of horror on her face."

Marty smiled then. "I remember that day. We were training a new mare and she came down to the corral and took over for me—trotted the mare in a circle for a good half hour. Did it right well too." He urged his mount into a gallop, suddenly more anxious than ever to find Nicki.

The two men said very little as they rode the Ryan land in search of her. They had no idea where to begin looking, but in both their minds they knew they wouldn't quit until they'd searched everywhere.

Lamplight bathed the room when she opened her eyes. She was lying on the bed in the cabin, and there was someone standing in the shadows at the foot of the bed. Her tawny eyes narrowed. He didn't have to step into the light for Nicki to know who it was.

As if he felt her heated gaze boring into him, he stepped around to the side of the bed. He raised the brim of his hat so he could better discern her face in the dim light.

"I'm glad to see you're awake at last. You had me worried."

Nicki scrambled to the far corner of the bed, clutching her knees to her chest. "How . . . could you . . . why?" she sobbed.

He made no other move toward her, just stood there looking terribly handsome, even as he set her heart to pounding in her chest with apprehension. He wore a long duster over his clothes, and she could see that he'd been riding hard, wherever he'd been. His eyes changed perceptibly when he realized what she was thinking.

"My God, do you actually believe it was me who tried to kill you?"

"I . . . don't see anyone else in this room," she replied, rubbing her raw throat. "And considering what happened the last time I saw you, I'm certain you can understand why."

"It could have been a lot worse. All we did was

stop Evanson from getting any closer to your land so that the K.K. Railroad could overtake him. It's a good road, Nicki Sue. They'll be fair, and take good care of you."

She was so upset she did not perceive what he was telling her. She was just staring at him accusingly, and Jesse was suddenly angry too, and provided no further explanation.

Nicki's eyes glittered. "Morris Skiles was killed brutally in that explosion. Or did you forget about him?"

"I take it by your tone that you blame me for that."

"As a matter of fact, yes, I blame you for a great deal," she asserted harshly. "Tell me, did you come here tonight to finish things with me—make certain that I don't tell anyone you were around the night Morris died, and give them an accurate description of one of the most wanted men in California?"

Jesse scowled. "I was trying to make certain you don't get yourself killed. And you have not made my job too easy. Hell, you ride all over at night, you cuddle up to my worst enemy—yours too, in case you have forgotten.

Nicki watched him with wary eyes as he took a seat in a chair next to the bed.

"And instead of being grateful that I chased that thug off tonight, you're acting as if I might strangle you at any minute."

"How do you expect me to react? You'd threatened to do just that any number of times in the past." She smiled unpleasantly. "Oh . . . I see now. . . . You expect me to believe there was another person here tonight that tried to kill me." She glanced around her. "Well—where are they?"

"I don't intend to sit here and defend myself to you," he stated flatly.

Nicki's eyes slitted. "I think you'd better state whatever is on your mind, and then leave. I don't know what to believe about you anymore. As far as I'm concerned, I don't owe you anything, and from now on, stay out of my life."

"Will you just shut up for a minute and let me talk?" he growled. "You always did give out orders, didn't you? I don't know how I could have forgotten so soon."

"I can manage to take care of myself just fine."

His grin was mocking. "Yeah—I saw, tonight, how well you do that."

Nicki felt her heart flutter strangely at his cold declaration. His eyes were burning blue, and condemning.

"Just go—leave me alone, and from now on stay off of my property, or I swear I'll have you shot," she stated harshly.

Jesse wasn't certain he recognized the woman before him. He tilted his Stetson farther back on his head and observed her silently. His coal-black hair spilled over his forehead, and Nicki's eyes were drawn there.

This was not the same woman he'd taken off of the train, ridden for days with, made love to with passionate abandon. This was an entirely different woman: tough, hard as nails, and determined to make her own way without anyone's help, and most especially, his. She really did hate him. He saw that

428

in the depths of her eyes. His own narrowed. Well, that was fine with him, for she was nothing but trouble anyway. He didn't think she knew the danger of her staying here. Obviously, Lars Evanson hadn't made his move yet. He could tell her, but then, she didn't believe anything he said, so what was the sense? Perhaps the K.K. Railroad might convince her, if she stayed alive long enough for them to reach her land. At the moment he felt like forcing her to go with him, but he knew she'd hate him even more if he did. He was drawn out of his brooding reflections by the sound of her voice.

"I'm leaving here, Jess, and don't try to stop me." Her hand was reaching for the rifle propped against the wall beside the bed.

Suddenly he was grinning. "You sure make it tempting," he said.

Her brow furrowed. "What are you talking about?"

"To take you with me."

Her eyebrows shot up in surprise. "You wouldn't dare! They'd hunt you down for certain this time — and I wouldn't be such a willing victim like before."

"Let's face it; I'd be a lot safer with you tucked away where I can keep an eye on you."

Nicki scrambled to her knees to dart off of the bed. Jesse was before her in an instant, leaning over her, chuckling infuriatingly.

"We had us some memorable times. . . . Maybe we could pick up where we left off."

"Don't you touch me!" she spat.

Ignoring the throbbing in her head, Nicki tried to scramble around him and off the bed. He grabbed her easily, imprisoning her against his hard body. He stared down into her luminous eyes.

"You'd soon get used to living with me. And it might be kind of nice having someone there waiting for me when I come home who can cook and clean . . . and to teach her a woman's place."

"When hell freezes over," she ground out from between clenched teeth, her head thrown back and her eyes spitting fury.

Something inside of him made him take her head between his hands and lower his lips to hers. That first touch of her lips sent a hot rush of desire tearing through him, and he kissed her hungrily until she whimpered softly and unclenched her teeth to allow their tongues to meet in a passionate dance.

Every fiber of her being was commanding her to resist, not to give in to the demands of her young body. His hands were upon her breasts, her flat stomach, the vee between her legs. Their breaths intermingled as one. No matter how much she told herself she hated this man, he could ignite a passion within her that simply could not be denied. She felt completely out of control, lost to everything but him. A soft whimper escaped her, but she was not even aware. Only when the sound of approaching horses and excited voices reached Jesse did they separate.

Nicki stared at him, dazed, uncertain what had happened to make him change so abruptly. Then she heard Marty and Pablo calling out to her.

His lips lifted in a mocking smile upon viewing her dazed expression. "Company's coming. I think

430

it's best if I don't stick around to welcome them."
He paused. "I'll be back real soon, Nicki. You can
count on it."

Before Nicki Sue could say a word, he had
slipped silently out the door and disappeared into
the night.

"Mrs. Ryan! Are you in there?" Marty yelled, as
Pablo leapt from his saddle.

Nicki tried to compose herself, and answered,
"Yes, I'm here—and I'm fine." At least I am physically, she thought, but emotionally, her entire world
felt as if it had been turned upside down once
again. And she knew very well the reason why.

"You fool!" Krystal was raging at Bart, sitting
next to her in the wagon parked high on the winding mountain road. "What happened? Where is the
Ryan woman?"

"I couldn't get her," Bart professed, gasping for
breath from his desperate flight.

"You yellow-bellied coward! She ran you off with
that gun of hers again, didn't she?" Krystal accused, her face absolutely livid.

Red-hot fire exploded in her jaw. Bart's fist
poised above her, threatening another blow. "Watch
what you say, lady; I don't take kindly to being called
names."

Krystal scrambled to the far side of the wagon,
her hand grasping behind her for the buggy whip
she'd laid there. Bart began to explain what had
gone wrong, but she was barely listening. All of her
pent-up rage at Lars had surfaced when Bart had

431

hit her. At that moment, she was as vicious as a coiled rattler, with fangs bared to strike.

"I almost had her! I waited for Bates and Lowell to take a smoke out back by the well before I went around to the opposite side of the house down to the corrals to stir up the horses. But damn it! it wasn't easy, like you said it would be! One of her men poked his head out of the bunkhouse to have a look see—he almost caught me. She came out of the house and down to the corral to saddle her horse. I got her to follow me to the cabin all right, but then I swear I heard someone come riding up just as I was ready to grab her, so I had to get. I barely got away from that cabin with my hide!"

"I don't want to hear your excuses, you oaf! You failed!" Gripped in the throes of her mad fury, Krystal began beating him with the buggy whip. The rawhide whipped through the air again and again, slicing across Bart's face.

He bellowed like a bull and began to slap at her. The horses bolted and went galloping down the narrow trail, the wagon careening dangerously behind them.

Too late, the two people realized their grave situation, Bart grabbing desperately for the trailing reins and Krystal clawing at his arms trying to grab them away from him. When she saw pale moonlight wavering before them on a twisting curve, she knew she must jump or lose her life. Moving quickly, she prepared to lunge from the wagon, and screamed in outrage when Bart's clawlike fingers grasped the folds of her skirt and aborted her plan.

"You ain't goin' nowhere,"he snarled hoarsely.

"We're in this together, lady!"

The team of horses kept running, thundering around curves and shifting the weight of the wagon back and forth on the weakening axle. Finally, on a hairpin turn, it snapped completely, sending the wagon with its screaming occupants plunging over the rim of the mountain.

Bart let go of Krystal to grasp the sides of the seat. Krystal was thrown from the wagon onto the rocky mountainside, where she rolled and tumbled like a broken rag doll, her piercing shrieks of anguish intermingling with Bart's roar of frustrated fury.

Their piercing cries tore sharply through the night, sending birds winging upward from the trees in noisy flight. Then all was still.

Chapter Twenty-three

Vincent Kardel was at the K.K. Railroad construction sight before sunup to catch the first view of the crew members, who were predicated to round the mountain with the sun glinting off the newly laid rails. He was standing on the tall stacks of steel rails that had been delivered earlier in the week. Elizabeth was sitting in their buggy beside the rails, pencil and paper in hand.

As soon as he viewed the sun rising, Vincent tensed, waiting. He had been visualizing this moment for a long while. His bank had invested heavily in the railroad's bonds, but he had complete faith in the enterprise.

"Do you see them yet?" she asked her husband.

Vincent trained his field glasses on the pink-gold horizon. "I . . . see something . . . wait — yes! They are heading this way!"

He swung his gaze briefly to meet hers. A tense look passed between them.

"The waiting is just about over, darling." He smiled widely.

Elizabeth felt a rising sense of anticipation. "How long will it take them to lay the track this far?" she

434

inquired, the enthusiasm evident in her voice. She had been waiting a long time for this. Her hand shook as she made notations on her writing pad.

"I'd say from the reports I've been receiving about that crew, they should be here in about four hours."

"My, that is impressive.".

"They're paid well for their loyalty and hard work," Vincent said.

"I've heard their boss is a generous man with his money."

"Yeah, he is at that," a man who'd ridden up on horseback answered with a half grin.

Vincent's mouth lifted in a wide smile when he met the man's eyes. "How's it going, Bill?"

"Fine, Vince. The crew should easily lay four miles today."

"I'd like you to meet my wife. Bill Hickok, Elizabeth Kardel."

Hickok nodded and touched the brim of his hat. "Nice to meet you, Mrs. Kardel."

"And you, sir." Elizabeth smiled up at him. "Might I talk with you sometime? Do a piece in the paper perhaps on your exciting life."

Hickok grinned and shook his head. "I don't think so, ma'am. My name draws too many undesirables. And we have enough with Evanson and his men."

James Butler Hickok, known far and wide as Wild Bill, had signed on as a troubleshooter for the K.K. Railroad. He was a personal friend of the K.K.'s head man, and his work came highly recommended. He was fast on the draw, played a mean game of poker, and didn't back down from any man, no matter his size.

"I'm surprised you're still around," Vince said. "I thought by now you would have gotten bored with this dull work and have moved on."

"Sooner or later, I imagine," Hickok admitted with a wry smile. "There seems like enough excitement around here to keep me hanging on a little longer."

Elizabeth was busy writing on her pad when another rider came galloping over to join them. It was Red Sinclair, the foreman for the K.K.

"The boss sent me to check on the supplies and also to let you know some of Evanson's boys were snooping around the rail site earlier. He wants you to keep them away if you can." Behind them a wagon rumbled onto the site.

Hickok observed the Gatling guns and stacks of rifles in the wagon's bed, and the flame-haired beauty sitting next to the driver. His eyes revealed his pleasure. "Well, now, this is a surprise — I haven't seen that gal since Abilene. She worked at the Bull's Head saloon until she got married and left town."

"Friend of yours?" Vincent grinned.

"In a manner of speakin'," Hickok drawled, his eyes now resting on the guns in back of the wagon. "Looks like we're expecting trouble."

"Just a precaution," Vincent told him.

"Can you handle it, Bill?" Red asked with a knowing grin.

"Oh, I believe so," Hickok chuckled; then, nodding at the Kardels, he kneed his horse toward the heavily laden wagon.

"Good man there," Red said. "I don't expect we'll have much to worry about with Hickok on the job."

Elizabeth stared after his retreating figure. "The man is never as big as his legend, is he?" she pondered aloud.

Red considered her words before replying. "No, ma'am, and that's what makes it tough for fellas like Wild Bill. They're painted almost bigger than life—most of them get in the habit real quick of sleeping with their back to the wall every night."

Elizabeth could not help but think of her own sons, and said a silent prayer that this would not be their legacy.

Nicki Sue knew she must continue to believe that everything would be fine. But every time she heard a sigh of the wind or a creak in the house late at night, she imagined it was Jesse come back again.

She would recall the night the deputy had been found murdered, and then she would get out of bed, with her stomach feeling as if it were in knots, and pace back and forth in her room fighting the truths inside of her.

No matter how hard she tried to convince herself that Jesse no longer mattered to her, she admitted to herself, when night fell and she was alone in her room, that he did. She could easily recall the way he walked, his bold, handsome features, and the passionate way he made love that took her breath away. She wanted him even as she feared him. Dear God! What a mess he'd made of her life! He couldn't care . . . not the way he came and went in her life.

She stood looking out of her window at the half moon reflecting a cloudless sky. Lars Evanson had placed four of his men around her place to stand guard. One of them, Sam, had informed her of this with an almost gleeful grin.

"Mr. Evanson doesn't want anything happening to his lovely bride-to-be," Sam had told her. "He wasn't happy about you giving Bart a lot of guff the other day. Said whatever it took to make you behave, I was to do it." He'd peered hard at her with beady eyes before adding, "I guess that means if you act up, sis, you lose something you care a whole lot about."

With a sheer effort of will, Nicki Sue had straightened her shoulders, her eyes returning his hard glare. "And I suppose Evanson sent four of you to 'make me behave' after he found out I almost shot Bart's head off."

"You have an uppity way about you, you know that? I'd say you'd best work on changing it if you ever expect to catch yourself another man to look after you." He was red-faced with suppressed anger.

Nicki had tossed her head defiantly. "I don't think I need the likes of you to be telling me how I should act. Now, if you're finished—" She'd pointed toward the front door. "Keep away from my house, or I just may mistake you for a coyote skulking around and pepper your mangy hide with buckshot."

Sam had jammed his hat back on his head and spun on his heel.

A tight-lipped Maria had immediately appeared, grumbling under her breath in Spanish, to show him out the door and slam it soundly behind him.

And Nicki Sue had been left trembling with the knowledge that if Jesse came around the area again, they would be waiting to kill him.

Later, watching the sun come up from the windows of the study, where she'd gone to seek an escape from her memories, Nicki found she almost wished Jesse had come last night. What would she have done—demanded answers, been fearful of the hard-faced, blue-eyed outlaw . . . or forgotten everything for the moment, as in the past, and eagerly gone into his arms? She was saved from an answer by the sight of Marty striding toward the stable. A new day had begun, and she had to forget her need of Jesse, for she had the ranch to worry about.

Glancing down at the miniature train set and the replica of the water tower, Nicki began to think that perhaps Patrick's dream would be realized after all. She had no idea who this enigmatic railroad man was, or how to thank him, but he had sent a courier to tell her that the construction on her water tower would begin in the next few days.

She recalled Lars Evanson bragging of soon having his own town. But with this new railroad giving him competition, and the Kardel gang hampering his efforts to expand, she would be the one to soon have a new town—as Patrick had intended for his heir. And with a reputable railroad to back her.

Her husband's vision of Los Paraiso truly had been of a paradise. Her hand strayed to the model train set, one slender finger tracing the entire circumference of Patrick's imaginary town, and the tranquil lake that dominated the lovely setting.

"A train . . . needs water to keep its steam locomotive running. And Los Paraiso . . . has the only water in miles to guarantee a locomotive enough steam to cover the distance between towns." Her heart was racing now, and for the first time she was beginning to fully realize the legacy Patrick had left behind.

He had claimed this land and stayed here because he was simply biding his time, waiting for the PGC to get near enough to deal with Evanson. Perhaps he'd imagined offering Evanson passage over his land beside the lake. Later on, settlers would come and a brand-new town would emerge. The Ryans would be the planners and the builders. And then her eyes strayed to the mansion perched on the cliff overlooking the town.

"This was to have been our new home, a mansion to rival any of those found in San Francisco."

Who more than Lars Evanson had reason to have wanted Patrick dead? Nicki's eyes took on a faraway look. She owed it to Patrick's memory to realize his dream and make certain that Lars Evanson was stopped once and for all.

In thinking about it later, she supposed she formed her scheme to kill him out of desperation. It came to her plain and simple, however horrid. Poison, that was the only way. She would end his life by putting poison in his food. An unexplained sudden illness could prove fatal with a doctor so far away. There was a small bag of white powder in one

440

of the tool sheds, which they used to kill off the ever-pesky rats that fed on the horse's grain. She thought then of her dead husband and the unborn child that had died as a result of the stable fire.

"May God forgive me for what I am plotting to do, but it is the only way to save lives. Someone must stop him before he kills again."

Feeling a settling calm, Nicki left the study and went to her room to dress for the day. She had much to accomplish, having also decided to go to Evanson on the pretense of having him ship her horses to Sacramento to sell them. It wouldn't appear suspicious, and her own people would not question her motives too closely.

She was surprised when she entered the kitchen at four A.M. to find it was already occupied. Pablo was sitting at the table drinking a steaming cup of coffee while Maria stood in front of the stove adding sliced peppers to a large pan of frying potatoes. Maria smiled when she noticed Nicki in the doorway.

"Sit down; I will get you some breakfast in a *momento*."

"Just coffee will be fine, Maria," Nicki said, taking a chair next to Pablo.

"You're up earlier than usual, señora. Is everything okay?" Pablo asked.

"I guess I'm a little concerned how we're going to sell those three yearlings. We can't put it off much longer. Money is real scarce, and I owe a lot of my neighbors." She sipped at her coffee. "I want

441

to pay them as soon as possible."

"It does not appear to me that Mr. Evanson will let you out of his sight," Maria murmured, ignoring the girl's chastising glare.

"Something will just have to be arranged," Nicki said. "This ranch can't be maintained much longer without an income. And I refuse to take charity from anyone again."

Marty came through the back door and joined them. "I wish you wouldn't worry so about money. We'll get by for a while longer."

She rolled her eyes. "I haven't seen any growing in the garden, have you?"

"Did I say something wrong?" he snorted.

Nicki shook her head and sighed. "No, of course not. It's just me. I've got a lot on my mind."

"It does not look good, I think," Maria commented, setting a plate of scrambled eggs and fried potatoes before Marty.

"There has to be a way," Nicki Sue mused aloud.

Pablo spoke up. "Arabians are a tough breed, señora, and even though the weather is very hot, maybe we can still take them across-country to Sacramento."

"Short of puttin' wheels under their hooves, I don't see how we could make it that far in this heat with such valuable animals without taking a chance of something going wrong," Marty drawled as he reached for a fluffy biscuit.

"Marty's right, I'm afraid," Nicki stated despondently. "There just doesn't seem to be a sensible means to transport them."

Everyone fell silent. Nicki appeared deep in

thought, and then suddenly a crafty light appeared in her golden eyes.

"What's going on in that head of yours?" Marty asked, a grin spreading across his weathered features.

"Marty, you've given me an idea. I think there just might be a way, after all."

"Whatever are you talking about?" Marty scratched his chin as he considered her words.

"Wheels, you said?"

"I did."

"Then wheels we'll have."

"I'm not following you, ma'am," Marty admitted, perplexed.

"Pardon me, señora," Pablo intervened. "I don't think I understand either."

"We will take the horses by train," she told the astonished trio.

"There's only one railroad around here—Evanson's," Marty grumbled in disbelief.

"It's the fastest, safest method to transport the horses that far," Nicki countered, "and I haven't any other choice. And how can my future bridegroom refuse my request?"

Inwardly Maria groaned. "I don't know about this . . . I don't like that man." She favored Nicki Sue with a worried frown. "I think there is something about your marrying him that you are not telling us, hmmm?"

"It is my responsibility," Nicki stated firmly. "You three stay out of it. I have to do what I think is right."

Marty took a deep breath, then said, "We know

you can't stand that man, and none of this makes any darn sense."

Nicki wished that she could have told them the truth, but she knew that they would intervene to save her if they became aware she was doing it to save them and the ranch. She looked at Marty. "It is my choice to marry him. And don't worry—everything will be fine in the end."

"Looks like her mind is made up," Pablo sighed, and then, smiling weakly at Nicki Sue, "If he is threatening you . . . I will kill him myself."

"No, it isn't that," she barely replied, thinking once again of the desperate mission ahead of her. She glanced over at Pablo. "Will you have one of Evanson's men escort you to his train? Tell Evanson that I wish to speak with him on an important matter tonight, and that I will be there at seven."

When Lars Evanson sent Pablo back to Los Paraiso with an invitation for Nicki Sue to join him for dinner in his private car, she knew a moment of panic. But she quickly stifled her feelings, knowing that the only way she would succeed was by staying calm.

She went to the tool shed and opened the bag of poison marked with a skull and crossbones. Scooping out only a small amount of the arsenic, she put it in a little bottle and capped it. After tightly securing the bag, she replaced it on the shelf, and then went directly to her room to wait until it was time for her to leave.

The rest of the day passed in a blur, and then she

was dressed and waiting for Marty to bring the buggy around to the house.

"You must not go, señora," Maria pleaded one last time, wringing her hands.

"Stop it, Maria," Nicki replied, gently firm. "I have to go. And as long as Marty is going to drive me and wait for me outside, I can't foresee there being a problem.

Pablo shook his head slowly. "I do not like this man at all. And while I was there this morning, I saw many men around the camp, and they look more like *bandidos* than railroad men."

"I'm beginning to wonder if there is a distinction," Nicki said. "The power and money one acquires with a railroad draws many unscrupulous men."

"I have heard the K.K. Railroad crew are nothing like the Pacific Gold Coast men," Pablo said. "When some of the K.K. men delivered the supplies for the water tower, they stayed around to talk for a while. They said you were not to worry about a thing, their boss would be in town later in the week to discuss terms with you. He was a nice young man, that one. Reminded me of my cousin Manual with his black mustache."

Nicki was so engrossed in her own troubled thoughts that she had not heard the last of Pablo's words.

On the drive to the campsite, Marty did his best to keep his opinions to himself. Once or twice he looked over his shoulder to glare at Sam, who was riding behind them. When they arrived at the railroad camp, Marty favored Nicki Sue with an encouraging smile.

"I'll make myself scarce, but I'll be nearby. If you need help, just give a holler."

"I'll remember," she assured him, but she'd already convinced herself that she could handle Evanson, and that nothing was going to go wrong.

She was nervous, even though outwardly she appeared cool and calm. She knew she looked her best when Marty's eyes had lit up with appreciation upon seeing her dressed in a lovely silk gown.

Lars was waiting for her, and just as soon as the buggy was spotted by one of his men, and this reported back to him, he dismissed his personal porter. He had been anticipating this evening all afternoon.

"We are going to have a splendid evening," he muttered to himself as he checked his appearance one last time in the wall of mirrors in front of him. He assessed his image closely. Were those dark circles beginning to form beneath his eyes? No! Of course not, he silently reassured himself. He appeared as confident as ever, although every muscle felt taut with urgency. Krystal's untimely demise, coupled with Cathleen's sudden disappearance, had shaken him; there was no denying it. And his secret files were missing too. Not many people had access to them, and possessed the nerve to steal them.

Lars had questioned Cathleen's boss regarding her whereabouts after having searched her room, finding nothing. He'd insisted Cathleen had told him that she was leaving town to tend to a sick aunt. Lars wondered about that. And then there was the Widow Ryan, in whom he had a vested interest. How had so much gone wrong so quickly? His empire was crumbling; he no longer could visualize that last spike being driven at the junction of the Central Pacific in Nevada. What had happened? When had it all begun to go wrong?

From all reports, Cathleen was a respectable woman, but there was some question as to her last name. The wire he'd received from the detective he'd put on the case stated he could find no evidence of a Cathleen Kramer ever having lived in Chicago. Lars had sent a return telegram to keep digging for clues—he had to discover the truth about her. He wanted so to believe in her.

Against his will a vision of her filled his thoughts. He recalled how she'd always worn her silver-blond hair fastened in a prim roll, until she was alone with him and he sent it tumbling like a silken waterfall down her naked back as he pulled loose the pins and prepared to make love to her. Her pale turquoise eyes could melt a man's heart or freeze it into fear that she might find him wanting. Yes, she was a quiet seductress, and even now fired his blood.

When the knock sounded on the door, Lars waited several seconds before answering it. Then, brushing a piece of lint from his impeccably tailored coat, he reached for the latch.

Nicki was trying to calm her riotous nerves, and when the door opened at last to reveal Lars Evanson smiling amiably at her, she swallowed her rising panic and stepped inside. The luxurious interior was just as she'd remembered it. For a moment she almost lost her nerve as she recalled the last time

447

she'd been here. She felt him watching her and for a fearful minute thought he could see in her eyes what she was planning.

"Good evening, Mr. Evanson."

"Yes . . . isn't it," Lars responded huskily, his astute gaze noticing that her face bore a slightly distressed look, and that even though she had cleverly applied a hint of rouge to her cheeks to try and conceal it, she appeared pale from exhaustion.

"Thank you for agreeing to see me," Nicki stated stiffly.

"I can't tell you what a delight it was to receive your message," he said as he showed her to a seat at the exquisitely set table. He held out her chair and she sat down. "You know, I knew somehow that sooner or later you and I would be able to set aside our differences and work toward a common goal." His smile was now completely charming. He withdrew a magnum of champagne from a silver container and reached for her glass. "This is the very best that money can buy. That's why I wanted you to come here. This champagne is only a prelude. After we are married and our futures combined, there will be nothing beyond our reach."

Nicki glanced around her. There was no one but the two of them.

"You trust being alone with me, don't you, my dear?" he drawled.

"I am here because you have left me no choice," she replied evenly. "Somehow we must work out our differences."

"And we shall," he murmured, his eyes glittering as they assessed her closely. "You are a woman with

448

spirit, and while I admire that, I must tell you, some of that must be tempered for us to get along."

She had to bite back the words she wanted to hurl at him, and watched as he filled her glass to the brim with champagne. Somehow she managed to stay calm and keep concentrating on the moment when she could use the poison. She saw his approval of her appearance mirrored back at her in his gaze. He wore a gold chain around his neck, a solid gold locomotive hanging from it and gleaming back at her. Her gaze was riveted there. She couldn't help staring at it. How much blood had been spilled for him to realize his dream? she found herself pondering. And knowing with certainty that she would be the one who would stop him. Had to be, in fact, before he killed yet again.

Lars smiled smugly to himself at the direction of her eyes.

Nicki picked up the delicate crystal glass, and he touched it briefly with his.

"To a very pleasant evening," he said softly.

At last she found her voice. "And might I also add: to new beginnings." Of course he could not understand what she really meant. And she knew she had to be very careful this evening how she presented her proposal. This was the moment she had been anticipating all day. She forced herself to smile encouragingly at Evanson.

"Well, shall we eat?" He waited for her to remove the silver cover from her plate.

"It smells heavenly," she said as she did so.

All through the magnificent dinner of roasted lamb with mint and saffron rice, Evanson talked of his plans for the PGC. He was a man obsessed with a purpose. And tonight, she was also.

Lars began talking about her ranch, and how he had not expected her to hold out as long as she had. Nicki's eyes were again drawn to the tiny gold locomotive on the chain. He leaned forward and it began to sway back and forth on the end of the chain. Her vision seemed to narrow, center on the golden gleam flashing in front of her. It seemed she could hear people screaming . . . and gunshots . . . and sinister laughter. She heard Lars now through a sort of fog and, with supreme will, forced her gaze upward.

"An after-dinner liqueur," he was saying in that whisper-soft way of his that she felt certain other women must find enthralling. "It is an exclusive brand found only in San Francisco."

"Just one," she replied.

He extended a tiny crystal glass toward her.

"I am just so pleased by your presence here," he stated, as though she never again would have anything to fear from him. "We must let everyone know that we have set aside our differences. It will do a lot to improve my image here."

"I did not know that we had." Her voice was colorless.

He only shrugged, and said, "With the K.K. Railroad breathing down my neck, I would say the sooner both our names are on the deed to Los Paraiso, the better for the PGC. And then I'll have the pleasure of telling their men to stay off of my property."

She knew he would have liked nothing better than

to oppose them immediately, but he must realize the K.K. was not without its own force. Evanson's manpower was fast dwindling. After the last explosion, there were many men who had quit his employ, fearing for their lives.

Taking a deep breath, Nicki said, "You may have that after I have sold my horses in Sacramento. As you have mentioned, I am a very independent woman, and I wish to pay off my debts before we go ahead with any wedding plans."

He stared at her, appearing to be weighing the truth of her words. Finally he said, "I see — well, I suppose you leave me no choice but to agree. But let me ask you, how do you propose to get them there?"

She kept her features perfectly controlled as she replied. "The faster I get them to Sacramento, the quicker we set a date."

Judging her shrewdly for a moment, he finally said, "I knew there had to be another reason for your coming here tonight. I was waiting to see how long it would take you to let me know what it is. I must say I am relieved that I can help you obtain your objective. I will arrange to take the horses to Sacramento on board the PGC."

Nicki sat back in her chair and sipped at her drink. Lars rose from his chair and walked over to his desk to pick up a cheroot. He stood there with his back to Nicki, and struck a match. Nicki reached inside the deep pocket almost hidden in her skirts, and grabbed the cold bottle of lethal powder. *Now! sprinkle it in his drink before he turns around!*

"Dear lady. I am relieved that we have at last been able to come to amicable terms."

Lars had not been taken in by Nicki Sue's charm tonight. The lady had every reason to hate him, and want to see him dead. He deliberately turned his back on her, watching her out of the corner of his eye through the mirrors beside them. He saw her hand dart into the pocket of her skirt and withdraw a tiny bottle. She removed the cap, glancing nervously at him before holding it over his drink. She had come to kill him! He was enjoying observing the tortured look on her face. The truth would come out now. Did she really possess enough nerve to go through with it? Her face went pale, and then she withdrew her hand. She could not kill him — she was weaker than she led everyone to believe. Lars knew she would never intimidate him again with her threats.

"You've changed for the better, my dear," he said as he dragged deeply on the cheroot.

Nicki felt as if she had failed. She could not eliminate this man, not even for the people she loved.

He turned around to face her, studying her slowly in the amber-gold light of the overhead chandelier before saying, "And I think I like this new one a whole lot better." He paused, then added silkily, "And I'm certain you will wish to travel with your horses, so you may have the use of my private car."

"That's very generous," Nicki managed to reply calmly. "But it won't be necessary. My horses are very spirited animals, and I wish to supervise every aspect of their transport."

"Whatever you wish, pet," he replied, picking up his glass of liqueur and putting it to his lips. "This has been an evening to remember."

Nicki Sue agreed, although she was never more anxious to leave. She didn't like him or trust him, and knew she'd be wise to call an end to the evening. She placed her napkin on the table.

"It was a lovely dinner. But I'm afraid I really must be going now. My days are quite long since I have a ranch to run, and daybreak comes much too soon."

Evanson came to his feet and cast her a slanting look. "I wish you wouldn't rush off so soon . . . Why, the night is still young and we haven't even had dessert."

"I must, for I have much to do tomorrow." She walked toward the door.

"Of course; forgive me for being so reluctant to let you go, but I've not enjoyed an evening so much in a long while." He reached for the latch and opened the door. The night air rushed into the room.

"I'll be ready to take the horses within two days. Will that give you enough time?"

"The PGC is at your disposal," he replied with a congenial smile.

Nicki Sue was shaken when he moved to drape an arm around her shoulders, his hand sliding across her back. She had a sudden desperate urge to turn and run away, but she knew she could not.

He directed her over the threshold, the two of them standing on the platform. "Goodnight; I'll see you in two days."

"I'll be here," she told him.

He took her fingers and pressed them to his lips. "Until then."

To her dismay, he walked with her to her buggy. She could see Marty was not happy about it, but he didn't say anything as they approached, just stared stonily ahead.

Lars helped her into the conveyance. "We will soon become very close, you and I," he said with confidence. "And nothing will come between us again."

"We shall just have to bide our time and see what transpires."

A man coughed in the shadows, and Nicki's head turned to stare at the group of rough-looking men lounging under a tree several hundred yards away. The glow of a cigarette arced through the darkness, and she turned to meet Lars's eyes.

He smiled down at her questioning look.

"I need my bodyguards as well."

Touché, she was thinking, but said nothing.

The men were so intent on Lars and Nicki Sue that they failed to see the dark figure far off on a jagged cliff whose eyes followed every move that Lars Evanson made toward Nicki Sue; and narrowed even more when they saw Lars Evanson take her fingertips and bring them to his lips.

All the way home she was angry with herself. When it came right down to the actual minute and she was ready to put the poison in the liqueur, she had not been able to. Her stomach had churned and her heart had beat rapidly; she'd lifted the bottle over the drink and then snatched her hand back before any of the powder came out of the bottle. She just could not cold-bloodedly kill anyone. No matter what he had done. Lars Evanson would have to face his own judgment day.

As they turned the bend in the road that led to her ranch, Nicki thought for certain she heard a horse some distance behind them, and could not help envisioning the dark-haired, captivating bandit who had sworn he would come back for her.

Chapter Twenty-four

Staring at the sampler she'd been stitching since her return from dinner with Lars Evanson, Nicki Sue reflected on the evening. He was an evil man who certainly deserved to die, and she had longed to put that poison in his drink, but just could not. Unconsciously she pushed her wire spectacles back in their rightful place on her nose. She would never submit to Evanson's plans, or his lust. Perhaps she should just do what Jesse had taught her so well. Bide her time, and wait until it was the right time to strike. Maybe she wouldn't have to kill him; maybe another solution would present itself if she just waited, and watched. She prayed that it would be soon, before it was too late for her.

Jesse Kardel stood concealed behind several trees and observed the light go out in Nicki Sue's room. Still he waited patiently another hour before glancing covertly around him and making his move toward her bedroom window. Evanson had men standing guard around her place, but tonight they seemed more interested in their bottle and cards than they did watching for intruders. It had been easy getting past them. He grinned sardonically.

Silently, he slipped inside, carefully avoiding a bright shaft of moonlight spilling across the floor. Keeping to the dark shadows, he advanced to the four-poster bed and stood staring down at her. Wavering moonbeams caressed her slender form and played about her alluring features. The night breeze stirred wispy tendrils of her hair about her face, and unconsciously she brushed the back of her hand across one cheek. Long, sooty lashes feathered against golden skin, and for a brief second her half-parted lips held his gaze riveted. It was a hot night. She'd kicked the covers to the back of the bed. The thin lawn gown she wore hid little from him. It wasn't difficult to imagine making love to her again, but he knew that after she'd been with Evanson, it could never be the same between them. And there had been no mistaking the intimacy she and Evanson must have shared. He'd seen the way Evanson had pulled her close to him as they were saying goodnight.

What a fool he'd been to feel sorry for her, and to have worried about her so much, he had found a way to keep watch over her without her being aware. She used her body to get exactly what she wanted from him, and Evanson. This godforsaken piece of land meant more to her than anything! Hell, he wasn't worried about her survival any longer. She was like a cat with nine lives—no one could get the best of Nicki Sue.

Why had she let Evanson make love to her? And he knew that she had. He remembered how they'd stepped from Evanson's car, and the sight of his arm wrapped possessively around her waist. Jesse had wanted to kill them both where they'd stood. Now he wondered why he'd felt that way. She wasn't worth it. And there were other, more effective ways to make her pay. He withdrew the knife he kept sheathed at his side and, with several quick moves, cut strips from the sheet and bound her hands and legs together.

Nicki Sue awoke confused, but when she saw Jesse standing over her, a cold, hard gleam in his eyes and a knife in his hand, her eyes rounded in acknowledgment. She opened her mouth to scream, and immediately his hand came forward to stifle her. He stretched his leanly muscled body over hers and lowered his face until they were staring heatedly at each other.

"You seem surprised to see me, Tiger Eyes. Did you truly think I'd forget the charms you offer so freely?"

Nicki Sue was frightened, but she was angry too. She struggled against the bindings that kept her from scratching his eyes out. How dare he do this! She tossed her head from side to side in frustration, her body twisting and writhing in an effort to loosen her bindings.

"I'll take my hand away from your mouth if you promise not to scream." When he saw those tawny eyes narrow with fury, he laughed mockingly. "It's really up to you, Nicki Sue. What I have in mind doesn't require talking."

She closed her eyes then, and he felt her heart fluttering rapidly against his chest.

"You weren't afraid with him tonight . . . were you, sweetheart? And you should have been—for he would have just as soon cut out your heart." His tone was belligerent, almost menacing. "And we had to part so suddenly the other night, there wasn't time for proper good-byes."

Nicki was trembling so violently that Jesse tossed aside the knife ansd removed his hand from her mouth.

"This isn't the way it should be between us," he stated in a harsh voice. "I don't want to get rough with you—don't make me."

"I'm not afraid of you," she hissed venomously. "You should know that by now."

"I don't want you afraid . . . but I do want you willing." He trailed a finger from her lips downward across her throat to trace teasing patterns across her full breasts. "You still can make a man want you like hell despite the fact he'd like to strangle you."

She watched him closely with bated breath, saw the reckless lights in his eyes dim, and become dark with desire.

"You may want me willing, Jesse, but you won't have me that way."

"I've heard that from you too many times, Nicki. And in the end, you're always more than willing."

"Why can't you just get out of my life and leave me alone?" she flung back at him, stung by his callous words.

"Leave you to him, you mean, don't you?" he snarled.

"I don't know what you're talking about." Her eyes were hard.

"Oh yes you do," he shot back heatedly. "I saw you with Evanson tonight, so don't try and deny it."

Her first reaction was to tell him to go to hell, that she didn't owe him any explanations, but she was wise enough to keep quiet and let him vent his rage. He was beyond reasoning at the moment, he was so furious.

He reached out and she held her breath, but she did not say a word.

"What? No pleas for me to understand? Not even a whimper," he said with a sneer, his fingers snaking around the ribbons at the neckline for her gown and slowly, but deftly, unlacing them.

"I only have one thing to say," Nicki said quietly.

Jesse was fascinated by her cool nerve. More than ever before he wanted to make love to her, but damn it! Not with tender regard; she deserved to be taken like the role she'd portrayed earlier. And yes! All along he'd been feeling like he shared a sort of unspoken bond with this woman, while she had merely been teasing him with her charms.

"Say whatever you want; it won't stop me from taking what is mine." The ribbons were all curled loosely across her heaving breasts, the gown falling open to his appreciative gaze. His hunger for her made his breath come fast and his loins tighten with need.

"This vendetta you have against Evanson has blinded you to the truth about us from the very beginning. It's affected your ability to feel, Jesse, and that's why I never want to see you again." She lay there staring up at him unflinchingly as his lips

460

lifted into a cynical smile.

"I'll try and remember that . . . afterwards," he drawled softly, his lips brushing across hers like a hot flame. With a quick movement of his wrist, he stripped the gown from her and sent it fluttering into the shadows. She lay naked beneath his assessing gaze; beautiful, defiant, his Tiger Eyes.

The heat between them would always be this way—Nicki knew that—but as for love, that they would never have. But when he was holding her, caressing her in this way, she began to think she could settle for less with Jesse.

His lips lingered on her cheek, her eyelids, then nipped at the lobe of her ear. She felt his tongue, moist and wet, caress the delicate shell before moving in circles along her arched neck. And his hands; they were all over her, doing things to her that drove her wild with desire for him, making her arch upward to coax his fingers inside her. Never had she felt so on fire for him. It felt as if liquid heat surged through her veins: tiny pinpricks of warmth that, when his fingers caressed there, nearly drove her out of her mind with need. Never had she wanted him like she did at this moment. Her skin craved his touch, and she could not stop the desperate sounds coming from within her, which, had she been aware of them, would have made her want to die of shame.

Jesse saw her throw her head back and bite down on her bottom lip to keep from sobbing out her pleasure when he moved his fingers in that way he knew she craved. It was enough to almost tear him from her and send him in a killing rage to Evanson.

Every inch of flesh on her body belonged solely to him! His lips plundered her mouth to still her soft cries.

Strong arms held her tightly as their mouths clung in a hungry kiss. His caressing hand delved deeper between her thighs, rubbed gently velvet-soft folds as his finger explored. Free of any thoughts except those of exquisite pleasure, they felt at that moment as if no one else existed but them. Nicki started to protest softly when his lips left hers, but the words died in her throat as she felt the wetness of his tongue on one quivering nipple. His teeth nibbled the tight little bud, felt it welcome his kiss, eliciting panting gasps from her. Her hands lay tied over her head clutching the bindings, and her legs twisted to be free. She was excited beyond endurance, yet half-afraid to surrender all to him. But he would settle for nothing less. He wanted her completely his, and she felt her strong will weakening. It was unbelievably sweet torture. He kissed the valley between her breasts, then suckled slowly the other love-starved peak. Beneath his ardent assault she trembled violently, and gasped for him to stop, then at last, to take her.

"Please . . . Jess, unbind me, let me touch you." Her passion was so overpowering she thought she might die from it.

He lifted his head to shake his head and smile knowingly. "It's much too soon; you'd turn on me in a minute, sweetheart. Hush now . . . let me love all of you."

Jesse took his time and explored every satin inch of her body. He suckled the ripe fruit of her lush

462

breasts, worshiping them completely. Her smooth, flat belly quivered beneath his lips, her hips already moving in the age-old rhythm of desire. He knew now that she would deny him nothing. Opening like a morning flower to the sun's kiss, she eagerly encouraged his questing hands and lips to explore every inch of her. He gripped her slim waist, kissed the hollows on either side of her hips until she was writhing mindlessly beneath him. He laid his cheek there, felt her shaking with her need of him, and turned his lips to nuzzle the firm silkiness. His hands stilled her trembling flanks as his tongue dipped inside her to savor her musky sweetness. He lathed the warm, moist flesh until she thought her shattered nerves would explode. Just when she had reached her peak, he moved away, his knowing tongue exploring the smooth inner curve of her thigh, her trim calve, the sensitive place behind her knee, kissing the graceful arch of her foot and each one of her toes before working his way slowly back upward once again and tearing the binding from her ankles to firmly grasp her legs. He buried his lips between her spread thighs, seeking the dusky pink core of her. Slowly he parted her moist pouting flower whose womanly essence was like an aphrodisiac to him. He kissed it, swirling his tongue over it until her head was thrashing from side to side. He drew back to watch her helpless writhing with heavy-lidded eyes. She was the most desirable creature on the face of the earth. He bent his head once more and Nicki groaned. With infinite patience, he teased her and abandoned her, and then finally, she could stand no more.

"Now, Jess . . . let me feel you inside." And when he heard her plead with him to come to her, he unbound her wrists, for he wanted to feel her arms go around him at that first hard, driving thrust to her body.

At that first powerful lunge, Nicki felt all of her nerve pulses go crazy. With a small cry she felt him drive into her yielding flesh, pushing upward until the seeking tip of him touched her womb. God, he was driving her out of her mind with her need for him. She grasped him tightly, her slender legs wrapping around his buttocks to draw him closer. She opened her eyes when he whispered.

"Look at me, Tiger Eyes. . . . Let me see the fires in your eyes while I move inside you."

Golden orbs flared hotly with undisguised passion as they met his. "Damn you, Jess . . . for making me want you so terribly."

He kissed her hungrily then, pinioning her arms above her head and reveling in the feel of her sweet breasts caught tightly beneath him. The rigid nipples seared into his, stimulated the flat male nubs to hard buds. Jesse sucked in his breath as he felt her body begin to shudder in the first throes of her orgasm. She was like a wild thing, untamable and unconquerable. He abandoned his careful control and immediately his loins responded. Never had another woman fired his passion in such a way. She was magnificent, and Jesse knew he would kill any man who ever tried to claim what was his alone. Harder, faster, he moved in and out of her until the sweat poured off his body onto hers.

The earth appeared to shatter around them and

end them hurtling through a vast prism of un-
bounded desire. Nicki moaned again and again in
rapturous pleasure, her cries mingling as one with
his. Their hearts were united for the breadth of a
second. Nicki trembled and quivered with ecstasy
and, completely spent, fainted in his arms.

Jesse's dark head was lying near hers when Nicki
awoke. She saw that as soon as she opened her
eyes, and her heart hardened. It seemed as if she
could never get enough of his passion, but she was
wise enough to realize that lust did not make a
relationship. Her body was his slave, but her will
was her own. Feeling once again in absolute control, Nicki Sue started to rise from the bed, intending to retrieve another gown. She knew her other
one lay ruined, for she'd heard the delicate lawn rip
as he'd impatiently yanked it off her. His deep voice
stopped her.

"Don't dress, I like you just the way you are."

Nicki froze in motion and sat up on the edge of
the bed. "You shouldn't have come here tonight,
Jesse."

She felt his fingers caress the curve of her back
and failed to halt a shiver.

"Damn it, Nicki, can't you just enjoy the time we
have without telling me what to do? Or do you
want me out of here before your bodyguards discover me and word gets back to Evanson?"

She whirled on him, eyes narrowing, warning him
that he was in for a fight. His face darkened as he
met her glare.

"I'm not defending any of my actions to you ever again. I do what I must to stay alive, and protect those I love—just as you do."

"I'm going to kill him, you know—just as soon as I destroy him financially." He swung his legs over the side of the bed and drew on his pants, then reached for his shirt.

"You make it sound so simple, as if taking a life means nothing to you!" Nicki hissed. "I know why you came here this evening—and it wasn't to look out for me. You're just staking out previously claimed territory, and making certain Evanson doesn't take it away from you this time." It was a cruel thing to say to him, but Nicki was feeling so trapped by her emotions, she lashed out with the only hurtful thing she could think of. She was panting and out of breath, but it did not stop her from grabbing up the sheet and wrapping it around her, then walking around the bed to face him. "You wanted to make certain I was still branded exclusively your property, for you couldn't stand the thought of him having me." She vented all of her pent-up anger and frustration at him.

Things she'd thought and hadn't been able to say came pouring out in a fury of accusations. His cool, almost distracted gaze never once revealed a hint of rage, but Nicki saw the muscles in his jaw clench tightly and knew she'd managed to hit a nerve. "You are an outlaw . . . and one of these days you won't be able to elude them. . . . They'll finally catch you, and hang you." Despite her best efforts, her voice broke in the end. "And then, I'll be free of you at last."

He sprinted forward to grasp her shoulders and throw her back onto the bed. The sheet fell away, and she was left naked and panting as he straddled her, one leanly muscled leg on either side of her waist.

"Are you through?" he snarled, a menacing sound that sent a shiver along her spine.

But she was too overcome with emotion then to stop, and half sobbed, "You bastard! Why did you come here? Why didn't you just leave me alone? I hate you! I hope they hang you!"

He shook her roughly, snarling, "Shut up before you wake the household."

Nicki Sue's eyes dilated as she viewed his menacing face hovering above hers.

"Evanson will be through soon. I have given names of his political supporters to the governor; he's heading an investigation to expose him. I want you to stay you of it, Nicki. If you don't, you'll be involved with him."

She wanted to beg him to help her keep her loved ones safe from Evanson until then, but she knew even Jesse could not do that.

"I want to . . . but I can't," she breathed raggedly.

For a moment she thought he might slap her, he looked so enraged. But he only gripped her shoulders tighter. "You should have left, Nicki. You're way in over your head, and you don't even realize it."

In a lithe moment, he released her and was on his feet, pulling on his boots and buckling on his guns. He was beginning to realize she was not a woman whose words could be taken lightly. She had become independent and strong, and even while it angered him that she defied him, he had always admired her bold courage. He thought it was this daring that had first attracted him and, even now, prompted him to return. Her passion ensnared her, but after the fires became embers, she soared free and without a doubt would go on with her life quite well without him.

"I'll leave you alone—you're damn right I will," he said in a too soft voice that should have warned her what to expect next. Suddenly he jerked Nicki to her feet and crushed her to him, long fingers tangling in her riotous hair to draw her head backward. "But let me tell you this—if you breathe a word of what you know to anyone, I'll be back. And you'll be very, very sorry you double-crossed me."

He was gone before Nicki could blink, slipping from the room with that cat-silent tread and out of her life.

She felt the color drain from her face, and her iron will crumpled. Nicki sank back down upon the bed and drew the covers up around her neck.

Chapter Twenty-five

It was nine-twenty in the morning, but already the sun beat down relentlessly on the riders waiting beside the train tracks. Jesse kept his eyes trained on Smiley, who was down on one knee, his hand covering the iron rail.

This would be the last ride for the men of the Bardel gang. They had turned their efforts to a legitimate and more profitable enterprise. Railroading. What money Jesse hadn't turned over to those who had suffered because of the havoc wreaked by PGC, they'd invested in the K.K. Railroad line. It would be an empire of spectacular proportions to serve the needs of many people from Sacramento upward through Nevada to connect with the CP. It had been Jesse's dream since he'd undertaken the task of bringing down Lars Evanson and his railroad built from other people's misery.

His crews had worked long, hard hours laying roughly eighty miles of track a day along a route acquired by selling valuable railroad bonds to interested investors. Land acquisitions amassed the K.K. thousands of miles of land—much of it in the rich Sacramento Valley. Its founders, Jesse and Robert

Bodine Kardel, were fast on their way to becoming rich and powerful men.

Smiley turned to Robert Bodine with a gleam in his eye.

"Feel anything yet?" Robert Bodine asked, wiping his sweating brow with the back of his arm.

Smiley was a study of quiet concentration, then suddenly he grinned widely. "Let's git it! It's time to ride!" he yelled.

Without another word, the tight group of riders pulled up their bandannas over their noses and wheeled their horses around and into a gallop alongside the winding rails.

Jesse's sleek sorrel led the way, Dakotah and Robert Bodine's horses trailing close behind. Smiley's little dun had been cutting around, and it took him longer than he'd intended to get a foot in the stirrup. He saw with distress that the others were already far ahead. He knew his timing had been all shot to hell, and he cursed the stubborn filly under his breath. He wouldn't be there in time to gather the horses after the men made the cross-over to the moving train. That could spell trouble when the time came for them to make a quick exit.

"If you've caused me to mess things up for them boys, Jezebel, you'll be crow's bait come evening," Smiley grumbled in the mare's twitching ear.

He didn't know if she understood or not, but she stretched out into a smooth gallop, and Smiley could only hope it was not too late. When he finally caught sight of the other horses, the sound of the train could clearly be heard rumbling toward them.

Jesse had only one thing on his mind as he urged Max onward to intercept the moving train. Taking his woman away from Lars Evanson. He knew Nicki was right when she had said his hatred for Evanson had been more intense than his love for her. It had been; but maybe that could all change. He wanted her to give him a chance to learn how to love again. This hatred was eating him up alive.

He tried not to think about the things she had said to him, or the contempt he'd seen in her eyes. She'd had a right to say them, and even more. Neither of them had ever mentioned the word *love*, although he felt her love for him whenever he was near her. He felt bad that he never gave her the same in return. But hell! he could admit it now. He had been scared to death of it. There had been too much pain to bear whenever he thought of love. Perhaps she had realized that, and never spoke aloud of her true feelings for him because of it. He hoped he was right. For in almost losing her, and having lost their child, he had experienced just another depth of grief. Sorrow was a part of life, perhaps unprecedented at times and difficult to accept, but a fact nonetheless. He should never have allowed it to rule his other emotions, and become more necessary to him than living.

He had a terrible feeling inside him. It was the way he always felt when there was death in the air. But this was worse. Nicki Sue didn't know the position she had placed herself in by trying to protect the people she cared so deeply about.

Jesse had ridden over to her ranch several hours earlier to have it out with Evanson's men and force Nicki Sue to go away with him. But when he had arrived, the only person he'd found was Maria. She told him that everyone had gone. The guards had ridden away with Nicki Sue and her men to take the horses over to the PGC for the trip to Sacramento. Reluctantly, Maria had handed him a bottle she said was filled with rat poisoning, explaining that she had found it in Nicki's shirt pocket.

"It was the very same skirt she wore the night she had dinner with that man," Maria had sobbed. "Oh, señor, I am so afraid she is going to do something today that she will regret — or even get killed over."

The train came rumbling down the tracks toward Jesse, and he kneed Max into a thundering gallop. Evanson's private car, elegantly black and sleek, was easy to spot. He knew his Tiger Eyes would put up a good fight, but she really didn't stand a chance with a vicious animal like Evanson. The man was desperate now; he might do anything to get Los Paraiso away from her, even kill her."

Killing was not easy, and for someone like Nicki, it was virtually impossible. Evanson had the advantage; he found it quite easy.

God, how could he have been so blinded by his hatred that he hadn't seen what she had had on her mind for some time now? Nicki had been plotting to kill Evanson to free them all from further bloodshed and death. That night he'd gone to her room and accused her of being with Evanson had been the night she had tried to kill him. Why did she

472

always have to take on the world by herself? But then he knew why. She was as proud and independent as he was. What needed doing in her life, she did, without asking for anyone's help if at all possible.

"Well, you may not appreciate my help, but you're getting it anyway," Jesse murmured under his breath.

Cathleen Kramer had bought her ticket for Sacramento and boarded the PGC without Lars or any of his men being aware. Today she was going home, *really* going home. And after she did what she had to do, she would once again be Cathleen Simmons, older sister of Allison Simmons, whose family had been killed by the direct order of Lars Evanson.

She stared out of the window as the town of Bodie was left behind. No one had known that she was still in the area; she had taken a room in Middleton and waited for this day. Her work here was over. She had delivered into Charlie Starr's capable hands enough evidence to issue a warrant for the arrest of Lars Evanson and his men. She hoped she could get to Lars before the Pinkerton detective and the area marshal.

She was certain Charlie Star knew who she was by now. He had been asking a lot of questions regarding her life before she'd come to Bodie. And after she'd given him the files that Evanson had on all of his associates, and the families he'd had murdered who had opposed the PGC, Star had inquired why she had placed herself in such danger to help

473

him uncover evidence to convict Evanson. She had told him that she wanted to make certain he was punished for his crimes. Although she already had it in her mind that he would. Lars Evanson would never see a jail cell. Cathleen had already judged him guilty, and was going to carry out his sentence before he hurt anyone else. She remembered Star's tired smile when last they'd met. He was glad it was over too, she could tell.

"It was Elizabeth's articles that first drew my attention to his abominable crimes," she had told him. "I hated what Evanson had done, what he would have continued to do unless enough evidence was obtained to put him away forever."

Charlie had gripped the files tightly. "Well, I believe we've got enough to do just that now. I've gotten sworn statements from several victims who have survived his attacks, and were willing to speak out at last. Mrs. Kardel did a commendable job bringing the facts to the public attention. Hopefully it will help prevent this sort of thing from happening again." He had thanked her, then he had added softly, "Have a safe trip home, Miss Simmons. Perhaps we will meet again."

She thought about his parting statement, and wondered if she would ever go back to Chicago to resume her law studies. Someday perhaps, if she lived through this day.

Cathleen thought of the derringer in her reticule. And how she was going to kill Lars Evanson, and let him know who she was, and why he was going to die. With perfect calm, she rose from her seat and strolled down the aisle, through the door and into the next car.

Nicki Sue had just entered Evanson's private coach to tell him that the horses were all loaded and that she would be traveling in the car near theirs to oversee their safety.

"No, I don't think you will be doing that," he said, his coldly glinting eyes lighting upon her. He laughed at her expression. She still does not know, he mused to himself. An exasperated sigh escaped him. "You just pushed me too far, my dear. I really can't wait any longer to have your land. I must have it now."

"What are you going to do . . . ?" Nicki posed anxiously.

He smiled coldly. "You are going to be the one to do it all, Nicki Sue. I know you've only been civil to me to pacify me so that I don't harm any of the people and things you love, but now it's time to pay the full price. You despise me, and your hope was the K.K. Railroad would destroy all of my plans. Well, they won't. I have one last chance to succeed. We're transporting the payroll from the gold mines in Middleton to Sacramento. I was able to get the contract, but it took a great deal of persuasion. My reputation is rather soiled, you might say, but redeemable." The baneful intent in his gaze warned her too late, and she could not escape his arm that snaked out to grab her.

"Let me go!" she hissed.

"I don't think I can do that," he drawled, grasping her back against him; snatching a knife from inside of his coat, he brandished it before her wide eyes. Slowly, he lowered the blade against her throat.

Cold shivers ran along Nicki's spine. "Put the knife down . . . We can talk this over. You don't want to hurt anybody."

He shook his head. "No . . . I don't think I can do that. For you see, I know how badly you have wanted to kill me. You haven't quite worked up the nerve yet—it's hard the first time, but then it gets quite easy. I'll show you very soon what I mean."

Nicki tried to keep her calm, but it was impossible with the knife blade pressing into her flesh. She knew she must keep talking to him, do anything to persuade him that she would do whatever he said. "You're wrong . . . I told you we could work out our differences. . . . We still can; just give me a chance."

He laughed shrilly. "Like I did the other night at dinner. I tested you that night, my dear—and you failed. I know now you never had dinner with me to discuss transporting your horses to Sacramento. You came to kill me."

Nicki made an inarticulate sound, thinking then of reaching downward for the gun on her hip.

"You were so obsessed with the thought of killing me, you forgot about the mirrors on the wall, didn't you, sweet? I saw you out of the corner of my eye reaching in your skirt pocket to withdraw that little bottle. And then struggling with your conscience as you held it over my drink."

She reached for her gun, but he anticipated her action, and knocked the gun out of her hand.

He kept rambling, almost gleefully, and she was certain he was enjoying her terror. "What kind of poison was it . . . hmmmm? It doesn't really matter now, I suppose." He sighed with feigned regret. "I really wasn't planning on killing you so soon. Later, after we were married awhile and everyone saw how devoted I was to you. Then it wouldn't have looked so suspicious when you had your accident. But now you've gone and spoiled all of my plans with your stubbornness.

"You can't possibly think you can continue to eliminate whoever stands in the way of your railroad and get by with it?"

"I have friends in high office in California. Political people who will help to squash any charges that might be brought against me. That shouldn't surprise you. They hold PGC bonds; they can't afford to take a beating with so much of their money tied up in my railroad."

"No doubt, crooks and swindlers, like you," Nicki could not help but snap.

"The railroad does have a small, brilliant group of us, but then, it has been common knowledge for years. I've sought to maintain as low a profile as possible, but your outlaw shed so much publicity on me, it became impossible. Now I am overindebted; I have to expand to absorb my losses and acquire enough profit to make the payments to my bondholders as well. Your land will bring in a large amount of new investors. They take more of an interest in the land being offered for track laying than they do the railroad. Your land has been my only stumbling block to success. After I have it, I'll expand rapidly, and soon connect my line with the CP. I'll have doubled my profits with a connection to the mainline."

"It's over, Evanson; they'll catch you if you kill me. Let me go and I'll give you whatever you want."

"No they won't . . . they haven't so far. But I will let you live for a few minutes longer while you sign a paper that will leave your land to me."

Through the mirrors Nicki saw the door open silently, and Cathleen stepped into the car. She had a derringer pointed at Lars's back.

Nicki's eyes widened in disbelief, and she must have made some small sound to alert him, for he forgot Nicki and spun around to face Cathleen.

"Cathleen . . . my beautiful wild rose, I've been searching for you everywhere," Lars breathed softly, the knife in his hand momentarily forgotten until he saw the little gun. Then he gripped it tightly before him.

"Hello, Lars," she smiled at him, but it was a cold uplifting of her lips. "I'm back, and I think just in time." Her eyes swung briefly to Nicki Sue.

"Get out of here, Nicki, while you can. This doesn't concern you."

Lars read the intent in her eyes and took a step toward her. The derringer jerked upward to point at his chest.

"Don't you even move, you bastard. I don't want you to die so easily. And you can drop that knife now."

Lars hesitated, then did exactly as she demanded, for the gleam in her eyes was one he could not deny. She *would* shoot him if he didn't. His eyes were brimming with unshed tears.

"You took the files! Why did you do it—to blackmail me? I'll give you money if that's what you want," Lars pleaded. "It's really only you that I've wanted."

Nicki scrambled away from him, to stand with her back against the wall

"You can quit acting now, Lars. I'm not falling for it. And by the way, it wasn't for blackmail!" she disagreed. "It was to help them to discredit you before everyone so that nothing like this can ever happen again. You even had poor Morris Skiles killed, a helpless soul. And I heard that with my own ears. Your guards were talking about it one day—laughing, actually." Her eyes shot silver fire. "I wonder if they'll laugh about you when they hear how you died."

"Why? I was good to you," Lars shrieked.

Cathleen laughed harshly. "Oh yes, very good—so good, in fact, that you murdered my entire family to get the land that you needed for your railroad! My name is Cathleen Simmons; I'm sure you remember the Simmons family from the Sacramento Valley."

Lars began backing away from her, and by the look on his face, Nicki knew he remembered all too well. "You can't prove it!"

"I don't have to prove that you were behind their killings, although I have given enough proof to Charlie Star of your other misdeeds to discredit your name until the end of time." Suddenly she inclined the gun just a bit toward the door, keeping her eyes fixed on the man before her. "Outside, now."

"Cathleen, don't, please!" Nicki Sue pleaded, unable to stand by and watch her friend kill Evanson without trying to stop her.

"I have to, Nicki; please don't try and stop me. I don't want to hurt you." She waved the derringer at Lars. "Go on! I think I shall watch you jump from the trestle that should be coming up just ahead."

"Don't do this, my wild rose," Lars implored her desperately. "I'll forgive you. . . . We'll go somewhere and start over."

"Shut up and keep moving," Cathleen ordered, deadly soft.

Nicki watched in breathless anticipation as Cathleen made Lars walk outside on the platform; then she cast Nicki Sue a sad smile and closed the door behind them. Nicki braced herself for the scream of anguish she was certain would follow. It never came; instead a series of rifle fire erupted, and men's voices rang out in the air.

The fireman saw them waiting, and leaned out of the cab window to take aim with a carbine. Jesse shot the weapon from his hands before he had time to get off a single shot.

"Cut your speed," Robert Bodine yelled as he galloped alongside the cab, his .44 leveled at the man.

Needing no further convincing, the engineer slammed the throttle down, and the train came to a bumping, screeching halt.

On the platform outside Evanson's private car,

480

Cathleen lost her footing and fell against the rail, the gun slipping from her fingers and tumbling over the side of the train. Lars Evanson went dashing forward into the passenger coach to escape Cathleen's fury.

The train halted, the Kardel gang spread out to do their tasks.

"Don't do anything you're going to regret!" Jesse told the white-faced crew staring down at his intimidating figure. A long duster concealed his clothes and a mask covered the lower half of his face, but his midnight-blue eyes glittered with deadly lights that none of them looked brave enough to challenge.

Jesse and his brother quickly dismounted.

Robert Bodine climbed on board the steam locomotive behind Jesse. The engineer lunged for the rifle lying nearby, but Jesse's glare gave him pause.

"I don't aim to hurt you, mister," Jesse said, a savage gleam in his eyes, "unless you'd rather have it that way. But hear me well. I don't want this train to start moving again unless we give you the order. Otherwise, I'm going to change my mind about some things."

The engineer and the fireman quickly agreed.

"We don't want no trouble," the engineer exclaimed shakily.

Robert Bodine leaned over the side and saw the rest of the men coming alongside the cars. Jesse scooped up the engineer's rifle and tossed it over the side to one of his men. Then the four men left the cab, Jesse sending the engineer and fireman trotting down the road.

"And don't look back, boys; just keep on moving until you reach the next town!"

Robert Bodine had already darted for the express car, where the men appeared to be meeting resistance from the express messenger, who was locked inside the car. Dakotah tried the door.

"Open up in there!" he demanded.

"By whose order?" came the muffled reply through the bolted door.

"Let's just say from the fella that's trying real hard to save your life," Dakotah replied.

"Mr. Evanson gave strict orders this door was to stay locked," the express messenger responded bravely.

"Mister, if you value leaving that car with your bones all intact, I'd say you open up — and right fast! Otherwise I'm going to blow that door clean off its hinges!" Dakotah called forth.

For a few tense moments there was silence, then came the sound of the bolt sliding free. Dakotah couldn't help a wry smile as he saw the young express messenger peek around the open door.

"Just throw out them black boxes, son, and nobody will hurt you," Dakotah ordered.

"Can't do that . . . ," the young man warbled, his face fusing crimson.

"Tell me that again," Dakotah growled, the hammer clicking back on his big gun.

The express messenger immediately started stuttering. "I-I'll be aiding . . . and ab-betting . . . your c-crime . . . sir. If you're going to take anything out of . . . this c'car . . . you'll have to c-come . . . in here and g-get it yourself."

Shorty leaned over his saddle toward Dakotah and said softly, "Don't like this—something's not right here."

"Oh hell," Dakotah growled. "The kid's just scared of losing his job; I'll go get the money myself. The rest of you boys spread out and keep your guns trained on the passenger coaches just in case someone tries to act the hero."

Shorty glanced nervously down the track toward the engine, then back at Jesse, who was running for Evanson's private car. He just didn't feel right about this one, maybe because it was their last job and he didn't want anything to go wrong. Or maybe he was just getting too damn old. Sweat popped out on his brow. They were going to show Evanson, though—with this last robbery they would destroy every last shred of his credibility. No one would ever create havoc again in the ruthless manner that he had.

Swinging his gaze back to Dakotah, he saw that he'd already vaulted up into the express car. He had just taken a step toward the car when Jesse whirled around and yelled.

"Get to the horses! I see a lot of dust kicking up back there! It looks like someone is headed this way!"

"Dakotah!" Shorty yelled. "Let's get out of here—now!

"There's a lot of gold in here!" Robert Bodine shouted.

Whirling around, Jesse expected to see Smiley nearby after having gathered the scattered horses. He was not anywhere around, and their mounts were still spread out, too far to reach safely with horsemen hot on their trail. Smiley rode onto the scene then and was doing his best to gather up the skittish horses.

Dakotah sprinted out of the car, clinging tightly to a bag. When he saw there were no horses, his expression tightened. His eyes flew to Jesse. "What went wrong—damn! This job wasn't right from the start."

"Sometimes they go that way, partner," Jesse replied in a grim voice. "Let's just keep our heads and hope we all get out in one piece."

Robert Bodine stuck his head out of the express car to glance furtively down the tracks. "Riders getting mighty close! I'll try to hold them off until you get away!"

"Don't be a fool!" Jesse snarled. "Get out of there!"

But Robert Bodine ignored his brother and instead had climbed up on top of the express car and fired off several shots, hoping to slow down the approaching riders.

Smiley had done a remarkable job gathering up the horses and now hurried forward to the men. They wasted no time swinging into their saddles and putting their heels to their mounts.

"Go on!" Jesse told Dakotah, who'd reined in beside him. "I'm heading after Nicki Sue!"

"Be careful, Jess," Dakotah cautioned. "It could be a posse after us—and they'll be shooting to kill."

As Jesse galloped past the passenger coaches, he noticed the passengers all had their faces pressed to the windows. He gazed at them with cool, steady eyes, thinking how any one of them could grab for his weapon and sight down on him before he had time to react. "Just hold on to your trigger fingers," he said heatedly under his breath.

He was suddenly shaken by the sight of the woman dashing inside of one of the coaches several yards behind Lars Evanson. At that moment she looked so much like Allison, it gave him pause.

And where was Nicki Sue? Had they hurt her? Reaching the private car, he breathed a tremendous sigh of relief when she came running down the steps from Evanson's coach.

"Nicki!" Jesse called to her, reining Max in beside her.

Her eyes flew to his, and unhesitatingly she accepted his outstretched hand and allowed him to draw her upward into his arms.

"You're safe, sweetheart; I've got you now."

"Oh, Jess, he . . . he was going to kill me because he found out why I had come today. . . . And then Cathleen, she came in with a gun . . ."

"I know, but there's nothing we can do about it now. I've got to get you out of here before that group of riders catches up to us."

Pablo and Marty dashed out of the dining car, where they had been held prisoner by one of Jesse's men during the robbery.

"Madre Dios!" Pablo groaned; the train robber has her!

If it had been possible, Robert Bodine would have turned the air blue with his swearing upon seeing Jesse thundering down the tracks toward the express car.

"Get out of here!" he called out. "I'll keep you covered!"

"I'm not leaving until you do, little brother," Jesse growled.

Robert Bodine glared at them, grumbling under his breath, before leaping fluidly from the rooftop to his waiting mount's back. "Just once I wish you'd let somebody tell you what to do." He cast a furtive glance behind them, and saw the distinct outlines of men and horses not more than five hundred yards away.

Firing off a volley of shots, the Kardels turned their horses toward the distant mountains, ducking as several wild shots were returned. Glass shattered behind him as one of the bullets careened through a window. The passengers ducked back inside, hands covering their heads.

Robert Bodine let loose with a triumphant yell as they sprinted safely away, their powerful mounts carrying them into them surrounding mountains, where they would quickly lose themselves in a snarl of unending trails.

Charlie Star was in the telegraph office at Bodie when the message clicked across the wire, from a town only five miles due south, telling of the train robbery and the bloody shootout. He had just returned from Chicago after attending a memorial service for his longtime friend Ed Daniels, who'd been killed by Jim and John Younger in a shootout in Monegaw, Missouri.

But he knew now he had a whole 'nother set of

problems to deal with. Damn! Maybe he was getting too old for this stuff. It was losing some of its appeal.

"Guess you're going to have to go after them again?" the clerk said.

"Yes, I guess I am at that," Charlie grunted.

"Well, good luck to you. I wouldn't trade places with you to go after them boys . . . no sir-eee."

The Pinkerton detective left the telegraph office and hurried across the street to the nearest saloon. He had a feeling he was going to get the same response from everyone in this town. He slapped the telegram on the polished wood bar. All eyes turned his way, for they'd heard he was in town.

"I have authorization to deputize any man in this saloon with the guts enough to ride with me and apprehend the men who have just robbed the PGC! All of my men have gone back to previous cases — it's just me, folks. And I could use some help." He stood with his legs apart and his thumbs hooked in the lapels of his buckskin vest. "Do I have any takers?"

Of course there was nary a peep in the place.

Charlie Star didn't appear too surprised by the lack of enthusiasm. Surprisingly, he was losing his passion for this job himself. He knew much of the story now: the train robber's bitter hatred for Evanson, how years ago Evanson had slaughtered people the bandit had cared about, bringing the man's wrath down on him. But it was his job.

"There's a substantial reward being offered — ten thousand dollars for the leader, five thousand for any member of the gang."

487

The townfolk all mumbled and shook their heads. But several of the miners, whose wives had complained no end about their fear of the desperadoes, volunteered to ride with Charlie.

Twenty minutes later, Charlie had seven men behind him and an awful feeling about the whole damned thing. He was thinking of the job he had to do, and how, for the first time, it left a bad taste in his mouth. Pictures from his own past flashed in his mind, moving images flitting painfully across his mind's eye that would not be halted. He confronted the ghostly figurations, feeling his eyes moisten and burn. It was the only part of his past that could still make him want to sleep.

Many years ago, when he'd been young and in love, he'd been faced with a similar situation to that of the outlaw he was now chasing.

He had been a sheriff in Sweetwater, Arizona, then. His love, Rebecca, was living with him in a little cabin outside of town. One night while he'd been away chasing down some desperadoes who'd shot up two men in the local bar, a man broke into the cabin. He raped and stabbed Rebecca to death, then stole whatever he could carry, and left her nude, mutilated body for Charlie to discover three days later.

Charlie hunted the man for six months, and when he found him, he killed him slow, much in the same manner as the filthy scum had done to his lovely Rebecca.

Star almost wished Elizabeth Kardel had not shown him those clippings from the Sacramento paper that reported the horrible story of the Simmons family massacre, and that of Elizabeth's son. She said she had simply included them in the file of reports she had compiled for him so that he was well aware of the danger a man like Lars Evanson posed to the people of Bodie, and even to Star himself.

But he had his duty to apprehend the outlaw for robbing the PGC, regardless of the fact the man had never intentionally killed anyone that he'd heard of. For the first time in his career, Charlie Star hoped he did not get his man.

Chapter Twenty-six

Jesse was leading them along a narrow mountain pass high above the PGC tracks when they heard the speeding sound of a locomotive roaring through the dangerous pass at a frightening speed.

"It's the PGC," Jesse said.

"It can't be," Nicki gasped, her voice cracking with anxiety.

"Look down there," Dakotah exclaimed. "It's the PGC's locomotive. Someone must have uncoupled the engine from the rest of the cars."

"But why?" Nicki asked, clearly confused.

Without explanation, Jesse gripped Nicki Sue around the waist and swung her onto the back of Dakotah's horse. When she saw the glint of steel in his eyes, she knew what he was going to do.

"No! Jess, let it go. It can be over. I heard Cathleen say she had turned Lars's business files over to Star. With all of the evidence he's got compiled against him, he'll be punished."

"You don't understand, Nicki," Jesse said. "It isn't over between Lars and me until one of us isn't breathing anymore. I don't want him to have a second more of life than I have to. I appointed myself his executioner years ago, and I'm going to see it finished today."

"Do you think that Lars is engineering that locomotive?" Dakotah asked.

"Yes, I do." He ignored Nicki's small sob, and told the men to take her to the K.K. camp and look after her until he finished what he had to do.

"No! No! Jesse!" Nicki was struggling in Dakotah's arms, but he refused to let her go.

Jesse was already plunging down the steep mountain trail toward the tracks below.

"He'll be back," Dakotah murmured to soothe her, but there didn't seem to be any way to do so. She fought him, causing his horse to dance about nervously. She managed to break his grip and fling herself to the ground. She took off running after Jesse.

Robert Bodine had leaped from his saddle to run after her. He caught her in his arms and held her tightly against him. She sobbed brokenly. Dakotah left the two of them alone and rejoined the men. He knew it would be better if he and the men rode on ahead.

Cathleen had managed to pull herself up into the engine with Lars just as he had pushed the throttle forward to set the engine in motion. When Evanson saw her, he roared in fury and struck her a glancing blow that knocked her down at his feet. He was occupied with trying to get the steam engine to gather speed, thinking that it might not have been his men behind them, but Charlie Star and a posse

491

coming to get him. She grasped at his legs, and he kicked her viciously. Dazed, she fell back and was still.

Jesse reached the bottom of the mountain trail and lay low over Max's neck, urging him onward for that last bit of speed that he new the valiant stallion had yet to give.

Lars Evanson cursed the fates with a mighty roar when he saw the man on horseback galloping alongside the locomotive. Jesse took his feet out of the stirrups, and balancing on Max's back for breathless seconds, he leaped lithely across the empty space and into the open cab, boot-kicking Evanson and sending him sprawling into the wood piled on the floor. Lars immediately grasped a heavy piece of wood and came at Jesse with a snarl.

Jesse's gun hammer clicked, and Lars froze in motion.

"Come on, Evanson, make your move," Jesse taunted mockingly. "You'll die a little quicker if you get it over with now . . . and you are going to die."

"Who in the hell are you?" Lars growled.

"You wouldn't remember, I guess. It was a long time ago—and I'm certain you never thought I'd come back to haunt you."

"Tell me . . . surely you have a name?" Lars was almost pleading now.

Jesse's lips lifted in a feral smile. "Jesse Kardel. Does that stir your memory?"

Slowly, Lars's eyes widened in dawning recognition. "The Valley . . . years ago—but you were dead! They told me they killed you!"

Jesse stared coldly into his eyes. "I came back from hell just to look into your eyes when I pull the trigger — just the way your men did Allison when they shot her."

Lars was shaking so badly, his teeth were rattling together. "I . . . I . . . will . . . give . . . you anything. Money . . . my . . . my railroad. Name it!"

"I already have it all, Evanson," Jesse drawled. "The K.K. Railroad is mine. I've used your money to help a lot of people, and kept a little bit for myself." He reached behind him and slowly shut the throttle down. The locomotive came to a grinding halt, the steam engine hissing in protest.

"Don't kill me . . . Have mercy, please . . . Let me live," Lars begged. "I'll even drop the wood . . . see?" He tossed the wood aside.

"She wanted to live too, and so did Reed, and how many others you butchered." He shook his dark head slowly back and forth. "Uh-uh — I found you guilty a long time ago; I've just been waiting to carry out your sentence, that's all."

"Jesse . . . do you know what you are doing?" Cathleen gasped, sitting wide-eyed and breathless watching the scenario before her.

"I know *exactly* what I'm doing," Jesse replied.

"You are *really* going to pull that trigger, aren't you?" Lars's eyes never left Jesse's.

"Yeah, I really am."

"That's murder."

"I guess I'll have to answer for it on Judgment Day."

When Nicki Sue arrived at the K.K. construction site with Robert Bodine, it was nightfall and the area was quiet. Soft light glowed from within each tent, and some of the crew members sat around outside playing cards, drinking whiskey, and swapping long-winded stories about their railroad experiences.

Robert Bodine rode immediately to the back of the camp, where there was one tent set off from the others beneath some tall trees. She assumed even before he told her that the tent was Jesse's.

"I reckon you'll be staying here for tonight," he said, dismounting and assisting her from the horse.

She was bone-weary and emotionally spent. Why argue about the accommodations when she was so exhausted? she thought.

"Do you think Jesse will be back tonight?" she had to ask.

In both of their minds was the fear that he might never come back; each knew what the other was thinking, but neither of them mentioned the fact that Jesse might never return. Only once had they voiced their apprehension, and that had been when Bo was with her alone on the mountainside. But they would not voice their troubled thoughts out loud again.

"I can't say, honey," he returned gently. "But when he does show up, I know he'll be looking for you first thing."

She cast her eyes downward so he could not see the spark of joy his words brought to her heart. "I hope you're right. He and I have a lot of talking to do about many things."

"Don't push him too hard at first, Nicki Sue," Bo advised softly. "I expect he has a lot of healing to do after what has taken place the last few weeks. The past is behind us after today. It's all over, for good. Everything here belongs to Jesse and me. He can give you a good life."

"Would he have come for me if I'd have stayed at the ranch, Bo — or would he have just ridden out of my life?" she posed with tears threatening.

He didn't know how to answer her, for he truly *didn't* know what Jesse would have done in the end. He had been concerned for her safety, and he appeared to care for her. But with Jesse, it was just too hard to say. He had been alone for many years now, and it wasn't easy to change a pattern of life once you'd adopted it. The K.K. would keep him very busy in the future. And of course he had Deidre if he felt a need for a woman. Robert Bodine looked at the woman before him. Proud, beautiful of spirit, and a nice person to boot.

"I'll tell you what, Nicki Sue," he answered her with a devilish smile. "If that brother of mine doesn't welcome you into his life with open arms, you tell him he'd better watch his step or he just may lose you to another Kardel."

Nicki knew he was only saying that to lift her spirits and make her feel wanted. And he had. She did like Bo; he had been closer to her in many ways that Jesse would not allow himself to be.

She smiled back at him before she stepped inside the tent. "Thanks, Bo, for everything. Goodnight."

A woman's sultry voice halted Nicki Sue just inside Jesse's tent.

"That was a touching scene. Tell me, though, which one of the Kardel men are you really after, sugar—Jesse or Bo?"

Nicki could not believe her eyes, although she did not know why she should not have been expecting it. A flame-haired woman, with green eyes that mirrored the seduction in her soul, was smiling challenging at Nicki Sue. The dim lantern light fell on her bare skin and bathed it tawny gold. And Nicki had to admit, there was a lot of her that was bare. She was sitting on the only cot in the tent, a sheet draped carelessly around her full bosom, one lithe leg fully exposed, and meant to be.

"Cat got your tongue, little one?" Deidre McCain drawled, examining her nails one by one.

Nicki finally recovered her voice enough to reply. "I . . . I . . . that is, Robert Bodine didn't tell me this tent was occupied."

"He didn't know, I guess." Deidre glanced up at Nicki. "Jesse and I like to keep things between us kinda quiet."

Nicki saw the wedding ring on the woman's finger and could assume why. Her ire began to rise, and she glared at Deidre. "I suppose you can deliver a message to Jesse for me, since you will be here when he returns."

"Oh, I'll be here, all right, so whatever you want him to know, I'll just pass it along for you."

The insinuation was hard to deny. Nicki knew this lovely creature had been sharing Jesse's bed. Damn him! He *had* only been after her ranch for his railroad. Bo had told her how they were expanding the K.K. and hoped to become even bigger once

496

they obtained other valuable land grants. Was that why they had all been so nice to her?

Nicki Sue wanted to scratch the woman's eyes out. She heard the throaty voice ask again, and with a suggestive leer, what she would like to pass along to Jesse. It was that husky, insinuating voice that made her do it. She was beside the cot in three steps, the green-eyed temptress watching her warily now.

"Just this." She swung her open palm forward as hard as she could and slapped Deidre soundly.

There was a stunned gasp of outrage from the woman, and then Nicki Sue was spinning on her heel and stalking from the tent. To hell with all men! She had said it before and she'd say it again. She was going back to her ranch and live there, and by God, she was going to be happy, too!

Bill Hickok saw the young woman storm out of Jesse's tent just as he was riding past on his final check of the yard for the night. He heard the angry hiss from inside the tent, the string of curses that exploded in the night, and knew who it was who had been brawling again. He halted his horse before Jesse's tent and announced his presence before entering.

"I'm coming in, Deidre, so you'd better make yourself decent."

Deidre didn't move a muscle. The sheet was still barely covering her obvious charms. She was sitting in a huffy pout, nursing her sore cheek. Her flashing eyes met Hickok's.

"That little witch almost broke my jaw," she hissed.

He couldn't help but grin at her tawdry, tousled beauty. "Now, why do you have your rump in Jesse's bed again? Didn't he make it plain to you the last time you came callin' that he just wasn't interested in what you were offering?"

Deidre nodded miserably and sniffed. "I just got lonely . . . and wanted someone to talk with."

Bill reached out and tilted her chin upward to meet her eyes. "I know somewhere you could come where you would be welcome."

She was once again the seductress, sliding into his arms with a contented little sigh. "Oh . . . Wild Bill, if I would have only known sooner. Why didn't you tell me, honey?"

Hickok laughed deeply and swept her up — sheet and all — and carried her through the night to his tent.

Summer swept past, then fall, and winter was approaching. Nicki Sue involved herself in working around the ranch and tried to forget about Jesse. He had come to the ranch the day after he'd returned to the camp to find her gone, and tried to explain to her what Deidre had done, and why. But Nicki was too stubborn, and too certain he was lying, to believe him. They'd had angry words. Of course, she had expected all of that. Wasn't it always that way between them? When they' weren't making love, they were quarreling. Finally, after she had refused to talk to him the last time he'd stopped by the ranch, Jesse had stayed away. It wasn't because she didn't want to see him, for even though they bickered, she still loved just to look at him. But it was becoming more evident every day that she was pregnant. This, she did not want Jesse to know. She would not use women's tricks to hold him. She would worry about everything after the birth of her baby in April.

Robert Bodine came to see her shortly after the horrible stories surrounding Lars Evanson surfaced in the papers and swept over the town. He wanted to reassure her that everything would be fine, that she should just stay calm and Jesse would make certain she wasn't implicated in any way. If he had noticed that she had put on a little weight and wore fuller clothes instead of her usual form-fitting outfits, he didn't mention it. She said nothing about the baby. Jesse really didn't want her, and now that she had agreed to give Robert Bodine the land the K.K. needed to lay their track, she never expected to hear from Jesse again. She had done what was necessary to secure her child's future. The water tower was already built, and the groundwork laid for the town beneath the bluff. The K.K Railroad would secure the future for Nicki Sue and her child.

They never found a trace of Lars Evanson. Nor of the train robbers. It seemed that they'd simply vanished into the wilderness that day, and were not heard from again.

Nicki had read a story in the paper not long after that horrible day, written by Elizabeth Kardel. It announced the return of her son, Jesse Kardel, and told of how he had had amnesia from the trauma he had suffered in the shootout. She told of how he'd been traveling the country and had become involved in the railroad business. He had returned to California just as the story about Lars Evanson went to print. The article had stirred his memory, and when the K.K Railroad moved close to Bodie, he came looking for his family.

Nicki had been happy for Jesse and his family. She was glad their nightmare had come to an end.

The evidence that Charlie Star, Elizabeth, and Cathleen had compiled clearly proved that Evanson had made so many enemies through his ruthless business practices that many people thought he had disappeared to save himself, perhaps to resurface somewhere else one day. Charlie Star finally closed the case after searching for the train robbers through the surrounding mountains for weeks, and never finding a trace of them. Everyone was surprised that he didn't appear too upset, but left in a right good mood.

Nicki had received a letter from Cathleen. She wrote that she had returned to Chicago and her schooling. She mentioned that she and Jake were writing each other. And that the future looked promising for them.

Folding the letter and laying it aside, Nicki could not help but feel envious, in a small way, that everyone's lives had fallen into place. Feeling a need to escape the confines of the house, she decided to get some fresh air.

Bundled against the brisk wind and cold mountain air, Nicki went to the bluff to check the progress of the K.K. She told herself that she wasn't going there each day to watch Jesse . . . no! She would not do that.

With a resigned sigh, Nicki Sue leaned back against the tree on the bluff overlooking the lake and watched the railroad crews laying the track across her land.

She tried not to allow her eyes to search the throngs of men for Jesse's tall, broad-shouldered form, but somehow, it was impossible. She saw him; he always stood out in a crowd from other men, riding along beside the tracks on Max. He looked the part of the railroad baron.

His thick black hair was blowing in the crisp breeze, lying wild and curling around his ears. But that was all that appeared familiar about him. He wore a dark jacket of impeccable cut, and trousers that appeared to cling to his muscular legs like a second skin. He slipped his hand inside of his waistcoat and withdrew a watch on a chain to check the hour.

Bo had mentioned that Star had left the timepiece with Elizabeth; as a memento of the case, he'd said.

Nicki's eyes were drawn to Jesse's hips. She noticed with a smile that beneath his coat he wore no guns.

As she sat there lost in thought, the sky began to darken and the clouds turned black and threatening. Before she could tear her gaze away from Jesse, fat droplets of rain began to fall on her. It was time to seek shelter.

With a wistful sigh, she rose slowly (her round

figure demanding it), and picking up Krya's reins, she secured the mare in the lean-to and then hurried up the path to the little cabin. She hadn't been there since that last time with Jesse. It seemed now like another lifetime ago.

Chapter Twenty-seven

Jesse stood looking down at the sleeping woman on the bed. When he had first glimpsed her sitting up on the bluff, he had tried his best not to allow his gaze to stray upward to where she sat beneath the tree. But of course, it was hopeless. She still filled his thoughts, and his dreams. He saw her struggle to stand when the rain started to come down, and then her cloak swirling about her in the wind, and the distinct round outline of her abdomen. And now, the proof was before his eyes. Nicki Sue was carrying his child.

With agonizing slowness he studied her closely. One hand lay back over her head, the other cradling her abdomen. It did something to him to see her heavy and round with his baby. Her hand on her abdomen fluttered, then did so once again. The child was moving inside her! My God, what a wondrous sight!

She stirred languidly, then opened her eyes. Her delicate nostrils widened perceptibly and her breath came in a gasp. "Jess . . . why did you come here?"

Jesse knelt down on one knee beside the narrow bed. "Nicki, how could you have kept this from me?"

She knew very well what he was implying.

"I didn't keep it from you. . . . You just never were around to tell you," she said defensively, sitting up and drawing the folds of her skirt around her feet.

"You could have sent a message that you wanted to see me."

"Why?" she returned infuriatingly.

"Because, damn it! I had a right to know you're pregnant!"

"Don't you take that tone with me; I'm not one of your men."

"I can see that very well," he said, softer now, sick of the time they had spent arguing in the past. He wanted to reach out and touch her, kiss her, but did not. "You're quite beautiful for a very pregnant lady, you know that?"

She was staring, narrow-eyed, at him, looking for the world like a spitting little tiger cat. "Don't patronize me, Jess. I am not Deidre. Go to her with your sugar phrases; she'll lap them up like cream."

"Deidre is not my type of woman—never was, never will be," he stated levelly.

Her expression softened somewhat, and she considered his words for a moment before replying. "I . . . couldn't live with a man who had his eye on other women all of the time."

"When have I ever looked at another woman when you were around?"

"And I wouldn't tolerate ever having *that* woman within fifty miles of you."

"She took off with Bill Hickok for Deadwood

over a month ago. They both got bored, looking for more excitement now that things quieted down around here."

She was moving closer to him now, her eyes still wary but her love for him impossible to deny any longer. He let her make all of the moves. She had to see by the look on his face how much he loved her, needed her.

"Jess?"

"Yes," he murmured as her head lowered slowly toward his.

"Can we just have a small wedding, nothing fancy? Just your family and a few friends?"

"Whatever you want — with one condition."

One dusky eyebrow arched upward. "And what would that be?"

He couldn't keep his hands off of her any longer. A snarl rumbled in his chest and he gathered her gently in his arms. Midnight-blue eyes gazed deeply into tawny gold. "That we have a very private honeymoon."

They kissed hungrily, all of the months of longing for each other, needing to feel close like this, at last being satisfied.

Much later, lying, contented and warm, beneath the blanket with a fire roaring in the hearth, he turned to kiss her tenderly and murmured the words she had waited so long to hear.

"I love you, Tiger Eyes."

Her arms held him close. "I love you, Jess, more than I ever thought possible."

Epilogue

Three years had passed since Jesse Kardel had hung up his guns to take Nicki Sue Ryan for his bride. Many changes had occurred — all of them wonderful.

There was a big, stylish mansion on the bluff now, the little cabin taken down board by board to be rebuilt on another secluded section of the property. For when Jesse and Nicki Sue came to Los Paraiso, the two months they spent there each year, they sometimes wished to recapture a bit of their stormy, passionate beginnings. And the cabin held many of these memories.

They were very wealthy. Jesse and Robert Bodine had been successful in securing valuable land grants across California. Bo had met a girl the last time they'd all been in New York. He decided to settle there and open a branch office of the K.K. in the East. With things changing as fast as they were, and the railroads expanding everywhere, prosperous businessmen had to pay close attention to the competition.

Jesse and Nicki Sue traveled all over the world. And with them they took their two children: their

506

son, Robert Jesse, and their daughter, nine months old, Elizabeth Leigh. They were very proud of their beautiful children, as were their grandparents, who insisted they visit them often. Jesse and Nicki did visit everyone in the family, including Aunt Lorna, who had mellowed when she had learned of the fine man (and rich too) whom her niece had married. And they were at home anywhere, whether in a Mojave wickiup while visiting Doris and Dakotah, or in their posh coach trailing behind the K.K. It didn't matter where they called home, just as long as they had each other.

EXPERIENCE THE SENSUOUS MAGIC
OF JANELLE TAYLOR!

FORTUNE'S FLAMES (2250, $3.95)
Lovely Maren James' angry impatience turned to raging desire when the notorious Captain Hawk boarded her ship and strode confidently into her cabin. And before she could consider the consequences, the ebon-haired beauty was succumbing to the bold pirate's masterful touch!

SWEET SAVAGE HEART (1900, $3.95)
Kidnapped when just a child, seventeen-year-old Rana Williams adored her carefree existence among the Sioux. But then the frighteningly handsome white man Travis Kincade appeared in her camp . . . and Rana's peace was shattered forever!

DESTINY'S TEMPTRESS (1761, $3.95)
Crossing enemy lines to help save her beloved South, Shannon Greenleaf found herself in the bedroom of Blane Stevens, the most handsome man she'd ever seen. Though burning for his touch, the defiant belle vowed never to reveal her mission—nor let the virile Yankee capture her heart!

SAVAGE CONQUEST (1533, $3.75)
Heeding the call of her passionate nature, Miranda stole away from her Virginia plantation to the rugged plains of South Dakota. But captured by a handsome Indian warrior, the headstrong beauty felt her defiance melting away with the hot-blooded savage's sensual caress!

STOLEN ECSTASY (1621, $3.95)
With his bronze stature and ebony black hair, the banished Sioux brave Bright Arrow was all Rebecca Kenny ever wanted. She would defy her family and face society's scorn to savor the forbidden rapture she found in her handsome warrior's embrace!

Available wherever paperbacks are sold, or order direct from the Publisher. Send cover price plus 50¢ per copy for mailing and handling to Zebra Books, Dept. 2349, 475 Park Avenue South, New York, N.Y. 10016. Residents of New York, New Jersey and Pennsylvania must include sales tax. DO NOT SEND CASH.

ROMANCE REIGNS
WITH ZEBRA BOOKS!

SILVER ROSE (2275, $3.95)
by Penelope Neri

Fleeing her lecherous boss, Silver Dupres disguised herself as a boy and joined an expedition to chart the wild Colorado River. But with one glance at Jesse Wilder, the explorers' rugged, towering scout, Silver knew she'd have to abandon her protective masquerade or else be consumed by her raging unfulfilled desire!

STARLIT ECSTASY (2134, $3.95)
by Phoebe Conn

Cold-hearted heiress Alicia Caldwell swore that Rafael Ramirez, San Francisco's most successful attorney, would never win her money . . . or her love. But before she could refuse him, she was shamelessly clasped against Rafael's muscular chest and hungrily matching his relentless ardor!

LOVING LIES (2034, $3.95)
by Penelope Neri

When she agreed to wed Joel McCaleb, Seraphina wanted nothing more than to gain her best friend's inheritance. But then she saw the virile stranger . . . and the green-eyed beauty knew she'd never be able to escape the rapture of his kiss and the sweet agony of his caress.

EMERALD FIRE (1963, $3.95)
by Phoebe Conn

When his brother died for loving gorgeous Bianca Antonelli, Evan Sinclair swore to find the killer by seducing the tempress who lured him to his death. But once the blond witch willingly surrendered all he sought, Evan's lust for revenge gave way to the desire for unrestrained rapture.

SEA JEWEL (1888, $3.95)
by Penelope Neri

Hot-tempered Alaric had long planned the humiliation of Freya, the daughter of the most hated foe. He'd make the wench from across the ocean his lowly bedchamber slave—but he never suspected she would become the mistress of his heart, his treasured SEA JEWEL.

Available wherever paperbacks are sold, or order direct from the Publisher. Send cover price plus 50¢ per copy for mailing and handling to Zebra Books, Dept. 2349, 475 Park Avenue South, New York, N.Y. 10016. Residents of New York, New Jersey and Pennsylvania must include sales tax. DO NOT SEND CASH.